Zach

THE BRASH BROTHERS BOOK FIVE

JENNA MYLES

Copyright 2023 by Jenna Myles

All rights reserved. No part of this book may be reproduced, distributed or transmitted in any form or by any means, including photocopying, recording, or other electronic or mechanical methods, without the prior written permission of the publisher, except in the case of brief quotations embodied in book reviews.

Publishers Note:

This is a work of fiction. Names, Characters, places and incidents are a product of the author's imagination. Locales and public names are sometimes used for atmospheric purposes. Any resemblance to actual people living or dead, or to businesses, companies, events, institutions, or locales is completely coincidental.

Published by Myles High Publishing

authorjennamyles.com

To all the people hitting up my inbox, telling me how much they love the world I've created.
-Thank You.
I really needed to hear it.

THE BRASH BROTHERS READING ORDER

CHARACTERS

Ransom Kyle: The 'dad' of the group. He brought together a group of misfit boys and turned them into a family. He's the big idea guy.

Kade Dixon: The CEO, in charge of operations. Favorite word is Fuck and he manages to work it into nearly every sentence. Girlfriend is Becca

Becca Tyler: A teacher at a Dojo and runs a lot of self-defense classes. Colton trains with her, and she makes him cry at least once a week. Often referred to as a Ninja.

Micah James: Works on custom projects out of the Knight Street garage. Was beaten by his father as a child, and suffered brain damage. He will often use ASL to supplement his speech. Big reader, has a kitty named Minnie (as in mouse). Girlfriend is Holly.

Holly Clarke: Escaped her abusive husband and hid from him for two years. He's now in prison with Joker. Holly works at Knight Street with Micah.

Colton Miles: He's the overprotective Golden Retriever of the group. Had a history of underground fighting. Girlfriend is Evie.

Evie Collins: ER nurse and mom to Mia. She has a no-bullshit attitude that the guys find equally terrifying and hilarious. She's the one that helped Holly escape her abusive husband, and as a result, had her life torn apart.

Declan Wilder: The hacker/computer geek. He can find anything on anyone. Obsessed with video games. Notorious for losing bets with his brother Jonas, leading to Mohawks and ass tattoos.

Cara Davis: Ransom's right and left hand. Owns her own club *Curves Ahead*. Obsessed with Declan and after years of chasing him, they are finally together.

Bree Davis: Cara's sister. She's a physiotherapist and often works at Cara's club in the evenings. Cara raised her from the age of sixteen. Had an abusive boyfriend and she's still recovering from his attack.

Zach Lee: Head of marketing. The playboy of the group. Very image-focused and loves his expensive suits and beautifully decorated home. His younger biological brother is Jonas.

Maya Miller: Marketing Guru. Zach's new hire. Brilliant. Incapable of keeping her shoes on her feet. Awful sense of direction.

Jonas Lee: The CFO, the numbers guru. On the Autism Spectrum. He tends to be reserved around new people. Huge fan of puzzles.

Nick Diaz: The fixer. He could convince a nun to marry him in ten minutes flat. No official title, he goes where Ransom needs him to.

Maverick Walker: The lawyer. He and Nick are often sent out to handle problems that Cara can't solve.

Johnny (Joker) Miles: Older brother of Colton. He's been in prison for eighteen years.

AUTHORS NOTE

Content Warning: This book deals with the loss of Maya's dog. It happens off the page, but it's still sad.

I love hearing from readers. If you spot a typo, or you just want to complain about how long it's taking me to get to Ransom's book, email me at: jenna@authorjennamyles.com

1

MAYA

Can a person survive without a heart?

Until last week, I would have said no, but I'm still here, walking around, existing, breathing, without one.

So it must be possible.

I'm a medical miracle. Maybe I should update my will and donate my body to science. They'll want to study a woman with no heart. Maybe they'll write an academic paper about me. At least then someone would remember me when I'm gone.

I'm alone in the elevator, and it's a small blessing. I deliberately came late to work today. I need to push off the uncomfortable questions and the sympathies for a bit longer. People mean well, I know. But I just don't have the capacity for sympathetic smiles and chit-chat.

The doors open on my floor, and I step off into chaos. It's always busy here, but this level of panic is new. Something is happening, and I'm lost. What I am *not* is bombarded by sympathetic colleagues. Whatever is happening trumps me being away all week.

Weaving through the maze of open desks, I search for my

assistant, Abigail. She's normally right outside my office, but her desk is empty. Upon closer inspection, I realize it's not just empty, it's bare. No plant, no pictures of her boyfriend, no coffee cups.

I spin in a slow circle, minor details adding up. It's not just Abigail's desk that's empty. About half the desks are. The rest have clusters of people around them, whispering. A little spark of interest flares in my chest. Something is happening, and I welcome it. I can work on solving this little mystery and forget about my missing heart for a bit.

"Ms. Miller."

I turn and find a man in a tailored suit smiling at me from a few feet away. I don't like the smile. It's fake. I can tell. It doesn't crease the tanned skin near his eyes. I've seen a lot of those smiles directed at me. The kind that curves the mouth and exposes the teeth but never touches their eyes.

My mother looked at me like that.

"Yes," I answer crisply, matching his tone. His lips are firm as he rakes them down my body, over my loose dress and simple black shoes. I know what he thinks of me. I look like a turd among the beautiful, well-dressed people around me.

I don't care.

Not even a bit.

I used to. Way back when I tried to be like everyone else. I wore designer clothes and spiked shoes. I slapped on makeup and spent hours on my hair.

And I hated every minute of it. After my fourth panic attack in one week, I decided fitting in wasn't worth it. So I searched for a company that would let me be me.

Mr. Williams and his forty-year-old marketing agency became my new home. And it's been everything I need it to be for the last decade. They let me be as creative as I wanted to be. They overlooked my quirks, and in return, I made them the top agency on the east coast.

That's not bragging. That's a fact. Thanks to me, we have a

waiting list of clients, all eager to pay a ridiculous amount of money to work with us. Mr. Williams was happy. I was happy. Everything was going fine.

I don't think they're fine anymore.

Mr. William's eyes are kind when he looks at me.

The man in the suit's eyes harden. "Ms. Miller. If you'll come with me." He spins on a shiny, pointed shoe and walks away, confident I'll follow him. And I do, because I'm more than confused right now. I need to understand what's happening around me and where Abigail is.

I follow him to the executive end of the office, straight toward Mr. Williams's office. But the nameplate is new. I stop. "Liam Callaghan, President. Is that you?"

"Indeed," he says, amusement coloring his words. But not the funny kind. The kind that says *you're a bug beneath my heel, and I will toy with you for my own amusement.*

I'm not really interested in being toyed with. I'm too broken. Too sad.

He motions to the chair across from the massive oak desk, and I drop into it. I don't betray my whirling thoughts. Despite what Abigail said, I am capable of putting a social mask on. I don't like to, but I can. This time, I wear it gladly, only the wiggling of my toe inside my shoe betrays my discomfort. The lights in here are so bright, I wish I had my sunglasses. They're tucked in my desk for situations exactly like this.

"Well, Ms. Miller. We finally meet. You can imagine my surprise to arrive Monday morning, eager to meet the head of the marketing department and discover she's missing." His tone is challenging, like he thinks I'll stumble through an explanation of my absence.

"You can imagine my surprise to come in this morning and find the entire office in upheaval." My coworkers looked like they'd just sighted *Voldemort*. "I can't say I was eager to meet you since I don't know who you are."

A little twitch in the corner of his mouth. He's not amused anymore. "Yes, well. Until the takeover was finalized, Williams was forbidden from speaking of it."

I lean back in the chair, waiting. His gaze turns more and more puzzled the longer I sit calmly. I see it, that moment when his curiosity outweighs the power play he had planned.

"You've worked here a long time. I expected you to be more surprised or upset. Do you not care that your mentor is gone?"

"Mentor? Mr. Williams? He was my employer." At one point, he may have mentored me, but that was years ago. I've been on my own creatively for a long time. The division of labor worked well. He handled the business, and I handled the projects. It worked for both of us.

"Ah...yes, I see." His brows lower into a semblance of a frown...as well as his Botoxed forehead will allow. He brushes a speck of dust off the lapel of his dark blue suit. "Well, Mr. Williams is gone, and you'll be reporting to me from now on. We'll be working closely for the next while until I'm confident we have things running smoothly."

I give myself a moment to feel that. The man I worked with for a decade is gone, and he didn't even say goodbye. The decent thing to do would have been to tell me. To speak to me personally.

I breathe deeply to push down the tendrils of anger. I have no right to feel that way. It's his company, and he can do whatever he wants with it. I can't say I'm eager for a new boss, but we should do fine as long as he stays out of my way. "Where's Abigail? My assistant? Her desk is empty."

A slight flash of a smile with an edge of glee starts my toe tapping again. "We've had to...trim the fat. We've let go of all the unnecessary staff. I'm sure you'll do fine without her."

He wants me to work without Abigail? She's the barrier between me and the world. She's the reason I can focus and be creative. And now she's gone? Just like that? I open my mouth to correct him on his stupidity when his next question rocks my world.

"You've been out of the office for four days. Where have you been?"

Saliva pools in my mouth, and I force myself to swallow it down. "My dog died." There. That wasn't so bad. A simple statement of fact. It came out clear, with none of the pain and bewildered loss I'm feeling.

Callaghan places both hands flat on his desk and leans forward. That frozen forehead isn't so frozen anymore. He looks a little like a cartoon movie villain about to say something dastardly. "Pardon me. Are you telling me you've been away from my business for four days, because your pet died?"

I could argue the word pet with him. Explain to him she was so much more than that. That she was my connection to the world. My reason for leaving my apartment. The light in my life. But he doesn't get that part of me. "Yes," I say flatly.

His lips pull back from his teeth in a snarl. Disgust coats his voice as he lectures me about my irresponsible choices and lack of professionalism. He has a vein over his left eye that bulges each time he yells. The yelling doesn't bother me. I don't like the volume, but long ago I learned to tune the words out.

He sounds like the teacher in the *Simpsons*.

But his next words snap my attention back to this room. "You ever leave this company in the lurch for some fucking dog, you will be out on your ass so fast, you won't know what hit you. You're being docked four days' pay."

"I had family days saved up. Mr. Williams said I could use them."

"Family days are for family. Not for a fucking dog. Do you really think I'm stupid enough to give people time off every time their budgie dies? Not bloody likely."

When I told Mr. Williams that Birdie was going to be put

to sleep over the weekend, he was sympathetic. He told me to take all the time I needed to grieve. I came in today because I felt I should, not because I feel better. It's going to take more than four days to adjust to losing my best friend. If Birdie hadn't just died, maybe I would care more about what he thinks of me. Maybe I'd care more about this job.

But she is gone, and no matter how much I wish that weren't the truth, it is. For the first time in a decade, I'm completely untethered. My future is stretching out before me, and while I'm not sure what I want, I know for sure I don't want anything to do with the man sitting in front of me.

All my reasons for temperance, for patience, are gone. I know for sure I don't want to spend the next decade getting sneered at by this man. Or his version of a sneer, I guess. It's actually a little grotesque. He could go on a billboard advertising the dangers of Botox.

I have a very healthy bank account —my homebody tendencies are good for something, at least— so I lock eyes with him and do something completely out of character. I leap off a cliff and hope I'll find somewhere safe to land.

"Fair enough," I say, proud of how level my voice comes out. "I'm not interested in working for you. I quit. Feel free to dock my final cheque." I stand and exit the office, ignoring his shouts, my mind already cataloging the items in my desk as I pass through the halls. The only things I want are the photo of Birdie and me, and the coffee mug Abigail gave me for my birthday last year.

It takes less than a minute to grab them, then I head for the door. I murmur some goodbyes and good lucks to the staff that's left, stopping to assure one co-worker on the verge of a panic attack that he is more than capable of stepping up, though truthfully, I'm not sure he is.

Maybe I should be more professional about leaving. I should give formal notice, then work out a leave, but I don't have to. Long ago, Mr. Williams and I put an agreement in place that if I wanted to go, I could. No notice needed. And in the decade that followed, that suited us both just fine. So Callahan's threats of lawsuits don't phase me. I may look flighty —okay, sometimes I am— but I'm no pushover.

I'm outside in the crisp fall air in minutes, photo and mug clutched to my chest. It's 9:30 on a Friday morning, and I have absolutely nowhere to go. Nearly without thought, my feet carry me the six blocks to the dog park. We always came here. It was a brisk walk from my apartment and had the largest fenced play area in twenty blocks.

I drop onto a bench across from the off-leash area, staring sightlessly at the animals and their owners. I recognize some of them. When I had Birdie with me, we'd talk. I didn't have to struggle to find topics of conversation. We talked about our dogs and the weather and laughed while we watched them play. Often, those conversations were the only one-on-one human interaction I'd have outside of work. And when we were done, it was Birdie and me, heading home to our snug little nest.

Now, there's no reason to go home. No wiggling little tail, no happy yips...nothing. Just an empty dog bed and the toys I've been unable to pick up.

I'm not stupid. I know that she's just a dog. But I also know that she had all of my heart. That for twelve years, she loved me when no one else could. She was my family.

And now I have no one.

I feel the tears on my cheeks, but I don't wipe them away. I'm sad. I'm lost. And I don't care if anyone sees it.

Quitting my job is barely a blip. I have plenty of money, and I get offers from other companies and from headhunters constantly. One company has been particularly aggressive in trying to hire me. The Brash Group. I don't know much about them and honestly didn't care to. No way would I leave Birdie's vets. They'd given my girl three extra years with me, and I'm so thankful for that time. But now, my only tie to this city...to the world, is gone.

The future stretches out in front of me, long and lonely. I'm not sure what the right next step is for me, but the idea of staying right where I am, being forced to pass this park, to walk the routes I walked with Birdie, sounds horrifying.

I can't do it.

I don't want to.

When I return to my too-quiet apartment, I kick off my shoes and drop into my favorite chair. Its familiar softness settles me. I stare out the window at the brick wall it faces and contemplate the tattered remains of my life.

I have nothing tying me to this city anymore. No ties anywhere. Which should be comforting for a loner like me. But it's really not. Because I don't really think I am a loner. I like being around people. I just never seem to know how to interact with them. My whole life has been an exercise in avoiding sticking my foot in my mouth. It's only at work that I seem to know the right things to say and do.

Even this tiny hole of an apartment is an exercise in avoidance. I can afford better, even in the outrageous Manhattan market. But I've never moved because I know every crack on the sidewalk and every shop owner in a three-block radius. I never spoke to them, but we traded smiles. It made me feel like I wasn't completely invisible.

But now, doing nothing is more terrifying than doing something.

Plopping my computer onto my lap, I open up my email and tap on the *Ignore* folder I created. Dozens of unread messages from dozens of marketing agencies and corporations. All wanting to hire me.

I haven't applied for a job in a decade. Can I even do this? I'll have to go to interviews and let people judge me. I slam the computer closed and rest my head back on the chair, willing my heart rate to slow.

Change sucks.

I knew exactly who I was here. I was secure. And now that's all been ripped away. Everything and everyone's been ripped away. I need to talk to Abigail.

I don't think I've ever phoned her. We have each other's numbers to text, which we do often, but I think this warrants an actual phone call. It rings a few times before she picks up. Her voice is hesitant, guarded.

"Hello," she says carefully, like she doesn't know who it is. It's unlike her. She's always been outgoing and in your face, which somehow worked for us.

"Why didn't you tell me everything was blowing up?"

Her sigh is heavy. "I wanted to. I swear. But they made me sign some paperwork that I wouldn't contact anyone from the office or I'd lose my severance pay. It freaked me out. Plus, with Birdie," her voice trails off. She knows how much Birdie meant to me, maybe more than anyone.

"Right," I mumble, tracing one of the big pink flowers on my dress. I run my finger over the petals along my thigh, trying to think of the right thing to say. At work, I always know what to say. Being in charge, being in my element, is easier than this. "Are you...okay? I mean, you're out of a job too. What are you going to do?"

"I've got my half of the rent covered for the next few months, thanks to the severance. I've got a few interviews lined up, but Jason doesn't want me to worry. He can cover things. What are you going to do?"

What am I going to do? As I stare at the familiar walls around me, the space suddenly feels confining rather than cozy. "I'm going to find another job. I'm leaving New York." Abigail's gasp is appropriate. I've never left this city. Never. Not for a conference or for vacation. I don't travel. Honestly, I rarely leave Manhattan.

"Are you serious? Where are you going to go? Do you

think you can find a company that will..." Her voice trails off, and I can almost picture her reddened cheeks.

I give her a break and finish the sentences she cut off. "Do I think I'll find a company that will accommodate my quirks?"

"Yeah. That."

That's my worry too. But I have to hope that somewhere out there is a job that will let me be me. "I believe so. I have several possibilities."

"Good, that's good," she murmurs, sounding lost in thought. "Maya. If you're going to do this...then do it right."

"What does that mean?"

"I mean, that it's a chance to start over in every way. To build the kind of life you want for yourself. I know we haven't been super close, but I get the feeling that your life hasn't been...easy up to now. So if you want a chance to build something different, then do it."

"What are you suggesting I do?"

"Put yourself out there. Make friends. Fall in love. Live big, my friend."

My friend. The way she says that so casually, when I know I haven't been a very good one back, is humbling.

"I don't know if I can do that." But the idea is tantalizing.

"You'll never know if you don't try. What's the worst that could happen?"

What is the worst that could happen? Best case, I end up with a colorful life.

Worst case? I realize the problem has been me all along.

There's only one way to find out, though.

Opening a new note on my computer, I type out a heading for a new list: *Time to Get Living,* then I start typing.

Fly on a plane
Make a friend
Kiss someone

Laugh so hard I nearly pee my pants
Get a passport
Travel outside the country
Go on a date
Hold hands
Get a boyfriend
Have sex
Fall in love

The list feels overwhelming. I'm thirty-four, and my list is filled with things most people do before they graduate college. I'm pathetic, and I'm sick of it.

That's it.

I'm done being the weird loner girl. It's time for the new me.

2

ZACH

I feel a little disloyal walking into this place. It's opening
night, and this club is competition for Cara's club
Curves Ahead. I should go there instead. Keep it in the
family. But I can't get what I need there.

Not tonight.

The women there are luscious, but Cara's staff knows who
I am now, and I guarantee they'll report back to her. It
shouldn't matter. It's not a secret that I like women. That I like
variety and like letting them take me home. But doing it at
my friend's —now brother's woman's— club feels wrong.

As usual, the bouncers let me in with a smile. There's a
slim chance they don't know who I am, but even though it's
opening night, they're experienced enough to mentally add
up my shoes, my custom suit, and the watch on my wrist and
come up with dollar signs. The blacked-out Escalade that
dropped me off would be the other clue.

It's always the same. I'm ushered into the VIP area by a
beautiful waitress. She'll flirt and tease and do her best to get
me to spend.

It doesn't take much to convince me.

I have more money than I know what to do with. I can

drop a few grand in here…or ten thousand, and I won't feel it. But she will. I don't know her story. I don't know if she's got a family at home, if she's going to school, or if she blows everything she makes on drugs. I don't know, and I don't care. All I want from her is smiling service, and I'll reward her with a tip big enough to pay her rent for the month. I don't want to know anything about her or about her life. I don't want to get sucked in by some sob story and end up on her hook.

No, I don't want complicated. I want sex, sweat, and moaning. Then I want to get the fuck out and go home. Release and a little fun are all I'm looking for tonight. It's all I ever want.

So I do what I do best.

Lounge back on the sexy red couch in the VIP area and start fishing.

It never takes long. A glance at the expensive bottle in front of me, a flash of my quarter-of-a-million dollar watch, and a slow smile are all it takes to draw them to me. My brothers make fun of me for it, that smile. I get it. I practiced it in the mirror when we were kids and didn't give a fuck what they said. I always knew it would come in handy.

I'm not the smartest of us. Or the most strategic. I can't hack a computer or run complicated equations in my head. What I do have is a thick head of hair, a killer smile, and a powerful body honed by hours-long workouts in the gym. My looks are my asset, and I know exactly how to make them work for me.

And tonight, it doesn't take long to get something glittery on my hook.

She knows the game.

She's a master at it too, dancing by, ignoring me at first. Flirty smiles come my way on the second and third passes, and by the fourth, she makes her move. She approaches the bouncers guarding the VIP area and flashes a smile in my direction. With a nod from me, she's through the ropes and sliding sensuously onto the sofa.

I love this part. The teasing cross of her legs, the way she wets her lips, the little shimmy of her shoulders, making one of the thin straps of her dress fall off her shoulder. I know my role. With a small, seductive smile, I lean forward and run the tip of my finger up her bare arm, snagging the strap on my way up until it's back where it's supposed to be.

We exchange small talk, but neither of us has much to say. We know where this is headed, and the anticipation is thick between us. I toss back my whiskey, taking a minute to savor the burn, and turn to her.

Her features are unremarkably beautiful. She could have come out of the pages of any magazine with her golden skin, bleached hair, and blowfish lips. She's got the kind of face and body that would sell anything. I should know. It's my job to sell anything and everything my family needs me to, from oil changes to luxury condos, and I'm really fucking good at it.

Packaging matters, and hers is stellar.

She leans into me as we cross the club. The pounding bass, the crush of bodies, and the dimly lit room all blend together. This could be one of a hundred clubs I've been to around the world. They're all the same. Same music, same smells, same plastic people. No judgments, though. I'm just as plastic as anyone else here.

Maybe more.

I call my driver, and the second we're in the privacy of the Escalade, she's on me, uncaring that my driver is watching. He barely notices, eyes focused on the road, ferrying us to her place. He knows the score, and he's paid really fucking well for his discretion.

A few hours later, I emerge, slightly mussed, a hell of a lot more relaxed, with lipstick marks on some very pleasurable places.

She tried to get me to stay. They always do. But I slipped out easily, making noncommittal noises when she asked about seeing me again. It happens almost every time. Doesn't matter if she knows the score or not. By the end of the night, they always want more.

What can I say? I have skills.

And Billions of dollars.

I'm realistic enough to know my money probably has more to do with it. They're dreaming of the life I could give them. The exotic vacations and $50,000 purses. If they knew what life with me would really look like, they wouldn't be so interested.

I climb into the front of the Escalade, ignoring Luis's smile. "Home, boss?" he asks.

"Home," I mutter, propping my elbow on the door and resting back in my seat. It's late. After two. The roads are quiet as we make our way to the waterfront and the high rise my brothers and I built. I'm not sure when that stopped being weird, but somehow, in the last few years, the idea that we built and still own a big chunk of a high-rise, has become the norm.

Laying in my cot in that group home, rocking Jonas through a meltdown, worrying how the fuck we were going to make it, I never dared to dream this big. Thank fuck for Ransom. He saw value in Jonas and drew us into his circle. Fucker was smart enough to realize my brother and I were a package deal.

I might not have been Ransom's first pick, but I earned my spot in our family. All nine of us worked together to build our empire, but Ransom's vision is the one that got us here. I would lie down in front of a speeding train if he asked me to. I would for any of my brothers. They gave me the one thing I needed in life, Jonas's safety, and in return, I gave them my loyalty.

Jonas and I may be the only blood brothers in the group, but we're all thicker than blood now. We're family.

I SMOOTH MY HAIR IN MY BATHROOM MIRROR ONE LAST TIME, making sure every strand is exactly where it should be, then flick off the light and move through my apartment to my front door. I handpicked everything in here, from the color of the hardwood floors to the luxurious wallpaper. Everything is expensive as fuck and looks like it belongs in a magazine. Not bad for a poor kid from the South side of Chicago.

Shoving my feet into a pair of Converse, I pull open the door and cross the small entryway to my brother's door, knocking briefly before entering. We're all coded to each other's places, and it's not unusual to have someone popping in multiple times a day. Declan set up a privacy option for us, so if we need it, we use it. I never have. I don't think any of us did until this year, when my brothers started coupling up. Now, enabling privacy mode is the equivalent of putting a sock on the doorknob.

I expect to find him at the table, working on a puzzle. It's where he is most Sunday mornings. Jonas is a creature of habit. He wears the same type of clothing every day, eats the same food, listens to the same music, and does the same activities. That routine is comforting to him. Hell, it's comforting to me.

So when he's not at the table where he should be, my heart races. I don't go into a full panic like I used to, but the echoes of all the times that panic was warranted flash through my mind. "Jonas?"

No answer. Each heartbeat comes faster.

The condo is one massive open room, and he's clearly not here, so I head to his bedroom and push open the door.

"Shouldn't you knock first?" he says dryly. Just like that,

all is right with my world again. I mentally will my heartbeat to slow. He's ok.

He's laying on his back on the bed, feet bare, dressed in sweats and a black t-shirt. His shoulders and head are dangling off the bed. I cross the room and drop onto my ass on the floor next to him, looking out the same window he's gazing out of.

"Why the hell would I need to knock?"

"I could be entertaining a woman," he says dryly.

I shoot him a glance, but I can't tell if he's making a joke or if he's serious. And I usually can.

"Is that a possibility? As far as I know, you've never... entertained a woman here before."

"I could start."

"Never said you couldn't. But I thought you were..." I don't know how to finish that sentence.

"A virgin?" he asks, voice relaxed.

"Yeah."

"I am. But I think I'm going to change that. Soon."

A wheezing gasp escapes. The man doesn't even like shaking hands and how he's talking about having sex. "Fuck, brother. You could have told me you were going to clown school, and I'd be less shocked."

Jonas's whole body shivers. "That makeup is so thick. It's unlikely I could move my face. I think that's what being buried alive must feel like."

Chuckling, I nudge his shoulder with mine. He nudges back halfheartedly, still staring, upside down, out the window.

"Tell me what's going on in your head? You've never shown an interest in anyone before, so..."

His mouth tightens briefly. "That you know of."

I stretch my legs out and study the toe of my pristine white sneakers. That idea doesn't sit well. I know my brother better than anyone. I've been there for him from the day he was born. "What do you mean? Have you had a...crush before?"

He snorts, rubbing a hand over his stubbled cheek. "A crush? Do you mean, have I been sexually attracted to anyone before? That's really what you're asking, aren't you? If I have desires or if my dick hangs limp in my pants twenty-four hours a day, right?"

I grab his thick shoulder and give it a small shake. The thread of pain in his voice makes my chest ache uncomfortably. "Never, brother, never. I know you. I know you're packing heat in your pants, and you can do whatever the fuck you want with it. I just meant that you haven't shared much of that part of your life with me."

I can hear the smile in his voice. "Packing heat? Are you commenting on the size of my penis? I'll have you know I still have all the pages memorized from our dick ledgers from when we were kids. Mine was at the top of the girth list. I've read that girth is far more important than length, though I have also read that I'm far above the norm on that as well."

Not trying to hide my laughter, I shove him so he slides off the bed onto the floor. He kicks out at me, nearly nailing me in the balls. We wrestle around on the floor until we're both panting, neither one of us able to hang onto the upper hand for long. We flop to the thick carpet, laying side by side, staring up at the ceiling.

"So now that we've clarified that you've got the goods to please a woman, can I ask you what's going on with you?"

Jonas folds his hands under his head, eyes still fixed on the ceiling. "I'm struggling with an...attraction. I find myself fixating on a woman, and it's quite maddening. Apparently, it's been quite obvious. At least Declan seemed to think so."

I hold in my sigh. It is obvious. Janey's been working for us for a few years, but it wasn't until she helped us identify a thieving employee that she really hit our radar. She has a way of connecting with people that I'll never understand. Her gentle nature snagged Jonas's attention. The man asked her to call him by his first name —he never does that— so it's a big fucking deal.

"It's obvious to us, yeah, but only because we know you so well. You haven't paid much attention to women in the past, so the way you act around Janey is glaring."

"Yes, well. I find myself thinking about her far too often and at quite inconvenient times." He frowns, rolling his head to meet my eyes. "I don't think I like it. It feels...unsettling. Like a piece of me is not where it's supposed to be anymore."

I understand exactly what he means. That's exactly how I feel about Jonas. The fact that he feels that way about a woman? I'm not sure I like it either. Everything is changing too fast. Four of my brothers are coupled up in less than a year. And now Jonas has fallen.

"Have you talked to her about it...about how you feel?"

"Is that what I should do? Tell her she makes my chest ache?"

I sit up, resting my arm on my bent knee as I study him. I know the lines of his face better than I know my own. But this man looking back at me is a stranger, and I'm desperate to change that. To find my way back inside to the core of our relationship. "Fuck, brother. I don't know. Maybe? Or maybe, you should figure out what it is you're feeling and what you want. If you're just needing to scratch an itch, or if you want something more from her. Because if it's just an itch...then you have to make different choices."

He rolls over, resting his chin on his folded hands, and stares at the lake stretching out before us. "Explain choices. Be specific."

The familiar order settles me. "If this is just an itch...if it's just sexual attraction, then pursuing Janey isn't fair. There are plenty of women out there that could meet those needs." His grimace is telling. He doesn't like the idea of other women. "If you want Janey, then you're going to have to be careful. She's an employee, but she's also...." I don't know how to finish that.

"Fragile," he says softly. "She's one of the kindest, most nurturing people I've ever met. But she's also self-conscious and does not believe in herself."

Placing my hand on his back, I give him the truth he's looking for. "You're a man in a position of power, and Janey is just trying to find her footing at work. If you want her, if you want more, then we'll figure it out. But if you need a fuck, that can be arranged discretely, with someone who will give you exactly what you need, with no expectations."

"A professional," he says flatly, glancing back at me. I give him a nod, and he turns back to the window. "I don't like that idea. At all. I don't like the idea of touching a stranger. Of letting her touch me. That sounds...awful."

His words strike me, little daggers shredding the thin veneer I have around my core. His judgment of my entire lifestyle is implied. He may not mean to insult me. He's talking about himself. But that's what I do, don't I? I let a stranger touch me. I touch her. I bury myself in her and let myself get lost for a few hours. There's no emotion other than mild affection. And when it's done, I'm back to being cold.

For someone like Jonas, who guards his inner circle of trusted people like a dragon protects its treasure, fucking a stranger may well be a horrifying thought.

"Did I upset you?" he asks, brow furrowed.

I smooth out my unconscious frown and do what I always do. Push down my discomfort and say what he needs me to say. "No, I'm not upset." His eyes dart back and forth, and his face relaxes. "I don't have relationship advice for you, brother. Maybe you can talk to Micah about that. Or Colt. They're better equipped."

"Do...do you think I would be a good boyfriend?"

I drop onto my stomach and rest my chin on my hands, mirroring his pose. I've done this thousands of times. Moved to his level and laid with him in whatever state he was in. I've been present. At times in my life, it's been easy, but other times, it's been one of the hardest things I've ever had to do.

Today, it's hard.

He's growing away from me, and I would never do anything to stop it, but I'm terrified. Terrified that he won't find his way through this and terrified that if he does, I'll be left behind.

"You'd be the best boyfriend. I have no doubts." And he would be. Jonas is one of the most caring people I've ever met. Any woman would be lucky to be loved by him. But not every woman will take him as he is, and that's the part that scares me. The possibility that he'll end up with someone who will chip away at who he is.

His exhale is long and slow, carrying with it his tension and worries, at least for the moment. We both lay there, drifting, supported by Jonas's cloud-like carpet.

"She's coming today, Maya," he says.

"Yeah, she is," I say grimly. There's a pool of unease sitting in my stomach. Something about that woman bothers me. So why the fuck did I push so hard to get her here? *Because she's fucking brilliant.* And I want brilliant for my company. For my brothers. Sure, we have billions, but there's no reason why we shouldn't make more.

If only the woman weren't so difficult. I don't have room for difficult in my life. I've been chasing her for months. I don't chase. Ever.

"You don't seem happy about it," he says, frowning at me.

"I'll be happy if she sticks out the three months, and we can lock her into a contract."

"Isn't a three-month probationary period standard? I don't understand the problem."

I scrub my hands over my face. "Yeah, I guess they're standard. But they're usually for the employer's sake. To give us time to see if they're a good fit and are meeting the expectations of the job. But that's not what this is. She required a three-month probationary contract that allows her to walk away for any reason. I feel like I'm going to spend the next few months jumping through hoops for this woman. I don't fucking like it."

"That's why she's staying here, then?"

"Yeah. If she decides to stay after the probation is done, she'll find her own place. For now, the job comes with one of the apartments."

"Did you fix one up?"

I roll onto my side, propping my head in my hands. "Why would I fix one up? It's got everything she needs in it already."

"Colt fixed up Evie's apartment."

"Colt's an obsessive fucker who was half in love with Evie before he ever met her."

He hums. "There is that."

"Maybe we just give her that one." I peek at my watch. "She should be here soon. Her flight landed an hour ago."

Jonas grunts and does some weird plank to a one-handed handstand to rise to his feet.

"What the fuck was that, brother?"

He shoots me a grin, "I keep telling you, body weight exercises are all you need. It would improve your muscle tone and flexibility."

I rise to my feet, straightening my shirt. "The ladies like all my muscles just fine," I say as I aim a punch to his stomach. He dances back with a laugh, and just like that, we're back on familiar ground. "Let's go. We'll wait for her downstairs."

3

MAYA

I should have worn my work clothes. As I tug my t-shirt down under my heavy parka, I wish I'd thrown on something different. Something less casual than my Hello Kitty tee and leggings. But the idea of being stuck on a plane for any length of time in anything but my cozy clothes made me itchy. Not that I've actually been on a plane before today, but I did a lot of research. All the travel blogs suggest dressing for comfort.

Staring up at the high rise in front of me, nearly tipping backward trying to see the top, I realize I might be in over my head. I was so sure, after my video interview, that this was the right choice. It seemed like the kind of company that would let me work the way I wanted and would accommodate my quirks, but now I'm not so sure.

Because people who live in places like this, or who can afford to put employees up for free in a place like this, are not my kind of people. I'm not stuffy or formal. I don't care about designer labels, and I've never lived in a place that had a doorman.

My apartment back in Manhattan was a tiny one-bedroom with worn floors and radiant heaters. My windows looked at the building next door. This place has views for days. And it's right on the water.

The driver that picked me up is staring at me quizzically, trying to wave me through the huge glass doors. I shake off my anxiousness and follow him in, nodding and mumbling a 'thanks' to the man in the suit holding the lobby doors open for me.

Everything in here is shiny and expensive. I make sure to rub my boots really carefully on the mat. I don't want to be that person. The one tracking in the mud. That's all I need, a reputation as a mud tracker-inner. I would get glared at by the doorman each time I walked through. They'd talk about me behind my back, whispering and pointing. No, thank you. I'll be the obsessive foot wiper instead. That's a label I can live with.

Every bit of my nerves evaporate when the two dachshunds strut off the elevator, bums wiggling, tongues hanging. I register the well-dressed silver-haired woman holding their leashes, but the fur babies are the ones who have my full attention. As they approach, I drop to my knees on the cold marble floors. "Hi, sweet babies," I whisper, putting my fingers out.

It's heaven. The wiggly bodies, the soft wet tongues, the excited little yips. I lean down and let them sniff my hair and my face, laughing and rolling my lips in to avoid an eager lick at my mouth. I stroke their smooth dark coats and touch their small paws, all the while whispering to them how sweet they are. How wonderful.

A throat clearing snaps me out of the dog daze I'm in. I meet the eyes of the woman holding their leashes in one hand and an ornate cane in the other. A flush heats my cheeks as I realize I'm sitting on the floor in the ritzy lobby with her dogs still climbing all over me.

"I would stay and let you play longer, dear, but we're on a schedule today." Her lips are curled in a small smile, and there's warmth in her eyes. She's laughing at me, but it's not malicious.

"I'm sorry for holding you up," I mumble as I gently place the dogs on the floor, carefully untangling them from their leashes. "They're beautiful dogs." She smiles, murmuring her thanks, then they continue on their way. I spin on the floor, eyes blinking furiously, and watch them leave.

Pulling my gaze from the woman's back, I scan the ornate lobby, my eyes crashing to a stop at an imposing sight.

I'm not sure how I missed them, the two large men staring at me. They're immobile, standing in the small seating area near the elevators. Zach and Jonas Lee. I recognize them both from my interview. At the time, I was looking at four people crammed into a tiny screen, so somehow their impact was lost on me. It's not now.

They're two of the most physically imposing men I've ever met. Both over six feet, with straight dark hair. They're dressed casually but somehow radiate the same kind of power that most men need an expensive suit to pull off.

As I study them, they're busy studying me. The one with the scruff, Jonas, is doing so obviously, scanning me from top to bottom and back again. But he's doing so without judgment, like he's cataloging, deciding what mental box he wants to put me in. I get it. I do the same thing when I meet a new person. I'm doing it to him right now, actually.

Zach, on the other hand, the man I'll be directly reporting to for the foreseeable future, is unable to mask his...distaste. While he studies me, I study him right back. He has a powerful frame, but not like he lives in the gym and eats entire cows daily. His muscles are big but refined, with broad shoulders tapering to a narrow waist. Below that, hidden by his black athletic pants, is the outline of some not-insignificant thighs.

As we scan each other, our eyes finally meet. He's quick to wipe any judgment from his face, but not quick enough. I can't say I'm shocked. Of course, he's judging me. In my admittedly limited experience, men like him care a lot about their appearance. I do, too, despite what he may think. I did two armpit sniff tests on my way here.

I'm good.

But even I can admit crawling around on the floor is not the best introduction to my new bosses. I push to my feet and walk over to them, taking slow, deep breaths.

He smooths his features into a charming smile, and even though I know it's practiced, it unsettles me. I'm sure that smile gets him whatever he wants. I'm not used to something so powerful being directed at me.

"Miss Miller, welcome to Chicago. I hope your flight was ok? You...ah, have a little hair, there," he says, gesturing to the side of his face. I swipe my hands down my cheeks, catching the black dog hairs, then rub them off onto my leggings. He can't hide the little twitch at the corner of his right eye at the motion.

I stretch out my now hair-free hand. "I prefer Maya." He clasps my hand, eyes widening when I shake firmly. Was he expecting one of those limp hand clasps some women do? Not my style.

"Maya," he says, drawing out the final *a*. "We'll be working closely, so please call me Zach."

He releases me and steps back. The other steps forward but doesn't offer to shake. "You can call me Jonas," he says, dropping his hands in his pockets. There's something about his manner that I find soothing. I give him a smile, and Zach clears his throat. When I shift my gaze to him, he's looking at his brother with surprise. He catches me looking, and his features smooth out.

"Well, if you'll follow me, I'll take you up to your apartment." He takes my two large suitcases from the driver. "Marco will bring the rest of your things up."

"That's everything," I say, pointing to my brand-new suitcases.

He can't hide his surprise. "Excuse me? Is the rest of it being shipped later?"

"It's in storage."

"Well, we can arrange to have it sent for you. Just email me the details."

"I don't want it sent."

He sets the suitcases down and runs his fingers through his hair. It barely moves. It goes right back to where it was. Is it gel that makes it do that? Would it be crunchy under my fingertips when I touch it? Or maybe it's just been whipped into submission, terrified of not meeting up to his perfectionist standards.

His big chest expands with his deep breath. "I don't understand."

"I do," Jonas says. I forgot he was there. Not sure how, since he's gargantuan. Ok, not gargantuan, but at five foot nine, I'm not used to being loomed over the way these men do. To be fair, they're just standing there, but it feels like looming. It's a little unsettling. "You're taking the probation period seriously, aren't you?"

"Yes, I am. There's no point in moving everything if I don't like it here. And if I do, I can have my things sent to my new home, not the temporary apartment here."

"Logical," he says with a nod, looking over my head. I wait for him to say more, but he's done. Short, sweet, and to the point. I think I'll like him. His brother, I'm less sure about.

That tick is back next to Zach's eye. I have a feeling I'll be seeing a lot of it. "You're ready to give up that easily?"

"Give up? This job?" When he nods, I smile. "That's a very calculated choice of words. To give up implies loss. Very clever. However, if I choose to leave this position, I won't be giving up. I'll be choosing something different. Something better for me. So you can save the subtle manipulation for someone else. It won't work on me."

His eyes flare in challenge, but he pushes it down. Too bad, it would have been nice to see him less buttoned up. In my experience, people are always going to show you who they are, eventually. I'd rather that happen sooner rather than later.

He hums low in his throat and puts that charming smile back on as he picks my suitcases back up. "I see. Well, let's get you upstairs."

He waves me toward the elevator, lifting one of my very heavy bags to point. The muscles of his shoulder bunch as they easily adjust to the weight. We ride up in silence. Jonas stares at the wall, his fingers tapping rhythmically against his thigh, but not like he's agitated. More like it's a habit.

Zach doesn't look as relaxed. The tension in his shoulders and the twitch at the corner of his eye are telling me a story. It could have nothing to do with me. I'm a blip, a nobody. But I still think I'm the cause.

"You agreed to the terms of the probation. Three months, I can leave whenever I want. That's a good thing," I remind him. "If I don't meet your standards, all you have to do is ask me to leave, and I'm gone. It's simple for both of us."

"Simple. I suppose. But it sounds more like you've already got a foot out the door. I thought by accepting this job, you were agreeing to make an effort here. But you're right. I did agree to it."

I open my mouth to defend myself, to explain how big it is for me to be here, but the doors opening distract me. Zach steps off, followed by Jonas, who holds his arm against the door for me. I step off with a nod and follow Zach to the door on the right. I was so distracted on the elevator, I didn't register where we were, but the little placard next to the door gives me a clue 3401. The thirty-fourth floor.

Jonas swings the door open, waving me in. I shuffle in and

to the side, letting Zach in. He lowers my suitcases and shoots me a look. "There are two other available rentals on this floor, but we thought you might prefer this one. My brother's wife and her daughter used to live here. He furnished it for them, and it's...softer than the other two." I study the space, the comfortable couch, the rug under the coffee table. Everything in here is lush and luxurious. The kitchen is five times the size of the one I had in my place, and much, much nicer.

"This is lovely," I murmur. And it is. Unable to resist, I circle the couch and sit. It's nearly perfect, with just the right amount of bounce to the cushions, the fabric soft yet crisp. I run my fingers back and forth, enjoying the texture. I'll be petting this couch a lot.

Conscious of their eyes on me, I stand and clasp my hands awkwardly in front of me. "This will be fine. Thank you so much."

Jonas is studying me, head cocked to the side. He nods, more to himself, then moves across the way bigger than I expected-apartment. "The bedroom is this door, then you have the bathroom. This room," he says, placing his hand against the door on the right of the small hallway, "was Mia's room."

"Mia?"

"Evie's little girl. Evie and Colton got married six weeks ago, so they've moved upstairs. This was her pink princess room. Colton moved everything to his home, but the walls are still pink. If you need them repainted, let us know."

Curiosity drives me to the door. He swings it open, revealing not just pink walls, but sparkling pink walls. I can't resist touching them, my sensitive fingertips feeling the tiniest of bumps from the glitter. I stroke over them as I study the room, imagining it filled with the little girl's things. Maybe it's fanciful of me, but I can almost feel the joy in this room and hear her happy giggles.

So unlike where I grew up. Who would I be today if I

grew up in a family that cared enough to paint glitter on my bedroom walls?

Finally, I find my voice. "This is fine. I won't need this room." I turn my back on it and return to the front door, twisting my hands together. "Thank you for seeing me up. I'll see you tomorrow at work."

Zach's eyes are icy as they rest on me. Jonas moves to the door and pulls it open, shooting me a calm nod. "Understood. You'd like us to leave now. We will be leaving for work tomorrow at 8:15 am. Just push the P3 button, and you'll find us."

"Oh, no. There's no need for you to pick me up. I'll find my own way."

"We're not picking you up," Jonas says simply. "We live upstairs. We all go the same direction anyway, so there are always rides available."

My mouth is dry. "All go the same direction?" Who is all?

"Yes. There are nine of us. Well, eight. Our brother Micah works elsewhere. But the rest of us all work at the compound."

"Wait...so you all live here? In this building? I'm living in the same building as all of my bosses?" Yep, my voice cracked at the end.

Of course it did.

There is no escape from them. Am I going to have to be office me all the time? They're going to expect professionalism and propriety all the time. I can't live like that. I'll suffocate. I won't do it. I can't go back to the cold, reserved person I was in New York. I'm supposed to be different here.

It's Zach who answers. "We own the building. Where else would we live?"

Crap. Maybe I shouldn't bother unpacking.

4

MAYA

I arrive in the parkade at precisely 8:15 am. I nearly called a cab twice, but decided that offending my employers on my first day of work might not be the best strategy. I normally like to be early for things, but I did not want to get down here and meet more of my bosses before I'm mentally prepared.

I'm wearing my standard work clothes this morning. A baggy dress that falls to my ankles. This one is beige with vines along the skirt, and my black loafers. I'm not really sure if they match the outfit, but they're the only pair I have, so they'll have to do. My long black parka is unbuttoned for the ride. I'm really glad I brought it. I wasn't expecting the way the wind cut right through me yesterday.

Zach and Jonas are standing next to a blue minivan right outside the elevator doors. Jonas gives me a smile and nod. I return it, then turn to my other boss. He's holding the sliding door of the van, fingers nearly white, as he stares down at my shoes. I glance down, and yep, they're still there. He doesn't look like he can pull his eyes from them. I think he'll need a minute. "Do I sit in the front or the back?" I ask Jonas.

"Front. Zach can sit back there." I move for the door, but Zach's there before I can touch the door handle. I don't think anyone's ever opened a car door for me before.

"Morning," he mutters, giving me the smile again. Beneath it is consternation and confusion.

"Morning," I return.

The ride is silent, giving me plenty of time to ponder the men in this van...and the van. Finally, my curiosity wins out. "Why do you drive a minivan?" I ask Jonas. They're rich. They can definitely afford to drive something more expensive.

He glances at me briefly, then away. "It's one of the safest vehicles on the market, and almost all of my brothers can fit in it."

"Do you do that often? Drive all your brothers around?"

"Yes," he says simply, hands at nine and three.

"So you're telling me that this minivan is sometimes filled with a bunch of billionaires? Are all your brothers your size?"

His lips quirk into a small smile. "Or bigger. Micah and Colton are nearly six-foot-six."

A little snort escapes as I imagine it. "Oh my god, it must look like a clown car when you all get out."

He barks out a laugh. I hear an echoing one from behind me. "Yes. I had to upgrade the suspension...when we go over speed bumps, we'd occasionally bottom out."

Chuckling at that image, I nearly miss it as we pull through a security gate, the guard at the gate nodding at Jonas as we pass through. Then we're heading past a large outdoor parking area and around a large office building. "How many stories?" I ask as I peek up at it.

"Twelve," Zach answers. I crane my neck to look back at him. He's sitting in the backseat of a minivan, and he looks like he could step right out onto a runway. Does he ever look ruffled? I wonder what it would take? And I wonder why I'm wondering. That's...unusual for me.

We pull into a covered garage at the back, then cross a covered walkway and into the building. There's no snow on the walk, but the cold seeps through my shoes, and I make a mental note to wear my boots tomorrow.

The building is a bit of a blur. We're through the foyer and up on the twelfth floor before I know it. It's a massive floor, with executive offices around the outside and glass-walled cubicles and offices in the middle. They lead me to an office near the back. "This is yours," Zach says. "The marketing department is on the seventh floor, and there will be a work-space for you down there, but you asked for an office away from the busyness, so here you go."

I murmur my thanks and drop my heavy bag onto the desk. It's not a huge space, but it's nicely equipped and has a glass door that closes.

"You'll be spending this morning with Janey —you met her during your interview— then we'll head down to the marketing floor and spend some time getting you acquainted with everyone."

"I'll take you to Janey," Jonas says, fingers tapping on this thigh. Zach shoots him a look I can't interpret.

"I can take her. I'm sure you have other shit to do."

Jonas frowns at his brother. "No. I'll take her," he says firmly, then steps into the hall and gestures for me to follow. There's some subtext there that I'm not sure about, but it becomes clearer when we approach a woman on the floor below. She's a little shorter than me, dressed in black leggings and a gray silky top. She smiles brightly at us.

"You're here! It's so nice to finally meet you in person. Is it ok to call you Maya? I'm Janey. It's my pleasure to show you around today, and help you feel settled."

Her warmth loosens the tension in my shoulders. "Hi Janey, I'd love it if you call me Maya."

She beams and turns to Jonas. "How are you this morning? How did the puzzle go yesterday? How many pieces was this one?"

He clears his throat, the tips of his ears are red. "It went well. It was five thousand pieces."

Her eyes widen. "Five thousand? Oh my gosh, Jonas, that must have taken you forever to finish." She claps her hands. "Oh, I almost forgot. I found this stuff at the craft store this weekend." She grabs a bottle out of her desk and brings it to him. She places it in his upturned hand and wraps her fingers around the base of his palm. "It's for puzzles, so you can hang them up after you're finished. You just paint it on, and it will hold it together."

Jonas is frozen, staring at his hand. But I don't think he's looking at the bottle of puzzle glue. Janey drops her hands and steps back. "You don't have to use it. But I thought maybe—"

"It's wonderful. I'll try it this weekend." His throat bobs as his gaze skates over her face. "Do...do you like puzzles?"

"I do," she says with a rueful smile, "but I'm very slow. I don't think I would ever be able to finish the kind you do."

Ask her to do it with you, I mentally urge him. He's completely in love with her and has no idea what to do about it. I've seen that look on a few of my coworker's faces through the years. It's beautiful and heartbreaking at the same time, because she's not looking at him the same way. But even with my limited experience, I know that with a little coaxing and a little attention, feelings can change.

"Yeah. Well. Yes. It takes some practice." He swallows again, then tightens his grip on the glue. "Thank you. I'll leave you now." He spins and walks away abruptly.

Janey watches him go, a gentle smile on her face. When he's out of sight, she turns back to me and claps her hands together softly. "Now, Maya, I want to show you around this morning. And I know during the interview you had some worries about the environment here. We'll work together to make sure you're comfortable."

She doesn't seem put out. Or frustrated that I'll need some accommodations, and I release the last little bit of tension I'm holding. Maybe this will be ok.

I'M OVERLOADED BY LUNCH. TOURING THE BUILDING, I'VE MET more people than I can keep track of, though the rest of the brothers have made quite an impression. They're all large men, dark-haired, deep voices. But they welcomed me with kindness, insisted I call them by their first names, and let us continue with our tour. My nerves are humming now, and that low buzz is at the back of my head, warning me I'm going to suffer later. I rest my head back in my chair and close my eyes, trying to will the headache away.

"That bad, huh?"

My eyes fly open to rest on the woman standing in the doorway. She's tall but also wearing death-defying stilettos that put her head near the top of the doorframe. Her lush mouth is painted a deep red. Her white lace top is low cut, tucked into her leather skirt. She looks like sex. Everything about her is a mixture of soft curves and steel.

She's like a full-figured Barbie come to life.

"Ah, bad?"

"Yeah. You look like you've gone a few rounds, and it's not even lunch." Her eyes are dancing with humor. She's intimidating but doesn't seem mean.

"I think I met a hundred people today, and I can't remember anyone's names. And the lights are humming." I mutter the last part, but she catches it away. Her blonde mane falls off her shoulder as she tilts her head.

"Well fuck me, you're right. They are humming. Is that new, or did I just never notice?"

"It's not new," I say flatly. I asked about the lighting in my interview, but I knew I'd have to deal with some obstacles. But this is a big one. "Fluorescent lights provide poor task light, and can trigger headaches." *Like the one brewing right now.*

Her eyes are piercing. "They a problem for you?" Zach steps out of his office, across the hall, and a couple of doors from mine. He's close enough to hear, I'm sure.

"Sometimes I get headaches. They're not my favorite. And the noise always makes me feel like there's a swarm of bees working next to me."

She scowls, crossing her arms over her chest. "That sounds like a pretty big problem."

I shrug, but what can I say? "I'll survive." Zach turns and retreats into his office.

She hums, still studying me, then nods to herself. "You should come over for dinner tonight."

I stare at her, wondering why on earth this bright butterfly is even talking to a moth like me.

That's not a put-down.

I know exactly who I am, and I'm definitely more of a dark, blend into the background moth. This woman is not. "Who are you?"

She laughs. It's low and throaty, and I could totally picture her narrating a smutty book. "Cara. I'm Ransom's executive assistant. And your neighbor."

I peer over through my glass walls, searching for her office. She laughs again and points to the office right next door. "I'm there. We're office neighbors, but I meant at home. My sister and I live across the hall from you. You're in Evie's old place, right? I meant to say hello last night, but my boyfriend distracted me."

Her hazy eyes and pink cheeks tell me exactly how he distracted her. She has someone. Of course, she does. She's exotic and stunning. Her boyfriend probably wears expensive suits and flies her around the world.

"Does everybody who works here live there?" It's possible, right? It's a big building.

"Nah, just the lucky ones." Her smile drops, and her eyes get serious. "You're new, but I think you'll see that Brash operates a little differently. The brothers are great bosses, but there aren't a ton of boundaries."

My whole life has been one big boundary. More than once, I've been told I have a metaphorical *fuck off* sign over my head. I don't mean to be that way, but if I'm honest with myself, it's easier to stay in my little bubble. *People-ing* is hard.

But Cara seems in the mood to talk, and I have a lot of questions. Questions Janey and the Brash website have been unable to answer for me. "Are they all actually related?" It's nosy of me. But the worst she can do is say so.

"No, Zach and Jonas are biological brothers. They all met at a group home. It was massive. The way they describe it, it was more like Juvie."

I lean forward in my chair. "A group home? How on earth did they end up here?" I mean, to go from foster care to billionaires is a major accomplishment.

Her smile this time isn't sultry. It isn't full of laughter. It's soft and gentle, and it makes everything about her even more alluring. If I liked women, I'd be in love.

Who am I kidding? I already have a bit of a crush.

"They decided to be a family. They took care of each other. And they worked like mad." She taps her red fingernails on the doorframe. "Dinner at six. I'll make spaghetti." Then turns and saunters down the hallway. I'm still watching when a large man in a hoodie tugs her, laughing, into an office and slams the door. Either that's the boyfriend, or there's a hell of a lot more going on here than I ever imagined. What would that be like? Working with your boyfriend?

I can't even imagine what it would be like to go on a date.

Shaking off a little bit of jealousy, I scowl up at the lights again, then rifle through my bag, pulling out sunglasses I packed for just this occasion. I've only been here a few hours, and already this is the weirdest place I've worked.

But just maybe, there's room for my kind of weird here too.

5

ZACH

She's wearing sunglasses. Not a sexy pair. Not even an off-the-rack pair from Walmart. Nope, she's wearing full-on old-people sunglasses. The kind that presses against her forehead and wraps right around to her temples.

Who the fuck is this woman? And what the hell did I do, hiring her?

I stand in her doorway, waiting to be noticed. She brings an apple to her mouth and takes another big bite, a fine mist spraying from the crisp fruit. Her mouth, that luscious, too big for her face mouth, is completely distracting. I clear my throat, tired of waiting for her to acknowledge me.

She shrieks, her bite of apple flies across the small space separating us, and lands on the tip of my two thousand dollar Ferragamo loafers. I stare down at the offending chunk of fruit.

"Jesus, you scared me," she says, slapping her hand on her chest and sucking in a deep breath. My eyes are drawn to that bountiful chest, despite my best efforts to ignore them. Maya Miller is a distraction I was not expecting. The low-level buzz of attraction I've been feeling toward her today is inconvenient. The woman's not my type.

Ok, she is. But only because I like all women.

But the clothes and shoes are fucking hideous.

"You spit food on my shoe," I say flatly, pulling my gaze away from her and staring down at the offending piece of fruit.

"Sorry, sorry," she mutters. Her hands land in my field of vision, then the back of her head. Her dark hair falls loose, the ends trailing on the floor as she carefully picks up the chunk of apple, then uses the side of her hand to wipe off the juice.

She sits back on her heels and looks up at me, a rosy blush on her cheeks, eyes still hidden by those hideous sunglasses. "Sorry. All better."

She's on her knees in front of me, her head—

I'm snapped out of my stupor as she begins to rise. I reach for her to help her up. The loose sleeve of her dress falls back and I'm gripping her soft, warm skin. The tips of my fingers tingle, and I release her as soon as she's standing.

So fucking inconvenient.

She picks her apple up off her desk and takes another bite. Chewing as she looks at me...I think.

"Can you take...those off?" I ask, pointing at her face. She frowns, patting her face until she hits the glasses.

"Oops, yeah."

Her rich brown eyes meet mine, no hint of embarrassment left on her face. The slight flush is still in her cheeks, though. Does that mean she's good at masking it? Or is she used to little collisions like this? I stand there for too long, waiting for her to say...something. The dawning realization comes over me that she seems perfectly content to stand here, not speaking, just staring at me. And now I feel like a creepy fucker. Shouldn't she be trying to impress me or some shit? I am her boss, after all. Besides that, women are always trying to impress me.

I crack first. "If you're finished with your lunch, we can head down to the marketing department."

"I'm ready boss, let's go," she says cheerily, waving me forward. She doesn't put down the apple, happily munching as we walk down the hallway. Just before we get to Declan's office, his door opens, and a flushed Cara strolls out, followed by my brother.

"Is he your boyfriend, or your side piece?" Maya asks casually. Declan chokes, and Cara laughs brightly.

"You'll find out at supper tonight," she says with a wink. We all turn and watch her walk away, hips swaying, her husky laugh carrying back to us.

"She's a very interesting woman. I think I like her." Maya turns to Declan. "I don't think we've met yet. I'm Maya."

Declan, cheeks red from being referred to as Cara's side-piece, gives her hand a brief shake. "Yeah, no, we haven't. I'm Declan. I handle the IT end of things here."

"And you're another brother?"

"I am," he says, smiling at her. "If you need anything, come see me. I can find anything out about anyone."

She tilts her head. "Really? Did you learn all about me?"

Declan's eyes shift uncomfortably. "Uh…yeah, I did."

Is she angry about that? Embarrassed? Nope, apparently not. She laughs.

"That must have been boring research," she says.

Declan chuckles. "There weren't any skeletons in your closet. You're normal, not boring."

"Normal," she echoes, mouth twisted. "I don't know if anyone's ever called me normal before." She shakes her head and waves goodbye, wandering off down the hallway, munching on her apple.

"She's weird right?"

"Yeah," Declan mutters, watching her walk away. "But I think I like her."

"Okay," I say, drawing out the words. Declan shoots me a look and shakes his head.

"Sure, she's a little different, but that's not a bad thing, especially for you."

"What the fuck do you mean?"

"I mean, you're used to a certain kind of woman. All the women in your department flirt with you, even the older married ones. You're used to that dynamic. Maya seems different."

"She doesn't flirt, that's for damn sure. I don't even think she's wearing makeup. And that fucking dress." My lips curl in disgust as I stare at her retreating back. "A paper bag has more shape."

Declan's chuckles grate over my annoyed ears. I turn and aim a punch at his stomach, and he dances back with a laugh. "You sound like a douchenozzle," he says through his laughter.

"Whatever the fuck a douchenozzle is, it sure as hell isn't me." I rake my hand through my hair unconsciously, then carefully pat it into place again. "It's not wrong to have standards. She looks like she shops at a thrift store run by an eighty-year-old. She can't represent the company like that. They'll think we can't afford to pay our staff."

Declan's eyes turn serious. "I think you might find that no one pays as much attention to the way she dresses as you do. I wear jeans and hoodies every day. Jonas refuses to wear suits. We all have our things."

"Maybe, but my department is different. We're out there representing this company. She's going to have to fall in line."

He crosses his arms over his chest, eyes fixed over my shoulder. "Well, I guess you'll have to talk to her about that." His lips curve into a grin, "if you can find her."

Frowning, I spin in time to see the elevator doors close. "Fuck."

Declan's laughing words follow me as I jog down the hall. "Does she even know where she's going?"

No, no, she doesn't.

She has no clue where she's going, and it takes me fifteen minutes to track her down. I finally find her wandering through the accounting department. When I stop in front of her, my words come out harsher than I planned. "I've been looking for you. Where the hell did you think you were going?"

She looks at me innocently, her face serene. "The marketing department."

"You're on the wrong floor."

"Yes, I figured that out. I would have found it, eventually."

My eye is twitching. I resist the urge to slap my hand over it to get it to stop. "Waiting for me to escort you would have been a better use of our time, don't you think?"

Her head tilts, and a slight flush creeps over her cheeks. "Right. I thought I'd get a head start on meeting everyone. I just got turned around."

I bite back any more frustrated words and take her elbow, spinning her in the right direction. We're silent on the ride up to marketing, and I spend the whole time mentally berating myself for my decisions. I did the same thing last night. Why the fuck did I chase this woman so hard? Yeah, she's supposedly brilliant, but so far, she's not living up to the hype. I didn't expect her to be like this. So…scattered. Maybe this probation thing is a blessing in disguise. I can get rid of her and move the fuck on.

My brothers will never let me live it down if I do, though. I made such a big deal about getting her here, I can't bail right away. But maybe, once everyone sees how unsuitable she is for this role, I can send her off quietly. Dick move, maybe, but I won't let anyone fuck with this company. We've worked too hard to build it. I will protect it, and my brother's future, with everything I have.

Satisfied with my plan, I step off the elevator, holding the doors for her. The marketing department is my baby. It's a wide-open space with a few glass offices on the edges. The whole space is filled with light and activity. I'm conscious of Maya's deep inhale as she studies the people clustered around large desks spread with sample ad layouts and graphics.

Here we go.

SHE'S BARELY ACKNOWLEDGED MY EXISTENCE IN HOURS. AFTER introductions, I claimed one of the communal desks in the corner and sat back to watch as Maya worked the room. I didn't expect to see her smile at everyone or laugh with them. I didn't expect the way her eyes sharpened and the way the people around her responded. The more she talked with them, the taller they stood. Within twenty minutes, she had every one of them wrapped around her little finger.

That's when the fucking magic happened. She started pulling apart marketing plans and layouts. I clenched my hands and resisted the urge to barge in. They worked really fucking hard on that. The campaigns were good. Really good even. But in Maya's hands, they went from really good to astronomically amazing.

Unable to resist any longer, I stand and inch closer, examining the explosion of color on the table. She took something that was sleek and polished and breathed chaotic life into it. Everything about her at this moment seems different. Bigger. Bolder. Her voice is stronger, more in command. She's decisive and has everyone around her lit up in a way I've never seen them.

I might as well be invisible. No one's paying a bit of attention to me. It's a weird relief but also a little maddening. Everyone sees me. Everyone pays attention to me. They always have. I've made sure of it. At first, it was to deflect attention from Jonas. Now, though, I enjoy being flirted with. I like women's eyes on me. And I really fucking like being admired. I didn't have that before, and it sure fucking beats being looked down on.

I drift back to the corner of the room to wait. At five, things break up, and my staff packs up and moves toward the elevators. I get some smiles and teasing winks as they leave, which I, of course, return. Maya stands motionless in the middle of the room, watching them leave. Soon, it's only the two of us left.

"They're a really talented group," she says.

"Yeah, they are. I handpicked every one of them. Most of them have been with me for years."

"It shows in their work."

Something about the way she says that sets me on edge. I sit on the edge of a desk and cross my arms over my chest. "Why does that not sound like a good thing?"

She shrugs one shoulder. "It's not a good or a bad thing. It's just that they're all trying to please you, so they give you what they think you want. They're maybe sacrificing innovation as a result."

"We're pretty fucking innovative," I just barely contain my snarl. "We've had to be. We were a bunch of punk kids. We've been turning this industry on its head for a decade."

She nods, looking thoughtful as she weaves through the desks toward me, stopping feet from me. "Much of what you do here is innovative...for what it is. But you're missing a big part of the picture."

"What exactly am I missing?" I challenge her. There's not much heat in it though, because I think I know what's missing. I can see it in the jumble of ads behind her on the desk.

"Life. You're missing life and warmth. You're missing the people. You've got a bunch of sexy ads that don't have anything to do with the people who are actually going to buy what you're selling."

"Like?"

Another shrug. "If I were a busy mom needing an oil

change, then clean bays and top-of-the-line equipment are not what's going to sell me on Brash Auto. I'd be more interested in being treated fairly, in the convenience, and how easy you could make the process for me."

She's not wrong. I've never once thought about what a mom needing an oil change would look for. But that's why I hired a diverse staff. "I employ a bunch of moms," I say, slightly defensive.

"I'm sure you do. But you have an idea of what looks good. Of what sells. And maybe they're just looking to give you what you want, instead of what you need."

I drop my chin, studying the toe of my shoes, wondering if she's right. I can admit, if only to myself, that I run this department tightly. And maybe I have a certain aesthetic in mind. But — "Where the fuck are your shoes?"

Maya peers down at her toes, bare against the grey commercial carpet she's standing on. "I took them off."

"Why?" I mean, I've seen Cara walk barefoot at work, but she wears those sexy Jimmy Choo's. Pretty but not practical. Miss Ugly Loafers here, on the other hand, probably has orthotic insoles. Why the hell would she take them off?

She lifts the hem of her skirt to her knees, rocking side to side as she lifts one foot, then another. Her nails are short, bare. Not a drop of polish on them. I don't think I've ever seen a woman's bare toenails. Not in the last decade at least. Something about it feels too intimate.

"I don't like shoes very much."

My eye twitch is back again. I tear my eyes from her feet and spin for the elevator. "Put them back on. I'll escort you upstairs." She's liable to end up in the basement if I don't take her back myself. A little snort escapes at the image of her drifting through the pipes and boilers.

Picturing her bare feet getting dirty on the concrete floors down there kills my smile.

The elevator arrives, and I hold the doors open for her.

But she's not there.

I don't see her anywhere. Puzzled, I scan the space and see a flash of beige skirt on the floor. Striding forward, I glimpse a plump, rounded ass covered in hideous fabric. It's a fucking travesty — the skirt not the ass — the ass is…magnificent. And distracting. I shake off the interest and mentally slap my dick. We are not going there.

But she's on her knees again…and that's really fucking distracting.

Sighing, I duck down, meeting her eyes past the table legs. "You're on your knees. Again. Why are you crawling around on the floor?"

She barely spares me a glance, but I think I catch a roll of her eyes. "I'm looking for my shoes, remember?"

"You don't know where they are?"

She sits back on her heels and throws her hands up. "If I knew where they were, I wouldn't be looking for them, would I?"

I need a fucking drink.

Or three.

6

MAYA

"You can do this, woman. It's just a dinner. You go, you eat, you come home. People do it every day."

I stare at my reflection in the mirror, hoping my pep talk will have changed things, but nope, I still look terrified. Closing my eyes, I take a few deep breaths, reminding myself that I chose this. I wanted to shake up my life. Living my life in my tiny little bubble has gotten me exactly nowhere. I'm in my thirties, I've never been in a relationship, and if I died tomorrow, the only person who would care is Abigail. I promised myself this would be a fresh start and I wouldn't be such a loner in Chicago.

Phase one of that plan is to make friends.

I did really well today with the staff. It was strange at first, but I smiled when they did. Laughed when they did, and suddenly it wasn't so scary anymore. Maybe I can *people*.

So why am I still panicking?

Because this shit is hard. There's no Birdie as a buffer, so it's just me and my insecurities. How can I be so confident at work, and such a wreck in all the other areas of my life? I'm sure there's a diagnosis for what's going on in my head right now, but I don't have time to google it. It's already six, and Cara's waiting for me.

I throw my long, dark hair into a quick ponytail. I thought about curling it, trying to make myself more presentable, but there's no point in going to all that effort. The curls would fall out within minutes. With a sigh, I slap the light off in the ensuite and drop onto my bed.

Today was harder than I thought it would be. The actual work was great. The people in my department all seem pretty great, but the rest of it is overwhelming. Everyone at Brash seems larger than life, and I could feel the urge to shrink into nothing come over me. My tendency to fade into the background socially was riding me hard.

I know I wanted different, but maybe it was a mistake to change everything so quickly. Maybe I should have gotten a new haircut, or tried online dating.

But nope, I had to up and move my entire life.

I've spent one night in this apartment, and it was the longest night of my life. Tossing and turning, no hum of the traffic outside for white noise. No neighbor's footsteps. It was entirely too quiet. Humming the lyrics to *Don't Stop Believing* helped for a while. I hope tonight will be better so my brain can turn off and let me rest.

Moving to the front door, I stop and take a breath, then another and another, until my heart rate is back to normal. Here goes nothing.

I cross the hall to Cara's door decisively, raising my hand to knock. My hand freezes in the air as my doubts come storming back.

Nope. Not doing this. This is too much change, too quickly. I spin, retreat back to my door, and stop, hand on the doorknob, battling with myself. *Stop being such a chicken.*

Ok. I'm really doing it this time. Back to Cara's door.

Nope, maybe not. Got a little too cocky there.

I'm not sure how many trips back and forth I make, but

eventually the decision is taken out of my hands when Cara's door swings open. I keep my eyes fixed on my hand, raised to knock.

Maybe if I stay really still, she won't notice me. That could work.

"This has been endlessly entertaining, but dinner will be cold if we do this any longer."

Ok, crap. She's been watching me. Damn whoever invented peepholes. And she's laughing at me.

"Ah, right. Yes. Well, I just wanted to get some steps in, you know?" I pat my bare wrist for emphasis, then wish a portal would open and suck me in.

"You're a bit of an odd duck, aren't you?"

I meet her eyes, expecting to see scorn, and finding warmth and laughter instead. "Yeah. I don't *people* all that well," I admit, feeling my cheeks heat.

"Well, okay then. Come eat." She backs up and waves me into her apartment. From where I'm standing, it appears to be a mirror image of mine. Big living, dining, and kitchen with two bedrooms off a small hall. The air is scented with garlic and beef, and my stomach lets out a growl.

I let out a little *meep* when another blonde appears next to me. They're multiplying.

Cara introduces us through her laughter. At least she finds me entertaining. "Maya, this is my sister Bree. She lives here too."

I can't figure out if having dinner with two other people is going to be easier or not. Is it too late to bail? I've used the cramps excuse before, but that's usually more effective on men. At work, I know the protocol, but in social situations, I tend to struggle.

I end up sticking my hand out to Bree. Then instead of shaking her hand, I slap it in the world's most pathetic low-five.

Bree tilts her head, bemused, but a slow-growing smile

covers her face. "You're going to do just fine with this group. Come eat."

"YOU'RE FUCKING WITH ME. YOU HAVE TO BE." BREE'S EYES ARE popping out of her head.

"No. It's true."

"How can that be possible? Did you grow up in a commune or something? How have you never been on a plane?"

I take another bite of my garlic toast and scowl at her as I chew. She just laughs, which I secretly love. I've never done this before. Sat and had a meal with other women, and just been able to be me, metaphorical warts and all.

"I've been on a plane. I flew here." And I only hyperventilated twice on the flight. Better than I expected, truthfully.

"But didn't you go on family vacations? Or a spring break trip with your friends in college?"

I place the last of my bread carefully on the side of my plate. "No, I really didn't."

"How," Cara asks quietly, "does that happen?"

Picking up a tiny crumb from my legging, I roll it between my fingers.

"I'm trying to decide if I want to answer your question or not," I admit, scowling down at the floor.

"You don't have to talk about anything you don't want to, Maya. But we are curious about you. Zach made such a big deal over you coming to work here that we've been a little curious."

"I'm not that interesting," I mutter.

"You are to Zach. He still doesn't understand why you wouldn't talk to him or meet him before that interview."

I roll my eyes. Clearly, he didn't understand. The man sent me dozens of gift baskets, flowers, and makeup. I don't even remember how to put on makeup. "I had no reason to leave my job."

"So then, what changed?"

What changed? That's a loaded question. I lean back, studying the women. They're obviously sisters, but Bree has a more laid-back look. Cara's in leggings and a simple t-shirt, but she makes them look sexy and high-class somehow. Bree looks like she's ready to hit the soccer field in her sweats and long-sleeved T. They're both curvy like me, but they have a little less going on in the ass than I do.

"My dog died," I say. The words still hurt, but not as badly as they did. The weeks since Birdie's death have dulled the pain a little. I'm sure it's healthier, but it's also a little sad. I don't want to forget her.

Their faces turn sympathetic. "I'm so sorry," Cara says. "That must have been hard."

"Me too," echoes Bree. "We haven't had a pet since we were younger, but I understand how much a part of the family they can be."

"She…she was more than that to me. But thank you." I clear my throat and pick up the garlic bread again. "Besides, that was just the catalyst. My boss sold his company, and the new owner is a douche canoe. I didn't see the point of staying. I liked going to work before that. It was…good there. It was easy."

Cara's brow quirks. "So your easy job got more complicated, so the next logical step for you was to quit, pack up your whole life, and move?"

I put the bread back on the corner of my otherwise empty plate. Cara makes incredible spaghetti. "It sounds stupid when you put it like that."

"Then why did you make that choice? Something was driving you." How do you explain to someone this put together that you didn't fit into your own life anymore? Has she ever felt like that? I doubt it.

"I...have been living in a bubble for most of my life. I've never been on a plane because I never had any close friends to go anywhere with. Then I didn't want to go anywhere... well because Birdie was at home and she was my family."

"Birdie is...your dog?" At my nod, Cara's face softens. "So when you say your dog died, what you really mean is you lost your family?"

"Yeah, I do."

"Do you have any other family?" Bree asks, propping her chin on her hand.

"Not really."

She opens her mouth to ask another question, and Cara kicks her under the table.

"Ow! You miserable cow. How rude!" Bree's voice is laced with laughter. Cara's smiling too, dodging her sister's return kick. A little pang of jealousy clogs my throat at how easy they are with each other. I've never had that with anyone.

"Do you have other family?" I ask, curious but also wanting to stop talking about me.

Cara's smile fades, and turns sadder. "Our parents passed away a long time ago. It's just Bree and me."

"Cara took me in when I was sixteen," Bree says quietly. "We've been together ever since. She's been there for me no matter what. I wouldn't be here today if it weren't for her." Her voice is thick with emotion. Cara reaches for her hand, gripping it tightly on the table. There's a subtext here that I don't understand, but it feels too private to ask about.

Bree blinks furiously and shakes her sister's hand. "Besides, we have a ton of family now. The Brash Brothers have sucked us into their world. I have way too many big brothers now and they're loud and annoying and..."

"Chaotic," Cara offers.

"Yeah, that's the word. Chaotic." Bree leans forward and folds her arms on the table, her not-insignificant chest resting on top. "But enough about that. I want to know how your first day of work went. Was it what you expected?"

"Well, I expected it to be different, and it was."

"You say it like it's a bad thing, though. You wanted to change things up, right?"

"Yes, I did. I do." *Stop talking now. You can leave it there. Don't....* "I just didn't realize how hard it would be. Everything is different. I don't know where the bathrooms are. I don't know where anything is. And there are so many new people, and they all seem to know me. And the owners are... all so big. Why are they so big? What are they all eating?" I deflate in my chair now that all my anxieties are out on the table. I feel lighter.

"You sound pretty overwhelmed," Bree says.

Cara snorts, "She sounds freaked the fuck out."

"That's the one," I mutter, pointing limply at Cara.

"So, what are you going to do about it? I mean, you're here. I saw your contract. You can leave any time you choose. Are you planning to bail?"

"I didn't come all this way to run away," I mutter defensively.

"Ok, so you'll have to sit in discomfort. It sucks, I know."

I cross my arms over my chest. "What do you know about discomfort? You probably came out of the womb ordering men around."

Cara laughs brightly, not bothered by my snark. "Oh, honey, you have no idea. I spent nearly three years in love with a man I worked with. When I'd get close to him, he'd bolt. Like, literally run away from me down the hallway." She shakes her head. "I know all about discomfort. And now, seeing how things turned out, I wouldn't change a fucking thing. So sit in the discomfort, Maya. Soak it in. Because if you can find your way through it, you might just discover an incredible new life."

7

ZACH

I grip my glass tighter, trying to convince myself that I don't want to throw it at my brother's head. I'm not going to waste the precious whiskey. But it's really fucking tempting.

"I'm just saying, you've got her here. I don't know why you're so grumpy about it." Declan's smirk gives him away. He knows exactly why I'm grumpy about it. Fucker's going to make me say it.

"She doesn't fit in."

"You were convinced she would revolutionize our marketing department. You spent months chasing her. And now that she's here, she's not a good fit? How the fuck does that work, brother?" Ransom's voice is level, but there's a hint of frustration in his tone that only the men in this room...and maybe Cara...would catch. He's leaning back in his desk chair, fingers loosely interwoven over his stomach. They're all watching me, eager to hear my answer.

"It's going to sound fucking awful, I know it," I admit, "but I don't think I want her representing us out there. She doesn't fit the Brash image. She's too..."

"Too....?" Maverick prompts from across the room, elbows on his knees.

"Too frumpy, okay." I say, scowling. "She's scattered, she's frumpy, and she lost her fucking shoes tonight. We spent half a goddamned hour looking for them."

Ransom's lip twitches. "Where were they?"

I groan, lean back on the couch, and throw back the rest of my whiskey, savoring the burn as it blazes a path to my empty stomach. "They were in a planter in the lobby."

Laughter erupts around the room. "It's not fucking funny. That's time I'll never get back. I spent half an hour looking for the world's ugliest shoes. And the woman has no fucking sense of direction. I swear to Christ she'd get lost in a paper bag." How does she function in the world? Who the hell's been looking out for her? Because she sure as fuck needs a keeper.

"She seemed really sweet. Yeah, frumpy. But sweet," Nick offers. His tie is pulled loose, a few buttons on his shirt undone. "If she can do the fucking job, then I don't really see the problem."

"Seriously? Marketing is about image. What image do we want to project to our customers, to our suppliers, to the community? Because her image screams hippy housewife."

"You sound like an ass," Jonas says flatly. His tone takes me back, drying up the words about to come out of my mouth. "Is she good at her job?"

"It's only been a day," I mutter, staring down at the empty glass clutched in my hand.

"Are you saying you have no idea what she is capable of?"

The glass in my hand makes a cracking noise, and I loosen my fingers immediately and place it carefully on the glass coffee table in front of me. I straighten my cufflinks, then raise my eyes to look at Jonas standing at the bank of windows. He's immobile, his clenched hands betraying his frustration.

I've seen it plenty of times, but to have it directed at me makes my chest hurt.

"She spent a few hours with the team today…she's good," I admit quietly.

"Then you have no reason to ask her to leave. Right, Mav?" he asks, looking at our brother.

Maverick, the only one with a legal degree in the room, nods. "That contract is pretty clear-cut. It's an easy out for either party, but if you're asking her to leave because of the way she dresses, then Jonas is right, you're an ass, and you'll make us out to be assholes by association."

Jonas nods, satisfied. He knew the answer, but he's smart enough to get backup when it comes to family fights. "I don't dress according to corporate standards, but I am still perfectly capable of doing my job. Why couldn't she?" Jonas asks.

I rest my elbows on my knees and study his pinched features. How do I explain it to a man who cares nothing about society's opinions? "From what I can tell, she has a brilliant marketing mind. But do you want her representing us at the mayor's office? What about at a $10,000-a-plate dinner?" A collective groan travels through the room at the idea of those stuffy dinners. But they're a fact of life for me. I'm constantly out networking, schmoozing, and representing our interests.

"I know you guys hate them. But they're an important part of what I do."

"Does she really have to be the one to do them?"

I ease back on my seat and rub the back of my neck. "Maybe not, but it would be nice to not have to be the only one going to those fucking things. When I finally got Maya here, I thought I could turn some of that over. But I don't think that's going to happen."

"Do you really not like going? I thought you did? You always seemed fine going on your own?" Ransom's gaze is piercing. I shift on the couch, my suit suddenly feeling tight.

"It's fine, they're fine. I know you guys don't like them."

"Would everything fall apart if we stopped going? I mean, how much fucking money do we need?" Kade asks. He's unbuttoned, too, no tie in sight, but that's by design. The man can't stand them. My brothers chime in with assurances that we don't need the exposure.

"The food usually fucking sucks," Colton mutters, patting his stomach unconsciously.

He's right. It does. The inane conversation sucks. The being paraded in front of people to make speeches and hand over big checks and pose for pictures, sucks.

"We do a lot of fucking good in the world with our money. Yeah, there are some projects that we keep close to the vest, but most of the time, the good press is a win-win for the charities and for us. So no, we can't just stop. It's my job to represent us," I say with a wink, smoothing my tie, "and I'm really fucking good at it."

"You are. You're so pretty," Nick says, blowing a kiss at me.

"Fucking asshole," I mutter, hiding my smile. My brothers are dicks, and I wouldn't have it any other way.

"It's your department," Ransom says, tapping his fist on the desk. "You run it any way that you see fit. But if this woman can give us a new perspective and help us in any way, she should stick around. But if it's too much for you and if you think she's going to be a problem, then do what you need to. We'll handle the fallout."

"It's been one fucking day," Jonas says, glaring at me. My mouth dries up again. The rest of my brothers fall silent as Jonas's words land like a bomb between us. It's not the content of the words that shock us silent, but the combination of the contractions in his speech and the f-bomb he just dropped. Jonas rarely swears, and when he does, then you'd better take him really fucking seriously. I grip the couch cushion tightly. I feel like I'm in a boat in raging waters, and one rogue wave will send me crashing into the water.

"You barely know her. Why are you so bothered by the idea of her leaving?" I ask carefully.

His eyes close, and his shoulders slump forward in defeat. "What if it was me?" he says, his voice a whisper. "What if I was out there, and I couldn't wear a suit or talk to people the way the company wanted? If my boss were anything like you, I would be out of a job before I ever had a chance to prove myself."

My eyes are burning. I hate I made him think of that. I hate that he's got a point. "You're right. I know you're right. I'll figure my shit out." I don't know how, but I will. Because the idea of someone just tossing out my amazing brother because he doesn't fit some idea of perfection in their mind makes me want to punch something.

And yet I was about to do the same thing to Maya. How big of an asshole am I?

Colossal, apparently.

"It's a three-month contract," Maverick says. "Let's give this at least six weeks. And if you have some concerns, try and figure them out within that time." He turns to Jonas. "Can we agree that if Zach still wants to let her go by then that we support his decision?" Jonas's mouth tightens, but he drops his chin in agreement.

I scan the room, catching the rest of my brother's nods. They'll call me on my shit, but I know at the end of the day that they're always going to have my back. It's the only thing I know for sure, and I won't do anything to make them regret it. I don't know how I'll fix this or handle Maya, but I'll figure it out. Maybe I can fairy godmother that shit and get her looking more professional.

"Ok, now that we've handled that shit, can we talk about my brother?" Colton asks. Grateful for the shift in topic, I lean back in my seat and brainstorm with my brothers. Colton's biological brother Johnny, Joker, as he's known to most people, has been in prison for eighteen years. "I saw him again yesterday, and he still doesn't have any intention of applying for parole. He says he needs to stay in there and keep an eye on Brent."

Fucking Brent. My brother Micah's woman, Holly, was married to that piece of shit for too long. And she has the scars to prove it. She's well shot of him, and now she has an amazing man who would protect her with his life.

"Not that the effort isn't appreciated," Ransom says, "but he's paid the price for his crime. Brent's going to be in there for decades. Joker can't give up the rest of his life for that. Besides, even if he doesn't apply, his sentence will be up in a couple of years. What then?"

Colton grimaces. "I have a feeling, if it got to that point, he'd do something to make sure he has to stay. He could play that fucking game and end up staying in there until he's gray. I want a different life for him. I've spent too many years angry with him, and I don't think I can live with him in there any longer. But he's spent half his life in there. He's institutionalized."

"He can't picture his life outside," Maverick says. Colton nods, because yeah, that must be scary as fuck. The entire world, everyone he knew before, has moved on.

"So maybe we need to paint him a picture," I mumble, thoughts swirling.

"What do you mean?" Colton asks, rocking forward in his chair, the frame groaning in protest.

"I mean, we pull the same shit Ransom and Jonas did on us when we were building the tower." Most of us weren't sure about moving into our building. We'd scattered and had our own places throughout the city. But that disconnect wasn't healthy for us. We are unapologetically co-dependent. We thrive when we're together and up in each other's business. So they spent months casually asking us how we'd like our places designed and furnished, having interior designers showing us mock-ups. Before we knew it, we were totally invested and wouldn't think of letting anyone else live in those units.

"We need to paint a picture for Johnny. Show him what his life would look like on the outside. Have we thought about what he could do? And where he could live?"

"I want him with us," Colt mutters.

"Of course you do, brother. We wouldn't have it any other way." Ransom says, rising to put a big hand on Colt's massive shoulder.

"So we fix up an apartment for him," I say. "We figure out a few job options and slowly work on him. Play up how much we need him. Because in there, he feels like he has a purpose. We need to give him one outside those fucking walls."

I didn't know Johnny well. Honestly, from what I remember when we were kids, he was a dick to Colt, but what my brother wants, my brother gets. "We can design a kind of marketing campaign tailored just for him. I bet that within a month, we can convince him to apply for release. And we've got The Judge to put in a good word for him." The Judge being a corrupt fucker that tried to blow up Cara's life. He's ours now, and we'll damn well use him for this.

The tension seeps out of Colt's body. "Ok...ok. That's a good idea."

Our post-workday meeting breaks up soon after, my brothers scattering. The ones with significant others hurrying home to them. Jonas trails me to my office, clearly not done with telling me how much of a dick I am. He pushes the door shut behind him, and with a sigh, I sit on the edge of my desk. He glares at me, hands propped on his hips like superman. Fuck, if any of us were qualified to wear the cape, it's him. He is good and kind and so fucking thoughtful that I feel like a degenerate next to him sometimes.

"Promise me," he finally says.

I rub my hand over my stubbled cheek as I study him. "Why does she mean so much to you? You barely know her."

"I do know her. I know exactly what it is like to feel like the odd one out. I know what it is like to have people judge me. I know her, and I do not want to do anything to make her leave."

"Are you...do you have feelings for her?"

He frowns, giving me the *what the fuck you talkin' about* look. Why am I so relieved? "I have feelings for her. She's a human being and a co-worker."

Right. Forgot who I was talking to for a minute. "Do you have romantic feelings for her? I thought you liked Janey, but maybe y—."

"No. Maya is not Janey. My feelings for one have nothing to do with the other."

"Alright, no offense intended. I just wondered."

"Stop wondering." He moves to the door, swinging it open, his large frame filling the doorway. "Six weeks. Do not do anything to make her want to leave."

Clenching my jaw, I finally give him a nod. He walks away, leaving the door wide open.

I drop my chin to my chest, the next six weeks stretching in front of me endlessly. How do I convince a woman who seems to have one foot out the door on day one, to stay? I rise and lean in the doorway of my office, staring toward her desk. The image of her relaxing in her chair, wearing those ridiculous glasses and eating that bright red apple flashes in my mind, and I grin involuntarily. She is so strange. Nothing like the women I'm used to. I rub my aching chest and ponder ways to make her happy. I've already sent gift baskets and flowers and more shit that I can't even remember, trying to get her to move here. And nothing.

No, if I want to get her to stay...at least for the next six weeks, I'm going to have to start thinking bigger. Those sunglasses flash through my mind again, and I suddenly know just where to start.

It's going to be a long fucking night.

8

MAYA

The ride to work the next morning is uneventful. Zach sits in the back, lightly snoring, as Jonas and I debate vehicle safety. He has such a deadpan way of speaking day to day, but I'm starting to catch hints of humor. They're not glaring, but they're there. He has a dry humor that not everyone would get. But I do. I've already picked up a pattern in his speech. He tends to be more formal, but when he's more emotional, he'll use more contractions. Somehow, understanding that about him makes me feel a little like I'm a part of things. Like we might be friends.

Honestly, it's a relief not to have to speak with Zach. I'm finding myself quite overwhelmed with all the togetherness, and I know I'll probably be spending most of the day with him again. I can do it. I can do hard things.

But I'm grateful for the break right now.

Jonas honks the horn when we arrive at work, scaring Zach awake, and he cackles at Zach's scream.

"Fucker," Zach mutters, rubbing his hands over his scruffy cheeks. I haven't known him long, but the scruff seems out of place. From what I've seen, neat and tidy is the only acceptable look as far as Zach Lee is concerned.

I'm not stupid. I saw exactly how he looked at me yesterday. He covered it up, but not well enough. I know my outfits are killing him. Wait until he sees today's dress. He's going to shit kittens.

"Since when do you sleep on the way to work?" Jonas questions, spinning in his seat to pin his brother with an arched brow.

"I was up late," Zach says with a grunt, climbing out of the backseat of the minivan. I really need to figure out this commuting thing. Do I really want to drive to work with my bosses each day?

No, I really don't.

I take a minute on the elevator to pull my winter coat off and toss it over my arm. The groan behind me makes me smile. I tuck it away, then turn to him, eyes wide.

"Did you say something?" I ask innocently.

Zach can't hide the look of horror on his face. "What exactly are you wearing?"

"A dress."

"Could you have picked an uglier pattern?" Everything in him is cringing back. It's funny, but I didn't expect the little tendril of embarrassment in my chest. Why do I care what he thinks?

"There might have been one or two others to choose from. I think they had little hearts and little flowers, but I already have some flower dresses. I thought I'd branch out."

"To bugs?" he asks with disbelief.

"Huh. Look at that," Jonas says, leaning down and peering closely at my chest, and the small ladybug and beetle print running in rows. "From far away, they could be mistaken for stripes, but nope, bugs." His face is inches from my breasts as he studies the pattern. It occurs to me that it might be perceived as inappropriate if someone were looking at us. But Jonas isn't interested in my boobs. I have the feeling he'd pull a magnifier glass out of his pocket, if he had one, to get a closer look at the pattern. Zach's eyes dart from his brother, and back to me. A frown twists his handsome face. I almost feel bad for offending his sensibilities...almost.

The door opens onto the executive floor, and he slides off, stalking down the hall. We follow, close on his heels, trading amused glances. Maybe it's childish, but annoying this put-together man is satisfying.

As we near my office, my steps slow. I didn't see it when we got off the elevator. But now, I don't know how I missed it.

There, above my desk, and any desk within a twenty-feet radius, are light dispersing panels on the ceiling. I drop my things to my desk and sit in my chair to gaze up. It feels like I'm on the forest floor, looking up through the green canopy of trees to the blue sky above. And the glare I usually feel under fluorescent lights is nowhere to be found. Tears prick my eyes at the thoughtfulness.

"You had a late night," Jonas says, studying his brother. "You were here, doing this." It's not a question. The conviction in Jonas's voice is unarguable. Zach rolls his neck and pins me with a halfhearted glare.

"Maybe now you'll burn those ugly fucking sunglasses." He's trying for cold, but there's a faint flush on his neck that's interesting. He did something nice...maybe nicer than anyone ever has for me, and he seems embarrassed about it. Why? Because he showed me kindness? Or because he did it himself?

I doubt many men as rich as he is would have put in the time to do something this big. I can't decide how I feel about it. Grateful, yes, because this is going to make my day-to-day life so much better. But also...I have no idea where to tuck Zach in my mind. He doesn't fit in that self-obsessed playboy corner I had him in.

"Probably not," I say, thinking of the special-order glasses. But maybe I won't need them anymore. Zach's right. They're ugly, but they've saved me hours of pain more than once, so I'll keep them buried at the bottom of my purse, just in case.

He snarls at me, then spins and stomps into his office. "Thank you!" I yell toward his door. I exchange glances with Jonas. "Is he always like that?"

"No," Jonas says, sounding far away. "He's not. He's generally very level-headed and easygoing. Something about you seems to bring out a different side of him."

I rotate my chair from side to side, processing the hurt his comment inflicts. I never set out to be a nuisance. It's not like I search for opportunities to be annoying, but somehow, the same thing always happens. People end up annoyed and frustrated with me. They start speaking to me in clipped sentences and whispering about me under their breath.

"I don't know how to change that. I don't want to be...difficult."

Jonas pins me with a piercing stare. His brown eyes, framed by simple black rectangular glasses, glare at me. "Don't do that. Do not change who you are to please anyone. Not me, not my brother. Not Ransom. It is a bad idea. For everyone."

"That's what people do, Jonas. They adjust. They change to fit in." Or so everyone tells me.

His mouth tightens. "Is that what you want, though? You moved a thousand miles to a brand new city to be someone else?"

"Basically...yes. I want a different kind of life."

"And you think you're going to get that by changing who you are?"

I stand up and pin him with a glare, annoyed at the way he's pushing this. I don't have this all figured out yet. It's been two damn days.

"Why do you care so much?"

"Because I've tried to be someone different, and it doesn't work." He slashes his hand between us in frustration. "If people like you, it has to be because they know you and like you. The good and the bad. Acting like a different person is not sustainable. At all." He stares down at his hands and runs his thumb over his fingertips. "At some point, you will slip and return to the person you are. Then the people around you will disappear, complaining that you've changed. It is *not* worth it."

The conviction in his voice hits me hard. He's not guessing or theorizing. "It happened to you?"

"Yes. It is a mistake I don't care to repeat."

"Sometimes it's easy to forget that I'm not the only person in the world that struggles." I drop my gaze, staring at the neat surface of my desk. "I didn't have any friends. I didn't socialize. Outside of work, I barely spoke to anyone. And I didn't realize how lonely I was until," I slam my mouth shut, not wanting to explain about Birdie, "well, something changed. Besides, aren't we supposed to be trying to better ourselves as human beings?"

Jonas drops his head and plants his hands on his hips. "Yes. I am coming to see that if something is important, we need to...stretch." He smiles at me sadly. "It is a slow and painful process...for me, at least. I like you just as you are, Maya. If you are going to change, I urge you to think carefully about your reasons why." He turns and wanders to his office. I watch his retreating back as I mull over his words.

I came here wanting something different. To be someone different. Someone who has friends and a social life. And maybe, in the middle of the night, when I'm really honest with myself, someone who is loved. I haven't seen any examples of healthy romantic relationships, but that doesn't mean they don't exist. But I would like to have someone. To matter deeply to someone. But in my thirty-four years on this planet, I've never had that. I've never mattered that way to anyone.

Maybe it's not in the cards for me, but I can admit that I haven't actually tried. It's easier to keep to myself and dream about having something more, than to go out and try for it and fail. I can't stand failing at anything. Glancing up at the ceiling again, I can't help but smile. All of these worries will keep. For right this minute, things are looking up.

ZACH'S A CON MAN. THAT'S GOT TO BE IT. IT'S WAY TOO EASY for him to switch between shooting me dirty looks and flirting with his staff. He's charming, he keeps the flirting from being creepy with that smile of his, and everyone in this department falls at his feet. What would it be like to be that magnetic? To walk into a room and know that you can have everyone eating out of the palm of your hand in minutes?

There's a power in that I crave. Being able to make people like me feels like a superpower.

Too bad we're not living in a comic. I would look amazing in a cape.

"Where the hell are your shoes?"

I flail in my chair, nearly tipping back. Only Zach's quick grab of the arm stops me from hitting the floor. "Jiminy Cricket! You scared me."

He rears back. "What the fuck did you just say?" A grin flashes before he wipes it away. "Did you just use an animated character as a swear?"

"Ah...ummm...gee, look at the time." I tap my bare wrist —*mental note: buy watch so I don't look like an idiot every time I do that*— "looks like we're the last ones here. We should hit the road, Jack."

A choked sound escapes him, and my face flushes. I pop to my feet and glance around for my shoes. I think I took them off somewhere around lunchtime, so maybe I can retrace my steps. Except I got lost a few times today...so yeah, it might take a while.

I wander the floor, searching under tables and chairs in the now-empty marketing department. Zach's large form shadows me. I sneak a glance at his face, not finding the frustration he wore last night. That was embarrassing. Not the losing my shoes part —that happens all the time— but the having my boss searching for them part. Mr. Williams never helped me look. Not once in a decade.

"I can find my own way home tonight. You don't need to stick around."

One brow raises. "Can you? I'm afraid if I leave you alone, I'll find you curled under a desk in the IT department tomorrow morning. You don't have a very good sense of direction." The smirk on his face, combined with his words, makes me feel small. Carefully backing out from under the table I'm crouched under, I stand and face him.

"That's not fair," I say quietly. His head tilts questioningly, but the smirk stays firmly in place. Exhaling, I stare at him, carefully choosing my words. "I've spent my entire life in Manhattan. For the last decade, I lived most of my life within a twenty-block radius. I've been here two days." He drops the smirk, watching me steadily. "I'm trying to find my footing here, but apparently, I'm not doing that fast enough for you."

He crosses his arms over his chest and sits on the edge of one of the tables. The seams of his suit strain at those massive shoulders. Is it weird that I want to poke them? "You got lost getting off the elevator on the executive floor today. There's only one way to turn, but instead, you went straight for the wall. Your sense of direction is absolute shit."

My face flushes again. Yeah, I did do that. "I thought I saw a bird," I mumble, staring at my feet. A low, surprised bark of a laugh escapes him.

"You did not."

"You're right. I didn't."

For some reason, admitting I lied makes his smile grow.

"This is the first time you've smiled at me."

I wish I hadn't said anything because immediately, his

smile falls. "I smiled at you when we met and every day since."

"Yeah, but not that smile. This one is real."

He drops his arms and grips the side of the table with both hands. I stare at his hands. He has nice knuckles. They're not hairy…at least from what I can tell. I wonder if his chest is hairy. I squint at the middle of his shirt, but nope, I still don't have X-Ray vision. Such a letdown.

"I apologize if you've felt I haven't been welcoming," he says stiffly.

"That's the fakest apology I've ever heard," I say, laughing at how he forced out the words. It's awful. "Don't say sorry if you're not. There's no point. Neither of us believes it. Besides, you're easy to read. It's comforting."

"Easy to read?" he echoes, eyes wide.

"Yeah. I mean, it's pretty obvious that you're regretting hiring me." He sputters, but doesn't deny it outright. And that hurts a little bit too. Even though any denial would be a lie. "I'm not what you were expecting. That's obvious. My guess is you've gone over the contract a few times, trying to figure out how to get rid of me." I drop onto a desk and mirror his pose. "I'm really good at what I do. I think you've seen that. And so far, I like it here. But if you're thinking of firing me, then I'd appreciate it if you'd do it soon. Before…"

He clears his throat. "Before what?"

"Before I start to like it here too much. You don't really know me, but me coming here is…big. I'd really rather not get settled and build a life if I'm going to be out of a job and an apartment soon."

He studies me, frowning for achingly long minutes. "You didn't bring anything with you. You already seem to have one foot out the door."

"I can see how you would think that. But I'm just trying to be smart. I haven't moved in twelve years. I just…needed to be sure about this first. I've had a hard month and maybe needed to...protect myself." I shrug, not sure how to explain to this put together man that I'm an emotional wreck most days, and feel like running away from my life. Only I'm the problem, and there's no running away from me.

He hums low in his throat, staring off over my shoulder. I take the opportunity to study him. I still wonder if that hair is soft or not. I curl my fingers into my palms, tempted to walk over there and check. That would be a no-no. Do not fondle the boss. Pretty sure there was a clause about that in the employment contract. And if there wasn't, then there definitely should be.

"I don't mean to make you feel...unstable here," he says haltingly. I nod encouragingly. Not sure what I'm encouraging him to say, but he seems to need something from me. He rubs his mouth and locks his gaze on me. "Marketing is all about perception. I go out into the world and represent this company. That requires me to look and act a certain way. You..."

I wrinkle up my face and fill in the words he hesitates to say. "I don't look the part. I'm aware. You won't offend me if you just say it."

"Ok, you don't fit in. Your clothes are frumpy and your shoes are the most godawful things I've seen in my life."

"You don't like my dress?" I ask in mock surprise, satisfied to see his lip curl in disgust again. It's easy to handle people judging my clothes...because it takes the attention off me. Come to think of it, my baggy dress is a better disguise than Clark Kent's glasses.

I stand and take a few steps toward him. "I learned a long time ago that a person's appearance has very little to do with who they actually are. And that the finest clothes can hide the darkest hearts."

9

ZACH

The finest clothes hide the darkest hearts.

Doesn't that just hit me in the throat? Oh, I'm not dumb enough to think her words have much to do with me. But they hit close. My clothes, my hair, my smile, all of it is a costume I put on for the world. Ok, and maybe for me. Because I want people to look at me and see a strong, successful man, instead of the worry-riddled, selfish man I really am.

How can she stand there in her hideous outfit and not care? She knows people judge her and yet she doesn't change it.

"Your appearance may have nothing to do with who you are, but it tells the world a lot about you, Maya. And right now, you're telling the world you don't give a fuck."

Her head tilts, her shiny dark hair falling over her breast. I have to pull my eyes away from the ends, curled on the awful fabric. Who the fuck wears bugs on their clothes? Kindergarteners, that's who.

Her cheeks redden, and she closes the distance between us. "I meet the dress code as outlined in the interview. I made very sure of it. And as my boss, that's all you should care about. Nowhere in the employee handbook does it say I have to be pretty. So you can take your judgmental attitude and shove it."

No, she's not pretty. I know pretty. She's more...stunning, riveting...fascinating. And all I can wonder is what it would take to get her to poke me in the chest with that finger she's waving under my nose. I want to feel her touching me. I let a little of my inner asshole out just to see how far I can push her. "You could put a little effort in."

That does it. Her long finger with the blunt, unpainted nail pokes me in the middle of my chest, and that little fear niggling in the back of my head fires into full-blown panic. Because somehow, this mousy woman's touch lights me up more than any of the women I've ever fucked. And that's terrifying. How the hell does her finger on my shirt feel better than being buried inside the blonde from this weekend?

"Do you want me to go? Because I can. I can be on a plane to anywhere in the world in a few hours, and you can go back to life as you know it. Then you can find someone else to work for you. Someone who meets your standards."

I've never felt like this and wondering what else I might do to feel more of it is what forces me to slide away from her. Her words register and I can't stop the instinctive "No." I don't want her to go. For Jonas. That's the only reason. I made a promise to him.

Yeah, sure, that's the only reason. It's not because you're fucking fascinated by her.

She backs up and crosses her arms, rubbing her biceps. Her voice is low, sad. "Your brother gave me some good advice today. He told me not to change for anyone. That people have to accept me the way that I am." Her chin lifts, and she waves at herself. "Take it or leave it. Either way, decide soon." She spins and stalks from the room, and I drop into a rolling chair and drop my chin to my chest. *Take it*, my whole body screams.

Mousy Maya, as I've been calling her in my head, is easy to resist. Magnificent, fiery Maya is nearly impossible to. She fucking yelled at me, and I want more of it. What else is she hiding beneath those ugly dresses?

This isn't me. Jonas was always the one who needed to figure shit out. Who would needle and dig until he got to the bottom of things. But now, I want to chase her down the dead-end hallway she stalked down, and force her to reveal herself. To give me more of her. Because it's clear that there is a fuck of a lot more to Maya Miller than meets the eye.

"Ah...did you know there's a break room at the end of this hall?"

Closing my eyes, I drag in a breath and let her sheepish words wash over me. "Yeah, I did know that."

"Right. So...um, the elevator is that way?" I make a mental bet with myself, then open my eyes. Winner, winner, she's pointing down the hallway to the bathrooms.

The smile just won't fucking stop. "No, not that way."

She groans and stares at the ceiling. The panels are in here too. Those fucking things were a nightmare to find. I had to call ten different places to find enough, then search through six floors of maintenance closets to find a ladder tall enough. I didn't finish until three this morning. I've functioned on less sleep before, but usually because I was busy with more pleasurable things.

"I didn't know," she mutters.

"Know what?"

"That I had a bad sense of direction. I just...get distracted, or annoyed, and I don't pay attention to anything around me."

"Distracted by what?"

She wanders over and drops down into the chair next to me. "Everything," she says. "The lights, the pings of people's computers, the voices, the bright colors, my shoes."

It's hard, but I keep the smile off my face. "Your shoes?"

"Yeah, they pinch and annoy me."

"Is that why you're taking them off? You need better shoes, Maya." I like saying her name. *Maya. Mine.* Nope. Nevermind. Her name sucks.

"All shoes are the same, Zach. It doesn't matter which ones I buy. They're all the same. They're all evil and out to get me."

My laugh escapes, unbidden. How does she do that? I can keep my cool in any work setting. I know exactly when to smile, smirk, or tease. I know people and can manipulate them to suit me. But this frumpy...and yes, stunning woman shatters that. "Your shoes *are* evil. You should get rid of them."

She sighs, smiling up at the ceiling. "They're the only work shoes I brought." Rolling her head, she pins me with a look. "You ran away too fast this morning. I didn't get to say thank you. These panels help a lot."

I roll my shoulders and rest my head back. "You didn't get a headache today?"

"No, I didn't," she says, sighing happily. "It's kinda wonderful."

"I'm glad." And I am. I may be a dick, but the idea of her hurting didn't sit right with me. "You are doing a good job," I admit to her, meeting her eyes briefly. "You're giving the team a new perspective we really needed. For now, it's enough."

"So you're not planning to fire me?"

"No, I'm not." *At least not for the next six weeks.*

THIS FUCKING WOMAN.

I tug at my tie, loosening it further, and run my hand through my hair in frustration. I put aside my annoying reactions to her. I've been nothing but professional with her all week. But my fucking eye won't stop twitching. How the hell does she live like this?

Grabbing her ugly shoes off the top of the fridge in the Executive staff room, I spin and begin my hunt for her. The night after our talk, I held out twenty minutes before tracking her down and helping her find her shoes. Thursday, I promised myself I'd stay in my office and let her find her own fucking loafers. When she was still wandering past my office an hour later, I gave up and helped her search. Cara finds it fucking hilarious. Most people seem to. But not me.

I'm pissed.

Our building is well cared for, and we have a great cleaning crew, but the floors are still dirty. God knows what kind of germs are on the bottom of her feet each night. It's maddening. How the fuck has this happened every day this week?

Walking…okay, stomping through the hallway, I spot Cara packing up. Stopping in front of her, I glance briefly at Maya's dark office. I hold up the shoes so Cara can get a good look. She's one of the most stylish women I know. She has to be as offended by them as I am. "Where is she?" She shrugs, seemingly unconcerned that her co-worker is wandering around this building, lost and shoeless. "How does she do this? Just wander around and lose her shoes? It's completely unprofessional."

Cara rolls her eyes. "You say this every day. You told her there was no dress code, remember? She even cleared in with Janey."

"Don't even get me started on her wardrobe," I mutter, grabbing my hair again. I'm going to pluck myself bald and it's that woman's fault.

"There's nothing wrong with her wardrobe."

"No, not if you're fine with shopping at Frumps R Us."

"Zach, you're a complete snob." She's laughing at me, and I don't appreciate it.

"Cara, I simply have standards. Standards that she is not meeting."

"Oh, I see." She crosses her arms and leans her shoulder on the doorway. "So she's not performing? She's actually awful at marketing?"

I scowl at her. "She's amazing. Everything I hoped she would be, in that aspect at least."

"Then I don't see the problem."

"Cara, we travel all over the country for work. Looks matter. And her looks are…well, she's pleasant to look at, and she's…" Maddening. Distracting. Has the most kissable lips. And the shiniest hair. "Anyway, I need to do something about her wardrobe." I stare down at the damned shoes, "This can't continue."

The elevator ding draws our attention across the office. There she is. The bane of my existence. The woman who has taken up far too much real estate in my mind this week, wandering towards us, alternating between taking bites of her muffin, dropping crumbs, I'm sure, and ducking her head into cubicles. Searching, yet again, for her loafers.

I shoot a glare at Cara, who's snickering behind her hand, then turn to glare at Maya. Declan and Jonas have both emerged from their offices and are chatting casually with her as they help her search. I've complained about this at more than one of our evening meetings, and the fuckers laugh every time. Why aren't they as bothered as I am? Why can't they see how unprofessional this is?

She's smiling at them. She's chatting with *them* in a way she doesn't with me.

I don't like it.

Grunting a goodbye, I stalk towards the group, but I'm focused solely on her. "Missing something?" I ask harshly. As usual, she doesn't acknowledge my surly tone, simply nodding and taking another bite of her muffin. And yep, she drops some crumbs, one landing on the front of her dress. I tighten every muscle in my body. *Don't you fucking dare touch her. Don't you brush off that crumb dammit.* Busy staring at that crumb and imagining the lush bounty underneath the awful flower pattern, I barely hear her thanks, but I snap to attention as she takes her shoes and turns, wandering away.

I feel him at my shoulder. We're not twins, but our bond is forged in fire. I always know where he is. Jonas's hand slaps my back. "Let's go. She *will* get lost if we don't go with her." With a grunt, I follow him. We catch up with her at the elevator, and I listen to her and Jonas chat casually on the ride down. I hate that they're so comfortable with each other. I hate that she smiles at him, and I hate the jealousy that creeps up when they both laugh.

I don't get jealous, ever. It's not my style. Women try that shit on me all the time, talking about some other man when we're together, and I don't give a fuck. None of them matter. But this little thing they have going on bothers me.

A lot.

Maybe I don't like that Jonas is paying more attention to her. Yeah, that's it.

No, it's not. I'm jealous that he can make her smile.

So stupid.

Maya steps off on the marketing floor, and unbidden, my feet follow her. Jonas snickers and gives me a little finger wave as the doors close.

"Where are you going?"

She frowns, glancing back at me. "I have a few layouts I want to work on this weekend." I stand next to the elevator as she gathers a bunch of design boards and paperwork. She looks at home here. Somehow, in the week she's been working here, this space has become hers. Everywhere I look, she's there. In the colors scattered on the table tops, in the bright designs tacked to the walls. I've tried to keep my distance this week, but when I do check in, she's filling the place with her energy, taking up space, and being completely distracting. It's only when she settles at a table that her words penetrate.

"Wait. What? You're still working?" The building is empty tonight. We always have security on, but I don't like the idea of her here by herself.

"Yes," she says, distracted as she rifles through the pages in front of her.

"It's Friday night. You should head home. There's no reason to work late. The boss is already impressed."

She flicks me a glance. "I'm thrilled."

I want to take her by the arm and march her down to the car. That's not me. I don't manhandle. I flatter and flirt and wrap women around my finger. Except for this woman. "Maya, let's go home."

She drops the papers and pins me with her gaze. "You are my employer, not my father. Why are you insisting on ordering me around? Most bosses would be thrilled to have an employee stay later. Aren't you glad I'm so dedicated?"

"We don't require anyone to work overtime here. That's not what we're about."

"Oh, well, that's nice to know. Have a great weekend." Then she lowers her head back to layouts, and completely tunes out my presence.

"We're your ride, Maya. How are you supposed to get home."

She snorts, "There's an app for that. Besides, I'm not going home. I have plans."

"What plans?" I wish I could call it back. The demand is clear in my voice. And as oblivious as she is, she hears it. I can tell by the tightness in her shoulders.

Her eyes are hard, her gaze firm. "Goodnight Mr. Lee. Have a lovely weekend."

I've been dismissed. She's done it with a finality that unsettles me. Curling my hands into fists, I battle my instincts. Why the fuck does it matter if she stays late? She's a grown woman. And she's not my responsibility. With a muted snarl, I turn and stalk back to the elevator, stabbing the call button with way more force than necessary. I stare at the closed doors, determined to push her out of my mind, but like a fucking pussy, I glance over to see if she's watching me. Nope, she's not.

Stepping onto the elevator, I spin and glare at her, willing her to look up. Finally, just before the doors close, she looks up and, with a smile that takes my breath away, lunges for the remains of her muffin.

Even the fucking muffin gets a smile.

I'm in a shitty mood as I exit the elevator to the lobby, but seeing Jonas, head dropped on Cara's shoulder as she hugs him, chases away all thoughts of the maddening woman upstairs. I freeze, eyes darting from the back of Jonas's head to Cara's face. Something in her gaze reassures me that he's ok...mostly.

Jonas raises his head, "Thank you, Cara," he says quietly. I join them, bumping my shoulder against his gently, letting him know I'm here. He leans in slightly, accepting comfort, and exhales deeply.

"Anytime, Jonas," Cara says, eyes gleaming. "Jonas, can you tell me why Declan has your face tattooed on his ass?"

I lose it, folding forward, laughing hysterically. Jonas snickers as Declan gasps and orders us not to tell her. It was a bet. Another stupid bet out of hundreds we've made in the decades since we all became a family.

We tease Declan all the way to the parking area, waving as Cara and Declan pull out in her sporty car. Jonas turns to me, a smile on his face and shadows in his eyes. "Where's Maya?"

And just like that, I'm grumpy again. "She's working late. Said she has plans and will find her own way home."

He nods, unconcerned, and climbs into the driver's seat. I drop into the seat beside him. Everything feels off. This is Maya's spot. I should be in the back, staring at the back of her glossy black hair, imagining how it would feel running through my fingers or, even better, over my cock. Pisses me off to no end that all my dreams have been about her lately. But I'm going to handle that shit this weekend. I'll get a woman or two under me, and that will be that.

"Janey has a boyfriend," Jonas blurts into the silence between us.

Groaning, I lean my head against the headrest. "I'm so fucking sorry."

"Yes. Well. It's to be expected," he says stiffly.

Studying his profile as he expertly guides us through rush hour traffic, I wish I could fix it for him. Show Janey how amazing he is, and make her fall in love with him. Jonas wants her, and I want whatever he wants, even if it means I lose him.

"Wait for your moment," I say. "It must be fairly new. So watch and wait. There will come a time when you can make your move."

"I don't have moves."

Laughing, I punch him lightly in the shoulder. "Yeah, you do. Just pull some of your Jonas mojo on her, and she'll jump into your arms."

"I'm strong. I could catch her."

Smiling at his literal interpretation, I give him the words he needs to hear. "You are, brother. You really are."

That seems to cheer him up. He switches on the classical station and hums along with some concerto written hundreds of years ago. And I sit, staring into the darkness, wondering what's to become of us.

Fuck that.

I'm not spending this weekend all melancholy and shit. I'm going to enjoy my family, and later, when everything breaks up, I'll venture out for some very adult entertainment. A smile curls my lips as I wonder what stunning thing I'll hook tonight. Then lose the smile when a pouty mouth, glossy black hair, and magnificent ass are all that come to mind.

Not doing that. Not going there. I'm putting her out of my mind.

But first, I shoot a text to the security on duty tonight and make damned sure that Maya's safe.

There. Now she's out of my head.

My resolve holds....until Maya shows up at family dinner.

10

MAYA

"Give me all your money."

Everything flies from my hands as I spin with a cross between a shriek and a bellow, and brace for an attack.

I have a second to meet Bree's stunned eyes before she drops to the floor, howling with laughter. "Oh my god, Maya. Seriously? What is that?"

My heart rate slows as I take in the laughing woman rolling around on the carpet. My cheeks heat as I drop my foot back to the floor and lower my arms. "Ah, nothing. You're lucky I didn't kick you."

She snorts, choking a bit. "Listen Maya-san, that crane kick was hella cool in the movies, but you are not the *Karate Kid*. I think I'm safe."

Frustrated, I consider kicking at her anyway. She doesn't look like she'd care. But I do. Who am I? I don't kick people. I don't get angry. But I seem to be feeling all kinds of new things this week. Kneeling, I gather all my scattered design boards. "What are you doing? Why are you accosting me at my front door?" I ask her.

With a bright giggle, she sits up, her blonde hair a frizzy

halo around her head. "I just came down to grab some chips. We're all upstairs. You should come up!"

Dropping my hands into my lap, I stare at her. "Come up where? With who?"

"It's family dinner," she says with a grin. "We're all at Ransom's. We've eaten, but we're breaking out the dessert. Come up and have some. There are lots of leftovers." She stops and corrects herself. "There are a few leftovers. Those boys can *eat*."

"I see," I say, but I really don't. "It's probably better I skip. I'm not family. Besides, I have some work to do." I busily gather the papers again. Bree's tanned hand covers the paperwork, pushing it to the floor. Damn her for feeling so familiar. Two dinners, and all of a sudden she thinks she knows me.

It's equally annoying and comforting.

"You live and work with them. I'm sure they'd be happy to see you. Come on, come upstairs. Just for a few minutes."

"A few minutes," I murmur, more to myself. I can do a few minutes. I've never been to a family dinner before. I've always wondered what it would be like. Maybe I could go from more of an anthropological perspective and take some notes like a field researcher.

I can do hard things. I can do hard things. "Ok, yes. I suppose I could do that." Clutching my papers to my chest, I stand and ponder my next move. But as usual, one feeling overrides all the others. "I have to take my shoes off."

Bree grins and winks at me. "Go. Change into something comfortable. I'll wait."

I study her outfit, taking in the casual joggers and tank top. She has freckles right on the top of her shoulder. How does she have tanned skin at the end of November in Chicago? I don't think I've seen the sun all week. Finally, I nod and push my way into my apartment. Kicking off my shoes as soon as the door closes behind me, I moved to the dining table and dump all the paperwork.

I don't actually have to do any of it. The staff in the marketing department is amazing. Zach put together a great team and they can more than handle their workload. But rolling into my first full weekend in Chicago, I felt…anxious. Not wanting to give myself too much time to think, I figured bringing work home was a reasonable plan. A weekend alone in my apartment looms before me. Nowhere to go, and nothing to do. No reason to even leave the house, now that I don't have Birdie to walk.

A few times I've considered tracking down the woman with the Dachshunds. Maybe she'd let me walk her dogs. I even wandered toward the front desk to ask them what apartment she lived in, but I chickened out and asked for the time instead.

Planting my hands on my hips, I let myself breathe through my panic. *I can do hard things. So I go up, say hello, have a quick something to eat, then leave. Easy. I can do that. And if it looks like they don't want me there, it's no big deal. I have plenty to eat here, anyway.* Nodding as I cross the apartment, through my bedroom, to my closet, I stare at my limited choices. The few items of clothing I brought look ridiculous in this big closet. I spread out the hangers so they take up more space, but it doesn't help. Why didn't I bring a little more?

Because I was terrified I'd fail, and by bringing two suitcases, I managed to convince myself this was a vacation. So if I flew home, it would be no big deal.

But it's a big deal. I like it here. A lot. The people I work with are lovely. I've started to make friends with Cara and Bree and even had dinner with them again. A little seed of something has sprouted here, and I'm desperate to nurture it.

But that little voice at the back of my head, the one that protects me, is telling me it's safer to stay here, in my apartment. To avoid everyone upstairs. She's very convincing, telling me all the ways I could act like an idiot. How I'll screw up and cost myself my job. How no one wants me.

I almost give in. I almost let myself believe her.

She's talked like that my whole life. And sometimes she's been right. My mom didn't want me. That voice protected me when mom went on one of her tears. But I'm not a child anymore, begging for her mom's love. I'm a grown woman, and I'm beginning to realize that little voice has been hurting more than helping...maybe for my entire adult life.

"No more," I say softly. "I don't believe you anymore." I yank my dress over my head and reach for my favorite pants. Loose, flowy, and decorated with tiny pink hearts. They're so soft against my skin, it's like they're barely there. Throwing on a loose tee and shoving my feet into my favorite slippers, I move to the bathroom.

A puzzle with pieces put together not quite right. That's how my mom referred to my features. The mouth too big for my face, lips too thick. Wide-set eyes. I'm not pretty, not like the popular girls at school. My features are too bold to be called pretty. But my eyes are a striking dark chocolate brown, framed by solid eyebrows. I lucked out there, never needing to shape or pluck them like some women. Their shape naturally frames my eyes.

My hair is my best feature, I know. Long and straight, thick enough to be a pain in the summer. It's the only thing my mom ever praised. In my twenties, in a fit of revenge, I cut it all off. And spent the next two years growing it back. It doesn't matter what my mom thought of it. I like it, and that's all that matters.

Sweeping my hair up, I throw it into a high ponytail, then head to the front door, enjoying the way it swings against my neck. With a deep breath, I pull open the door. "Let's go." *Before I change my mind.*

Bree eyes me up and down, then gives me an approving nod and waves me to the elevator. She pushes the button and then leans against the wall, studying me. "How's your first week been?"

Her question isn't casual, so I give it the consideration it deserves. "All things considered, really good."

"All things?" she prompts with a smile.

"Well, I think I'll rent a car."

"Sick of riding to work with the boys?"

"Sort of. It's just weird, isn't it? To have your bosses drive you to work? Besides," I say, rolling on as her eyes fill with mirth, "it would be nice to have a car to explore the city. I haven't been anywhere but here and the office. I should go do...stuff."

"There are other people you could catch rides with, though." She laughs at my expression. "Come on, they're great guys."

Groaning, I rub my face. "They're fine. I just...it's a lot. They're a lot."

Tucking her arm through mine, she pulls me into the elevator. "Yeah, 'a lot' pretty much describes them. I can see how it would be overwhelming for you. They live in each other's pockets. They don't get the concept of personal space, like, at all. But they are incredibly kind and generous. And fun. Don't forget fun. But I fully support you doing what you need to do. One question though...you said you grew up in New York so...do you have a driver's license?"

Damn my fair skin. I feel the blush rise like a wave. She's found the hole in my plan. "Well...see...um....no."

Bree's still laughing as the elevator doors open into possibly the biggest apartment I've ever been in. Unlike the floors below, the elevator opens straight into the foyer of this place. The floors are polished concrete, and the ceilings must be at least twenty feet high. But somehow, as we enter further, it doesn't seem that big. Because there, crowded around a table that would fit easily into a castle, are nine huge men and a few women.

"Maya," a few voices call out. Searching the faces, I see warmth and welcome. I wave a little, skimming my gaze over

Zach. His face isn't that warm, his eyes are narrowed and fixed on me, but it's not screaming *get the hell out* either. A little more of my tension dissolves as I quietly return the greetings. Bree tugs me toward a large man I haven't met, holding a small, beautifully rounded woman on his lap.

"Micah, Holly, I don't think you've met Maya yet. Maya, this is Micah. He works out of the Knight Street location. And this is his girlfriend, Holly. She works there too, so you wouldn't have seen them at the office."

Micah smiles gently, and I'm immediately at ease. "Hi, Maya," he says, lifting one massive hand to shake mine. He holds my hand, giving it a gentle squeeze, then releases it, putting his hand back on the woman's belly. I didn't notice before, but there's a definitely swell there. My wide eyes fly up to meet her kind gaze.

"Hi Maya, it's so lovely to finally meet you. I've heard a lot about you." She pats the chair next to her. "Please, sit."

I drop into the chair and search for the right thing to say. *Come on, think.* "You've got a baby in there," I say, pointing to her stomach. "...or maybe not. It's ok if you don't. Tummies can be all shapes and sizes. All bodies are beautiful." I slam my hand over my mouth, unable to stop the flow of words otherwise.

Holly stares at me for a second, then dissolves into giggles, falling back against Micah's chest. His warm laughter travels the room, drawing everyone's eyes.

"I am so sorry. I'm so stu—".

"Oh my god, I love you," Holly says, cutting off my apology. "Yeah, I'm due in a few months."

"Right. Good. That's good. Yay. Congratulations."

We fall into a relaxed conversation after that, her and Micah's gentle nature putting me at ease. Whenever I fall silent, unsure of what to say, they easily draw me into a new topic. And through all of it, Micah's big hand rubs slow, deliberate circles on her stomach. Over the life they created together. Easily, naturally, Holly touches his hand or turns to place a gentle kiss on his cheek. They are so totally connected, clearly in love. There is no doubt or hesitancy. When one reaches out, the other is reaching right back.

My throat feels tight. It's jealousy. I know it. Another feeling I hadn't really experienced until recently. I've always been happy with my lot in life. I always told myself that I had a good life. That I'm respected, and that's enough.

But I want what they have...desperately.

As the shouts of the other brothers and happy laughter fill the room, I realize, maybe for the first time, everything that I've missed out on.

And I have no one to blame but myself. And that stupid little voice.

"So you're the new girl. Shove over. My ass needs more room."

I spin in my chair and find another woman staring at me. She's wearing workout clothes, her auburn hair in a ponytail like mine. She's tall, even taller than me. And while she's curvy, it's clear she's also packed with muscle. Dumbly, I slide my chair a little closer to Holly and Micah. With a sigh, she drops into the vacant chair beside me.

I've taken someone's spot, I'm sure, but no one seems bothered. There are at least ten empty chairs at this massive table, and everyone seems to be shifting around, moving into new groups, then breaking up and moving again. It's chaotic but clearly familiar to all of them.

I meet Cara's eye across the table, and she gives me a wink, then leans into Declan sitting beside her. He throws a casual arm across her shoulders and shouts at Colton in the kitchen, "Save some for the rest of us, asshole. Holly will murder you if you finish it."

Colton, looking like he's about to argue, meets Holly's suddenly hard eyes. With a slow gulp, he carefully lowers the ice cream scoop back into the container. "Yep. No, there's lots.

I saved you some, Holly. Let me get you a bowl." Moving slowly, not meeting her eyes, he scoops out a big bowl of ice cream and carefully carries it to her, putting it gently on the table in front of her. The light green color and dark spots register as the smell of mint hits my nostrils.

Colton turns to me. "Hey, Maya. Would you like some?"

I like him a lot. He's been nothing but kind when our paths have crossed at work. All of them have been, actually. They've created this easy, relaxed corporate structure I am not used to. I'm not sure I ever called Mr. Williams by his first name. So this is weird. But with Colton, it feels a little more natural. I see a lot of him since he likes to stop by Cara's office all the time. Their dynamic is strange, and more than once, I saw her try to twist his nipple. But who am I to judge?

I glance at Holly, who's got the bowl clutched to her chest, her entire fist wrapped around the spoon as she shovels in a massive mouthful. Her low groan makes me blush again. There's something…primal about it. It must be really good ice cream. I nod at Colton, who heads to the kitchen to get me a bowl.

"Jesus, Holly, you sound like you're shooting porn over there. Try to keep it PG, lady." Holly shoots the woman behind me a dark look, but dissolves into bliss again with her next scoop. I turn to the woman, hiding my smile from Holly.

"I'm Maya," I say, sticking out my hand. She smiles, shaking my hand firmly, her grip strong and confident. "I'm Becca. I'm married to…." she searches the room, finally pointing, "Kade, right there." I haven't spent much time with him, but this confident woman being married to him makes sense. Of all the brothers, he seems like he's the most uncomfortable in his suit. And his language…I've never heard so many *fucks* come out of one person in my life.

"I heard you're newly married. Congratulations."

She smiles, and she's beautiful. "Thank you. I'm pretty happy about it. So…Bree tells me you think you're some kind of *Karate Kid*. Care to come down to the dojo and try out your moves?"

My jaw drops, and I spin, looking for Bree, finding her in the corner with another of my bosses, Nick. She catches my glare, and with a cackle, ducks behind Nick. He smiles at me, then reaches back to tickle Bree. She laughs and dances away from him, slapping his hands.

"She's doing so much better," Becca says thoughtfully, staring at Bree.

"Better than what?"

"She was attacked by her boyfriend a few months ago. She's been struggling with it, but she's healing."

"Attacked," I repeat dumbly. I've had two dinners with the sisters, and both times, I thought about how blessed their life seemed. How worry-free. "What happened?"

"It's her story to tell. But it was bad. Cara was there, too. They're lucky to be alive."

Dropping my head, I let the idea that the two women, my new friends, were nearly killed wash over me. I might never have met them. The idea is inconceivable.

Becca nudges me. "Hey, *Karate Kid,* I'm serious. I teach self-defense, and the girls come to my class. So does Holly. You should come too."

"I've never done anything like that."

She nods. "There's a first time for everything. There's a class tomorrow afternoon. Come. Colton's volunteered to be a sparring dummy for us." *I can do hard things. I can do hard things.*

Looking around the room at the laughter and happy shouting, I jump.

"Ok," I say. "I'll come."

11

ZACH

I've never been this hyperaware in my life. I can't keep my eyes off her. No matter where she moves in the room, no matter who she talks to, I'm aware of her.

I hate it.

This was supposed to be my night. My chance to get that woman out of my brain. To fuck my way clear of my obsession with her. But here she is, in my family's home, distracting me again.

I should be angry. I expected to be. But when she walked into the room, all I felt was…happy. Isn't that a fucking joke? There's something about the way a tiny smile plays on the corner of her mouth that's riveting. She's engaged at work, especially on the marketing floor, but when she's around larger groups of people anywhere else in the building, there's a feeling of anxiety pouring from her. I can't figure out what she's afraid of, and damned if I don't want to figure it out.

Jonas drops into the chair next to me, rubbing Mia's back. She's been running around all sugared up for the last forty-five minutes, and she's finally wound down. It's close to bedtime, but none of us are going to remind Evie about that. We want more time with the baby, not less.

Mia's dark curls are resting on Jonas's shoulder. She's irresistible. I lean over and give her a kiss on her cheek. She smiles sleepily, reaching up to run her tiny fingers over my nose. "Zach," she murmurs, managing to add a *w* in my name with her lisp.

Catching her hand, I blow a soft raspberry into her palm, making her giggle. "You sleepy munchkin? Did you have fun chasing the kitty?"

She makes a dismissive sound that cracks me up. "I no chase kitty. We looking for hamsers."

"Hamsters," I correct automatically. I don't know why. It's been months, and she knows damn well how to pronounce it, but I think it's become a game to her now. "You still haven't found the last two?"

Jonas drops his cheek on the top of her head with a smile. "They are well and truly lost. Ransom and Mia have been leaving out food, and it's being eaten, but we can't figure out how to draw them out long enough to catch them."

"What did you lose?"

I felt her coming, so I don't react, but Jonas jumps a little, then shakes his head with a laugh and rubs Mia's back again. He doesn't look inclined to answer.

"My brothers and I got a little carried away a while back," I explain, smiling as I remember that day. "We were on babysitting duty while Colton and Evie went on their first date. And we got some hamsters for Mia."

"Lots and lots," Mia mutters, eyes tiny slits. She's fading fast.

Maya's brows raise. "Lots? How many are we talking?"

I stand, and Maya steps back with wide eyes. They really are beautiful, so dark I can barely see her pupil. If I get close enough I—. Mentally yanking myself away from her, I rearrange the chairs and pat one, urging her to sit. She does, carefully, and I'm caught staring at the material of her pants pressing against her thighs. Her dresses are hideous, not only because of their patterns but because they hide her shape.

These pants aren't hiding anything. The black material, dotted with little pink hearts, looks soft, touchable, and it clings to her thighs. *Thick, lush, they would probably feel amazing pressed against my ears as I—* Nope. Not going there. I shift my focus back to Mia and my brother, trying desperately to remember what we were talking about.

"Ah…right, well, we bought twenty."

Her mouth drops open. "You bought twenty hamsters?"

I scratch my neck and wince. "Yeah, well we didn't want to get just one because then it would be lonely. But then we saw there were other colors, and it snowballed from there." It seemed perfectly reasonable at the time, but later that evening, things got a little out of hand.

"Oh, my god. Where are they now?"

"We had them up here for a while," Jonas says, swaying gently to soothe Mia. "But then we lost two in here somewhere and thought we'd better set them somewhere permanent. So they were in my home for a while…"

Maya pokes Jonas in the elbow with a smile, her eyes soft on the munchkin. "Then what?"

"Yes, well, it seems we chose males and females, and when they get together…" he trails off with a grimace.

"No! Oh my god, how many did you end up with?"

"Hundreds," I tell her, lip twitching. I break into a full smile as she dissolves into peals of laughter. Her hands are over her mouth as she desperately tries to hold it in, not wanting to disturb the baby. "We had to bring them back to the pet store. They didn't mind taking them back…they should make a nice profit. Now Jonas has two male hamsters for Mia in his apartment."

Maya wipes her eyes with a sigh and sits back in her chair. "I get it now. I didn't see it as much at work, maybe because you're all scattered most of the time, but Bree said you guys are a *lot*, and she's totally right."

I shrug, but don't bother denying it. We are a lot. Always have been. We didn't name our company *Brash* for nothing.

"You're lucky that cat hasn't…found the missing hamsters," she says voice low as she eyes Mia. Jonas and I trade glances over the baby's head.

"We hadn't really considered that," Jonas says with a frown. "Minnie doesn't live up here. She's Micah's cat, but Mia insists that she be a part of family dinners. Do you think she'd E-A-T a hamster?"

"Enough with the hamster talk," Colton growls as he crouches next to Jonas. "They're D-E-A-D guaranteed."

"You wish they were D-E-A-D," I snicker. "You wouldn't be able to show your face in this room otherwise, you big baby."

Colton scowls at me. "Rude! Mia baby, let's get you home. Time for bed."

I will replay the next moment, over and over again, for the rest of my life. It will bring me sheer joy for years to come.

As Colton leans between us, reaching for Mia, in a moment of absolute divine timing, Minnie jumps onto my lap with a plaintive meow. It takes a second for us to register the large cream-colored spot on her dark fur. And another second to register the face and tiny hands gripping on for dear life. It's Mia that says it, just a second before we all realize it, and pandemonium breaks loose.

Her voice is pure joy, pure glee. "Hamser on Minnie!"

Colton's shriek comes directly from the bowels of hell. He throws his body backward in sheer terror, landing between Maya's chair and mine. Then he begins a frantic swimming motion, kicking his legs, trying to back crawl away from the tiny hamster clinging like a monkey onto the cat's back. For Colt, this is completely on-brand. Anything little and furry and he loses his mind.

He doesn't make it anywhere, and realizing the danger of his situation, the terrifying hamster only feet from him, he flips, bumping Maya's chair. I grab for her instinctively, dragging her towards me as Jonas scoops the cat, hamster still attached, into his lap with Mia.

Maya's warm, round, delectable ass lands right in my lap. I wrap my arms around her tightly as Colton's frantic movements continue below us. For just one moment, for a millisecond of time, everything slows as I register the softness of her skin, the warm weight of her.

And how perfect she feels in my arms. The kind of perfect I never imagined existed.

In that millisecond of time, my entire world changes.

Time speeds back up as Colt finally manages to flip over, and with another blood-curdling yell, wiggles forward like a snake until he's free from the chairs. Then, with a speed always shocking in such a massive man, he pushes up and bolts for the kitchen island, diving on top.

"He always goes for the island," Jonas mutters, staring at Colton, who's on his hands and knees on top of the kitchen counter, searching the ground frantically for another killer hamster.

Mia's softly petting the hamster as Minnie, settled in Jonas's lap, begins to lick the hamster, her rough tongue ticking Mia's fingers, making her giggle. Jonas carefully detaches the hamster from the cat, and cradles it to his chest.

"Look what we found," he whispers to Mia.

"Yay," she crows, throwing her hands up and calling out to Colt, "Daddy, you so silly. He little. See."

"Yeah, baby," he says with a gulp, "I see. You let Jonas take it back to his house and keep it safe."

"I don't know," Jonas chimes in, trying to look innocent. "This one could be female. We don't want to have more babies. Maybe it's better it go home with you tonight."

"You Motherf—" he clamps his lips shut, murder in his

eyes. "No, I think they'd be happier together. Micah, Code Red. Micah! I need you," he yells desperately, opening and closing his hands like a hungry toddler.

Micah, holding a giggling Holly, rolls his eyes and, with a gentle kiss to her shoulder, stands and lowers her into the chair. Then he strides across the room, beckoned there by Colt's frantically waving arms.

"He looks like he's *Vogueing*," Evie says flatly, staring at her two-hundred-and-eighty-pound husband. The corner of her lips twitch, betraying her.

Yep, that does it. We all lose it, falling into hysterics as Colton alternates between glaring and cursing at us. Finally, Micah gets close enough and, like it's a well-choreographed routine, turns his back so Colt can climb on and get a piggy-back ride right out of the penthouse.

"It's a core wound, assholes," he shouts over his shoulder. "Try to have a little sympathy. I hate all of you. Except for you, Mia, I love you. And Evie, I'm mad at you, but you can make it up to me later tonight. In bed. With the door locked."

And they're gone.

Looking around the room at all the people I love, I understand how fucking lucky I am. Ransom, Nick, Bree and Maverick are all collapsed forward, giggling on the table. Evie, a tiny smile playing on her lips, is shaking her head. Becca and Holly are leaning on each other, tears streaming. Cara's on Declan's lap and they're both laughing so hard they tip out of the chair onto the floor. And Jonas, the person that matters most to me in the world, chuckles quietly, shoulders bouncing as he clutches a toddler tightly to his shoulder, other hand carefully cradling the tiny hamster.

And still wrapped in my arms, Maya, her body shaking deliciously as she sputters and gasps through her laughter. I can't stop myself from tightening my grip, pulling her back closer to my chest. *Just so she doesn't fall off.* Yeah, right.

"Wait…what core wound?" Becca asks, staring around the table.

Ransom lifts his head, wiping his palms across his face. "You never heard this story?"

"No, I haven't. I asked last time this happened, and nobody clued me in!"

"Last time this happened," Maya whispers, turning to me.

"Yeah, the night we brought them home, Colt saw them and flipped his lid. Ended up on the island that night, too."

"Oh my god," she mutters, her attention on Ransom as he tells the story. She seems to have completely forgotten she's in my arms, and I'm not mad about it. I'm not in any hurry for her to move.

"God, it was at least twenty years ago, back when we all were bunking at Knight Street. We were all crashing on the floor in sleeping bags. Colt was already big back then." His lips twist with a grin. "Not as big as he is now, but still big. That sleeping bag was tight on him. So one night, must have been two or three in the morning, he screams. Like, bloodcurdling, about to be murdered screaming."

Nick, laughing, chimes in. "I've never heard anything like it. Ransom's bouncing around the room, diving for the light switch. We're all reaching for a weapon…shoes, knives, whatever we had on hand, preparing to defend ourselves."

"Ransom finally gets the light on," Maverick says through his giggles. He's always been the one that has the hardest time getting himself under control. Get him laughing, and it takes him forever to get a handle on it. He wheezes out a breath. "He gets the light on, and all we see is Colton, screaming, wiggling around in his sleeping bag. He liked to zip himself all the way up, then wiggle his arms down until he looked like a fucking mummy. So there he is, totally stuck and flipping the fuck out." Maverick dissolves back into giggles, unable to continue.

"What?" Evie asks, "What was happening?"

"A mouse crawled in there with him," Ransom says. "He didn't stop flailing around until that little fucker popped out of the top and ran under the fridge."

Declan and Cara climb back into their chair, wiping their eyes. "He didn't sleep the rest of the night." Declan says. "Just sat on top of the table and kept watch. He didn't sleep there again for weeks. Not until Ransom bought a dozen mouse traps and set them around the apartment. He's been a fucking wreck ever since. Anything small and furry, and he's a goner."

"Oh my god," Cara murmurs, an evil smile lighting her face, "this is going to be so much fun!"

12

MAYA

He'll shove me off if he doesn't want me sitting on him, right? Okay, so maybe not shove me because that would hurt, but maybe give me a little nudge? The way his arms are wrapped around me, I can almost convince myself he doesn't want me to leave. My mind is full of bees, buzzing and humming, making it impossible to think my way through this.

I've never done this. Sat on my boss's lap. Anyone's lap. Ever. Apparently, this is the week for me to try all the new things. And I get to cross *laugh so hard I nearly pee my pants* off my list. Not bad. Maybe tomorrow, I should get a tattoo. Something cute that won't look sad and pathetic when my skin is all stretched out when I'm eighty.

Zach's chest is still moving in quiet amusement, and the sensation pings through my back, up my ribs, and out through my fingertips. My hands are hovering, not quite sure where to land. Do I rest them on his? Do I let them dangle? What's the etiquette here? Cara and Declan are across the table, cuddled up, but Cara's back isn't stiff like mine. She's relaxing back. So is that it? Do I just...pretend like he's a chair? Somehow, I don't think I can or should do that.

I can't remember the last time anyone held me. I'm sure my mother did it at some point. She didn't always hate me. At least, I don't think she did. I barely remember my dad other than a vague impression of a stubble cheek pressing against mine and the faint smell of cigarettes lingering on his skin. I don't really remember his arms or the sensation of being squeezed, but I guess it was a hug. Those moments were nothing like this.

Nothing about this experience is vague. I'm too aware of the strong legs supporting me. And of the warmth of his body. He probably has to kick his blankets off at night just to cool down. He's so hot.

Ha, that's funny. I'm a comedian. Snorting out a laugh, I try to come up with a plan to extract myself from the bizarre position I'm in. This one, though, it's not my fault. I didn't screw up and put myself in yet another awkward spot. No, this one was all Colton, and that makes me feel infinitely better.

The last hour has been a complete revelation. If this is what all families are like, I've been missing out. But all the lines I thought I had drawn around me and this family have been completely blown up, and I don't know how to find my footing again. Once you've seen your boss flip out and try to swim his way across a concrete floor, can you really go back to professional distance?

I've gotten a glimpse behind the curtain, and I want another. I want to know more. And that's terrifying. I'm getting sucked into this group way too easily.

Panic bubbling in my stomach, I slowly, carefully lower my hand to the arm banded around my waist. Gripping Zach's thick wrist, I gently pull. He resists, arm tightening around me briefly, before releasing me, his hands falling to dangle at his sides.

I clear my throat. "Would you look at the time?" I say, tapping my bare wrist. *Dammit, why do I keep doing that?* "I'm about to turn into a pumpkin!" I say cheerily. My cheeks flush because I'm an idiot, and I carefully ease off Zach's lap. He doesn't help me, he doesn't touch me in any way until I stumble to find my footing. Then his warm hand cups my elbow, steadying me. I flash him a wobbly smile in thanks, but I'm not prepared for the look on his face. Something in his eyes freezes me in my tracks. It's gone quickly. I don't have a chance to catalog it. To analyze it. But oh my god, do I want to. No one has ever looked at me like that before, and while the little voice in my mind is trying to tear me down, another voice tells me that look wasn't negative.

Jonas gives me a curious look, then rises, moving away to who I assume is Mia's mom. He hands her over, then tucks the hamster close to his chest and heads for the elevator, nodding at the shouted goodbyes as he leaves. The rest of the people at the table don't seem to be paying us any attention, and I'm thankful for it. Tucking my shoulders back, I throw on my imaginary cape and meet Zach's eyes.

"Thank you for catching me. I um...good job." Wincing, I rush through the rest, "It was nice of you guys to let me come up. It was nice to meet everyone. Really nice." *Jesus, Maya, say nice one more time. Go ahead, do it.* "Have a nice night." Dropping my head, I wave at the rest of the people scattered around the room and make a beeline for the door...elevator. It's the billionaire's version of a door, I guess.

"Maya, wait." I slam my eyes shut and freeze in place. And there it is, that warm hand cupping my elbow again. "I'll walk you out." I nod and step forward at his urging. A few more steps and he makes a choked sound. "You know, it might be easier if you open your eyes."

"Oh. Whoops. Thought I went blind for a minute there." I open my eyes really wide, and shoot him an awkward smile. The smile that usually has people's eyes darting side to side, looking to make their escape.

But not him. He just shakes his head and leads me to the

elevator, pressing the button to go down. "We could take the stairs if you'd prefer. All our apartments are connected by a stairwell separate from the rest of the building. It's only a few — what are those?"

I stare at him blankly, then track his gaze to my feet. "Slippers," I say, the *duh* implied in my tone.

He plants his hands on his hips, still staring. "I can see that. They're very...furry."

I check his face quickly, looking for that tick in his eye, but it's not there. The corners of his eyes are crinkled. It makes him look more approachable, less perfect. "The tongues flap, see," I say, wiggling my toes up and down, making the tongues of my Weiner dog slippers bounce up and down. I watch them, giggling, patting myself on the back again for making such an awesome purchase. "They make me laugh," I tell him.

"I see that," he says, honey coating his words. I peek up at him, surprised to find he's staring at me, not the slippers. Again, there's something in his gaze that makes my stomach flip.

"Are you ok? Do you need an antacid? Some people can't handle dairy. My old assistant carried these pills, and she'd take them before she ordered her favorite milkshake for lunch. They seemed to work for her. She said she'd get the poops if she didn't." I slap my hands over my eyes and let out a scream of frustration. "I'd really like to go now. Please. Just let me go before I say anything else."

Chuckling, Zach guides me onto the now open elevator doors and settles me in the corner. I drop my hands and fix my eyes on the tip of my slippers. "I'm sorry. I didn't mean to imply that you had...that you might..." I wave my hand vaguely around the belly, then in the air behind my butt.

I shouldn't be out in public. Ever.

Zach's voice is choked. "Have lactose intolerance and be

on the verge of shitting myself? No, I'm good. Thanks for your concern, though."

"Yes, well, sure." Meeting his grinning eyes, some of my frustration with myself dissipates. "I am sorry. Sometimes I get uncomfortable, and words just bubble up."

"Is that what I have to look forward to the first time I take you to a work function?"

"Oh god, no. I swear I know how to behave at things like that. They're not my favorite things to go to, but I can handle them."

"Then why was tonight so hard?"

"Because it is," I say, frowning at him. "There are rules for business functions. Small talk, business talk, all that is easy. But tonight? I didn't know what the rules were...though apparently, there weren't any. So I struggle."

"Are you like this in all social situations?" He asks curiously. It's the lack of judgment in his tone that allows me to answer honestly.

"I'm never really in social situations. Other than dinner with Cara and Bree, I've never been to a gathering like this."

His eyes widen, mouth opening to...I don't know. We're interrupted by the doors opening. Glancing out, I see the abstract art piece on the wall on my floor and step out of the elevator.

"Well, goodnight. Thanks for escorting me home. I'll see you on Monday." I wave and dash to my door.

"Maya," he says quietly, so quietly I freeze, not wanting to miss anything he has to say. "You're welcome at family dinner anytime." I frown at him, and he shakes his head. "I mean it. Anytime."

I give him a pained smile and reach for my door handle. He growls and pushes his hands through his hair. It doesn't land right back in place like it usually does. He looks a little messy. A little more human. "You're not wearing a suit," I say with a gasp, staring at his sweatpants. They're expensive, tailored sweatpants, but still sweatpants.

"You're just noticing that now?"

I push my hair back over my shoulder. "Yes, well, I was distracted before. By the adorable little person. Then there was the screaming and all the rest of it. You look nice like this," I say, waving at him. "You should dress like that more often."

"I'll take that under advisement." He pushes his hands into his pockets and rocks forward onto the balls of his feet, eyes steady on me. "Go on in. I'll see you on Monday."

Nodding dumbly, I fumble for the handle. With a slow grin, Zach stalks forward, crowding me against the door. Reaching for the handle, his hand covers mine, and his head dips down, putting his mouth next to my nose. "Goodnight," he breathes, pushing the door open. He doesn't move, just stands sentinel, waiting for my brain to come online.

Finally finding my breath, I choke out a goodnight, then push past him into the apartment. I turn, and slowly, carefully, while staring at him and those rich caramel eyes, I push the door shut and twist the manual lock. It's got fancy biometrics, but I just can't get used to them.

"Oh my god," I whisper, resting my head against the door. "What was that?"

Seriously. What was that? Why was he looking at me like that? Why did he touch me? And why is there so much pressure on my chest? *Is this what a heart attack feels like?*

Dashing to my laptop, I look up signs of a heart attack, somewhat reassured to realize that I don't exhibit any of them. But I feel different. It's a strange feeling, but not bad. And when I think about the way Zach's hand felt touching mine, it roars back.

It's him.

He did this to me with his smile, and smiley eyes, and sweatpants. Why couldn't he have stayed the disapproving, aloof boss he seemed to be all week? That man didn't bother me. He was just like all the other people who judged me. Easy to ignore.

Standing, shaking out my arms, I hop around the living room, trying to work off the tension. When that doesn't work, I throw on some music and dance it out. Flailing, stomping and generally looking like I'm being attacked by a bee.

But long minutes later, when I drop, panting, onto the couch, that pressure in my body has released.

It's just a fluke. Nothing more. If I'd fallen into any man's lap, I would have reacted the same. I'm sure of it. It's natural.

Slapping the couch, I rise and move to my closet to figure out my options for tomorrow's self-defense class. I'm dreading it, but I also really want to go, and those two emotions are warring for supremacy. I don't know which one will win out tomorrow, only time will tell. But the idea of going to a class to hit people wasn't on my *Time to get Living list.*

Maybe it should have been.

13

ZACH

What the fuck was that? Seriously, what the fuck? She's my employee. She's frumpy, and so fucking awkward.

So why am I hard as a fucking rock? The feel of her ass on my lap has etched itself into my memory. And the smell of her hair…like sunshine and cherries.

I should not have crowded her.

And I really shouldn't have let myself get that close. It's those fucking lips. They drew me in. I want to know what they taste like. I want to bite.

This is really fucking inconvenient. I don't have time for this. For obsessing over her. For obsessing over anyone. I don't have the capacity to care for anyone else. I have to be there for Jonas and for my family.

Slamming into my apartment, I jog to my closet and strip, pulling on a blue suit, the expensive fabric nearly shimmering under the lights. I have to get out of here and find my footing. And I know just how to do that. I tap out a quick text to my driver, then throw on a Rolex and push my feet into soft Italian loafers.

This is the right move, I'm sure of it. I've let this woman

turn my life upside down this week. I haven't been to the clubs at all. Come to think of it, it's the longest stretch I've been away...maybe ever. That's why I'm feeling so off. Best thing to do is get back to what I do best, flirt and fuck.

My plan is solid on the elevator ride down to the lobby. I'm convinced it's right on the drive to one of the hot new clubs in town. But when we pull up in front, I can't seem to make myself open the door. It's not a big deal. It's just sex. I've done it a hundred times. Just go in, fish for something sparkly, and take her home. It's easy.

So why does the idea of going in there and touching any woman but the one occupying my thoughts make me break out into a full-body sweat?

"Boss?" Luis asks, "Should we go somewhere else?"

Pulling my hand from the handle, I curl it into a fist and drop it into my lap. "Just drive for a bit, Luis."

"Sure thing, boss."

He pulls smoothly away from the curb and back into traffic. I stare out at the city lights, wondering what the hell is happening to my life. How did I get myself in this position? Here, in the dark of my Escalade, I can admit that I created this. I fixated on Maya for months. I had this idea that she would take our business to the next level, and it made me... not me. Every time she refused to see me, it sucked me in deeper. And that was before I ever met her. Now? I don't know what the hell to do. How do men do this? Handle this kind of want?

"You married Luis?" I know he is. I clocked the ring on his finger the day I hired him, but I ask all the same.

"Thirty-five years to the most beautiful woman in the world," he says proudly. I whistle low because, seriously, thirty-five years with one woman? I didn't think people did that anymore.

"Kids?"

"Three. They're grown now. They've got kids of their

own." His pride in his family is evident in his wide smile, visible in the rearview mirror.

"How did you know? I mean, there are a lot of women out there, so how did you know she was the one?"

He chuckles softly, "I understand now, Mr. Lee. You've got woman troubles."

Groaning, I prop my forehead on my fist. "Something like that."

"Congratulations," he says far too cheerily. "The night I met my Rosa, I looked a lot like you do right now. Like the breath got knocked out of me, and like the world tilted sideways." Jesus, is that what I look like? I feel it, but I didn't realize it was that obvious to everyone else. My mask never slips, and that alone is a reason to straighten the fuck up.

"Did it get better?" I ask desperately. It has to get better. I can't keep feeling like this.

"It did. And it got worse. She is the reason I get up in the morning, Sir. The reason I come home every night. I love my kids, but that woman is my world, and if I ever lost her, there would be nothing left of me."

That's the most terrifying thing I've ever heard.

I know exactly what he means because that's how I feel about my brother. If he's not ok, I'm not ok. The idea of feeling that way for someone else sends ice down my spine. I won't do it.

"I don't want that. I don't want to be that dependent on another person. It sounds horrible."

Luis hums low in his throat. "It is horrible sometimes. It's like having your heart outside your body, just hoping that the person holding it will take care of it. There have been moments so...terrible that, for a second, I wished I could escape. Go back and make it so we never met in that diner. But then all the good stuff floods in, and I realize I'll take the bad moments because there were so many more good ones."

I groan and scrub my hands over my face. "You couldn't

have just told me it's horrible and let me live with my illusions, could you?"

Luis chuckles, shaking his head, and meets my eyes briefly in the rearview. "You pay me enough, so I'll say whatever you want me to say. But that won't change the truth. Human beings are built to be in relationships with other people. We need the connection. You're proof of that."

"Me? How the fuck am I proof of connection? What I do has nothing to do with connection."

He makes a dismissive sound. "You're wrong. It's all about connection. You may not want long-term with these women I see you with, but you do want something from them. Warmth, touch, sex. They're basic needs. We all crave them."

"Maybe," I mutter, slouching in my seat. "I don't have room in my life for the kind of relationship you're talking about, though. I have my brothers, and now their women. I have lots of people to care about already." Too many to care about. Too many to worry about. It all adds up to sleepless nights and antacids to battle the stomach ache.

"There's always room for more, boss. People are like that green guy from the Christmas movie. You know the one? His heart grows. Ours do too."

"Are you seriously comparing me to the Grinch?"

"Yep, that's the one. You're not a grump. But you do guard yourself against people. You keep them at arm's length. I see you hiding, even with Mr. Jonas."

"I don't hide anything from my brother," I say flatly, done with this conversation and the armchair psychologist driving my car.

"Really? My mistake, sir." The grin curling his lip tells me he's not at all sorry. Fucker. Why the hell did I think having this conversation was a good idea? I don't hide anything from Jonas. *Do I?* This conversation has killed the urge to hook up tonight. I can't deal with any more woman drama. All of it is too big for me to solve, though as an iconic sign catches my eye, I realize there is one problem I can solve.

"Pull over," I mutter. "I have to make a quick stop."

"Here, sir? Really?"

I glare at him, and he nods, pulling to the curb at Saks. I have a little shopping to do.

IT'S NEARLY MIDNIGHT WHEN THE ELEVATOR DOORS OPEN ON MY floor. I cross the foyer on autopilot when Jonas's "Hi," makes me fumble my package. I spin, seeing him laying in the entryway of his apartment, legs and feet on the open door.

"Holy fuck. Jesus, don't do that shit. You're going to give me a heart attack."

"Unlikely," he says absently, staring at me. "Where have you been? You're not usually back this early. And you don't look like you've had sex."

Dropping my head, I turn and open my door, placing the bag down carefully. Then I peel off my suit jacket and kick my shoes into my place. Then I return to Jonas. "Move over," I order him. He walks his bare feet across the door, wiggling his back along the floor. I slide down, propping my sock feet next to his, and lay down on the wood floor next to him.

"What's up? You don't usually wait up for me."

"You're usually predictable. I don't need to wait up."

"Predictable?" Something about that rubs me the wrong way.

"Yes. You go out, come home relaxed, and do it all over again a few times each week. This week, you haven't. Why?"

"Why haven't I gone out to fuck? Really? That's what you want to know?" I'm being a dick, but I don't want to have this conversation with him.

"No, not really," he says easily, staring up at the high ceiling above us. "I want to know about your feelings for Maya."

I suck in a breath, choke on my spit, roll over to cough it out, then lay there gasping, mind whirling. "What makes you ask me that?"

Jonas rolls his head toward me. "Why wouldn't I ask it? You asked me the same thing a few days ago. Only I would argue that you had less reason to ask it of me."

"Really? How's that?"

He snorts, "I'm not the one that can't seem to stop talking about her. You talk about her, a lot. And tonight, as soon as she walked into the penthouse, she was all you could look at."

I flop onto my back with a groan. He's right, and I hate that he is. That I was so obvious. "You can be so fucking oblivious sometimes, and then times like now, you're too fucking perceptive. It's annoying."

"I'm oblivious when I'm uninterested," he says with a jaw-cracking yawn. "You and Maya? That's worth paying attention to."

"Why? Why do you care?"

"Because you do," he says softly. "You're different since she arrived."

A dozen brush-offs spring to my lips, a dozen different ways to convince Jonas that there's nothing there. I've done it in the past, convinced him things were fine even when they weren't. Because I thought that was best for him.

"When did you grow up?" I ask him, startled all over again at the man beside me.

"I don't know how to answer that. I grew up a long time ago. But I feel...different since Janey. Maybe that is why I'm noticing it more in the people around me."

"Noticing what?"

"Attraction. Affection. Touch. The way people in love look at each other. I didn't pay attention to it before. And now, we have four brothers with significant others. And I am drawn to

Janey. It is very top of mind for me right now. So do you? Have feelings for Maya?"

"Maybe," I admit reluctantly.

"What does that mean?"

"It means there's something there, but I don't plan to pursue it. There's no point. I don't want a relationship, and Maya is a relationship woman."

Jonas sits up, spinning to face me. "Why don't you want a relationship?"

"Because my life is full. I have you and work. I don't need anything else."

"You need sex," he points out, one eyebrow raised in challenge.

"Yeah, but I can get that anywhere."

Jonas curls up his nose, and I want to punch him. "Do you really prefer sleeping with strangers? You'd choose that over Maya? Over being with one woman? It doesn't make sense to me."

"I don't know why. It's not that complicated. I can't let anyone else into my life."

"Why?"

I hate that fucking word. "Because! I can't fucking worry about another person."

The silence stretches tight between us, the tension nearly unbearable. He raises his knees and wraps his arms around them. "Because you worry about me. Right?"

"Yes," I say, giving him the full truth, too tired to pretend.

He actually growls at me. "I am not a child. I know that I have differences, but I am fully capable of operating in the world. I don't need you or anyone else worrying about me."

"Too bad. You're my brother. I've been worrying about you for your whole life, and I'll worry about you for the rest of mine."

"Do you think I'm incapable? That I'm so feeble-minded I can't take care of myself?"

"No! Never."

"Then why are you spending so much of your life worrying about me? I am a fully grown man."

"It's...you just...," I groan and shove up, resting my back on the doorjamb. "Sometimes you get so overwhelmed. And people have taken advantage of you in the past. I just don't want you to have to deal with all of that. I just want to protect you from that shit."

His face falls, making my gut clench. "I have had trouble with people. But I am not incapable of learning from those experiences. I know how to be more careful now. I know what to watch out for." He pushes to his feet, suddenly looking exhausted. "As for the other, I haven't had an anxiety attack in public in years. And even if I did, I would handle it." He grabs the door and slowly pushes it closed, forcing me to move back into the hall. But before he shuts it, he deals the death blow. "Stop using me as an excuse to avoid living your own life."

Attempting to slam my front door on that little truth bomb, I'm frustrated by the fancy soft close. Dumb doors. My bedroom door closes with a slightly more satisfying thunk. Why the hell does everything have to change? Life was good. Everyone was happy, and nothing got between my brother and me.

But now, everything is wrong. Everything is broken. And I don't know how to fix it. The only thing I do know is I'm going to avoid Maya at all costs.

At least until this stupid attraction dies.

14

ZACH

So much for keeping my distance.

"Why the fuck did I agree to do this again?" I ask Nick, shooting him a glare when he laughs. I don't think he has a clue about how I'm feeling right now, but he can tell I'm pissed, and that's enough to entertain him. The man doesn't seem to get bothered by anything. It's annoying as fuck, but also the reason he's excellent at what he does. He can get anything from anyone when he puts his mind to it.

"Because our sister-in-law asked, and you don't want to get on her bad side."

"Right. There is that." I admit. Becca's not scary the same way Evie is, but she's a hell of a lot meaner. She'll twist a nip in a heartbeat if she's pissed at you. So far, I've managed to avoid that particular torture. Colton has not been so lucky. "But why did Colt bow out? Doesn't he normally do this?"

"I don't know, man. He said something about Mia being under the weather. I think he was planning to call a chopper to take her to the hospital."

I spin on him, gripping his shoulder, my heart thumping in my chest. The thought of anything hurting that little girl.... "Jesus, then why are we here, and not at the hospital?"

Nick shakes with silent laughter. "Relax, I texted Evie. She said Mia sneezed a few times. It's probably just a cold. She was going to try and talk him off the ledge."

The muscles in my neck relax, and I drop my chin to my chest. "Yeah, that tracks." Colt is a bit of an overprotective bull when it comes to Mia and Evie. It would be just like him to lose his shit at the first sign of a sniffle.

Suddenly, the door opens behind me, and immediately my shoulders tense up. I shouldn't be here. This is not a good idea. But I'm stuck. My nipples are depending on me.

"Welcome ladies!" Becca says, sounding not at all like her typical ball-buster self. I turn and watch the women file in. There are a variety of shapes, sizes and ages. All dressed in comfortable workout clothing. A few are eyeing Nick and I like they'd like to make a meal of us. A few others steal quick looks, seemingly uncomfortable, before looking away. A few are dancing on their toes, smiling and laughing.

Our women come in last. Holly, her rounded belly leading the way, is first, followed by Bree and Cara. Maya, looking unsure, and absolutely delicious, trails in after them. She's in tighter leggings, tighter than I've ever seen on her, and I'm desperate for her to turn around so I can get a look at her ass. I'm sure the material is hugging it in just the right way. Nick's chuckle breaks my concentration.

"What?"

"Look at Maya's shirt!"

Pulling my eyes from her legs, I move up to her white t-shirt. The material is worn and soft looking, and right in the middle of her chest is a cartoon picture of a hot dog with legs. Below it, in the script, reads *Ask me about my Weiner.* Surprised laughter escapes me. I do not get this woman at all. She wears the most absurd work outfits...ok, not absurd, but not flattering. Then outside of the office, she's a Weiner dog slipper, dirty t-shirt-wearing enigma.

The women I've dated wouldn't be caught dead in

anything Maya's worn so far. Except maybe the leggings. But as she gets closer, I see the little bugs dotting the dark fabric. Jesus, this woman. She's so completely herself, it's a little terrifying. What would it be like to not give a fuck what anyone thinks of you?

I catch her worried eyes and immediately want to reassure her that everything's going to be ok. Except that would mean getting close to her. And I'm not going to do that. It's a bad idea. I end up giving her a quick nod, then yank my eyes away to focus on Becca.

"We have some new faces today, so welcome. You are in the right place. This class is all about reclaiming your power and your sense of safety. By the time we're done today, you should feel a little more confident in your ability to handle a sketchy situation. But," she says, planting her hands on her hips, "if you come back, then come back again, I can help you become a literal badass."

Some of the uncomfortable women crack smiles at that. I haven't seen this version of Becca. At home, she's more of a joker. She doesn't seem to take much seriously. But here, with these women, she is steely-eyed and focused.

"So today is about getting you over the fear of an attack. When we're in a dangerous situation, our bodies can tend to take over. I don't want that for you. I want your mind to be in control and for you to develop some instinctive reactions. That's why these handsome gentlemen are here." Nick and I smile and nod, still not sure what the hell we've actually signed up for. "We're going to suit them up and then give you a chance to beat the hell out of them."

She laughs evilly at our expressions and throws her hands up placatingly. "Relax, I'm joking. We're not really going to wail on you." She turns to the women. "We're going to focus on systematic strikes designed to incapacitate as quickly as possible, so we're mostly going for the groin, throat, and eyes today."

Trading panicked glances with Nick, and with decades of history between us, we smile again, take a step away from each other, and bolt for the classroom door. Fucking Becca anticipates us and moves like the ninja she is to intercept us. She plants herself in front of the door and folds her arms over her chest. The slightly deranged smile on her face sends us back a step.

"There's two of us," Nick says stupidly. That terrifying smile grows.

"Yes, there are. Do you really think that's going to help you?"

An involuntary squeak escapes me. I cover it with a manly cough, conscious of the women behind us. Talk about a rock and a fucking hard place. The only way out of this room is through Becca, but I've seen her make Colton, a man who's got a good forty pounds on me, cry like a baby, and beg for mercy.

Eyeing Nick, I wonder if I could get by if I tossed him at her. It's not a bad plan, except for the fact that *she* is watching. This is about self-preservation, so why the hell would I almost rather be kicked in the balls than have Maya see me run out of this room?

Pushing my shoulders back, I cross my arms over my chest, trying to look intimidating. It doesn't work on Becca. At all. She just smirks and raises an eyebrow.

"Listen, Bec, we're happy to help, but we didn't sign up for knees to the groin. Can't you find someone else to do it?" There, that was totally reasonable.

"No, I can't. There's nothing to worry about. Would I hurt you?" She dissolves into snorting giggles at our nods because, yeah, she would. Sighing, she wipes her eyes. "Seriously, the padding is designed for these classes. The suits will protect all your dangly bits, I promise."

Her smile drops, and she moves in closer, making Nick... ok, us, flinch. "This is really important. I wouldn't ask you to stay if it wasn't. But some of these women have lived through some horrible stuff, and they need you to man the fuck up and let them kick you in the nuts."

Nick groans and folds over, dropping his head between his knees. "My balls are crawling back into my body as we speak." *Mine too, brother, mine too.*

"Good, they'll be nice and safe there," Becca says cheerily, turning and shoving us toward a couple of padded suits in the back of the room.

THIS WAS A TERRIBLE IDEA. AS ONE OF THE BOUNCY WOMEN darts in with another knee to my groin, I kiss any children I may have wanted to have someday goodbye. Yeah, the suit's absorbing some of the impact, but not all of it. This shit is not comfortable. Nick and I are wearing thick padded suits that make us look like the Pillsbury Dough Boy, only not as cute. The very thick diaper piece is particularly attractive. The end result is a suit that absorbs most of the impact but also leaves me completely unable to bend my arms or legs.

Most of the women have cycled through with various levels of enthusiasm. The bouncy ones are the worst, coming at me with gleeful aggression. It's like they've waited their whole lives for this moment and don't want to waste it, aiming the biggest, most powerful kick they can muster at my junk. How the hell does Colt do this?

As Nick and I are being repeatedly attacked, with knees and elbows and shins, Becca circulates through the room, softly encouraging — I didn't know her voice could be that soft — or cheering for her students, depending on what they need.

And Maya? She's somehow avoided coming anywhere near us. She's punched the bag half-heartedly, but whenever it's time to line up, she disappears. Somehow, Becca hasn't noticed, or if she has, she's letting it slide, and it's bullshit.

These women are here for a reason, so why the fuck won't she just make Maya come over and knee me in the balls? I mean, is it really that hard?

Apparently, it is. Maya's one of the ones getting soft Becca, but I think that's a mistake. Maya's not soft...not really. She has no problem standing up for herself at work, and I don't see any reason why she couldn't do it here, either. Finally, after she sneaks away from another line-up, I call her out.

"Maya Miller. Where the hell do you think you're going?"

She freezes, hand on the handle of the glass door.

"Ah...just needed to use the washroom. When you gotta go, you gotta go," she says, breaking into some sort of pee-pee dance. No way, that cuteness is getting her out of this. Becca clues in and moves to Maya at the door, talking to her softly. Then she takes her hand, pulling her back into the room. Maya keeps her grip on the door until the very last second, her body stretched into a starfish. Finally losing her grip, she slams into Becca's back with a grunt. Becca barely acknowledges the hit, which is impressive since Maya's not a small woman. But neither is Becca.

Apparently, my brothers and I have a type. Wait. No. Not me, because I am not getting involved. She is not my type at all. Too lush, too earthy. Too much to hold. But Jesus, is it ever a seductive package, pee-pee dance and all.

I need my head examined.

Becca pulls her to a stop in front of me. Then moves to stand behind her and grip her shoulders. "What are you afraid of, Maya?"

"What? Nothing, never mind. I kick butt all the time. Woo." She rolls her eyes at herself and then slumps into Becca's hold. "I'm not really physical. This just isn't my thing."

Becca squeezes her shoulders gently. "Maybe it needs to be your thing. I've been watching you, and Maya, you need to get into your body."

Maya frowns, craning her neck to meet Becca's eyes. "Huh? I am in my body. I live here. I should know."

Becca smiles. "You are *not* in your body, my friend. You're somewhere up here," she says, waving her hand above Maya's head. "You're so busy worrying about everyone and everything else that you haven't bothered to sink in and feel who you are. You're treating your body like it's something you have to haul around rather than loving it for everything that it does for you."

The pucker between Maya's brows deepens. "My body and I don't have the best relationship."

Becca shakes her head. "There you go again. It's not separate from you. This is you...for the rest of your time on this planet, this is your home. Why aren't you treating it with love? Why aren't you appreciating everything it's capable of?"

Maya snorts, "From what I can tell, all it's capable of is irritation and hypersensitivity. That's not really something I want to celebrate."

"Oooh, lady, there is a dance party in our future. I'm going to get you connected in if it's the last thing I do. But for right now, turn around, and wail on your boss."

"You had to call him my boss, didn't you?"

"Why won't you do it?" I ask, desperate to understand her.

Her shoulders slump again as she meets my eyes. "I am not a violent person. I don't hit anything. I don't raise my voice. I don't get angry."

"That's the biggest pile of bullshit I've ever heard." Her eyes flare in challenge. I attempt to point at her with my heavily padded arm. "There, that's exactly what I'm talking about. You're full of fire and feelings. You've challenged me more than once. You have no idea who you are."

"Are you seriously trying to tell me you know more about

me than I do?" She plants her hands on her hips and stares me down.

"Apparently, I am. Because this calm, level person you're talking about? I certainly haven't met her. And to be honest, she sounds like a bit of a bore."

I have a second to brace before her hands are on my shoulders, and her knee nails me in the crotch. "That all you got?" I wheeze out. And she's off. With Becca's encouragement, she attacks me like her life depends on it, striking anything and everything she can, Becca adjusting her form when she's about to hurt herself.

This isn't like the other women. There's something happening here that's deeper than self-defense. Through the layers of padding I'm wearing, it feels more like she's fighting her way free of something. Maybe free of her past or her misconceptions. I don't know exactly what, but judging by the slow, steady roll of tears down her cheeks, it's big.

She's killing me. I mean, yeah, my balls are taking a beating, but I hate seeing her hurting. So far, though I've seen her emotional, I've never seen her crack like this, and all I want to do is wrap her up in my arms and tell her how amazing she is.

15

MAYA

The sob is trapped in my chest, but I don't want to let it out. I'm on the verge of a breakdown, I can feel it, but doing that in front of the man I'm currently beating on seems wrong. Winding down, my muscles twitching and cramping, I can't force myself to stop. Every strike on the padded suit reverberates down my arm and into my chest. The chest that's felt hollow for so long.

Becca's right. It's not just Birdie's death…I've felt disconnected from the world for a long time. Maybe my whole life. But now, the physical sensations are bombarding me. I feel everything.

And it's terrifying.

And exhilarating.

And terrifying.

Did I mention terrifying?

How do people live like this? Just raw and exposed to the world? My skin feels so thin, like the brush of a feather would tear it open and spill me out.

My body's heavier than it's ever been, my feet almost feeling weighted to the ground. Is this what the rest of the world feels like? All these aches and pains, and rushing blood and tight fingers?

I think I hate it as much as I crave more of it. The rush of sensation has me whirling, spinning, finally forcing me to stop, hands clutched tight to Zach's padded shoulders. I stand there, head bowed, forehead nearly touching his chest as I breathe. His arms, covered in padding, steady me, lending me his strength.

Zach's been a revelation today. The women in this class are diverse, and he seemed to pay special attention to the quieter ones, the timid ones. Watching his face through the caged helmet he's wearing, I could see the softness in his features.

After dinner last night, I'm less surprised by that. There's a softness to him that hasn't been evident at work this week. Maybe it's egotistical, but it seems obvious that my presence is the difference. He's been tense around me most of the week, silently disapproving. But with his family, with the beautiful little Mia, he lit up.

Someday, I want someone to light up when they look at me.

I'm vaguely aware of the room quieting and Zach's slight movements.

"Maya," he says softly. "Look at me."

The bubbly, heavy feeling is fading, making room for embarrassment. But I gather up the tattered remains of my pride and raise my head.

Someone's removed his helmet, and he looks…stunning. Oh, his hair is flat and there are lines running down the side of his face from where the helmet pressed it. He's sweaty and not at all put together, and I think he's the most beautiful man I've ever seen…with the most kissable lips.

That thought sends lightning bolts to my toes. *I have to get out of here now.* Except I underestimated how exhausted my muscles are, so when I try to step away, I wobble. Zach's shout echoes in my ear, and suddenly we're falling and twisting. We both groan at the impact, and I take a second to breathe and orient myself. Fingers and toes are wiggling. Check. Can I bend my knees? Check again. Twisting my head back and forth, I'm relieved to feel no pain.

The gasp below me freezes me in place. It's then that I realize my mouth is pressed to something soft...really soft. My eyes fly open and lock on Zach's rich brown ones. I suck in a breath but don't move. Maybe I'm locked in place with embarrassment, or maybe I just want one second. One more second to enjoy the tingling in my lips...and in other parts of my body.

Zach doesn't move, eyes searching mine. Something wild comes over me. Wild for me, at least. I brush my mouth over his again. *He's your boss*, that little voice reminds me, but I don't listen. Because this feels too good. So I do it again, then again. Just feather-light brushes. It's not even a kiss, not that I'd know much about those, so it doesn't count. It's not wrong.

The breath in my body explodes out as Zach moves, taking my lower lip between his teeth and biting. Then does the same to the top lip. I've never felt anything like it or the pressure it creates low in my stomach. The way it makes it clench.

I sort of know that feeling...but I've never experienced it with another person in the room.

I don't move, letting him take the lead as he nibbles and sips from me, murmuring like I'm the best thing he's ever tasted. It's ridiculous, of course. I'm a mousy, introverted, weird woman. And men like him don't fall for women like me. It's perfectly insane. But for a second, just one second more, I'm going to pretend.

Ok, so maybe ten seconds.

I probably would have laid on top of him, perfectly still, for the rest of my life. But suddenly, his tongue darts out and licks along my bottom lip.

I'm not conscious of it. I don't realize I'm doing it, but before I know it, I've rolled off of him and all the way across the room, only stopping when I hit the wall.

"Well," Nick murmurs from the doorway where he's standing with a gleeful-looking Becca. "That was interesting."

"Shut up," Zach mumbles, head turned to stare at me. He flails briefly, raising his arms an inch off the floor, rocking side to side. He's turtled. Completely. "Would somebody get me out of this fucking suit?"

Laughing, Nick — already out of his suit — and Becca help him sit up, so they can pull the heavy padding off of him. I take the opportunity to push to my shaky feet and quietly exit the room, breaking into a run as soon as I clear the door. I fly around the corner to the changing room, grab my purse and coat, shove my feet into my shoes, then run out the front door. I came with Bree in her old Jeep, and I'm so thankful that she's still there, waiting for me.

She smiles as I hurriedly climb in. "Hey, Cara went home with Holly. How are you feeling?"

"Great," I squeak, eyeing the front door of the Dojo. "Let's grab some food."

Her eyes widen. Understandable since I've had to be convinced to have a meal with them so far, but she doesn't question me, just starts the car and pulls out of the parking lot. And if my heart stutters to a stop in my chest when Zach runs out the front door of the Dojo, locking eyes with me as we pass, then I don't let on.

We're quiet, both lost in our thoughts as we drive through the industrial area. "So," Bree says, breaking the silence, "are we going to talk about the way Zach just ran after my Jeep?"

Inhaling, I break into deep coughs as I choke on my own spit. Bree passes me a water bottle and I sip gratefully. "Ah, yeah, what?" I mean, he came out of the door. He didn't run after the jeep like in some romance movie. *Did he?*

"Seriously? You're going to play dumb?" I stare at her,

mouth open, considering doing just that. "You don't have to tell me anything, but if you want to talk, I'm here." Want to talk? Do I ever? Maybe I do, but I don't have any practice with any of this.

"I don't know how," I mumble, crossing my arms over my chest and staring out the window.

"Don't know how to what?"

"Talk," I shout, then shoot her an apologetic smile. "I haven't had...friends. I don't really know how to do this."

"Oh, right," she says softly, glancing at me briefly, then back at the road. Her blonde hair is in a ponytail like usual, but little wisps of hair are fluttering around her face. She looks sweaty and happy. Two things I didn't think could go together.

"Well, if you're new to this, there are a few things you should know. First," she raises her forefinger off the steering wheel, "Girl Code."

"Girl code," I echo.

"Yep. When we're talking about boys, girl code says there is a cone of silence. I'm on your side, and what you say will never make it back to Zach. So if you want to complain, or talk it out, or whatever, you can do that. I'll keep my mouth shut, I swear."

"That...that might be good. The talk it out part." I wet my lips, unsure how to start. "I think...we just kissed in there. In front of Becca and Nick." I press my hands against my cheeks, trying to cool them. Bree's quick inhale echoes how I feel. "I know, right? It's crazy. It's certifiable. I have no idea why I did it."

"So you kissed him?"

"Um. Yes and no. I mean, I pressed my mouth against his. It's this whole thing. We fell over and whoops, our mouths touched."

"Oh, ok," she says, lips twitching. "So it was an accident."

I push at a cuticle on my bare nails. "Well, yes. But then no."

Bree dissolves into laughter, then, glancing in her mirror, swings into a random parking lot and turns off the ignition. Dropping her hands in her lap, she turns to me and asks through her giggles. "So, it was an accident, then it wasn't?"

"Well, yeah," I say, then proceed to explain the past few minutes in vivid detail. It's so completely unlike me to open up, but the words won't remain unspoken. This whole day has turned my world upside down. Why not spew every thought and fear I have on a sort of friend?

"Woah," she mutters, staring blankly through the windshield.

"Exactly. So you see, it was nothing. It meant nothing."

Her lips twist as she turns to me. "Um, no. A man doesn't run after a woman if it meant nothing."

"He really did that?" I ask quietly, maybe a little…thrilled. Who would have imagined frumpy me getting chased by a man? I mean, chased in a good way, not a creepy serial killer way.

"Yeah, he did. And obviously, it meant something."

"Maybe he wanted to fire me," I mumble. "I've stepped so far over the line, I can't even see it anymore. I've been to a family dinner. I yelled at him. I hit him. And then the kissing." My voice is rising with each word, and I can't stop it. "I don't even recognize myself anymore."

Bree's hand covers mine, and I freeze, staring at it. Her skin is tanned compared to mine, her hand clearly strong. Her nails are bare like mine, and there is a little cluster of freckles at the base of her thumb. "Hey," she says gently. "It's all ok. It'll be ok."

I search her gaze desperately. "How can you say that?"

"Because you're still breathing. As long as you're breathing, the rest of it will work itself out." Becca's words from last night rush back into my head. Here I am, freaking out about a kiss, and this woman was nearly killed a few months ago.

"You've been hurt."

Her hand trembles slightly, and I grip her tightly, covering her hand with mine, making a hand sandwich. I can't remember the last time I held hands with anyone.

"Yes," she says softly. "It was bad. It took a long time to come out of it."

"Was he punished?" I'm not sure I could do anything, but I'd happily plan his murder and help pay for someone else to do it.

"Yes," she murmurs, staring down at her lap. She sits in silence for a moment, then raises her head and locks shining eyes on mine. "Cara killed him and saved our lives."

I slam my mouth shut when I feel it drop open. What do you say to that? I have nothing, so I just squeeze a little tighter. Her shoulders relax as we sit there and breathe together. Finally, with a smile, she draws her hand back to her lap.

"There's no rulebook, you know," she says, staring out the windshield. "We just come onto this rock and bounce around, knocking into each other. And sometimes, the people you knock into change your whole life. For better or worse. But Zach, he's a good guy. I don't know him as well as some of the others, but he's always been truly kind. He won't fire you for kissing him, especially since he crossed that line, too. But I have to be honest, I'm shocked as shit that he ran after the car. From everything I've seen, he's very much...a man whore."

I flinch back, and Bree grimaces. "I don't mean it like that. Well, I do. But I have a point. Just stick with me for a second." I give her a tiny nod, and she smiles. "Ok, so I've worked in bars for years. My sister Cara owns a club. I don't think you knew that, did you?" I shake my head because, no, I didn't know that. She's younger than me, and she's built so much for herself. How did I let myself get so behind?

"Right. Ok, so her club is hot, and Zach, I've seen him in action. He's so smooth, he's like butter. All the women flock to him, and he knows exactly what to do. Nothing gets to him, nothing flusters him. But Maya, he looked pretty damn flustered just now."

I make a non-committal sound because, yes, he did look flustered. But it probably doesn't mean what she thinks it does. That's the only thing stopping me from getting on a plane today and vanishing. "Bree, thank you. That helps a lot. It was a mistake, and that's it. He's experienced in these things, and he probably didn't want me to get the wrong idea. I'll talk to him later and apologize, and I'm sure it will blow over." I nod to myself because it makes perfect sense, but when I meet Bree's eyes, she doesn't look convinced, but she doesn't correct me.

"I'm sure it will all work itself out," she reassures me. "Talking to him is a good idea, actually. The sooner, the better. You don't want to go to work on Monday with it unresolved. Can you imagine how awkward that would be?" She laughs, and a little pool of unease settles in my chest. Because yes, I can imagine exactly how awkward that would be. "The smartest thing would be to knock on his door when we get home, so you can hash it out face to face."

"I could just send him an email," I say hopefully. She shakes her head and gives me a gentle smile.

"There's a lot of nuance that's missing from an email. In-person is better. You can do it, Maya, I have no doubts."

Her confidence reassures me a little. If this strong woman thinks talking to Zach in person is the way to go, then I have to believe she's right.

"Ok," I say with a heavy sigh, because yes, I'm a strong, capable woman, but today's been a lot. "But not yet. Let's just…go somewhere for a while. I'm not ready to go home."

"I know just the place," she says, starting the car. "It has amazing Enchiladas, and then there's this fun store next door."

"Sounds perfect," I murmur, resting my head against the seat. I'm exhausted and, internally, already rehearsing what I'm going to say to Zach. I need to get it just right. I don't pay any attention to the road because I'm hopelessly lost already. I can't imagine driving at all, let alone in this city and that puts a serious crimp in my plan to buy a car. But that's an issue for another day. For right now, I'm going to eat Enchiladas and do some shopping with my friend.

The lack of motion finally registers, and I look up to see a tiny strip mall right in front of us. With a small Mexican restaurant with a line out the door and, next to it, a sex shop.

"Um, Bree...what kind of shopping are we doing exactly?"

Glancing at me, she wiggles her eyebrows and laughs, swinging open her door, letting a blast of cold air in. "The best kind. Now come on, move your ass. I'm starving."

It's ok. You can do this. It's just a shop. It's not going to kill me.

Who knew you could almost die of embarrassment?

ZACH

The brake lights of the Jeep flash briefly, then Bree swings onto the street and they're gone. Leaving me standing in sweaty workout gear in the icy parking lot. Do I look as pathetic as I feel? Touching my sweaty hair, I'm sure I do.

"Zach," Nick yells from the front door. "Get your ass in here before you freeze to death."

I drop my chin to my chest and contemplate walking home. It's only fifty blocks. I could do it.

"Zach, come on."

"Fuck," I mutter, turning and jogging back to the doors. Nick grins at me, and I elbow him aside, making him laugh.

Goddamn it.

If Kade or Jonas were here, I could get the fight I need right now, but Nick just laughs and follows me back into the training room. I kick at the stupid padded suit as I pass, then drop onto the floor in the corner, stretching my legs out and leaning my head against the mirrored wall, right at the spot Maya rolled to a stop.

When we were kids, I was obsessed with bugs. I loved the Roly Polys, because when you touched them, they curled into a ball. I force back a grin as I think of the way Maya rolled away from me, all curled up, just like those little bugs. Fitting since the woman seems to love bugs as much as I used to.

Becca walks in, zipping up a hoodie. "Hey, you're back. Didn't catch your bride?"

I glare at her, which, of course, bounces off her. She drops to the floor next to me and bumps her shoulder into mine. I bump her back a little harder, which just makes her laugh. Nick drops onto the padded mats and stretches out flat on his back.

"Thank you for coming, you guys. I know it was rough, but it meant a lot that you stayed," she says. We grunt, not bothering to explain that we stayed under duress. She knows, she just doesn't care.

"Soooo…you and Maya, huh? I didn't see that coming."

"There's nothing between us. Nothing."

"No, there was definitely nothing between you," she says with a choked laugh. "Not a millimeter. It was hot."

Growling, I bump her shoulder again. She turns to me with a smile that makes my balls crawl back into my body. A smile that warns me she can fuck me up for life. Then it drops, and she's back to sunshine. No wonder Kade's obsessed with her and put a ring on it. He needs her, someone strong and terrifying. All the women he had in the past were all too needy, too weak for him, but he couldn't see it until he met her.

"I'm glad you married him," I murmur, "even if you are deranged."

"Awww, thank you. You're so sweet." She claps her hands. "So, you want to bang Maya. Let's discuss."

I kick out at Nick, who's shaking with silent laughter at me being Becca's target. I can't take her, but I can hold my own with him. He rolls out of the way onto his side and props his head on his hands.

"Yes, Zach," he says with a shit-eating grin, "let's discuss.

You've had a hard-on for her all week. It was bound to happen eventually."

"I don't know what the fuck you're talking about."

"Seriously? You've been fixating on her from day one."

"Because she's a walking disaster! The woman loses her fucking shoes every day."

"She does?" Becca asks, looking intrigued.

"Yes. It's ridiculous. What grown woman can't keep shoes on her feet."

Becca rolls her eyes and lifts her bare foot, waving it in front of me. I grab it and tickle, immediately regretting it when she rolls and her other foot connects with my ribs.

"How the fuck are you so flexible?" I drop her foot and rub my aching side. "Besides, it's not the same. Your job requires no shoes. Hers does not."

"Fair point," she mutters. "I wonder why she can't keep them on."

I drop my head against the wall, replaying our conversation earlier in the week. "I think they're just uncomfortable. But it doesn't make much sense. Why not buy a pair she likes, then wear the fucking things?"

Becca hums noncommittally and stretches her legs out in front of her, flexing her toes. "Is that it? She won't wear shoes, so she annoys you. And you kissed her because....?"

"She kissed me first, for fuck's sake. You saw it. What the fuck was I supposed to do?"

"Um...not kiss her back?"

I stare at her, baffled, because how the fuck could I do that? It would be easier to flap my arms and fly myself to the moon than pull away from those incredible lips of hers.

Jesus, I've never felt anything like them.

When was the last time I kissed a pair of bare lips? Most of the women I've...been with, wear that never kisses off lip stuff. Tastes a little weird, honestly, but you get used to it.

With Maya, all I could taste was Maya. It's impossible to resist her.

Nick's back to laughing, forehead pressed on the mats. Becca's grinning, eyes darting between Nick and me. "Right. So clearly, that thought didn't occur to you." Her smile dims a bit. "Why are you so against liking her?"

"It's not about liking her, Becca," I say, slapping my knee in annoyance. Why can't they grasp such a simple concept? "I like my life the way it is. She's a complication I wasn't looking for. Yes, I'm attracted to her, but that's all. It's just a product of being in such close quarters this week. It'll pass." I'm nodding, trying to convince myself it's true.

"You don't think a woman like Maya could make your life better?"

"No," I say, ready to shut this shit down. Becca, of course, doesn't pay attention to the *fuck off* in my tone.

"Aw, my dear sweet brother-in-law, you're talking out of your ass now. You have no idea how amazing life can be with the right person."

"It doesn't matter. I don't have room in my life for that," I say stubbornly.

"Why? Your schedule all filled up banging women from the club? What if you stopped spending time with those women and just focused on one?"

"That's the problem, though, isn't it?" Nick says softly. "All those women don't require shit from you...they may want it, but it's easy to brush them off. This isn't a Maya issue, it's a Zach issue."

"Issue? It's not an issue to like variety, asshole. I can have any woman I want in my bed, any night of the week."

"Sounds really lonely," Becca murmurs.

I rear back and stare at her because...what the fuck? "I live surrounded by everyone I love. I'm not lonely. I'm barely ever alone, for fuck's sake."

It's true. There are a million people around all the time.

Though the days of popping into any apartment I want are gone, now that there are women added to the mix. I'm happy for my brothers, truly. I love all their women, even Becca, but it's changed everything.

"It's different, though," Nick murmurs, staring up at the ceiling. "I want it. I'm not afraid to admit it. I see what it's like to be in love and be loved back, and I'm a little jealous. If I found a good woman, you can bet I'd snatch her up."

"Just like that? What about everything else? What about all the relationships you're managing already?"

"Managing?" Becca asks with a frown. "What do you mean?"

"All the headspace the relationships take up," I say, honestly confused that I have to explain this shit. "When you love people, they have a permanent spot in your mind. They're always there, needing you, taking space from the rest of your brain, using up your resources, taking away from everything else you are."

"Jesus," she breathes, eyes wide. "I never, not once, looked at it like that."

"What other way is there to look at it?" I ask, wiping my suddenly damp palms on my pants.

"Zach," she says softly. "Loving people shouldn't feel like a sacrifice. The people I love take up space in my brain, yes, but that doesn't give me less capacity to be me."

"But don't you worry about them?"

She presses her lips together briefly, glancing at Nick. "Want to help me out here? I feel like I'm missing something."

"Worry," Nick says calmly, his gaze knowing. "Based on decades together, I can tell you that Zach worries more than almost anyone I've ever met. He worries about all of us...but he spends a fuck of a lot of time worrying about Jonas. So I get it, I think."

Becca's brow wrinkles. "But...why? I mean, I love Kade. I

want him to be happy and healthy. Everyone thinks about their partner. And yet somehow, I'm a fully functioning person, anyway."

"Jonas is different, though," I interrupt, ready to be done with this fucking conversation. "He needs me more. He requires more from me. I just can't give that level of attention to anyone else."

Becca rears back, frowning. "Wait. I'm sorry, I just don't get it. Jonas is an amazing man. What exactly does he need from you? Like, are you doing stuff for him all the time?" Seeing my frustration, she puts her hand on my arm. "I'm not trying to be an ass, honestly. I just...am I not seeing something? Are you doing a lot for him every day?"

"It's not about that. He's a grown man, he can handle his shit. But I need to be there for him. He's always needed me. His whole life."

"Meltdowns, you mean?" Nick asks.

Jonas used to get overloaded and lose his shit, but that doesn't happen that often anymore because I try to make sure he stays level and doesn't get anxious. "Yes. But also, just helping him navigate the world."

"That's a lot to take on," Becca murmurs. "Too bad you don't have anyone else who can help. It's so awful to have to shoulder such a burden on your own."

Burden.

That word, when applied to my brother, sends rage coursing through my entire body. Shoulders tensing, hands curled into fists, I lock eyes with her and freeze at what I see. It's not sympathy or judgment.

It's disgust.

"You are an asshole," she says flatly. "Your brother is amazing. Yeah, he needs support here and there, but I can tell you, from my short time in this family, that your brother is one of the kindest, most thoughtful, engaging people I've ever met. Granted, I've only seen one of these so-called meltdowns when I wanted to give Evie my shitty car, but he handled it. I've seen people fall apart far worse for far less."

"You don't understand," I say, feeling one hundred years old. "You weren't there when I'd have to hold him to stop him from hurting himself. Or when he'd scream for hours. You weren't there, and you have no idea how much he needed me."

"You just said it, though," Nick says, sliding up to sit right at our feet, smack dab in the kicking zone. "Needed. He needed you desperately for a long time. We all know that. But Jonas is not that little kid anymore. I don't think you need to worry about him nearly as much as you do. I mean, I don't know for sure, but at work, it feels like you spend the whole day checking on him. What exactly are you looking for?"

"He might need me," I say dumbly. This conversation is not going the way I thought it would. At all. "I want to make sure I'm available to him."

"Right. But do you think he doesn't know where you are? Or how to use a fucking phone? Will he just sit in his office and scream until you find him?"

"No."

"So then, what are you so afraid of? Why do you worry so much?"

"Because I don't know any other way to be! He's *my* brother. He's *my* responsibility."

A throat clears, and my head snaps up to lock on the figure in the doorway. Everything in me collapses as I meet his gaze and see the hurt swimming in it.

"Jonas," I whisper.

"Is that what I am? A responsibility?"

17

ZACH

I'm vaguely aware of Becca and Nick exiting the room. Jonas steps in further, letting the door fall closed behind him. The shouts and grunts from the dojo's main sparring area are muffled. The frosted glass of the door and glass wall lend us privacy, but I still feel like there's a spotlight shining on us.

"Is that how you see me? As a responsibility?" Jonas asks again. The pain lacing his tone tears through me. I open my mouth to reassure him, but he shakes his head. "No. No more telling me what I want to hear. No more lying. Just tell me the truth."

"The truth?" I ask. "What do you want me to say? I've been responsible for you since Mom and Dad died. That's all I meant."

He presses his palms together and rotates his hands back and forth, betraying his anxiety. I hurry to soothe him. "It's ok. It's exactly the way it's supposed to be. You don't need to worry about it."

The lines between his brows crease. "Why would you imply I'm worried?"

"Jonas, really? Look at your hands."

"What about my hands?"

"You do that when you're anxious. Rub them together like that."

He looks down at his hands and their motion, then looks back at me, a hard light in his eyes. "Maybe you don't know me as well as you think you do. I do not stim just because I'm anxious. I do it to help me think. Or to help me focus on something. I may have done this while I was anxious in the past, but it serves many purposes for me now."

I swallow past the lump in my throat. "Really?" He nods, and I push off the floor, moving to stand in front of him. "I didn't know that. It always seemed to be part of a meltdown. I just assumed that the two went together."

Jonas stares at my forehead for a minute, processing. "So every time you've seen me rub my hands together over the last decade..."

"I thought you were struggling."

"And you tried to make it better."

I nod, and he frowns, dropping his hands and pacing away from me to the mirrored wall. I follow, standing next to him as we study our reflections, him in his tight black shorts, bare chest on display, me in my track pants and t-shirt. His hair is all over the place, as usual, probably forgetting his last barber appointment. We're nearly the same height, with dark hair and eyes, bodies strong. It's obvious to anyone who looks that we're brothers.

"When I look in the mirror," Jonas says, "I am proud of who I am. I see a strong, capable man." His gaze shifts to me in the mirror. "When I look at you. I see my brother. My best friend." His lips tighten. "When you look at me, you see a child. The child I used to be. The one that struggled to function in the world. The one who needed you to stand between him and all the danger and distraction."

His eyes are challenging, and I can't hold his gaze, dropping my eyes to the blue mat we're standing on. I blink quickly and take a deep breath. He just called me out and shined a big fucking spotlight on our entire relationship.

And I don't like what I'm seeing.

But as I always do, I raise my head, turn to face him, and tell him what he needs to hear. This time, that's the truth.

"I didn't know I was doing that...but yes."

His eyes shutter. "It is a habit. One you need to break yourself of. Quickly."

"Maybe," I say, forcing the words out through the tightness in my throat.

"Not maybe." His words are clipped, hard. "You have to stop. Because now that I know about it, I will be watching. I will feel crushed by the weight of your worry."

"I don't know how to stop worrying," I admit, studying his features, so familiar. And yet, beneath them, there is so much more going on that I can't touch.

"I worry about you too sometimes, you know."

"You do?" Why does that feel so earth-shattering? Am I a complete dick for thinking that he was as oblivious to me as he is to most of the world? But maybe I *have* had my head way up my own ass. His next words prove that I have.

"Yes. I can tell if you are not feeling well. Or if something is bothering you." He rubs a hand over his stomach, frowning at my cheek in the mirror. Sometimes, like in moments like these, highly charged and emotional, his dislike of holding my gaze for long is a blessing, giving me time to regroup.

"I want to make it better for you, too," he says quietly. "But I trust you to manage your emotions. And to come to me if you require help. Can you not do the same?"

He's not oblivious...at all. "I didn't think you saw when I was...struggling. You never mentioned it."

"Was I supposed to?" he asks uncertainly.

I open my mouth to tell him it's fine, that it doesn't matter. But I stop. This is exactly what he's asking me to stop doing, isn't he? Stop protecting him and treating him like a child.

"Sometimes," I say, wetting my lips and looking him dead in his eyes, "it feels like you're not interested in me. Like I don't matter. You asking me how I'm doing and showing me you notice when I'm having a bad day would…be nice."

Jonas's hands start the rubbing motion again as he looks up at the ceiling. "It would make you happy…to have me mention that you are emotional?"

"Yeah, it would. It would let me know you see me."

He frowns, "As long as I have my glasses on, or my contacts, I can see you very well."

Chuckling, I lay it out for him. "You are a brilliant man, Jonas. Your brain is probably doing a million things at a time. So sometimes, even when we're in the same room together, I feel like you're looking through me. As if I don't exist."

His face falls, and he suddenly looks ten again. My urge is to smooth it over, and make him feel better, and I grip the side of my pants to physically hold myself back.

"Many times, I do not see you," he says softly, staring at the floor. "When I am working through a problem, it's like there's a big screen in front of me, displaying what's happening in my mind. Everything else disappears."

I've never heard him describe it that way. "Is it like that all the time, in your head?"

"No, not all the time. But a lot of it. But I do see you."

Moving closer, I put a hand on his shoulder, gripping tightly, giving him a playful shake to let him know we're ok. He cracks a smile and sighs. "The next time I see you twist up your face, I'll ask you what's wrong. Will that work?"

"Yeah, brother. That'll work." Sizing him up, finally registering the fact that he's not wearing a shirt, I ask, "What are you doing here?"

"Trying out various martial arts," he says, like it should be totally obvious.

"Trying them out. What does that mean exactly? I thought you had to wear one of those outfits when you train?"

"A Gi," he says, scrunching up his face. "I don't like them. The seams are too thick in the shoulders. I don't like the way it rubs. So they let me train without one. I have been coming for a few months. I have to try them for a while to see if I like them."

"I had no idea."

"I already told you that you do not know everything about me," he says, rolling his eyes.

Laughing, I move to elbow him in the ribs, feeling on more familiar ground. "I know, I know. I heard you. I guess I'm just realizing that maybe that doesn't have to be a bad thing. It just means there's more of you to get to know. Think of all the long…deep…intense conversations we can have."

Jonas easily dodges the elbow and kicks out at me, forcing me back. "We have to talk about feelings?"

"Might be a good idea."

"Ok," he mutters, already heading for the door. "But no more than six percent of the conversations may be about feelings." He's already done the math, counted up all the time we spend together, and come up with a percentage of *feelings* he can handle.

Jesus, he's weirdly brilliant.

I am so fucking proud of him.

"Wait," I yell after him, chasing him out of the room, laughing. "Is that an aggregate total, or is that limit per conversation? Like, can we cry on each other's shoulder one night, then do manly shit the rest of the week?"

His snarl and tackle are expected. The moves he uses to pin me after aren't. All too quickly, I'm laying on the floor panting, staring up at Nick and Becca's dumb faces.

"Looks like you need to get your ass to a class, dude," she says with a smirk.

I stick out my tongue at her, then roll away as she comes after me. When she's pinned me in seconds, I admit defeat. "Sign me up for whatever will teach me to kick your ass the fastest," I mumble into the mat my face is currently pressed into.

She pats my head like a child and hops off me. I roll over with a groan.

"This is going to be fun," she says, eyeing me with a calculated gleam in her eyes.

"Oh, I very much doubt that," I say, already wishing I'd run instead.

"MY EYEBROWS HURT," I WHINE, LEANING MY HEAD AGAINST the window. Jonas snickers from the driver's seat, but Nick's groan from the back is full of the same pain I'm feeling.

"Mine too. Why the hell did we agree to stay for three classes? I don't think I can lift my arms."

"You need to spend less time with the weights," Jonas says smugly, "both of you. I keep telling you, body weight exercise and real-world challenges are better for you."

I curl my lip and mimic him in a whiney voice, but it's halfhearted at best. He worked his ass off in those classes, picking up the movements way quicker than we did.

"I'm pretty sure I coughed up a lung when you threw me that last time, Jonas," Nick says.

Jonas doesn't reply, just shoots him a smirk in the rearview mirror.

"You're right," I say quietly. "You are a strong, capable man. I'm sorry it took me so long to see it." He grins bashfully. "But brother, I am going to learn how to kick your ass, then we're gonna spar. And I'm going to make you cry."

His smile breaks over his face. "Unlikely, but it sounds like fun."

"You're as crazy as Becca is," Nick mutters.

"Crazy like a fox," he says with a snicker.

"Jesus, you're spending way too much time with her."

Nick's right. He's sounding more like Becca and Colton every day.

God help us all.

The trash-talking and complaining continue as we haul our sore asses to the elevator. Well, Nick and I haul. Jonas walks normally, the asshole. The doors open on our floor, and Jonas and I step out. I attempt to wave bye to Nick as he continues up one more floor, but my arm just flops around. Shit. This is bad.

I blame the pain and the worry over having to live the rest of my life with floppy arms for missing her. It's Jonas's "Hi, Maya," that clues me in. I freeze, scanning the landing, but totally miss her. On the second pass, I spot her sitting on the floor near the elevator.

"Hi. Um. I didn't know which door was which." Her eyes flash to mine, then away, and everything that happened before the hellish workout flashes through my mind. Her sobs, her fists striking the suit, and her kiss. That devastating kiss.

I clear my throat. I don't know what to say. Everything I thought I knew about the world and the way I walk in it has been turned upside down in the hours since I saw her. So what do I go with?

"Hey neighbor, fancy meeting you here."

Fuck. The awkward is catching.

She's infected me.

18

MAYA

"**I**t's like a museum in here," I whisper, wrapping my arms around my stomach. Not only to comfort myself, but to stop myself from flailing and breaking something. "Pretty sure some of the stuff in here is worth more than I make in a year. And I make stupid money."

Zach, arms dangling at his sides, still in his sweatpants and t-shirt from earlier, but both significantly sweatier, frowns, glancing around his apartment. I stopped in the foyer, afraid to go further after he asked me in. I don't know the etiquette for this. Am I supposed to go into my boss's house? Is that done?

Mentally slapping myself, I remember that when it comes to this group, it doesn't matter.

"What was that?" Zach asks sharply.

"I said, it's like a museum—"

Frowning, he flails his arms, "Not that. I heard you, but your face just did something weird."

"Oh, yes. Well, I was just contemplating etiquette." At his baffled look, I rush to explain. "I wasn't sure I should be here. You are my boss, and this is your home. I'm sure it's quite invasive having me here. Actually, now that I'm thinking about it, I should just go. Yes, that's exactly—."

"Maya." The low demand in his voice brings my head up to meet his searching gaze. "What brought you here? It's ok that you're here. But did you have something you wanted to say?"

His tone is almost hopeful, like he wants something from me, and now I'm panicking again. Does he want my resignation? An apology? What? I need to move, but without breaking everything in sight. Maybe I can just shake out my hands a b —.

"Is that a Ming Vase?" I ask, pointing.

He glances at the vase on a sleek black pedestal in the corner and nods casually, like, *of course, it's a Ming Vase. Is there any other kind?*

"I can't be here," I mutter, staring at the vase in horror. I back up, banging against the door. Zach rushes after me, doing that weird flailing thing with his arms again. "What is that? What's wrong with your arms?"

He freezes, inches from me, eyes tracking along my finger. He wets his lip, and my finger trembles the slightest bit. I wrap my arm around my waist again and wait.

"I...um worked out with my brothers. We did a few too many classes, and my arms are sore. I can't lift them."

I stare at him longer than I want to admit. "Why would you do that?"

His lip curls and he shakes his head. "I don't honestly know. I started with one, then Becca pissed me off, so I agreed to the second. Then the rest of it is a blur. I have no idea what happened. It was stupid."

"Stupid," I echo, wondering how hard he had to work to have his muscles fail so completely. That would have been an incredible sight to see...so much sweat and.... never mind. "Right. Well. I came to say sorry for today. I lost my mind for a second. My lips were possessed by a hussy, but it won't happen again."

A choked laugh escapes his wide chest. "Hussy? I haven't heard that word in forever."

I drop my chin to my chest and stare at the dark hardwood floor. "Yes, well, it seemed appropriate."

"A kiss doesn't make you a hussy. It was an innocent kiss. About the most innocent thing I've ever experienced."

Everything Bree said about his life filters through my mind. The women, the clubs. Of course, he'd call it innocent. He's used to doing so much more. Everyone's used to doing so much more. "Right. Either way, I'm sorry, and it won't happen again." *Why is he frowning again?*

"Won't happen again," he echoes. His face showing…frustration? Anger? "I see. Yes, that's fine. No big deal. Let me show you out." His arm flails out again, but he's unable to grab the door handle. He stops, dropping his head against the door in frustration.

"You really overdid it. Come on, let's get you some water." A little devil, one separate from that awful little voice, hopped up on my shoulder the second he said our kiss was no big deal.

I know it was no big deal, but he didn't have to say it.

That devil makes me reach for his hand and slowly pull him toward his sleek kitchen. The shiny black cabinets paired with the dark floors are sexy. But it's the countertop that draws my eye and my fingertips. I brush my fingers along the oiled wood countertops, marveling at how perfect they are.

"You must use cutting boards all the time. The wood is still pristine. I had an old block countertop in my apartment back home, but it was scuffed and marked up. It was still beautiful, though." I glance over at Zach, but he's not listening to me. His gaze is narrowed in on our joined hands, and I draw in a silent breath, bracing for the moment he pulls away. Shocked, I watch as, with effort, he curls his fingers to wrap around mine loosely, his thumb barely brushing back and forth over the back of my hand.

I did not think this through at all. Do I pull away? I probably should. Do I want to? No. I really don't. Today is a banner day. Holding hands twice in one day.

I should buy a lottery ticket.

Holding Zach's hand is nothing like Bree's. His hand is so much larger than mine, his fingers easily wrapping around me. And the warmth...my god, it feels good. My hands are usually cold from November to April, always desperately searching for a warm pocket or a hot cup of tea to wrap around. But none of those come close to the warmth Zach's radiating. I stare at our joined hands for too long, only pulling away when Zach licks his lips again.

"You're dehydrated," I whisper to our hands. His slight startle ripples through our hands.

"Right, yeah, I am." He pulls away slowly, his body trapping me against the cabinet as he tries and fails to reach up.

A giggle escapes because this is ridiculous. His head bows, and he grins. "Can you get me a glass, please?"

I nod and turn, reaching for the handle. I expect him to move back, to give me some space, but instead, he does the opposite, moving the tiniest bit closer so I can feel the warmth of him all along my back. My fingers tighten on the knob as I battle with myself. My instincts are telling me to push back into him, so I can feel all of him, but that little voice is telling me to get the hell out of here, to escape back to my apartment and hide under the covers.

But I've done that too many times. Run away, hid from sensation, from fear, from anxiousness. Any emotion other than *fine* was to be feared, to be avoided at all costs. Today, right now, I don't want to listen to that voice.

I want to feel.

Drawing in a breath, my chest expanding, I pull open the cupboard and reach for a glass. As I pull it down, I casually lean my body back into him, and I'm rewarded by a barrage of sensations. We both freeze as our bodies are pressed together, his chest to my upper back, his thick thighs to my ass. I swear he's radiating fire as a full-body sweat breaks out.

I'd rather burn than pull away.

I want to feel all of it. The heat at my back, the low-level shiver running through my body. All of it.

A tiny whimper escapes me as Zach's cheek rubs against the top of my head, then travels down until his mouth is tucked right next to my ear. "Fill it," he rumbles. I feel the words more than hear them. I stare blankly down at the glass clutched in my hands, honestly wondering what he's talking about.

"Water," I gasp, darting my eyes around the room, trying to remember where water comes from. Thankfully, before I can make too big a fool of myself, I spot the sink a few feet away. I pull the glass into my chest as I contemplate the distance. I'm not ready to lose this connection between us, but I want to help him, to take care of him, even if it's only by getting him something to drink.

"Water. Yep, let's get some water." I step carefully to my left, his cheek still pressed against mine, and almost as if we'd rehearsed it, he steps too. I do it again, and he's moving at the same time. One more step, and I'm there. I fill the glass on autopilot and pull it back to my chest again as I slowly, carefully turn into him.

Zach lifts his head away, giving me room to move, but he keeps his body right where it is, forcing me to rub along him as I turn. The look on his face makes me wheeze. I've never seen that look. Not even in movies…at least not the kind of movies I watch. The ferocity and the need there make my hands tremble.

Agonizingly slowly, Zach's hands come up and flop on the counter behind me, completely caging me in. I swallow heavily and push the glass into his chest. "Here," I croak. A slow, sensual, knee-shaking smile curves his lips.

"Can't lift my hands, remember? You'll have to do it."

Dumfounded, I stare at him. "You want me to... uh...help?"

"Yes Maya. I do." The way he draws out my name, nearly stroking the letters, short-circuits my brain. I raise the glass, pressing the rim against his full lip. His eyes lock on me, and he drinks slowly, steadily. I vaguely register the motion of his throat as he swallows, but I'm far more interested in the single drop of water slowly sliding from the corner of his mouth. I watch as it beads at his chin, threatening to drip.

It happens again. The hussy takes over. Before I can even consider the consequences of my actions, I lean in and lick the drop of water off his chin, my tongue scraping against the shadow of stubble.

His eyes flare, and a low groan escapes him as he rears back from the glass. I fumble it, managing to spill most of it between us. The liquid splashes against our chests. Neither of us cares, though, as we stare at each other. He presses closer to me, and my brain comes online again, and it's my turn to lean away.

His mouth twists. "What game are you playing?"

"I don't understand," I murmur, nearly laying on the counter behind me.

"Come on, Maya. You come onto me, then you pull back. Is this your play? Draw me in, tease me, make me desperate. It's a good fucking play, but I'm not interested in games. If you want me, just tell me, and I'll be happy to scratch that itch."

"Scratch," I repeat dumbly, stuck on *want*. I do want him. Desperately. I haven't felt this way before, but this aching, pulling feeling in my abdomen can't be anything but desire.

That sexy smile is back, and he glides over me, his chest hovering over mine. "Whatever this game is, I like it. Let's go to my room and play more."

19

ZACH

"Let's go to my room and play more," I murmur, completely sucked into her vortex. What kind of strange magic does this woman have? She draws me in so easily, using none of the practiced moves I'm used to. Swear to christ, the way she watched me as she held that glass to my lips was the most incredible turn on. I am primed, and ready to give her exactly what her body is asking for.

I'm unprepared for the hands that shove me up and off of her, or her sudden drop to the floor. I lunge toward her, honestly freaked the fuck out. Is she hurt? Is she sick?

Is she playing another game?

My arms are useless, but she's faster than I am anyway, crab walking away from me.

"I should be going now. Take care. Hydrate. Use a straw. That will be easier." She spins, rising to her feet, giving me a glimpse of that truly epic ass.

"Freeze," I bellow, losing my cool. I'm grateful when she stops, but the second I step toward her, she backs up. I stop, desperate to figure out her play. "Seriously, what the fuck is your deal?"

"My deal?" she asks, wetting her lips. "I don't understand."

I'm so tired of games. Why do women do this? Pretend like they don't know the score? "Please don't try that shit with me. If you want me, fine, let's do this. But this innocent little act you've got going on..." How do I finish that sentence? I fucking love her act, I want more of her wide eyes and breathy sighs, but I hate the pulling away.

Her cheeks flood with color, and she folds her arms over her chest, drawing my eyes right to her luscious breasts. "I'm not playing games."

"Sure you aren't. What would you call this, then? Kissing me, then backing away? It's a classic push and pull, and you're a master at it."

"I wouldn't know," she murmurs, eyes locked over my shoulder. "I've never done any of this before."

A laugh almost escapes, but I bite it back at the last second as those words and the way she's holding herself register. "Wait...what?"

Her mouth trembles the faintest bit. She pulls herself taller and looks right at me. "I don't have any experience with any of this. With men."

I have to run it through my mind a few times, like she's speaking another language, and I'm mentally translating it into English. "Jesus. Are you saying you're a virgin?"

She frowns. "I don't like that term. In a clinical sense, do I have a hymen? No. Did I get that way because I had sex with a man? No."

I have no idea what's happening. *Hymen* is rattling around in my mind, and I can't gather a clear thought. "But... wait....what?"

She spins, running for the door, and this time I'm too slow to stop her. I end up face-planting into my front door as it slams shut behind her. Groaning in frustration, I slap at the door handle, my arms about as useful as a T-Rex's, just flapping.

What an epic shit show. Sliding to the floor, I drop onto my ass and ponder my major fuck up. How the hell is she a virgin, and how the hell did I not realize? Though, to be fair, it's not really something that's obvious. Sure, she's awkward, but so are a lot of people. That doesn't mean anything. But to somehow remain a virgin this long, fuck, how does that happen? Is it a religious thing?

"It's none of my fucking business," I yell at the ceiling, my voice echoing back at me like it's mocking me. I want everything about her to be my business, and isn't that just a kick in the ass? I have no idea how to navigate this. But one thing is clear. Maya has saved herself for some reason, and I know for a fact that someone like me, someone who treats sex so casually, is not the man she needs.

And that hurts.

MOST OF SUNDAY IS SPENT LYING ON MY BED, LETTING MY BODY recover from my stupidity while running every moment I've spent with Maya through my mind. Every time I do, I think I've come up with some clue or key to her. I think I understand her better. Then I realize I'm full of shit, and start back at the moment I saw her face on that video interview.

She seemed so cold and analytical. She fooled me into thinking that's who she really is. But she's the furthest thing from cold, and under that calm facade, there's a well of deep feeling. It was obvious at family dinner on Friday how much she really wants to be a part of something. So who the fuck am I, trying to get in her pants? I'm her boss, as she so rightly pointed out, and that is so out of line.

I went too far with her in my kitchen. I shouldn't have gotten near her. But when she pushed back into me, I lost my mind. I really thought I knew my type. The women I go for at the clubs are nothing like Maya physically, and I've been missing out. That ass is just...everything.

Sick of myself, I sit up and place a food order, then flop down to wait. I'll stuff my face and pretend everything is fine and that tomorrow at work, everything will go back to normal. I'll realize this little obsession is an overreaction, and Maya will pretend nothing happened.

It'll be fine.

But as I lay in bed, carb loading, eating a three-foot French baguette straight from the bag, the end of it resting on my bare chest, I realize I'm a fucking loser, and I maybe, just maybe, might be obsessed with Maya Miller.

Isn't that a kick in the head?

AS THE DOORS OPEN TO THE PARKADE ON MONDAY MORNING, I'M determined to act normal. I'm not going to do anything that might freak Maya out. Because I may not know what the hell is happening with me, but I do know I'll do anything to make sure she doesn't leave me.

Leave Brash, I mean. Not me. We're not together. *She's not for me. She deserves someone better.*

I paste my most charming smile on my face, ready to pretend my ass off, only to see my brother sitting in his otherwise empty van.

"Where's Maya?" I bark at him. Thankfully, he lets my shitty tone pass and answers me.

"She went in with Cara. Declan drove himself today."

"Oh. Ok. That's fine. Totally fine. No worries."

That gets a reaction. Frowning, Jonas studies my face, searching for some hint of what's happening. He shakes his head and turns away, then freezes, hand on the button to start the engine. "Wait. I'm supposed to ask what's wrong, right? Because your face is weird right now. Something's wrong with you."

I splutter and halfheartedly deny it, but I'm also really happy that he said something. That he noticed. "I'm not really ok, but I don't think there's anything you can do about it."

He nods and starts the car, pulling carefully out of the garage after making sure I'm belted in. As always, when Jonas is driving, I'm able to fully relax. When our parents were killed, I wasn't in the car with them. Jonas was, though. He was a tiny four-year-old, thankfully strapped into the best carseat on the market. My parents barely made ends meet, but somehow they always scraped together enough money to pay for things Jonas and I needed.

And Jonas needed a lot. His therapy and special early learning programs weren't cheap, but I didn't fully understand how expensive they were until Jonas and I were on our own and I was trying to figure out how to pay for them myself.

Ever since my parents died, I've been...particular about cars and about driving. I can drive. Ransom made sure of it. But I would much rather be a passenger. All my brothers are excellent drivers, but when Jonas is behind the wheel, when we're together, it feels like everything will be ok. Yeah, he's a fucking sharp driver, so that's a part of it. But the bigger part is more dysfunctional. When we're in the car together, I know that if the worst happens, we'll go together.

I always thought it would be better to die with my brother than to have to live without him.

Only recently am I coming to realize how fucked up that really is. How dependent on him I truly am, that I didn't believe I would survive it if I lost him.

"Are we supposed to be talking about feelings right now?" Jonas asks.

"Do you want to talk about feelings?"

"Maybe we should get it over with on Mondays, so the rest of the week we can go back to normal. Plus, statistically, the work week is busy and allows for very little variance.

You're likely to be more emotional on Mondays after a weekend of non-standard experiences."

"*I* am more likely to be emotional? What about you? Are you just level all the time now?"

Jonas frowns at the red light. "I am not...level, as you put it. I feel things all the time."

"About Janey?"

"Yes. I feel...many things for her. It's difficult to want something and know that you will never have it."

"Never is a long time. You just need to wait for an opening, remember? If you want her, just wait."

"I am not good at waiting for things. I find I am struggling to stay focused, and that's not at all like me."

"Focus and fixation are your superpowers. We've put them to good use over the years," I murmur. Ransom was ruthless, pulling us into his group. Well...pulling Jonas into the fold. He saw Jonas's potential and came after him. But I knew Jonas needed me and that it would be a cold day in hell before I'd let him go anywhere without me, especially at twelve years old. The rest of the boys Ransom collected were alone. No one cared if they didn't show up at their foster homes or group homes. But Jonas and I were a team. No way would I let him disappear with some teenager with big ideas by himself.

When we were in the fold, Jonas became the center of our group. He needed more protection, especially at the beginning. We all learned that if we let him settle into his strengths, we all made money. Didn't matter if it was gambling or business. Jonas had a calculation for that. So many nights, I'd find Ransom sitting on the floor next to the little workstation we set up for Jonas, talking quietly to him. I stayed away, and gave them their space for one reason only. The complete and utter awe on Ransom's face when he looked at my brother. That alone earned him my loyalty.

"They were my superpowers," he mumbles, accelerating

through the now green light. "I don't really need them anymore. Everything's too easy now."

"Running the finances for a multi-billion dollar company and all of its subsidiaries is easy?"

Jonas hums as he turns into our compound, nodding absentmindedly at the security guard. As he rounds the long drive, I glance at the main employee parking lot, searching for Cara's car, finally spotting it right near the door. My stomach does a little jump, knowing Maya's in the building and I'll be seeing her soon. Really soon. Jonas pulls into his spot and leans back, staring through the windshield at the busy loading docks beyond.

"Yes, it is easy," he says. "Everything runs on autopilot. There's very little needed from me anymore."

"If you tell Ransom you need a challenge, I'm sure he'd pick up another company for you to overhaul. You love digging into the finances of his acquisitions."

Jonas cracks a smile. "Yeah, I do. People always think they're so clever, hiding their money. I always find it." He does, and usually with a skill and speed that leaves the former owners of the business stuttering and trying to explain themselves. "But even that's not interesting anymore."

I squeeze his shoulder because I don't know what else to do. There's no easy fix for what's ailing him, and as his brother, I hate that.

I'd run in front of him with a sword, hacking and slashing if it meant he had an easy path to the princess.

"I don't know what to say. I wish I could help."

Jonas's eyes widen in surprise, "You do help. I do not need you to fix anything for me, but I like when you check on me. It helps me remember you exist."

Bursting into laughter, I shove him. He barely moves, strong fucker. "Can you explain that one to me?"

"You do not have that problem? Getting so focused on what you are doing that you forget the world exists?"

"Sometimes, but I'm thinking not the same way you do. When I'm focusing, thoughts pop in, breaking my concentration."

"What kinds of thoughts?"

"A little bit of everything. Something someone said that annoyed me. What I'm going to have for lunch. I think about you, wondering if you're ok. I think about the weekend. Just the regular, everyday stuff everyone thinks about."

"That sounds awful. No wonder most people's productivity is so low."

Snorting because, yes, the entire world's productivity sucks compared to his, I turn to him, leaning on the door. We've never talked like this, and I'm incredibly curious to understand the way he experiences the world. "Is it really not like that inside your head? When you're working, you're just thinking about work?"

Jonas puts his palms together and spins them. The familiar sight sends my heart racing, and I force myself to breathe out. *It's not a bad thing. It's ok. He's fine.* "Well...yes. When I'm working, I'm only thinking about what I'm doing. The rest of the world disappears. Nothing else exists."

"And nothing breaks you out of that?"

"Only a few things. Usually, it's sensory. If something is too loud, or if a seam is bothering me. Most of that kind of distraction has been eliminated, so I don't have to worry. Oh, also, elimination. If I need to use the bathroom, I'll notice, but only when it is absolutely urgent."

"I've seen those fast walks. You've done them since you were little," I say, laughing. "I look forward to them. They're funny as hell."

His face scrunches up. "They don't feel funny. They feel urgent and uncomfortable."

Covering my eyes with my hand, I dissolve into laughter, picturing him turtling it all the way down the hallway. "Jesus, Jonas. Why don't you go sooner?"

"I just told you, I don't notice." He scowls at me, and pushes open his door, letting a wash of cold air in. "The sensation has to be strong enough to make me break focus. By then, it's an immediate concern. Let's go to work." And he's gone.

Guess we're done talking.

20

MAYA

Waving to one last team member, I wait until she's out of sight before I slide down the wall and drop onto the floor in the corner of the marketing room. Everyone's gone, and I finally feel like I can breathe.

My nerves are frayed.

This is not sustainable. I'm going to have a heart attack before the end of the week.

I didn't realize it would be so hard to avoid him. I mean, obviously, I can't do this forever, but for the last four days, I've managed to avoid being alone with Zach. There's been a lot of ducking down behind desks or hiding in supply closets.

I'm not proud of that one.

The way he stared at me today in this room is…upsetting. It's my fault. I'm the one that put that look on his face. When I ran out of his place on Saturday night, I was so embarrassed. Everything spun out of my control so quickly that I didn't handle it very well. I don't have any reason to be embarrassed about my lack of sexual experience, I know that, but the shock on his face was just too much to take.

I promised myself I would go back to our professional

distance, but seeing him walk in on Monday with that little smile on his lips when he looked at me, I just…panicked. I ran off. Then I did it again later in the day. Then again, after work, riding the bus in loops until I thought it was safe to go home. It's unlikely he was going to knock on my door, but on the off chance he did, I needed to be prepared. So I rode until I felt like I had my speech perfectly rehearsed. Only I didn't get to use it, the elevator and my floor were empty of tall, dark, disapproving men with pillowy lips.

Tuesday, his smile was gone. He started watching me with his arms crossed over his chest, a frown on his face. Wednesday, he didn't try to approach me at all, and today, he mostly ignored me. He was still polite and professional, but he didn't smile at me or otherwise look at me at all.

Maybe it's for the best. We can go back to polite strangers and forget all about the kiss and the other…moments.

But I wish we didn't have to. I wish that I were someone else. Someone braver, who could walk right up to him and tell him that he gives me funny feelings, and I'd like to see where those lead. And yes, that could be career suicide. But for the first time in my life, I don't think I'd care.

If I was braver.

"As entertaining as your hiding from me has been, we need to talk."

I *meep* like the roadrunner and bang my head against the wall as I search for Zach. I find him, hands in his pockets, standing a few feet from me. He winces as I rub the back of my head, then smooths his expression back into the polite one I've gotten to know so well this week. Who knew I would miss him scowling at me?

"Ah…talk. About?" I wince because, of course, I know what about. I take a deep breath and mentally put on a bravery cape. *I can do hard things.* "Actually, I wanted to talk to you about this weekend."

"Did you?" he bites off, scowling. "Could have fooled me.

What, with all the running away and hiding." He pulls his hands out of his pocket and tugs at his light blue tie. "It doesn't matter, anyway. This weekend was a whole series of mistakes, and it's best we just move on."

Mistakes.

Being the woman without a heart was easier. Maybe I should go back to being her. I didn't want to move on or forget...but it's not just up to me, obviously. And my cowardly lion act this week obviously killed any chance we might have had. It's just as well. Maybe skipping all this male-female drama my whole life was the smart move. Who knows where I'd be right now if I'd met some guy in high school? I could be married with three teenagers right now, yelling at them to pick up their dirty socks and being chased around the kitchen by my husband.

It actually sounds pretty nice.

"We have an event to go to tomorrow night," he says flatly, moving to sit on a desk a few feet from me. All I can see is the top of his head. He doesn't seem inclined to accommodate my spot on the floor, so I stand and move to the large design board, so I don't have to look right at him. It's covered with images of harried mothers, minivans full of stuff, and happy families. All things I know nothing about.

"Yes, I remember. For the hospital."

He nods and stares at me like I'm a frog pinned to a dissection board in tenth-grade biology. "This is one of the biggest events of the year. Brash is the biggest donor and the only sponsor for the event. All eyes are on us." He tips his chin at me, eyes roaming down the dress I'm wearing. It's the bug one, his least favorite of all of them, judging by his wince every time he looks at it. I have an inkling of where this is going, and I'm already feeling itchy.

"You're there representing us. The way you look...everything about you reflects on The Brash Group. You've proven yourself to be a brilliant marketer, but first impressions and appearance matter."

"I understand that," I say, crossing my arms under my breasts.

"Do you? Because it doesn't seem like it from where I'm standing." He cuts off my attempt to defend myself. "It doesn't matter. You need something suitable for tomorrow. You're coming with me."

Dread pools in my stomach, and a rough chuckle escapes him. "Jesus, you'd think I just kicked your dog." I flinch at the mention of dogs. Does he know? Did he say it on purpose? *No, he's not cruel. It's a coincidence.* "It's just shopping, Maya. A free outfit. Most women would kill for an all-expense paid shopping trip on me."

"Right, it's just shopping. No big deal." I can do this. I can be the person he needs me to be tomorrow. I move toward him, mentally preparing myself for the ordeal to come, but he stops me with a hand on my arm. My eyes fly to his, and he lets go like his fingers are singed.

"Where are your shoes, Maya?" he asks, eyes flicking from my feet back to my face. I curl my toes into the rough carpet and drop my gaze. His heavy sigh doesn't surprise me. What does surprise me is the heat rising in my cheeks. I stopped caring about what people thought of me a long time ago. Even last week, his disapproval and frustration with me didn't penetrate that deeply. But today, I feel exposed. Like I've let him down, and I'm embarrassed with myself.

I open my mouth and do something I promised myself I would stop doing. Apologize. "I'm sorry. I'll find them." I spin, ducking down to search under tables and in corners, my face on fire.

A fairy godmother would come in handy right about now. Someone who could wave her wand and turn me into someone normal. I don't need to be exceptional or beautiful. Just a normal human being who can wear anything and keep her shoes on her feet. But my life isn't a fairy tale, no matter how much I wish it was.

"Maya," he says. I ignore him, furiously blinking back tears. "Maya." His tone this time makes it clear ignoring him is not an option. I stand, arms dangling, and stare at the middle of his chest. He sighs, and my hands curl into fists.

That one's different. I've heard that kind of sigh directed at me too many times. It's a sigh that says I'm too much trouble. Too annoying. Taking up too much space. It never feels good, but coming from him, it feels like standing outside in the middle of a blizzard, icy snow pelting me.

Busy blinking the tears out of my eyes, I miss his approach. But I don't miss his warm hand curling around mine, lifting. I stare, dumbfounded, as he uncurls my clenched fingers and places a pair of soft, delicate suede shoes in my palm. I twist them in my hand, dumbfounded, studying the seamless stitching and the soft rubber soles. My fingers stroke the luxurious suede, enjoying the texture.

Zach clears his throat. "You have to stop taking your shoes off. People spill things on these carpets all the time. You could get hurt."

"You," I lick my dry lips, dumbfounded. "You bought me shoes?" Maybe he's a wizard and can just conjure things out of thin air. That would make more sense than him going shopping for me, then carrying them with him until he found me.

"Yes," he says, dropping the hand holding mine and putting a desk between us again. When I just stare at him, he groans and rakes his hand through his hair. "Put them on, Maya. Please."

The *please* cuts through my fog. I drop into the chair behind me and lean over. *Please let them fit. Please let me like them. Please, please don't be pinchy.*

I run my fingers over the fabric again, enjoying the feel, and Zach mutters something under his breath. Then he's on his knees in front of me, pulling the shoes from my hand. "We don't have all day. People are waiting for us." His words are clipped and hurried, but his touch is gentle as he lifts my foot and carefully slips the shoe on. I stare at the top of his head and his thick black hair, realizing I've stepped into a fairy tale. My very own Prince Charming, on his knees in front of me. But there's no glass slipper, and no marriage in my future. But for a second, just one second, I want to pretend.

I memorize every brush of his hand, the low creak his jacket makes as he shifts and strains the seams, and the brush of his breath over my ankles as he focuses on sliding the shoes over my feet.

"The saleswoman said these are going to stretch and mold to your feet, but I made sure to get them big enough so they'll be comfortable right away." He slides his finger into the shoe, between the leather and my instep, and runs it down the side of my foot to my heel, checking the fit. "There," he murmurs, satisfied, sitting back on his heels. My suede-covered feet are resting on his knees.

"You know my size?"

His head bows, his voice is low. "I pay attention. Too much."

He sees me.

I should move. I should thank him. But my body's pinging with sensation, and I want another moment. I've never been a greedy person, generally satisfied with my lot in life, but he's changing that. Who knew the simple act of putting on a shoe could make my heart race like this? Cinderella must have been all tingly when the prince kneeled in front of her. I wonder what their wedding night was like. Did he make her wear the shoes?

Now I'm blushing again.

He's totally talking to me, and I missed it. "What?"

He rolls his eyes, which, to be fair, is a totally appropriate reaction. He's been so kind, and all I can think about is how soft his lips are. "I asked you how they feel."

"Oh!" I peer down at my suede-covered feet. *Moment of truth.* I wiggle my toes, then reluctantly drop my feet to the floor and stand. I pace away a few feet in one direction, then the other. Then I crouch and twist and spin. The shoes flex and move with me, not rubbing or pinching anywhere. "They're miracle shoes," I breathe, staring in awe at the pretty nude suede. "They feel like slippers."

Zach's hoarse chuckle wraps around me. "They're not miracles. Shoes are supposed to be comfortable. I don't know why the hell you bought those other ones in the first place."

I just shrug because the truth would only make him look at me like I'm an alien. How would this man ever understand the anxiety I felt going into a mall? By the time I managed to find clothes that felt good, a full marching band had taken up residence in my head. I beelined into the first shoe store I could find and bought the first pair I found in my size.

"You didn't have to do this, but thank you. No one's ever done anything this thoughtful for me before. You're incredibly kind." Yep, I'm teary. I blink furiously, refusing to bring attention to it by wiping my eyes. Zach frowns as he studies me, his gaze lingering on my cheeks.

"It was nothing," he says, moving toward the elevator. "Let's go *Pretty Woman* you."

Wait...what?

21

MAYA

I try to hide my reaction, but I'm not successful, judging by the scowl on the saleswoman's face. We've been in this change room, together, for nearly an hour, and so far, not one outfit has been good enough to show Zach.

Not because they're not beautiful. They are. Gorgeous, glittery gowns line the walls of the giant change room, mixed with more sedate tulle and crepe gowns. All beautiful, and all making me feel like I want to tear them off within seconds. "Isn't there anything made of cotton? Just plain cotton? There's got to be something?" I ask desperately.

The woman, not a seam or a lock of silver hair out of place, lifts her nose and sniffs at me. "Evening gowns are not made of cotton. If you want a t-shirt, I'm sure you can find it elsewhere. Here, I only deal with couture."

Oh, she wants to be snippy? "Are you telling me, Ma'am, that couture designers don't use cotton?"

She sniffs again and frowns. At least, I think it's a frown. Her forehead doesn't move, but there's a little twitch in her eyelid that makes me think she's done with me. "Mr. Lee instructed me to prepare for an evening event." There's that eye twitch again. "I suppose I'll have to inform him that nothing I have offered you has been suitable, and he'll have to go elsewhere to clothe you."

Crap, she's got me. I can't handle more of this. I've never shopped like this, and if it weren't for the type of clothing on offer, I could get used to it. No endless racks of clothes. No cramped change rooms. No crowds. Just one snooty woman and Zach and I in what looks like a bridal salon, without the wedding dresses. It's quiet and private, and I would really enjoy it under different circumstances.

I pull my patience around me like a cloak and try to explain. "Look, I have sensitive skin. If I wear any of these, I'll end up hurting all night. Can you please, please, find me something else."

She smooths her chignon, "There's not much available in your size." I don't miss the dig, but I don't give a shit if she's judging me. I just want something to wear that won't make me want to peel my skin off or embarrass Zach.

It's looking like I'll have to settle for one of the two.

"We can't all be chihuahua sized," I say with a hint of snark and watch a smile crack her porcelain skin.

"Thank you," she breathes, putting a hand to her stomach and bony hips. The woman took it as a compliment, who am I to correct her? She throws the curtain open as she leaves, and I'm left standing there in a too-tight satin robe, staring at my boss.

"Uh, maybe I should just close this." I reach out to snag the curtain, but he shakes his head curtly.

"There's nothing under there I haven't already seen hundreds of times."

The comparison to other women, the reminder of his experience, grates on my nerves. I should drop it, but I black out briefly instead. It's the only explanation for what I say.

"Really? I mean, I'm sure I have the same parts as any

other ladies you've been with, but I can guarantee you, you've never seen an ass like this." Then, to complete my moment of madness, I turn in profile and attempt a twerk. "Huh. It's a lot harder than it looks on TV." Zach's coughing and I rush over to pat him on the back, but he waves me off with wild eyes.

"You don't have to look so scared. I'm not naked under here or anything."

He presses the palms of his hands into his eye sockets. "Thank Christ for small favors." That should hurt, but something in his voice is…longing and rough. It makes the tips of my fingers tingle.

Rubbing them with my thumbs, I drop into the velvet chair opposite him and try one more time to convince him to give this up. "I promise, the dress I have for events is perfectly suitable. I wore it many times at my old job, and no one commented on it."

"You know the saying, Maya, if you don't have anything nice to say…" he says, smirking at me.

"Have you considered the possibility that it's fine and you're just a snob?"

He crosses his ankle over his knee and flexes his foot. "You're implying that because I care about appearances, I'm a snob?" He shakes his head. "Maya, I don't know how to break this to you, but everyone cares about appearances. Tell me," he says, dropping his elbow on the wide arm of the chair and rubbing his chin with his fingers, "has anyone ever complimented an outfit you were wearing? In the last decade, I mean?"

I search frantically through my memories, nearly crowing in delight when I come up with one. "Yes, actually, I have been. By a woman at the park." It must have been five years ago, with Birdie at the dog park. Had to have been there because that's the only place I ever stood around and spoke to other people.

He doesn't look defeated, merely smiling and leaning his cheek on his hand. "I see. And tell me, how old was this woman?"

I break off eye contact with him and stare up at the ceiling. "Um...let's see...she...um."

He laughs, a true laugh that crinkles up the skin on the side of his eyes. It's compelling and beautiful. "Don't bother. I'm sure she wasn't a day under seventy."

"Probably closer to eighty," I admit, amusing myself by making patterns in the velvet with my fingernail, then rubbing it away. "I thought she was homeless at first, but it turns out it was just her style."

His chuckles turn to belly laughs, making him shake in his chair. "Jesus, Maya. If that doesn't say it all." I smile as I watch him fall apart. This feels way better than the way things have been this week.

"I'm really sorry I ran away from you," I tell him, begging him with my whole face to let me finish. He leans back with a small nod, and I suck in a deep breath, mentally tearing away parts of my rehearsed speech. "I told you I don't have much experience...I just got overwhelmed by everything that happened this weekend. Something about Becca's class got to me. I've never hit anyone in my life. Well, except for Lucas in the second grade, but he kept pulling my hair. I had every right to slap him...I think."

I peek at him to make sure he's still listening. He hasn't moved, but his face has warmed the tiniest bit. *Progress.* "Anyway, I really am sorry for," I clear my throat and squeak out the words, "Kissing you and...um, rubbing on you. I just felt...well, never mind what I felt. It doesn't matter. It was unprofessional of me." I feel it coming. I try to hold it back, but the chaotic jumble of words pour out, "Everything was tingling, and I got too curious, and I shouldn't have done it. I'm sorry."

"Maya," he says, hands moving to grip the arms of the chair, voice raspy. "Tell me more about—"

"Well," the saleswoman says briskly as she breezes into the room, "I managed to find one gown in your size that might work. It's not cotton." Zach's brows raise at that before he smooths his face back into the mask he's been wearing for the last hour. "But it should meet your specifications. If it doesn't, then I'm afraid I have nothing else for you."

"Nothing else? You had at least twenty gowns in there. Are you telling me not one of them fit her? I sent you her measurements." The bite in Zach's voice makes the woman's smile turn up to a calculated dazzle. Wait, how does he know my measurements? Is that a hot guy thing? Can they just eyeball it, or do they have to touch? I mean, he definitely touched.

Maybe that's his superpower.

"Mr. Lee, I assure you I have pulled many appropriate options. Unfortunately, Ms. Miller's quite…selective."

Seemingly mollified, Zach turns to me. "Why are you being so picky?"

"Ah, it's not really picky. I just have a hard time with certain fabrics."

His gaze is piercing. "I'm sure you can figure it out for one night. That's all I'm asking for, one night. After that, you go back to wearing whatever you want…at work."

"Right. Yep, one night. I can do that. No problem." I spin and march back into the changing room, determined to make this dress work. The saleswoman, Bridget, has a little smile playing on her lips, a bit of a *so there*, I think, but it falls away as I drop the satin robe.

"Oh, no. My dear," she says, moving to me, hand hovering over the reddened skin of my arm. Anywhere the satin robe was touching, the skin is hot to the touch. She looks up at me, an apology in her eyes, "I'm sorry. I truly thought you were being difficult."

"I know. It's ok, really."

She doesn't look convinced and pulls the dress bag closer to her body. "It's not cotton...are you going to have a reaction to this one too? I really don't have anything else. I could maybe try and find something tomorrow. What time is the event?"

I cover her hand and wait for her to look at me. "Thank you. I really do appreciate all of this. But I'm sure this will be great." I'm not actually sure. Not at all. But I'm at my limit. I can't handle anything more.

I pull the dress on, the soft fabric sliding over my body, the long sleeves hugging me like a second skin. I'm distracted by the feel of it. Bridget's gasp brings my eyes to the mirror.

"Wowzers. Is that me?" Stepping closer, I admire the way the Jade green fabric caresses my curves. It looks like velvet, but the fabric feels lighter somehow and doesn't immediately make me want to tear it off. The rich color compliments my dark hair and makes my skin look like it's glowing.

She steps back, pressing her hands to her chest with a smile. "He must see this one," she says, and turns, flinging open the curtain. "We have a vision, Mr. Lee!"

Thank god I turn in time to catch his reaction. It's worth every bit of frustration over the last hour. Never, not once, has a man looked at me like that. Like I was...edible. Zach's face is everything I never knew I wanted. I press my hand to my chest over my fluttering heart, and his eyes track the movement. His face tightens and gets harder in a way that I really like. I rub my hand experimentally down the dress, and yep, he follows it.

Is this how most women feel? Desirable, powerful? It's heady, and suddenly, I can't wait until tomorrow. "What do you think?" I ask quietly, vaguely aware of the saleswoman's exit from the room.

Zach stands, prowling over to me, gently turning me to face the mirror. He stands behind me, his blue-black hair shining under the bright lights above us. Slowly, carefully, I watch as he lifts his hand and reaches for my hair, gently brushing it over my shoulder until my neck and bare shoulders are exposed in the dress.

The contrast between us is jarring. His strong hand, my soft one. His broad shoulders, my gently rounded ones. His harsh breaths and my gasping ones. I raise my eyes to meet his in the mirror. He locks on me, his jaw clenching as he stares, hand hovering in the air as he moves it slowly, slowly towards my collarbone. The tension between us snaps tight, tighter than I've ever felt. It's nearly unbearable as I wait for his touch.

"I've found the most adorable clutch to go with that dress. You'll be the belle of the ball," Bridget says cheerily as she returns, fussing with the bag in her hand. She raises her eyes at us and freezes, "Ah, well, yes, let me just leave this right here for you." She drops the bag on the small chair in the corner, then hustles her tiny ass out of the room.

The moment is broken. Zach steps away, rubbing the back of his neck as he exhales heavily. "That will do fine. Change out of it, and Bridget will package it up for you. She'll arrange to get you another pair of shoes from that same line as those ones to match."

He spins, taking a few steps away, then stops. Glancing back at me, eyes glittering, he says the most incredible thing anyone's ever said to me, "You look beautiful."

I stand frozen as Bridget bustles back in, a small grin on her face. No one, not once in my entire life, has called me beautiful. And suddenly, I understand why women wear dresses like this and plaster on makeup.

For men like him.

So men look at them just like that. Ok, and maybe for themselves. But I don't think I'll ever get over the high of knowing Zach Lee, handsome man about town, billionaire extraordinaire, thinks I'm beautiful.

It's a dream. One I want to keep living in for a little while, so I ignore my even redder skin and Bridget's worried eyes. It'll be fine. It's the price of beauty.

And to get Zach to look at me like that again? It's a price I'm more than willing to pay.

22

ZACH

She's the most beautiful woman in the room, hands down. She's done something with her eyes that makes them darker, smokier. And her pinned up hair looks like it's on the verge of falling. I'm desperate to get my hands in it, and pull it apart.

"What do you think?"

I snap my attention back to the man in front of me. He's been talking at me for a while, and I don't think I've caught a word. This isn't me. Not at all. I'm always on, always negotiating, always looking for the next opportunity. But tonight, I can't focus on anything but her. And that's a big fucking problem since the collective net worth in this ballroom is a cool Trillion.

I smile easily at the man…*what the fuck is his name?* "Let me think on it. Why don't you send me all the details, and I'll take a look?"

He nods enthusiastically, snatching my business card out of my hand so fast the thick card stock slices into my thumb. I have no idea what he was yammering on about, and I have no clue what's going to hit my inbox in the morning. But it's a problem for another day.

At ten-thousand a plate, the people in this room are rich and generous, at least generous enough to buy a plate and put on their fancy clothes. The bigger donors will dole out extra funds as the night progresses. All it takes is a little flattery, and I'll have fifty million in checks in my hands by the end of the night. The hospital's donor engagement team has been working overtime tonight, only calling me in to nudge the odd holdout here and there.

I move to one of the bars scattered around the ballroom and snag a napkin, blotting at the blood on my thumb. Though my attention is on the minor wound, I'm aware of Maya moving toward me, weaving through the glitterati filling the ballroom. Her rounded hips sway through the crowd, her natural grace drawing attention as she moves. I don't think she has any idea how stunning she is.

She finally makes it through the throng, slumping beside me at the bar. Her skin has a weird flush that has me on edge. "How much have you had to drink?"

"I don't really drink," she says, scanning the rows of bottles behind me. I really don't like the way she looks. If she's not drunk, then something else is wrong. It's making me antsy, and the fact that I'm antsy is pissing me off. Turning, I catch the bartender's eye, "Two waters."

I press one of the glasses into Maya's hand, "Drink." She doesn't fight me, thankfully, taking large gulps. I take the empty glass and press the full one into her hand. "More."

She side-eyes me but complies, sipping slower this time. She shifts awkwardly, looking down at the toes of her sparkly black flats. "So," she says, "I hope you're happy with my performance this evening."

Was I happy to see her smile at everyone she talked to? I suppose, yes, it's a relief knowing that she's capable of networking when necessary. If I have a problem with the way all the men smiled back, then that's on me. "Is that what it was? A performance?"

"Well...of course it is," she says, absently rubbing her arm as she scowls out at the crowd. "Nobody's stripped bare at something like this. We all have an agenda, and we're doing whatever we need to do to meet our objectives. You should know, you're the master at it."

"Am I supposed to be flattered or offended?" I ask mildly. She seems like she's stewing for a fight. How is she so pleasant to everyone else, then she's grumpy at me? In the words of the divine Miss Taylor Swift, it's me. I'm the problem, clearly.

"That's up to you. I'm just pointing out a fact. But in this crowd, whatever you're feeling will be hidden by your charming, fake smile. No way will you show anyone what you're really feeling."

I straighten my pocket square as I absorb her words. "You say that like it's a bad thing. Being polite and charming works." I would know, it's gotten me to the highest heights.

"Maybe it is when you're hiding who you really are," she mumbles, sliding the now-empty glass onto the barter. "Can I go now? I really need to go." She's holding her arms out from her body awkwardly as her face crumples with pain.

"What's wrong with you?" I ask her, putting my hand on her back to guide her through the room. I catch her flinch when I touch her, and I immediately register the heat coming through the gown. She's burning up. "Are you sick?"

She pulls away from me as she moves faster through the crowd. "Not exactly," she says, flapping her arms.

"What the fuck is going on?" I whisper in her ear, trying not to draw any more attention. Too many people are watching me escort the stunning woman flapping her way through the ballroom.

"I need to get out of this dress," she says as she hits the doors, shoving them open into the hallway of the hotel. She spins in a circle, rivers of sweat pouring down her face, then darts for the washroom. I don't hesitate before I follow her in.

A perfectly coiffed, Botoxed woman, looking forty but probably pushing sixty, huffs and hurries out.

"You're freaking me out," I tell Maya. She's stopped at the sink, pulling at the neckline of her dress, nearly sobbing. "Jesus Christ," I choke out as she pulls the neckline away from her breasts. It's not the shadowed valley of her breast that's stolen my breath, but the angry red skin she exposes. "What is happening? Tell me right now."

She slaps her hands on the counter and drops her head. "I told you, I can't wear clothes like this."

My stomach is in my shoes. "I thought you were a fucking fashion victim, not that your skin would peel off!" It's my turn to spin in a circle as I look for options. Other than draping her in a toilet paper dress, there is nothing here that can help us.

She's moaning, and I carefully cup her elbow. My stomach rolls at the tiny sound of pain she makes. "Come on, please, Maya. I'll help, I promise, but you have to come with me."

I guide her to the front desk and pin the poor girl working there with what I assume is a less-than-charming look. "Get me a key to a suite right now."

"Of...of course, Mr. Lee, right away." She drops the keycard twice before she manages to program it. She hands me the key. "Room 2701."

I take it with a nod and guide Maya to the elevator. She's sweating and shivering, and I want to put my fist through a wall. All I can think about is stopping her pain.

I fucking did this.

The elevator takes way too long, but thankfully, we're alone. All I can do is hover, wince, and curse myself and this whole stupid situation. Why the fuck didn't I just let her wear what she wanted? *Because I was trying to exert a little control in a relationship where I feel I have none.* Damn Colton and his Psychology degree. Life was easier when I could just blame everything on other people and didn't have to look in the mirror.

I scan the card and let us into the suite. The door is barely closed behind us, the room only lit by the moonlight streaming through the windows across the room, before I put my hands on the two sides of her gown, right over her breasts, and pull, careful not to put pressure on her skin as I do.

The material is strong.

I'm stronger.

It gives with a howl that doesn't quite cover Maya's gasp. I pull the remnants down her arms and let everything pool at her feet. Her arms come up to cover her chest, but there's still way too much exposed.

I peer into her wild eyes. "What else? What do you need? How can I make this better?" It's my fucking fault. I was the one who insisted she dress up for this stupid party. "Maya, tell me. What do I do?"

With effort, I keep my eyes above her neckline, but I deserve a fucking medal for it. The woman's not wearing a bra. Though, after sneaking a glance, —I'm fucking human alright— I can't find anything sexy in this moment. The delicate skin of her breasts is bright red too.

"Cool shower. Lotion." She tells me the name, and I dial the front desk and order them to run out for a bottle as I guide her to the bathroom. I'm afraid to touch her, so I just circle the air around her back with one arm and point with the other like I'm guarding the Stanley Cup. She's silent as we step into the opulent bathroom. I move for the shower, but she stops me, her voice barely a whisper. "The water hitting my skin will hurt too much. A bath is better."

I drop to my knees next to the tub and adjust the water temperature to just above cool. "Is this ok?" Her pale, perfect hand, followed by an arm covered in angry red skin, reaches over my shoulder, testing the water. Her sigh of relief as it runs over her arm is all the confirmation I need. Setting the stopper, I turn to her, holding her hand as she hurriedly steps into the water, still wearing her plain black panties. "Cotton," I whisper, my voice lost in the rush of water filling the tub. With effort, I pull my mind away from her simple panties and the protected skin under it.

She's the sexiest thing I've ever seen, despite the fact that she looks like a cooked lobster.

She sinks down with a sigh, knees to her chest, and carefully cups water to pour it over her heated skin. She's lost in a haze of pain, her eyes cloudy with it. I step back and drag off my jacket, dropping it carelessly on the floor, then yank off my bowtie and shirt, dropping them both on top of the jacket. Crouching back next to the tub, I run my hand under the tap, water pooling in my palm, then slowly, carefully, I let it trickle over her back.

Her hands come to rest on the sides of the tub as she lets me take over. I turn off the water and continue scooping cool bathwater over her red shoulders, arms, back, and chest, moving in a slow circle, then back again.

"Thank you," she murmurs, exhaling a shuddering breath.

"You shouldn't be thanking me, Maya. You should be tearing a strip off me." She sighs and bows her head, leaving the nape of her neck bare to me. Her hair is still in those pins, and my fingers still itch to pull on them.

"It's not your fault Zach," she says tiredly, "not really. I could have explained to you what would happen."

Yeah, she could have. And now I'm pissed. "Why didn't you? I never would have pushed if I understood."

She shrugs, and I have to lean in to hear the whisper of her reply. "I know I'm not what you expected. For one night, I just wanted to be what you wanted. And I really liked the way you looked at me in that dress. It was ok...for a little while."

Hands freezing over her back, I let the water run out as

her words and the meaning behind them hit me. Despite her apology yesterday, there's been a low hum of anger under my skin all week. I don't get angry that often, and never at women. But she's the only woman who's ever avoided me. The woman actually sprinted to the janitor's closet. I've got a little more sympathy for Cara now, remembering all those times Declan ran away from her.

That shit hurts.

"You've had me off balance for a long time," I admit, scooping up more water and letting it run over her shoulder."

"You mean for the whole two weeks we've been working together?" She asks with a little snort. It's adorable.

"No, I mean for a long time. Months."

She frowns, tilting her head back to look at me. "I don't understand."

"No, I suppose you wouldn't." How do I explain it to her? And how much of myself do I want to give? Looking at her angry skin, I know I'm going to give her all of it...or try, at least. Because I'm really fucking tired of denying the feelings that rush through me when I'm near her. Or when I see her. Or when I think about her.

Which is all the time.

"It might surprise you to know I get what I want," I tell her. She rolls her eyes. "Yeah, I know. Anything I've gone after, I've gotten. Money, business, women. All of it. So having you turn me down for so long...even before I knew M. Miller was a woman, was annoying as hell. In most areas of my life, things come easily. You, Maya Miller, are not easy."

Slowly, carefully, she spins in the big bathtub, careful to keep her knees up. She settles facing me, hands on her knees, chin nearly resting on top of them. Everything's covered, and yet nothing is. I am *very* aware of how much lush, naked woman is in the tub. The lines of pain on her face have smoothed, so I let my hands drop into my lap, barely considering the damage to my designer tuxedo pants.

So not like me.

"Not easy. I can't tell you how many people have used those exact words to describe me." Her lower lip trembles the tiniest bit, and I sit back on my ass, clenching my hands in my lap to stop myself from kissing that tremble away.

"Have you always been..." The last thing I want to do is hurt her, so I don't know how to finish that question.

"Weird? Difficult? Yes, I think so. For as long as I can remember, anyway. Everything bothered me when I was a child. Noises, lights, clothing. The feel of things makes my whole body react."

"Do you mean like this?" I ask, gently pressing my forefinger to her red arm. A white circle appears, quickly eaten up by the red again.

She clears her throat and shakes her head. "No, not exactly. I always got rashes from clothing. I do ok in cotton, but I have to be careful about detergent. But I mean that the way things feel makes me react. Like the shoes you gave me. It's like my fingertips are hypersensitive. So if something feels good, like the suede, then it's almost like my whole body lights up. My scalp tingles, and little waves ripple down my back. It's the opposite for things that feel weird. They almost hurt to touch."

I rock forward, my body shuddering as I realize how sensitive she is. I try desperately to rein in my mind, to stop myself from imagining how her sensitivity could play out in my bed. I *want* to learn what lights her up and makes her shiver.

"Like?" I ask, wheezing a bit. She gives me a funny look.

"Velcro. That's a big one. I hate the way it feels, and the sound is awful. Certain metal, like the handle of some knives. Hate that." She shudders dramatically, a small grin on her face. "I really hate that microfibre material, too. The one they use for cleaning cloths."

"You remind me a little of Jonas," I say, leaning back on

my arms. "He has a few sensory issues, too. The obvious ones have to do with clothing."

"That's why he's in t-shirts and the cardigan all the time?"

"Yeah," I say, smiling. "You should have seen him the first time Ransom took him to try on a suit. He was willing to try. That's honestly one of my favorite things about my brother. He'll try almost anything...now, anyway." I still remember trying to convince him to eat a grilled cheese sandwich when we were kids. The way the cheese oozed freaked him out.

He's come so far. Why the fuck couldn't I see it?

"It didn't go well?"

"Started out ok," I say, smiling at the memory. "He let them put him in a suit. Buttoned it up and everything. He had the tie knotted, and stood there for a few seconds, then went 'nope' and stripped right there in the middle of the store. Just tossed everything at the salesman and strolled through the store in his underwear and socks."

She giggles, muffling them against her knees. She does that at work too. Cover her laugh with her hand, or cut it off.

"Why do you do that? Hide your laugh? It's a really good laugh, Maya."

A flush comes to her cheeks, one that doesn't have anything to do with that fucking dress. "I...I don't know. It's become a habit, I guess. One I never managed to get rid of."

"But why? Did you have fucked up teeth? Or snort when you laugh?"

"No, nothing like that. My mother just preferred I not make any noise."

"Wait...what? How does that work? Kids are loud and messy, and take up a lot of space." I should know. I raised one.

She twists her lips. "She couldn't handle that. She needed things calm."

"Then why the hell did she have kids?"

"I asked her that once. She said it was my dad's idea. She

wanted to keep him happy, so she agreed. In the end, it didn't matter, anyway."

I rub the back of my neck, realizing there is so much more to Maya that I know. "Why didn't it matter?"

"He died, and later she ended up dying alone from something that was totally preventable."

"She got sick?"

"Yeah. Pneumonia. She died in her apartment when I was twenty. By the time she died, she hadn't set foot outside of it in nineteen years."

23

MAYA

I didn't know men could be breathtaking, but Zach, sitting on the floor next to the tub, chest bare, warm eyes fixed on me? His picture should be in the dictionary next to the word. I miss dictionaries. There's something so hypnotic about turning the pages.

"Your mom was a shut-in? Your whole life?"

"Yeah, she was." Homebody, agoraphobic, anxiety ridden. All of it applies.

"How does that work? How do you have a kid and not go anywhere?" His perfect forehead is creased with confusion. I get it. Not a lot about the way I was raised makes sense. "Doctor's appointments and school plays and birthday parties. There's so much...I don't understand. How...what happened?"

His eyes are still tracing my body, but it doesn't feel creepy or bad. Even when he tore...*tore*...the dress from my body, I wasn't afraid.

Shocked, amazed, shy, embarrassed, yes. But not afraid.

I've read books where a man is so overcome with desire he tears the clothes from his woman's body. It was hot. I wish my skin hadn't been on fire. Maybe I could have appreciated the moment more. Though, if my skin hadn't been on fire, Zach never would have come near me. That thought brings me crashing back to earth quickly.

I loosen the grip on my knees and swirl my fingers through the cool water. This is the deepest tub I've ever been in, the water coming to the midline of my chest. Too bad I can't enjoy it. I'd love the chance to have a bubble bath in here...maybe with company. I should add that to my list.

"I don't really know why she was that way. My dad passed away when I was little. Mom hired drivers to take me to school. Mom was always...sensitive, so I learned to keep quiet. I spent a lot of time watching tv. And as I got older, and I got more difficult, she would so get angry. So I didn't do any of those other things. I went to school, and I came home."

He crosses his legs and leans on the edge of the tub, resting his tanned arm along the rim. "You're telling me that your very difficult mother would get mad at you for being difficult?"

That surprises a snort of laughter out of me. "Yeah. I guess I am. I never really thought of it like that."

"How did you think of it?"

I drop my chin on my knees. "Like most kids probably would. Like I should be quieter or easier. I would do everything I could not to be a bother. I'd try and wear the clothes she bought me, but then she'd be upset with me for being uncomfortable and needing treatment."

He frowns, eyes tracing over my red skin like a caress. I swear it heats up again everywhere he looks. "So, how did you ever go to the doctor for that?"

"I didn't. She's just order lotions to be delivered or send me to the store with cash and get me to pick something up."

"Holy fuck," he mutters, staring at me like I'm an alien.

"It wasn't the easiest way to grow up, but a lot of people had it a lot worse."

He scowls and grips the edge of the tub. "Don't do that.

Just because others had it worse, doesn't mean the way you were treated is ok. People always said shit like that to me. *Well, at least you have your brother. Well, at least you made something of yourself. Look how successful you are now.*"

The way he spits the words out makes me hurt for the little boy he was. I asked Cara enough questions to get the bare bones of his story. I can't imagine what it would be like to lose both my parents so young. In the lonely corner of my mind, maybe I understand people pointing out at least he had his brother. At least he wasn't completely alone in the world. "Maybe not, but it's easier to look at it that way. For me. I don't want to spend any more time looking back and wishing things were different."

"That's probably healthier," he says grudgingly, dropping his chin on his arm. "Doesn't make what she did ok."

"No, I don't think it was ok. I just can't be angry about it anymore."

He nods, staring absently at my knees. "But hey, look how you turned out," he says, making me laugh.

"I think I turned out ok. I'm not for everyone, but I've learned to live with that."

His eyes are so serious. "I think you turned out great."

I narrow my eyes at him. "Really? Because it hasn't felt like there's much about me you approve of."

He looks away, absently rubbing his cheek. "I fucked up, Maya. I shouldn't have been so hard on you. I don't have any excuse."

"It's ok," I say with a smile. I have to force it not to crumple. "I wasn't what you expected, and you had a hard time adjusting." Doesn't feel good to say. At all.

He shoves his hands roughly through his hair. "It wasn't that. Not really. You made me feel—." At the knock on the door, his head snaps up.

"Lotion," I whisper, wishing the hotel hadn't been quite so

efficient. I desperately want to know what he feels, and I'm cursing the interruption.

I may be cursing it mentally, but Zach doesn't bother keeping it inside. "Fuck," he says, rising to his feet. There, right before my eyes, is his more than impressive package. I don't know where to look, it's just right there, a foot from my face. I miss whatever he says, then he's gone. I collapse back in the tub, the tension in my body dissolving now that I don't have an audience.

Oh my god, what a weird night.

My skin is still uncomfortable, but the stinging sensation has lessened, so I take the opportunity to leap out of the tub — nearly falling back and knocking myself out — and grab one of the neatly folded robes on the counter, cotton, thank God. I'm tying it shut as Zach enters, holding a bottle of lotion. "Wait...how did they give you a key so easily downstairs? They didn't ask for your ID or your credit card. They just handed it over."

"We own the hotel," he mumbles, staring at the V of my robe. I glance down and snatch it shut with a squeak. *Nearly had the nips showing.*

"Wow. Own it. That's super convenient. Great place to bring the ladies." My mouth drops open at my own stupidity, and I consider diving face-first into the tub and drowning myself.

Brilliant Maya, remind him of all the Barbie perfect women he dates.

He frowns at me, shaking his head slowly. Can't blame him. He's probably desperate to get out of here. "Here," he says, holding out the lotion. I stammer out a 'thanks' and move to the door, pulling it wide. He just stands there, staring down at the space I just vacated.

"I can take it from here. Thanks so much. For helping me out of the dress. Paid you back with a peek at my boobs, so that's something, I guess. Not that they're anything special, but you know, they're still perky, considering how b—."

"You'll need help," he says.

Like, mental help? He may have a point there.

When I continue to stare at him blankly, he frowns and points to the lotion. "Putting it on...your whole back is red. You're not going to be able to reach."

"Oooohhh. Right, that's what you meant. Of course it was. I can do it myself. I have this whole routine I've perfected with a rolled-up towel. I can smear it on there pretty good." I had to figure it out. In the past, there were no handsome men in tuxedoes standing by, ready to leap to my aid.

He nods, gaze traveling over my face, but doesn't make a move to leave. "I'm here. Just seems more efficient if I do it for you. But if you'd rather do the towel thing, that's fine."

The man is offering to put those big tanned hands on my skin. Just to help, of course. Is it stupid of me to get so excited about that idea? I was late to the game, but apparently, I'm going through puberty at thirty-four because my hormones are raging. Am I ever going to be in a situation like this again?

Not a chance.

I'm nervous, but I want to feel his hands on me more.

"Oh, yeah. That would be nice of you. Great. Let's do this." My lips are stretched into a smile, but even I can tell how grotesque it is, but there's no hiding the eagerness in my voice. First time tonight, Zach cracks a smile. The reserve from earlier starting to crumble.

"It might be easier to do this on the bed," he says, moving next to the massive King bed, draped in acres of white. It's plush and inviting, nearly begging to be dived on, but I restrain myself. It takes a lot more restraint to stop myself from diving at the man. He should be in the movies. The theater would be filled with women at every show. The studio would make a killing. I can picture the storyline already. The gorgeous playboy, struck by love for the unassuming nerdy girl. He's overcome with passion and tears off his shirt, ready to ravish her.

I have a knee on the bed, robe still clutched tight between my breasts, completely lost in the fantasy, when he yells. "Wait…what is it made of? You don't want to get worse." He flips the corner of the comforter over, looking frantically for a tag. The sight of this massive, gorgeous man frantically flipping bedding snaps me out of my stupor. I laugh at my runaway brain. I'm having sexy thoughts, and he's worried about logistics. His eyes snap to mine.

He's not dreaming about me, imagining all the ways he wants to undress me. The man is just trying to fix his mistake.

"It's cotton," I assure him, rubbing the sheet between my fingers. "I'll be ok."

He locks his hands behind his neck, staring at me, throat bobbing. "Right. Ok. Yes." We both stand, staring, for way too long. A nervous giggle escapes me, and it brings that smile back. He drops his arms and shakes his head ruefully.

"I really can put it on myself," I say quietly, giving him an out. He doesn't look anything like the smooth, seductive man I'm imagining. And he isn't acting like a man desperate to get his hands on me. It's a little — okay, a lot — crushing. "I've done it before."

He looks torn, and I wish I understood what was going through his head. Does he want to touch me as much as I want to be touched? Because it doesn't really look like it. But maybe it's not about that. He's my boss, and he feels guilty for putting me in that dress. And as much as I want his hands on me, I don't want him doing it out of guilt.

With an understanding smile, I head back to the bathroom.

I don't make it.

Suddenly a wall of bare, beautiful muscle is blocking my

way. I freeze, holding my breath, and we lock eyes. It escapes in a gasp as his hand comes up to cup my cheek. His eyes are searching as his thumb traces over my cheekbone, then to the bridge of my nose and down. I can feel faint callouses on the pads of his fingers, and the way they rasp over my skin makes the top of my head tingle. I stay perfectly still as his thumb reaches the bow of my lip.

"Tell me to stop," he whispers. The lines of his face are stark, pulled tight in near pain.

I wet my lower lip, not quite brave enough to lick his thumb, which I really want to do. "I don't want you to stop."

His groan comes from deep in his chest and sends a shiver down my back. Then his thumb is gently, lightly tracing my lower lip. My breaths are coming out in little pants. There is so much unsaid in his eyes, and I want to know all of it.

"You…you were going to say something before, in the bathroom. You said you feel…"

His hand freezes, and he carefully brings his gaze to mine. He swallows heavily and drops his hand, leaving my skin feeling cold where before he warmed it. "I…ah." He wets his lips and breaks eye contact, stepping back to put distance between us. "Right. Maybe it's better you handle this on your own. I should go down and wrap things up."

I'm stunned by his sudden shift and by the way he pulls away. I stare dumbly at him, wondering what just happened. I can't get my bearings. He heads for the door. "Wait," I call after him. He freezes, and I slowly walk to the bathroom and gather his discarded clothing.

As I approach, he's almost vibrating with tension. I stop beside him, too confused and hurt to look at him. Instead, I stare at his chest as I carefully press his clothing to his stomach. "You'll need these," I say, proud of how level my voice is. In it is none of the pain or embarrassment I'm feeling.

He clutches the bundle to his stomach, and I step away. I can feel his eyes on me, but I have nothing left to give him.

It's taking everything in me to hide my embarrassment and disappointment. He pulled me in, then pushed me away. I did the same thing to him last weekend, so maybe, whether he knows it or not, it's payback.

Or maybe he just doesn't want me.

24

ZACH

I've never wanted anything as much as I want her. So, of course, I panic.

I don't know what I'm doing. The woman would have given me everything. *Everything.* I know that look. I've seen it on too many other faces. With very little effort, despite her still pink skin, I could have her under me, screaming my name. Virgin or not, I have the skills to make her want me. But it's those very skills, and the literal fuck-ton of experience I have that made me pull back. I can't bring myself to treat her the way I would any other woman.

Like she's a convenience.

Like someone to scratch an itch with. Because she's so much more than that, and only now do I realize how much more.

This woman, little ropes of hair falling from the pins, eyes wide, baffled, and a little hurt, has burrowed her way into the center of my heart in a matter of weeks.

And I'm terrified.

How did she get in there so quickly? And do I even want her there?

I fist my fingers into the jacket in my hand to stop myself

from reaching for her. I want to erase the hurt from her eyes, but I don't think I know how. I'm too confused about her. About what I want.

About what I'm capable of.

"I'll arrange for my driver to pick us up in an hour," I say, focusing on the V of her white robe.

"I don't have anything to wear."

Right. Shit. The robe is barely covering all her deadly curves. No fucking way do I want anyone else seeing her like this. "I'll have him come around back for us. I'll make sure you're not seen." She frowns, but nods, moving back to the bed to pick up the discarded lotion.

"I'll knock in an hour."

She tilts her chin up, looking like a queen despite the robe. "Ok. I'll be ready."

I nod, trying to convince myself to be a gentleman. To leave, like I know I should. My feet don't want to move...not away from her, at least. Everything about her draws me in, but my mind is screaming at me to *get the fuck out.* "Right. Ok. See you then." Before I can say anything dumber, I wrench the door open and bolt. I don't know where I'm going. There is no plan other than *away.*

I get a lot of looks in the elevator, still too rattled to put my clothes back on. I just hold them like an idiot while I call myself every name in the book. I'm spinning out, and it's not until I spot the tall tuxedoed man in the middle of the lobby that I realize what I need.

He watches me exit the elevator, a small grin on his face. But he doesn't say a word about my outfit, or lack of one. "Need a drink?" he asks simply.

"Yeah, I really do."

Ransom nods, and walks me to the dimly lit bar, speaking softly to the waitress. Heads turn as we pass, but as usual, he barely notices. Ransom has always, from the day he approached us in that group home, walked with absolute confidence. It's like he knew from day one who he was and what he wanted, and never let anything sway him. He brought all of us together.

He saved us.

I slide into a booth, drop my clothes on the bench, and pull out my shirt, shrugging into it. Ransom slides in opposite me, unbuttoning his tuxedo jacket. The waitress delivers two glasses of scotch, then backs away with a polite smile. Weird.

"What's that look for?" Ransom asks, taking a sip. The glass looks small in his hand. In mine, too, come to think of it.

"She didn't smile at me. Or flirt. It's weird," I murmur, spinning the glass, watching the flickering lights twist and shift on the crystal. All waitresses flirt with me. All women flirt with me.

"Not weird at all." I shoot him a confused look, and he laughs. "You didn't look at her, Zach. You didn't give her that stupid fucking smile you use on the ladies. You didn't encourage her in any way."

"Oh," I say dumbly.

Ransom's chuckling, a wide smile on his lips. "I didn't expect it from you. Honestly, I thought you'd be the last one to fall. Clearly, I was wrong."

"What are you rambling about?"

His look is knowing. He sees way too much. "Love, man. I didn't expect you to fall for a woman this quickly. Especially not one like Maya."

The denial on my lips when he says 'love' is forgotten as I glare at him. "What's wrong with Maya?"

That damn chuckle again. "Nothing. Absolutely nothing. I really like her, actually. She's a little odd, and weird shit pops out of her mouth. But she's a really nice woman. More than nice, she's real. More real than I imagined for you."

"What does that mean?" But I know. And by the look he shoots me, he knows that. The plastic women. The women who want one thing from me...well, my money too, so two things. "I don't know what the fuck I'm doing."

"Clearly," he says dryly, eyeing my still-unbuttoned shirt.

I take a swig of the scotch and savor the heat. "What the hell are you doing here?"

He quirks a brow. "I'm here for you. I didn't want you to have to do this on your own. What you said, about the events and shit that we leave you to do? You're right. It's not fair of us to put that all on you. So I'm here, ready to schmooze and shake hands. That's pretty much all you do, right?" He gives me a shit-eating grin, and the web of crazy I'm stuck in loosens, most of the tension draining out of me.

"You know damned well I do more than that. After tonight, the hospital expansion will be fully funded, thanks to me."

So typical of Ransom, he doesn't trash talk or give me shit. He just smiles. "Nice job, brother." And like I do every time he praises me, I squirm a little in my seat. What can I say? I'm a praise whore. "So we're not needed in there?"

"Not really. It wouldn't hurt to go in and shake some hands. You might be able to squeeze out a few more donations, but it's not necessary."

"Good. Then we can sit here, have another drink, and you can tell me why you're wandering around half-naked."

I groan and slump in the booth. "I need a double for that story."

"SHIT, IS SHE OK?" RANSOM ASKS WITH A WINCE.

"Yeah, her skin was a lot less red when I left. She'll use the lotion, and hopefully, she'll feel better."

He hums and studies me over the rim of his glass. "So... why exactly did you leave her, mostly naked, alone in the room? Seems to me you missed a golden opportunity there."

"I've been asking myself the same damn thing," I

mumble, staring at the bottom of my glass. That went down way too fast. I put it on the table and push it away. The waitress catches my eye, and I wave her off. I don't want more. My head needs to be clear when I knock on that hotel room door.

"Do you really not know?" he asks in disbelief.

I groan and scrub my nails through my hair. "If I'm going to do this, I mean *really* do this, then I can't treat her like the others. I have to be different."

He whistles through his teeth. "You have to *be* different? Or you have to *act* different?"

Hands still clenched in my hair, I stare at him. "Shit. I don't know."

He shakes his head and chuckles. "You're already a good man. I don't think you should change. But there's some shit you do that could go."

"Like?" I prod, frustrated by the slow sip he takes of his scotch.

"Like that stupid fucking look you do."

"The women love that, trust me," I say, flashing the model smile I worked so hard to perfect.

He sneers, making me chuckle. "Yeah, I'm sure they do. But it's an act. One you've relied on for a long fucking time."

"I'm feeling a little called out, brother," I say quietly, dropping my hands into my lap.

He winces and rests his elbows on the table, leaning into the space between us. "I'm on your side. Always. But you want something different now, right?" He waits for my nod before continuing. "Then that mask, and that's exactly what it is, isn't needed anymore."

"It's not a mask."

"Yeah, kid, it is." Something about the way he says *kid* loosens my muscles. The reminder that he's older and wiser brings me back to being a teenager, desperate for his guidance and stability. He's the steady North Star all of us gravitate to. And he's always, *always* spoken the truth, and only the truth.

"It didn't start out that way," I say, throat tight. "At first, I just wanted people to look at me differently. Then I liked the way it felt and kept doing it."

"I like your regular face. Those fucking fish lips..." he trails off, shaking his head.

"You are not my target market," I say with a grin. "Either way, I hear what you're saying. But the problem is bigger than all of that." Inhaling deeply, I bare my soul. "How am I going to be enough for her? She's so fucking smart, she runs circles around me at work. Other than looks and money, I don't have anything to offer her. And my past? She's..." I stop myself because her sexual history, or lack of it, is none of his business. None.

Ransom's lips pull back into a snarl. "That's the biggest pile of shit I've ever heard you say." This. This is the loyalty he showed us right from day one. He'll tell us to our faces we're dumbasses but would tear apart anyone else who says it, even us.

"I love you, man, but you don't know what you're talking about. You guys all call me a man whore, and you are not wrong. The face and fucking are all I bring to the table."

"It's a term of endearment," he says, cracking a grin. He sobers, thumping his fist on the table, making the glasses wobble. "I don't make mistakes," he says flatly, eyes laser-focused on my face.

"Random, but ok."

"Seriously, I picked you, brother. I hand-picked you all. This family works because you're in it. You bring a lot to the fucking table."

The air crackles between us as I flatten my hands on the table and scowl at him. He looks like he's ready to go to war. "We all play our parts now, but don't pretend you planned on me. That's bullshit. You wanted Jonas and got stuck with me."

Ransom rears back with a frown, "What the fuck? Do you seriously believe that?"

"Well...yeah. How else should I read it? You zeroed in on Jonas and spent a bunch of time with him. You barely spoke to me."

He snorts, rolling his eyes. "You dumbfuck. Even back then, you were a charming fucker. Remember that one guard? The one that used to sneak you chocolate bars? Your charm worked for you even back then. That's what I was after. Someone with your kind of natural charisma is invaluable." He folds his arms on the table and leans in. "Anyone with eyes could see how protective you were of Jonas. I knew you wouldn't go anywhere without him, so I spent a fuck of a lot of time getting to know him."

This is not computing. At all. "But...Jonas's math abilities..."

He shrugs casually. "Didn't have a clue about them until after I'd decided on you. It was like Christmas morning, the day that I realized what he could do. But make no mistake Zach, you were my pick. You have never been a tag-along. Fuck, if anything, Jonas was...for a couple of days at least. Then I picked him too. But even if he hadn't been who he is... I still would have pulled him into the fold because, without him, there was no you."

I stare at him dumbly, mouth open, catching flies for way too long. His low chuckles turn to belly laughs as he takes in my expression. "I just drove a freight train through your whole worldview, didn't I?"

I nod because, yeah, he did. I've spent the last twenty years trying to earn my place in this family, and he's telling me it was always mine.

Mind. Blown.

"I didn't know."

"I see that now. I didn't realize you were operating under that stupid assumption. I guess that's the issue with all of us, isn't it? We assume when we should just talk it the fuck out." He scowls down at the table.

"Christ. I've been doing the same damn thing with Maya," I say, realization dawning. "Maybe I should just talk to her."

"Brilliant idea," he says, sounding distracted. He's staring off at the corner of the bar. I follow his gaze and see a sultry brunette giving him eyes.

"You going there?" He's selective. The man has a dick and obviously uses it, but I almost never see him with a woman.

He drops his gaze, staring down at the bottom of his empty glass. "Nah, I don't think so. That kind of thing is losing its appeal."

"Yeah, it is." I press my lips together, thinking of all those nights, all those women. "I wish I could wash it all away and be...new for her. Instead of the jaded ass I actually am."

His massive chest expands with his deep breath. "There's no point in wishing the past away. I know. Better to work for the future you want."

"But that's just it. I don't know what I want." I want more Maya. But I don't actually know everything that goes along with that.

"Do you really have to figure that out right now? Why are you putting so much pressure on this? On her? Is it fair to her to be making decisions about your future, before you've even taken her on a fucking date?"

"When you put it like that, it sounds a little dumb," I admit. This is what I do. I plan, I strategize. I figure out how to get what we want. And usually, I'm totally fine with manipulating anyone who's in my way. But he's right, it's not fair to treat Maya that way.

"Has anything Maya said or done led you to believe she's on the hunt for a husband?"

I strain my slightly scotch-soaked brain. "Not really."

He taps the table with his knuckles. "Then talk with her. Tell her what you feel and what you want to do about it. Let her make up her own mind."

He's right. I know he's right. "But...what if she doesn't want me?"

He stands from the booth with a wince. "That's a chance you'll have to take. But I know one thing for sure. You do nothing, you'll regret it."

Yeah, I will.

25

MAYA

How long do stuntmen have to practice before they can roll out of a car? Can they do it at any speed, or is it just when the car slows at the corners?

I'm tempted to try it, except for the small matter of the robe I'm still wearing. If my roll doesn't go well, I'll end up on the news with road rash in some very uncomfortable places. I shift uncomfortably on the seat, my still-wet panties feeling just…wrong.

I peek over at Zach from under my lashes, only to find him staring at me. "Hi," he says suddenly, like he'd been holding it in, and it finally burst out.

"Hi," I say slowly, drawing out the H. The man runs out on me, comes back, and ushers me to a private SUV, all without saying a word. You tell me, what woman wouldn't want to tuck and run?

Or, in my case, tuck and roll.

He runs his hand over his mouth, frowning. His bowtie is long gone, the shirt is unbuttoned, and his jacket's split a seam. But this disheveled man in front of me still looks like every one of his billion dollars, and I still look like I got too much sun. No wonder he ran out. We're two totally different species, and I was completely delusional imagining there was anything between us. And that's sad, if not unexpected.

But I like it here. And I want to stay. So I need to clear the air. Tell him it's ok. Tell him that I misunderstood what was going on between us and that I won't cross that line again.

I open my mouth to do just that when Zach's voice cuts into the space between us.

"I think about you all the time."

I slowly, carefully close my mouth as his words reverberate through me.

He glances at me, then out my window at the city going by. "All the time. And I don't really know what to do with that. It's a completely new feeling, and…" He frowns, hands fisting on his thighs.

High and low in one little sentence. I need out of this car. I want to crawl into my bed and pretend this day never happened. "You…have feelings for me. And you don't want to."

He shakes his head slowly, "Maybe. It's not convenient. Before you came along, my life was exactly the way I liked it. And now that you've stomped into it, I can see how empty it used to be. And that pisses me off a little bit."

The consternation in his voice startles a laugh out of me. His answering grin ignites a little flame of hope. "So…what does that mean?"

"Whatever we want it to mean, I guess. Do you…are you. Shit." He groans and yanks on the hair at his temple, then dives forward and pulls something out of the seat pocket in front of him and hunches over it. I can't see in the dim light, but I hear the tearing of paper.

Zach reaches for my hand, carefully uncurling my fingers and putting a piece of paper in my palm. He doesn't say a word, just watches as I bring it to my face, tilting it until the lights from outside illuminate the words.

"Will you go out with me? Tick yes or no." I look over at

him, and he's silently holding a pen out to me. I slide it out of his fingers, and a world of possibilities pass between us. What I do next may very well change the course of my entire life. Do I check the box that leads to more of the same? The solitary nights, the loneliness, the predictability. Or do I check the box that leads to anxiety and thrills, and heat and awkwardness, and heartbreak?

Slowly, carefully, I put pen to paper, then fold the paper tight, pressing it into his waiting hand.

I don't take my eyes off him as he tightens his fist around it before carefully, deliberately unfolding it.

And I don't miss the slow, satisfied smile that curls his lips when he reads my answer. He traces his thumb over the paper, then tucks it into his jacket pocket next to the now limp pocket square.

"Oh," he says on an exhale. "Ok."

I saw a movie once where a woman woke up, and the whole world was different. She was desired by everyone and had everything she ever wanted. Subtly, carefully, I pinch the side of my leg, and yep, it hurts. Good. Totally not dreaming. This is very, very real.

Oh hell. This is real.

"I've never been on a date," I blurt. It's easier not to look at Zach as I stew in a mixture of panic and embarrassment, so I stare at the back of his driver's head instead. Other than a polite smile, he's been completely focused on driving so I nearly forgot he was there. Maybe this is just a regular Friday night for him. Maybe Zach has women in bathrobes in his car all the time.

"Neither have I."

My embarrassment is washed away by absolute disbelief. "Are you making fun of me? No way you've never dated."

He props his elbow on the window and turns to face me. "I don't date Maya. Ever. I meet women, I spend a little time with them, then we...." His lips firm, and he looks away from me.

I drop my eyes to my sparkly black flats. "You have sex. You spend a little time with them, then you have sex."

He looks at me grimly, eyes narrow, the hand on the car door gripping tightly. "Yeah."

I nod because, of course, I knew that. "So you just go out, and what...women just invite you back to their place?"

He shrugs, but the move isn't casual. "Something like that."

"I see," I murmur. And I do. This man is light ages beyond anything I know. He's been with so many people, and I kissed one boy in High School. We are not the same, not at all.

He shifts to face forward, and I study his profile. He looks as tired as I feel. The elation I felt at actually being asked out is fading, and all my insecurities about...well, everything come roaring in.

"Ransom was at the hotel tonight," he says. "We sat in the bar for a while, and he said something that stuck with me." He glances over at me, then away. "He said we need to stop assuming we understand someone and just talk to them."

"That's good advice."

"Yeah, it is." He runs his big hand along his thigh, smoothing along the still-sharp crease. He takes a deep breath, then turns to me. "I have spent a lot of years having meaningless sex with a lot of women. And now, you've come into my life, and I wish I hadn't. I wish I had done things differently."

"Why?" I ask, my voice barely above a whisper.

"Because I'm afraid you're going to judge me for it, and not give me a chance."

"And you want a chance?"

"I wouldn't have asked you out if I didn't. I've never done that. Not once."

He's never asked out a woman. Except me. I glance away

and wet my lips. I don't usually have a problem with honesty, but the stakes feel really high, and I'm afraid of being *too* honest.

"I...ah...I'm worried that I don't have enough experience for you. And that you're either going to want more from me than I'm ready for, or you'll get bored and change your mind."

"Bored?" he asks with a shocked laugh. "You're the most annoying, confusing woman I've ever met. Most days, you make me laugh while simultaneously making me want to tear my hair out. When you're around, there's no room for anyone else in my thoughts. And that's a really fucking weird experience. It's like you're living up here," he taps his temple, "and I don't know what to do about it."

He rubs his hand over his face, then drops it to the seat between us. Then slowly, he turns it palm up in invitation. I stare at it, then release my white-knuckled grip on my robe. Trailing my fingers over his palm, I slide them through his fingers, and my heart leaps a little when he interlaces them. I stare down at our hands, marveling at how it feels. Not just to hold hands, but to hold hands with a man who seems to like me.

Maybe as much as I like him.

He's staring down at our joined hands, too. "I won't ever push you farther than you want to go. I swear it."

"And you won't get bored?"

"You're more likely to get bored with me," he says, scowling. "I've recently learned that I'm not that interesting."

"What do you mean?" I find him infinitely interesting.

"I...um, haven't been with anyone since I met you. So I have a lot of free time on my hands. I have no hobbies. None. I didn't actually know that about myself."

"You," my mouth is so dry, "haven't been with anyone since you met me?" He shakes his head. "And for you...that's a long time, right?"

"Longest I've gone since I was sixteen."

My eyes widen at that because two weeks without sex when I've gone my whole life doesn't seem like a big deal. But apparently, it is.

He looks away. "See, that's exactly what I meant. You're looking at me like I'm—."

"I'm not judging you." I hurry to reassure him. "Would it be easier if you were as inexperienced as I am? Maybe. But then it would just be a lot of fumbling around in the dark. I don't want that. I just...don't have a frame of reference for you."

"For a man whore?"

"For a man," I say quietly, trying to tug my hand from his, not liking the bite in his tone.

He tightens his fingers until I give up, then he softly strokes his thumb over my hand. "I'm sorry."

I slump back into the seat, the top of my head tingling from his touch. "If we're not careful, we're going to blow this up before the first date. Between your insecurities and mine, it's a freaking minefield."

"I know," he says, frowning. "What if we just talk it out?"

"To each other?" I ask, not able to imagine spilling every insecurity I have onto this man. "That seems like a good way to ruin things." When he frowns at me, I snort and lay it out for him.

"Do you really want to discuss other women and your experiences with me?" His look of horror makes me laugh. "You're suggesting we make ourselves completely vulnerable to each other. To just strip ourselves bare...metaphorically speaking. I don't think either of us has earned that trust yet. We've only known each other two weeks."

"Right," he mutters, frowning. "That's a good point."

"You do realize we're doing this all backward, don't you?"

One of those perfectly arched brows raises. "What do you mean?"

"I mean, we skipped over the flirting and casual conversation over coffee, and went straight to tearing clothes and talking about feelings. I didn't realize it would be so exhausting. Aren't you tired?"

Chuckling, he brings my hand to his lips and presses a casual kiss there. The action almost...relaxed and absentminded. Like a reflex. The spot on my hand his lips touched is tingling.

"I'm not tired right now, but you're right. I don't know how to play this game."

"Neither do I," I remind him.

"That puts us on equal footing." He takes a deep breath, exhaling with a sigh. "So maybe we forget what we're supposed to do, and just...play it by ear?

"I like the sound of that," I say with a smile.

Spending time together, without a bunch of rules or ideas about what we should do, sounds like heaven. When my personality bangs against rules and expectations...that's when things start to fall apart.

And I really don't want this to fall apart.

26

ZACH

"Y ou told me this was casual!"

I hold in my grin and take her in. The flushed cheeks and wide eyes. *Finally.* Finally, I get that date. If it were up to me, we would have had it right after that night, the night everything changed. But Bree and Cara stole her away. Then we had family shit, and before I knew it, it was Monday. That was the start of the week from hell. We were so busy getting ready for a big auto show overseas that we ended up working late with the team every night. So now, finally, a week after I asked her out, I'm getting my date.

I glance down at my cream cashmere sweater and pressed slacks. "This is casual."

"No," she says, waving her hands up and down her outfit. "This is casual. See, jeans. Regular sweater. Plain old coat. Nothing I'm wearing is worth more than a rent payment. Why is everything you own so expensive?"

"Because I have a lot of money," I say, winking. She scrunches her face up.

"But do you have to spend it all on clothes?"

I shake my head and let my smile break free —something that happens a lot around her— and laugh. "As a proportion of our income, I'd argue that your outfit is significantly more expensive than mine."

She rocks back on her heels, frowning as she considers that. I take the time to admire her flushed cheeks —naturally rosy this time, thank god-- and the way her lips purse as she thinks.

She taps her finger on her lips. "So getting a ketchup stain on that sweater would be the equivalent of me spilling on a raggedy t-shirt from the thrift store?"

I frown, imagining the splash of red on my pristine sweater, and she dissolves into giggles. It's the best sound. Before, she was so reserved around me that I only got to hear it second-hand. But now, having her warmth and laughter directed at me just tightens that hold she has on me. She's like a spider, wrapping me tighter and tighter in her web, and I can't bring myself to mind.

Not even a little bit.

"You really like dressing up," she says, shaking her head, smiling.

I open my mouth to tell her that, yeah, I do. But I can't. Because I don't think that's true. Frowning, I tug her out of her apartment and guide her to the elevator. "I actually don't know. I've been dressing this way since I was a teenager." I catch her look and clarify. "It wasn't Cashmere then, but I always made a point of looking sharp."

"Most teenagers care about how they look. I know I did. I was very aware that I didn't fit in, in a lot of ways. Wherever I could, I tried to blend in."

"I don't think I cared about blending in. It was more about feeling…" The doors open, and I guide her onto the elevator, pushing the button for the lobby.

"More about feeling what?"

I lean back on the wall, frowning as I admit something I'm only just coming to realize. "Feeling like I was worth something."

Her face softens, and she reaches out, fingering the zipper of my jacket. "Why did *you* feel that way?" I hear it in her voice, all the times she felt less than. Maybe it's that shared experience and the empathy in her voice that lets me answer truthfully.

"Because I thought that Ransom only let me into the family because of Jonas. I spent all this time thinking I had to earn my spot and prove to him that it wasn't a mistake taking me in."

She frowns, searching my face. "How did you come to be a family? I don't really know the story."

The doors open to the lobby, and I guide her out, pulling her to the side as I reach for her jacket, carefully zipping her up. She smiles up at me, bemused, but doesn't stop me.

"I don't think anyone's zipped my coat up for me in thirty years…so many firsts."

I force a smile when the reminder of how little she's been cared for makes me want to hit something, and thankfully she seems to buy it. I zip up too. We've got a rare sunny day, but the wind coming off the lake is no joke.

"You really had to take care of yourself, didn't you?" Wishing she had better parents won't do anything. Won't fix anything. But I still do. If I could go back and give her a cookie-making, warm hug of a woman for a mother, I would. She deserves to be loved like that. She deserves to understand how amazing she is.

She shrugs casually, like it was no big deal. "Yes, I did. But it made me incredibly self-sufficient and stubborn."

"You say that like those are good things to be," I tease. She rewards me with a halfhearted glare and a casual swat to my stomach as we exit the building into a big plaza. Ransom bought this land a decade ago, complete with an aging apartment building. The location on the waterfront was always going to be a moneymaker, but when we opened up the sales for condos in our building, we set a record. I've lived here for nearly five years, and not once have I done what we're doing now.

Walk.

I live steps from amazing restaurants and galleries. To funky shops and coffeehouses. And not once did I bother to walk along the waterfront in my own neighborhood. I've bought art from galleries around the world and never bothered to look next door. Maybe I am a bit of a snob.

"I thought we could walk and pop into any shops that look interesting if that's ok with you."

I peek at her, and she rewards me with a big smile. "That sounds perfect."

I have to laugh. "I've been agonizing over this all week. Jonas talked me out of flying you down to Miami. He said that might be a little too much. This seemed too simple."

She shudders. "I can't imagine going back on another plane. The man next to me was wearing too much cologne and the woman on the other side of me fell asleep on me. I can't say I understand the attraction of flying."

I stop right there in the middle of the walkway as her words penetrate. "Wait...that was your first time on a plane?"

She spins, smiling at me. "Yeah. Shut-in mom, remember?"

With slow steps, I join her, stepping into her until our bodies are touching, liking the way she has to tilt her chin up to look at me. "But after she died, couldn't you have traveled?"

She winces, looking away for a minute. "I suppose I could have. But my life was small. My whole world was seven blocks between my house and my school. When I went to university, it was only a few blocks further. My whole life Zach, all of it, has been lived on the Upper West Side."

She smiles softly, seeing my confusion. "When you live your life in a room, a whole house can feel overwhelming. Then, when you're used to the house, the street can feel too big." She turns, taking my hand to pull me along. "Besides, compared to how small my world was, going to university, getting a job, and getting my own place felt like massive steps."

I mull that over, trying to understand the way she lived her life. I've been all over the world. My brothers and I went a little wild for a bit, hopping on a plane at the drop of a hat. I've always known the whole world is out there for the taking. And I can't necessarily imagine her not wanting to take it. Though, I guess she did. Something made her decide to leave everything she knew.

"Why did you take this job?" I ask, pulling her to a stop.

She scrunches up her face. "There was nothing left holding me there. Everything I depended on was gone, and I was in this place of…how do I put this?" She throws up her hands, "*Fuck it!*" she says cheerily. "That's it. I was in a state of *Fuck it.* There was no reason to stay and what felt like a million reasons to go."

"What was gone?"

She smiles sadly and runs her finger down the zipper of my coat. "I don't want to tell you."

Yep, there's the invisible punch in the nuts. "I see." But I really don't. Why is she hiding that part of her life from me? Why can't she tell me? "There's a coffee shop up here. Why don't we grab something?" I'm torn between letting her hand go and being desperate to pull her closer to bridge the sudden distance between us.

"Zach," she says softly. I straighten my shoulders, let my lips curl into my signature smile, and look at her. Her brow furrows, and she tightens her hand on mine.

"I didn't say that right, and I think I hurt you."

It's my turn to shrug, but it probably doesn't come off as casual. "You don't owe me anything, Maya. If you don't want to talk to me, that's your choice." I'm trying to convince myself more than her. This caring for people shit sucks. When you care, you can get hurt. Why am I putting myself through this again?

She tilts her head to the side. "It's not that I don't want to share, but I've been looking forward to our first date all week. And the answer to your question makes me sad to think about. So maybe, could we just save that for another time?"

Searching her face, I see echoes of that sadness, and I feel like an ass for my impatience. Wanting to chase away the sad, I wiggle my brows at her. "You've been thinking about me, huh? Maybe, thinking about me with my shirt off?"

She blushes, and just as I hoped, her eyes fill with laughter. "Humm. I wonder if it hasn't been you thinking about me in that bathtub."

The laughter drains out of me as heat replaces it. A soft gasp escapes her as I pull her in closer. "I've been dreaming of nothing but you in that tub. I've been imagining a do-over all week."

"A do-over?" she asks breathlessly.

"Yeah. I want you in that big tub, skin milky in the moonlight coming through the window. I want you looking more like the siren you are than a lobster boiling in a pot."

She drops her head against my chest, dissolving into laughter. She's snorting with it, making the people around us smile as they pass.

How did I get this lucky? And how is it I'd rather stand here on this sidewalk, freezing my ass off with this woman, then be anywhere else? Though...

"I'm going to get you on a beach in Miami," I tell her. "Think of it. Sun, sand, a sweet drink in your hand."

She drops her ear on my chest, smiling over the water. "Maybe I'd go on a plane for that. But promise me I don't have to sit next to anyone but you."

I shudder, imagining the horror of security lineups and crowded waiting rooms. "Honey, I haven't been on a commercial flight in years. When you fly with me, you fly private. It's a whole different experience."

She looks up at me, worry in her gaze. "On a tiny plane?"

"Nah, it's not tiny," I reassure her, wanting to wipe the worry off her face. "It's got a bedroom."

"A bedroom," she whispers, gaze distant. I groan, realizing exactly where her mind has gone.

"Don't do that to me, woman. We're supposed to be having a nice date. And if you keep looking like that, my pants are going to be too tight for me to walk in."

"Too tight for you to—" I see the moment she registers what I mean. And the pink flush that covers her cheeks is completely kissable.

A stronger man would resist her. A stronger man would turn her towards the coffee shop and shift the conversation to something benign.

But nothing about us is benign, and where she's concerned, I'm not a strong man. So, taking her chin in my cold fingers, I tilt her face up and do what I've been wanting to do all week. What those pink cheeks are begging for.

That wide mouth of hers is a fucking dream. I breathe in her soft gasp and savor the way she leans into me. That day on the mats, I was too stunned to really savor her. But I've had all week to dream of her. To replay that all too brief moment over and over in my mind.

But none of it prepared me for how intoxicating she is.

Her hesitancy mixed with eagerness is better than any blue pill. I'm hard as a rock from a barely there kiss. When I get this woman in bed, preferably before my dick is permanently blue, I can't imagine I'll last more than a minute. She's too amazing, and she tastes way too good. Maybe, if I kiss her a lot, I can desensitize myself just a bit. Just enough to hold out and blow her fucking mind in bed.

Satisfied with my plan, the fear of biffing her introduction to sex soothed, I cover her mouth with mine. Our groans mingle as I dive into her, content to spend the rest of my life right here, kissing her. The rest of the world can fuck right off as I sip and taste, memorizing the feel of her. Soaking in her low moans and light gasps.

It can't get any better.

Maya's teeth nip at my lower lip, and I realize I was wrong. This is better. Her innocently carnal exploration takes me right to the fucking edge of control. It's so different from anything I've ever experienced. So much more powerful.

I have never, not once, kissed someone I felt this deeply for. My reaction to her is terrifying.

Not wanting to be an ass…again, I use every bit of my experience to ease back slowly, giving myself a pep talk the whole time. *Don't do it. Don't you dare lay her down in the middle of the sidewalk.*

It works, and with a final groan, we pull apart. Her dazed eyes and reddened, parted lips draw me back for one more taste, then I force myself to back away from her, putting an arm's length between us. I see the hurt and confusion in her eyes and rush to soothe it.

"I can't handle anymore. We're too good together, and I'm about to lose my fucking mind already." Her confusion fades, and her lips curve into a smile, and I realize I am in so much trouble. More than I've ever been in. And I'm not planning to do anything to get out of it.

Something dangerous lights her gaze, and I squeak, dancing back out of her reach, making her fold over laughing. "Stop teasing me, woman. We're supposed to be on a date, not making out like horny teenagers."

She stands, casually tossing her hair over her shoulder, and I forget my name for a minute. How the hell did I think she was frumpy? Well, ok, her clothes are frumpy as fuck, but the woman in them is fire.

"I feel like a horny teenager. I had no idea." She shakes her head, voice full of awe. "No wonder the girls went under the bleachers with the boys."

"I...um, thought you'd be shy about all this."

She scrunches up her face. "I'm thirty-four. Just because I haven't been with a man doesn't mean I haven't done plenty of solo exploration."

Laughing at the thunderstruck look on my face, she tugs me toward the coffee shop, lit up on the corner. "Come on, my face is freezing."

I nod, but my brain is completely offline, her words careening around my skull. *Solo exploration.*

Jesus, I'm fucked.

27

MAYA

"**I**s this what it's like?" I whisper to Janey and Cara. We're huddled around my desk, running out the clock on the last few minutes of the day. "He's looking at me all the time. And his eyes…god, they're so intense."

Cara grins and leans her hip on my desk, resting one bare foot on top of the other. "Is this what *what* is like?"

"Dating. Having men look at you like they want to eat you. All of it."

Janey smiles, "It's pretty wild, isn't it? Having so much attention on you? Are you and Zach seeing a lot of each other outside of work?"

"A lot? Well, we ride home together and we went for a late dinner last night. It's been busy so we've been working late. But here he's just so…watchful." A shiver runs down my back as I picture Zach's chocolate brown eyes on me. Cataloging the different looks he gives me has become my new favorite hobby. There's the *I'm thinking something dirty*. And the *I'm so hot you can't resist me*. And let's not forget about the *I wonder what you're wearing under your clothes*. I think that one's my favorite. His eyes go all hazy as he stares somewhere around my chest, and he'll absentmindedly rub his fingers over his jaw.

So hot.

"Watchful," Janey echoes. "Sounds…intense."

"It is," I say with feeling. "But it's also weird."

"Weird, how?" Cara asks with a snort.

"I mean, I'm wearing the same stuff he used to scowl at. I'm the same person. But suddenly, he's looking at me like I'm dessert. And I've never had that before. It's just weird."

Cara frowns. "And you're wondering what changed?"

"I guess…maybe I am. That day at self-defense, things changed, but I don't really understand what he sees in me."

"How can you say that?" Janey asks, lifting herself to sit on the edge of my desk. "You're wonderful."

"Wonderful," I repeat dryly. "So wonderful I've never had a boyfriend. So wonderful that only a couple of weeks ago, he would scowl at me when he saw me."

"People are complex, Maya. I think you know that better than most," she says with a soft smile. "We all walk around the world stuck in our heads, mostly oblivious to the people around us. Then one day, something, or someone, shakes us out of our stupor, and suddenly, we see what's right in front of us. Maybe, that day at self-defense, which" she turns to Cara with a raised brow, "I'm really sorry I missed."

Cara rolls her eyes. "I'm sorry. I couldn't find you. You went off too quickly with Mr. Mysterious. Are we ever going to meet him, by the way? Why don't you see if he wants to double date with Declan and me? And maybe," she draws out the e sound, "Zach and Maya. It could be fun."

Janey blushes and kicks her heels softly against my desk. "I can ask him. He says he likes it when it's just the two of us."

"Just the two of you," Cara says thoughtfully. "How long have you guys been dating?"

"Six weeks."

"And you're seeing a lot of him?"

Another blush. "Yes."

Cara firms her lips. "Then it's time he meets your friends."

"Friends," Janey says, repeating the world like its rich ice cream on her tongue. "Yes, he should meet my friends." She stares off, a small smile on her lips. I can't figure out if it's because she's thinking about her guy, or because she's happy to have friends. I would be smiling for both reasons, so maybe she is too.

She visibly shakes herself. "What was I saying? Right, so maybe that day at self-defense, you shook him out of his bubble, and he saw how amazing you are."

Cara snorts and taps her lip. "Do you think it was the way you kicked him in the balls or the kiss that shook him up?"

I slap my hands over my cheeks, blushing furiously. That was an overwhelming, strange, life-changing day. "I don't know," I mumble.

"Hello."

All three of us startle and swing to the doorway to find Jonas staring at us.

"For fuck's sake, Jonas, I'm going to make you wear a bell if you don't stop sneaking up on us," Cara mutters, hand pressed to her chest.

Jonas smirks and pushes his glasses up his nose. "The walls are glass, Cara. Sneaking implies I made an effort to hide. I just walked." He frowns, gaze traveling over all three of us, lingering just a moment longer on Janey. "You should all be coming to Becca's class. Your complete lack of situational awareness is concerning." It comes out a little condescending, but I can see the concern in his tone.

"We're at work," Cara says with a scowl. "We're not supposed to have our guard up at work. Besides, from everything I've seen, there's nowhere safer in the world to be than here...unless maybe the White House bunker. You guys would never let anything happen to us."

Jonas's face hardens. "No, we'd never let anything harm you. But as *you* well know, outside of these walls, there are a lot of dangers we can not protect you against." Cara's face falls at the reminder of what happened to her and Bree.

"I hear you. I promise we'll go to the class…but could you please try humming or something, to let people know you're there? I swear a tiny mouse makes more noise than you do when you walk."

He flashes a smile full of mischief but doesn't agree. I have a feeling he'll be walking even softer from now on, just to annoy Cara. They seem to have a wonderful dynamic. Both very comfortable with each other, but without the overt teasing and annoyance she and Colton seem to have. People…these people especially…are infinitely interesting.

His smile falls as he looks at Janey. "You should go too. You need to be safe."

Janey smiles at him warmly, and Jonas seems dazzled by it. "I will, I promise. I was just complaining that they didn't include me last time." She curls her hands into fists and puts them up like a boxer. "I'm ready."

Jonas steps forward until Janey's fists are nearly touching his chest. Something about the moment makes me want to look away. It's too charged, too intimate. He brings his hands up, wrapping one of her fists in his, covering it completely. He inhales sharply, and his eyes close for a moment. Carefully, gently, he peels her fist open, moving her thumb from inside, and wraps it up again. "Like this. If you keep your thumb inside, you will break it when you hit someone." He rubs his thumb across her knuckles and steps away. "There are more effective ways to defend yourself, though. Becca will teach you."

Janey, looking a little dazed and blushing furiously, nods. Jonas seems satisfied, turning to leave, but he stops, his hands gripping the doorway tightly above his head, and pins Janey with a look. "He should be opening the door for you."

She tilts her head, brow furrowing in confusion. "I'm sorry?"

He clenches his jaw and spells it out. "Any man you're dating should open the door for you. Your man doesn't even get out of the car when he picks you up."

"Oh," she breathes, fussing with the hem of her silky grey t-shirt. "Well, he's in a hurry."

Jonas closes his eyes and swallows. When he opens them, he pins her in place with his stare. "You're worth waiting for, Janey. If you were mine, I would open the fucking door," then he's gone.

"Oh my god," Cara says, fanning herself.

I pull the neckline of my dress away from my skin. "Is it just me, or was that totally..."

"Hot?" Cara says. "Yeah, that was scorching. If I didn't love Declan so much, I would be all over that. Jonas is a fucking catch. And that intensity in bed? Gawd!" She shakes her head. "The man is a freaking onion. Just when I think I've gotten to the core of who he is, he shocks the hell out of me with another layer."

Janey's still staring at the doorway, hands curled around the hem of her shirt. Frozen in place. Her breaths are low and shallow. The day I met her, it was obvious she didn't return Jonas's feelings. But now...I'm not so sure. I think the woman's eyes just got opened. Cara and I trade a knowing glance, which secretly thrills me. I'm actually in the know! I'm on the inside of one of these looks, not watching it from across the room. I love this new life.

"Zach opens the door for me," I say, shifting my gaze to Janey. "Even when he was grumpy, he always did. It's a courtesy I appreciated. When he does it now...then smiles at me when I walk through. I love it."

"I don't touch a door handle anytime Declan's with me." Cara purses her lips, "Or any of the brothers, come to think of it. Ransom raised those boys right."

Janey, breaking free of her paralysis, stares down at the floor. "Yes, he did." She looks up with a tumultuous smile. "Well, I should be off. Have a great weekend."

Cara puts her hand on Janey's arm as she passes. "You deserve a man who treats you like a Queen Janey. You deserve someone who opens doors and makes you feel like you're the most beautiful woman in the world."

Janey smiles sadly. "Maybe. But not every woman is going to find that. Some of us have to settle for someone who makes us feel good. Queen is a high bar."

Cara squeezes softly. "Yeah, it is. But it's so worth having. Better than anything you can imagine."

Janey's lips twist. She pats Cara's hand and steps away. "Goodnight, Maya," she calls over her shoulder, a forced cheeriness in her tone I haven't heard before.

We watch her go. Head bowed all the way to the elevator. "Jonas is in love with Janey," I murmur. "I thought he had feelings for her the first time I saw them together, but…"

"Yeah," Cara murmurs. "He does. But she has a boyfriend."

"Not a very nice one, by the sound of it." Though honestly, what do I know about the dynamics of a healthy relationship? Close to nothing. My parent's relationship was about as far from healthy as one could get.

She shrugs and sits on my desk. "I don't really know. She doesn't talk about him much. She seems happy, so who am I to judge? But I agree with Jonas. The man just pulls up to the curb for her, which isn't a big deal, I guess. But knowing these men and how they treat their women, that would never fly."

"It doesn't seem like a big deal. I've lived my whole life mostly by myself. I open my own doors the whole time."

Cara chuckles. "I used to sound like you. Now I have someone who spoils me rotten, and I love it. I never want to go back. You can bet I'm keeping that man so fucking happy. He'll never want to leave me."

The way she says happy and the way she winks at me makes it clear exactly how she's making Declan happy.

And now I'm blushing.

Again.

Cara laughs and nudges me with her foot. "You're pretty shy about that stuff, aren't you? Bree mentioned the little shopping trip she took you on."

"Oh god," I groan. "That was so embarrassing. She kept yelling at me from across the store, waving...things... around." By the time we left that shop, my head was tucked so far into my shoulders that I looked like a human turtle.

Cara throws her head back, laughing. "That's my girl. There's no need to be shy about any of that."

"I know. I'm all for women being comfortable with their sexuality. But I'm just...private, I guess."

"Private or shy?" she challenges.

I shrug and swivel my chair from side to side. "I don't know. I'm inexperienced, which is fine, I know that. But now that I'm dating Zach and he's...not inexperienced...I find myself worrying more about all of that."

"Did you talk to Zach about it?"

I stare at her, horrified, because, "NO. Why would I do that? We've been dating for a week. It's way too early for that. He knows I'm...well, a virgin. But I don't think it needs further discussion."

She frowns. "Look, it's not my place to give you advice. But if things start looking like they're moving toward the bedroom, you're going to have to talk to him. Don't let whatever worries are in your head ruin things between you."

"Ruin?" Have I been worried about the wrong thing? I thought spilling my guts was the worst thing I could do.

"Yes," she says, wincing. "Really great sex is about communication. The books where the hero just magically gives the heroine an orgasm are not reality. Your first time can be awkward and overwhelming. So if you don't have a partner who's right there with you, tuned into you, and ready to listen, then it's not going to be good. I don't want to think about Zach in the bedroom. He's like my brother, so...ew, but he's a good man. He is so in tune with Jonas, and he's an amazing brother. So I have to think those qualities will carry over into other areas of his life."

Did someone turn the heat up? I'm sweating. "Right. Ok. I'll think about it. Good talk."

"Ok, fine," she says with a little laugh, throwing up her hands. "I get it. I'll mind my own business. But if you need to talk, come to me, please. I raised a teenager, remember? I have a bit of experience with this stuff."

"I'm not a teenager," I say flatly, folding my arms over my chest. This having friends thing is good, I think, but it's also maddening. "I somehow made it to thirty-four without interference in my life. I'm sure I'll figure it out." Her face shuts down, and I immediately want to slap myself in the face. "I'm sorry. That came out wrong. I'm not used to all this."

Cara stands, moving to my doorway and looking down at me with a raised eyebrow. *Please don't leave. Please don't stop being my friend.* "Not used to all this? What does that mean?"

"I don't have friends. Well," I qualify with a wince, "I sort of have one friend. But I haven't talked to her in a while. But I'm not used to so much...input into my life. I appreciate your intentions. I do. But going from being the sole decision maker in my life to having people with *opinions* is more challenging than I expected."

Cara's eyes soften, and she nods. "Get used to it," she says with a wink, then turns and strolls off to Declan's office.

Get used to it. Good advice. I'll just get used to it. Because now that I have a taste for life as a normal person, one with friends and a social life...and a man friend, I don't think I ever want to go back.

28

ZACH

Her skin is so soft. Maybe all women's hands are like this, but I can't remember any touch but Maya's. She's staring out the window, seemingly lost in thought, but her fingers are playing over my palm, maintaining a connection to me. I sit back, unbutton my jacket, and just look at her, the passing city a blur over her shoulder.

I haven't done this much, just look. Before, it was all about the chase. I could always find something about a woman to compliment, but it was vague…their hair, their smile. I never spent the time with them to truly see them, not like I do Maya.

I amuse myself by tracing my eyes over all my favorite freckles. She doesn't have a lot of them, not like Becca, but the few she does have are positioned in all my favorite places. There's the one right behind her ear. I can't wait for the opportunity to press my lips against it. Then a little further down, another, right where her neck meets her shoulder. And the last one, my favorite, is the little dot right at the neckline of her dress over her left breast.

If it weren't for the hideous dresses, the view would be the best in the world. Ok, maybe even with the dress, it's still the best view. When did Maya's face become the only one I want to look at? I need her eyes on me, so I give her hand a playful tug. She turns to me with a distracted smile.

"You ok?"

She looks down at our joined hands, then up at Luis. "Why do you use a driver all the time? Do you have a car?"

Her question rattles through me, bouncing off memory after memory. This has been who I am for so long, I haven't had to think about it. No one asks because everyone who's close to me knows exactly why I have a driver.

This is what it takes. You want her, you're going to have to let her in.

I clear my throat, but I can't meet her eyes. I can't remember the worst experience of my life while looking at her sympathetic face. "You know my parents were killed in a car accident?" I catch her nod from the corner of my eye. "I wasn't with them. I was in school already. And that day, no one came to pick me up. The school tried to reach my parents, but eventually, they had to call social services. It was the social worker that took me to the hospital. To Jonas. He was cut up, and bruised, but he was ok. He was hysterical, though, fighting anyone who came close. I don't know how long he was like that. I can't imagine they would let a kid stay that worked up for long, but when he saw me, it was like his whole body deflated like a balloon."

I run my fingers along the buttonhole of my jacket as images of that day run through my mind like a horror movie. "I still remember what shoes I was wearing that day. I was so proud of them. I saw them in a thrift shop, and I begged my mom to get them for me. They were blue, and they had flames up the side. I remember staring down at them as the social worker walked me through the hospital."

"How old were you?" she asks softly, hand tightening on mine.

"Seven. Jonas was four."

"So young," she murmurs. I hear the sympathy and sadness in her tone. "What happened after that? With you and Jonas, I mean."

"We spent that night at the social worker's office. The next day, they took us to a foster home. She told us she'd search for family, but even then, I could have told her there was no one."

"You didn't have any family at all?"

I shake my head. "On my dad's side, there might be some distant relatives in Korea, but no one that could take two little kids. My mom didn't have anyone, either. There were no grandparents or siblings." I turn Maya's palm up and trace over the lines. Lifelines I've heard them called. I wonder if people like my parents, people who die too young, really do have shorter ones.

"You're Korean?" she asks softly.

"A Quarter, on my dad's side. My mom was white, but I don't know anything about her ancestry. She never talked about it. I looked into her," I admit, "I wanted to know where she came from. There's not much. It's like she appeared one day when she was sixteen. I think she must have run from something and just wanted a completely new life, so she picked a new name. I don't think I'll ever know anything more about her."

"What happened to you? After the foster home? How did you end up with Ransom?"

"We bounced around a lot. Jonas…was a challenge that not a lot of foster parents were prepared for. My mom and dad were amazing. They had nothing…*nothing*, but they did so much for him. When they died, he kind of…disappeared inside himself for a while. He refused to communicate with most of the foster parents. It just was a lot for most families to take on. So we'd end up moving. I learned to run interference. If I charmed the adults, they'd usually let us stay longer. But things kind of blew up one day, and we got sent to the group home."

"What happened? How did it blow up?"

My lips twitch, remembering that day. "It literally blew up. Jonas was researching the war or something...you'll have to ask him, and he ended up blowing up our foster parents' garage. He was still little enough that he didn't get in trouble, and his eyebrows grew back. He looked so fucking funny," I say, laughing. "But we got kicked out that night. Ended up at the group home, which in the end, was a blessing."

"What was it like there?"

"It was one step down from a jail. There were guards, only they didn't call them that. We all slept in these big open rooms lined with steel bunk beds. But I figured out who the players were and made friends, and we were mostly left alone. We were there for nearly a year when Ransom showed up. Everything changed the day he asked us to join his family. I don't think I realized at the time he meant actual family. I had it in my head that it was going to be more like the mob."

She laughs and turns, putting her back against the door. "Ransom seems to care about you all very deeply."

"Yeah, he does. He took on the parental role for a lot of us. And in the end, it all turned out."

"Yeah, I suppose it did. You don't...wish things were different?"

She does. I can see it in her eyes, the wishing she'd had something better. "I used to. All the time, actually. I used to imagine who we might have been if they hadn't died. But that can be...hard, living in the what-ifs. So I try not to let myself go back there anymore." Her eyes drift away over my shoulder as she nods. "You seem...off today. Everything ok?" I ask.

She hums and tucks her hair behind her ear. "Just a busy brain."

A little trickle of unease hits the back of my neck. "Busy brain. Anything you want to talk about?"

She sighs and faces forward, leaning into the black leather

seat. "I don't know. I've just come to realize that all this *peopling* is harder than I thought it would be. And it's clear that I'm not doing a great job."

"You moved permanently out of your comfort zone, Maya. It's ok if you don't get it right sometimes." Her lips tighten at that. She doesn't look convinced at all.

"That's the problem," she says, frowning. "I think I've been getting it wrong for a long time."

"What do you mean?"

She groans, pulling her hand from mine and running it through her hair. I immediately miss her warmth and stare at that hand in her lap, wishing it back to me. "I think I've had a friend. A really good one, all this time. And I did not treat her well."

"Who is she?"

She smiles slightly. "Abigail. She was my assistant in New York. And somehow, I didn't realize how important she is to me until now. And I have not been good to her."

"Not good? What does that mean? Did you put salt in her coffee? Pull her hair? Talk about her behind her back?"

My teasing does exactly what I intended. She scowls at me, a small smile breaking through. "We're grown women, so no, I didn't pull her hair. I just...she was always so kind, she'd share her life with me. And at work, I really liked that. But now I'm realizing it was so one-sided."

"And you regret that?"

"Yes, I do."

"So do something about it. If it's that important to you, then don't wait. If I've learned anything, it's that you might lose your chance if you wait too long. People can be ripped away from you too easily. So you have to hold on tight."

Her lips twitch. "So that saying, *let them go, and if they come back to you?*"

"Fuck that. Why the hell would you let someone you love

go? I say hold on tight, and if they fly away, you better damn well follow them."

The smile bursts as she dissolves into giggles. "You'd get along really well with Abigail." Her laughter is infectious, and I can't keep the grin off my face. She's beautiful. She also thinks I'm joking.

I'm not.

"Do you have her phone number?" She nods. "Then text her. Don't wait. Tell her how you feel."

She rifles through her purse. "Isn't this rude? We're on a date, and I'm texting someone else."

"You planning to let her kiss you?"

"She's not really my type," she says with a snort.

"Then it's fine." I give her a bit of privacy, turning my gaze out the front of the car. I catch Luis's amused eyes in the rearview. I glare at him halfheartedly, then stare out at the road.

"There. Done." She tucks the phone back into her brown leather purse — even the fucking purse is ugly — and turns to me, tucking her hair behind her ears. "It's been so busy. Even though we work together, I feel like I haven't seen you."

"It's always like that ramping up to a show. It's a great place for us to meet with suppliers and new customers, so we want to make the best impression possible."

She bites her lips as she studies me. "The staff mentioned that you're usually part of the group that goes. They all seemed shocked that you were staying back this time."

Yeah, I do go. Every time. Except now I'm really fixated on this baffling woman in front of me, and I don't want to leave her. "I think the team can handle it. And I just...wanted a break." My brothers may have a point. I've been so busy running myself ragged trying to be the face of the company that I've sucked a lot of the fun out of it. I just hope I don't live to regret it.

"I...I could try the plane again. If you need me to go, I mean."

"Nah, if you go, I go. Then we'd take the jet." I wink at her. No fucking way would I let her out of my sight. She's this odd mix of capable and innocent, and no way do I want her wandering around in a foreign country unprotected. "We're just pushing the chicks out of the nest. I'm sure they'll be ok."

She smiles and takes my hand and everything in me settles at the same time the hair on my body stands on end. I want her hands all over me. "You gave me some of your past. Thank you for that. But I'm not clear on how that ties into you having a driver?"

I frown down at our hands. "I can drive. I own this SUV and another car, but if I'm going to have anyone else in the car, I won't drive."

"Why?"

I shrug, "The idea of getting into an accident...of hurting someone is..." paralyzing, terrifying, the stuff of nightmares, "unpleasant. I just...don't want to. Jonas handled it differently. He's very focused on vehicle safety. He researches all our cars before we buy them, making sure the safety standards are up to snuff. And he likes to drive. He feels in control, and he's incredible behind the wheel. It works for us."

Her smile is soft, understanding. "That makes sense," she says. "I've never driven a car, and the idea of being behind the wheel is a bit nerve-racking. So I get it, a little at least."

Luis pulls to a stop, and Maya turns to look out her window. I can't see her face, but her shoulders drop, and I realize I may have made a massive mistake.

"I thought maybe we could have a do-over," I say slowly.

"Oh," she says quietly. She squares her shoulders and turns to me with a false smile. "More shopping. Yay. Let's go."

Yep, this was a stupid fucking idea.

29

MAYA

B ridget breezes into the curtained-off change room with another armful of clothes. "Here we are. These are all the finest cotton I could get my hands on." She smiles softly and puts her hand on my arm. "When Mr. Lee called me, I was so happy. I very much want a chance to find you some things you'll love. Then you'll be able to burn the clothes you walked in with. Except the shoes. They are, of course, exquisite. But I would expect nothing less from Mr. Lee." One thing about this woman, you know exactly where you stand with her. I think I admire it as much as I find it annoying.

She claps her hands and comes at me, pulling and tugging, and before I know it, I'm in an outfit that admittedly is much nicer than anything I've ever worn and feels like cotton balls against my skin. She spins me toward the mirror, putting her hands on my shoulders and popping her head out beside my arm. "This is just lovely. The fabric is very forgiving and so silky. It fits you perfectly." Her satisfaction with a job well done is clear in her voice.

She spins and tears open the curtain, revealing Zach in exactly the same position as last time. All of this feels the same...ok, not all of it. My skin is perfectly fine this time, which is no small thing.

"She's just stunning," Bridget gushes to Zach. He nods, but he's not looking at her. His eyes are on me, heating my skin and making the back of my neck tingle. This level of attraction is baffling to me. How did I go my whole life, barely noticing people, and then suddenly be so hyper-aware around this man? Is it him? Or am I finally just waking up to the world?

Maybe it's about timing, and any man would give me the same reaction now.

I snort, slapping my hand over my mouth when Zach's face turns questioning. The thought is ridiculous because I already know the answer. Definitely not. I am surrounded by many men at work, and Zach is the only one that makes me feel things.

It's terrifying.

Daily, I resist the urge to pack my bag and retreat back to the world I know. It would be so easy to go back, easier than staying. Moving everything I own out here and finding an apartment? It all feels like a lot.

But leaving would mean leaving Cara. And Bree. And Janey. And Becca. And all the other people that I'm starting to develop friendships with. How can I let them all go? And then, of course, there's Zach.

"Maya," Zach says, bringing my mind back to this room. And to the billionaire looking at me like I'm lickable. There go those tingles again. "You look beautiful," he murmurs. The approval in his eyes is satisfying, and that pisses me off. Bridget smiles and makes herself scarce.

"Thank you," I say, unable to inject any real warmth into my tone. Why am I so angry?

He stands with a frown, scanning my face. "Is that a bad thing to say? You're acting like I just told you that you remind me of some hag I used to know."

I wander over to the seating area and drop down into the chair he just vacated. He turns, arms crossed over his strong chest, and studies me.

"Would you stop looking at me like I'm a bug under a microscope and sit down? I'm getting a crick in my neck, staring at you," I mutter grumpily.

His lips twitch, and he sits. Where I dropped into my chair, he sits with an easy grace and control that I'll never manage. Not even with etiquette lessons for the rest of my life.

"Why are we even dating?" I ask sadly, truly wondering.

He freezes, hands gripping the chair. "What do you mean?"

"You don't seem to like much about me. I...I'm not who you want. Not really."

"What the fuck would make you say that?" There's a little vein popping out above his left eye, but the rest of him is ice cold.

I rub my forehead, wishing I hadn't brought it up. I should have just taken the free clothes and kept my mouth shut. People change all the time, don't they? Changing for him doesn't seem like such an awful thing. "Why did we come here today?"

"Because I forced you into a gown that nearly peeled the skin from your fucking body and I wanted you to have a better experience this time around."

"This isn't a gown, though."

"No, but it's the same principle. You could use some new clothes, so why not let me get you some?"

I shrug and rest my elbow on the arm of the chair, dropping my temple into my hand. Why did I bring this up? This conversation will not end in anything good.

"Maya, please, tell me what's going on in your head. I thought this would be fun."

That surprises a chuckle out of me. "Fun? Clothes shopping isn't fun. Though," I grudgingly admit, "this is better than going to a store." His dark hair is tousled, and I want to run my fingers through it. I don't know if I'm allowed to, though. Is there a certain number of dates you have to go on before that kind of intimacy?

"What's going through my head?" I exhale and rub at my brow. "I feel like we're so different, and you're bringing me here for clothes, so I don't embarrass you when we're out together. I feel like you want me to be someone else."

He rises, looming over me with fiery eyes, jaw clenched, then turns and walks away, further into the store. The intensity rolling off of him in waves is a little shocking, but I don't blame him. He's doing something nice, and I can't help but question it. But aren't we supposed to be honest with each other? Isn't that what we agreed on?

He stops near a rolling clothing rack filled with men's suits. Suits very much like the kind he's wearing. Suits that probably cost more than most people make in a month. Zach rakes his hands through his hair, fingers clenching at the back of his head. Tension is in every line of his body and I regret every word I said.

Why did I have to break it? Why couldn't I just enjoy it, for a little while more, at least?

"You wear outfits a seventy-year-old cat lady would admire."

I squeak, so lost in my thoughts I completely miss him coming back. Hands braced on the back of his chair, he's scowling at me, itching for a fight. I've never really been a fighter, so he's going to be disappointed. Another thing to add to the list.

"That's a fair point," I say, looking him straight in the eye. I've been picked at and picked on by masters, so nothing he can say will truly get a rise out of me. I'm sure of that.

"Why? You're beautiful. You're in your thirties. Why do you dress like that?" I resist the urge to scoff at his assertion that I'm beautiful. Each and every time he says it, I feel the same way. Like he made a mistake, or he's half blind. But he's right, I'm in my thirties. I've been out in the world, out around men, and it's just a fact; his attraction doesn't make sense.

"You saw my skin, Zach. You know exactly why."

"Bullshit. You're in marketing. I've seen some of the campaigns you've handled. You've worked for some of the best designers in the world. No fucking way did you believe the only clothing that would work for you were those fucking dresses. So why? Why do you continue to wear them?"

"Because I'm tired of trying to live up to everyone's expectations, and failing!"

Ok, so maybe he can get a rise out of me. I press a hand to my throat, shocked at my outburst.

His shoulders slump. "I don't expect you to dress differently." He holds up a hand, shutting me up. "Yeah, at the charity event, I pushed. I already apologized for that. But now, this is not about expectations."

"That's not true, but I can't figure out if you're trying to convince yourself or me." He scowls at me, and the little devil on my shoulder encourages me to push this. To go ahead and blow everything up. "Appearances matter to you. A lot. That's a fact."

He softly pounds his fist on the back of the cushioned chair. "Appearances matter to everyone Maya. Everyone. Our clothing choices say a lot about who we are. It's not a bad thing to use that to your advantage."

"Is that what you do? Use it to your advantage. Or do you dress that way so people will think a certain way about you?"

"They're the same thing," he says flatly. The twitch in the corner of his eye betrays his frustration with me. It happens all the time around me. Maybe that's a bad sign. What man wants to be with a woman who annoys them?

For that matter, what woman wants to be with a man who's always trying to fix them?

"No, I don't think they are. I think you dress the way you do because you want people to see your worth."

"By that logic, what does that say about you and your clothing choices?"

That hurts. More than I'll ever let him see. "I tried, you know," I say quietly. "I wore what everyone else was. And I was miserable. So my clothing choices now reflect me."

He groans. "No, Maya, they don't." He sits on the edge of the chair, bracing his elbows on his knees. "You are an incredibly dynamic woman. You're thinking five steps ahead of anyone else in my department, and you seem to understand people's needs and motivations in a way that most people can't. But for someone so observant, you have a pretty big block when it comes to yourself."

My chest feels tight. I cross my arms over my chest, sinking down into my chair. "And what is that?"

"You use your clothes to push people away. I think you almost take pride in not fitting in. In being different."

"It's not pride," I whisper.

"What is it?" he whispers back, nearly begging me with his eyes to let him in.

"It's easier. I know what to expect from people now. It's predictable. I like that."

"So you'd rather stay in the little box you created for yourself than try something new."

"Yes," I say mulishly.

He shakes his head, staring down at my toes. "Those shoes I bought you are better than your old ones, aren't they?" I nod, but I'm sure he doesn't need it. I haven't lost my shoes since he gave me the new ones. They feel like slippers... almost as comfortable too.

"They've made your life better?"

Another grudging nod.

"So what if a few nicer pieces of clothing could do the same? Not because you'll look different, but because you'll feel different."

I already feel different. Like I'm outgrowing my skin, and I'm not sure I like it. The old me was safe and predictable. "And it's not because you don't want to be seen with me?"

He shakes his head, but something shifts on his face and makes me push him. "Really?"

His sigh is long and a little annoyed. "I've walked down a street with my brothers covered in body paint. I've been kicked out of buffets and bars. I have a high tolerance for embarrassment, and if you were really happy in your clothes, I wouldn't push this."

My stomach is resting somewhere around my ankles. We're ill-matched, and I'm starting to realize everyone sees that. "Would it make you happy to have me wearing things like this?"

"Do what you want Maya, but yes, it would make me happy. You look beautiful, and you seem comfortable, and I like that. I like that I can give you that."

I run my fingers over the soft pants. They look fancier than anything I've worn but feel like pajama pants. It wouldn't be a hardship to wear them. So why am I still unsettled by this?

"How much are they?" I ask, pinching the pants between my fingers.

"You don't want to know," he says with a dawning smile. "Same as you going to a thrift store, remember?"

"I remember," I say as Bridget comes back with more clothes. "But if I let you buy me these, you need to let me buy you some things too. I'll order them online. You'll love them." Then, with a smile, I follow Bridget into the changing room. Zach's hand at my waist stops me from closing the curtain.

"What exactly are you going to buy me?" he asks nervously.

I grin, feeling like I have my footing again. "It'll be great. I promise." My smile falls. "I thought you were going to walk out on me...when you got up, I mean."

He nods and presses the softest, most barely there kiss against my eyebrow. "I don't leave people I care about Maya, remember?"

"And I'm on that list?"

He hums low in his throat and steps back, pushing one hand into his suit pocket as the other grips the curtain. "Right near the top," he murmurs, his words cracking right into my chest. Then he pulls the curtain closed and I'm left reeling. Bridget chatters in the background as I stand stunned, wondering how that happened so fast. And wishing desperately to be the first person on that list. I almost can't imagine it, being someone's number one.

But I'm also realistic enough to know that I don't usually get what I want.

This relationship shit is hard.

For the first time in my life, I want to see a woman again. And again. Which apparently means dealing with shit and not walking away.

I'm excellent at sticking it out…with my family. For so long, they're all that matters. But this dynamic? Feeling like I have to chase Maya, like she's on the verge of bailing, is stressful as fuck.

But also really fucking refreshing.

I've never chased a woman. Not once. Once I developed my fishing strategy, I just let that sucker roll. I didn't need to do anything but flash my watch and my smile, and the women jumped on my hook.

Now I had to go and fall for probably the most unlikely woman on the planet. She's right. People do look at us when we're together, and I've heard more than one person wondering what we're doing together. And okay, for a man who's always needed to be admired and looked at, that kind of attention stung a little. But it didn't take long for me to start not giving a shit. Growing up with Jonas, I learned to develop a very thick skin. I learned not to give a shit what anybody else thought of me...as long as they kept their fucking thoughts and opinions to themselves when it came to Jonas. When it comes to Maya, I just forgot those lessons for a minute.

I'm coming to realize that being in Maya's orbit is worth whatever shit she puts me through. She has a way of looking at me that makes me feel like I'm the most interesting person on the planet. *I* am, not Zach Lee billionaire, just me, just Zach. And I want more of it. But I'm going to have to learn how to pivot, because this woman just doesn't react the way I expect her to.

Case in point.

"For fuck's sake, Maya. Sit down."

She frowns at me from the corner of the living room and shakes her head. "Nope. I'm not leaving this spot. Not happening."

I peel off my jacket, the custom-made suit feeling too tight lately. I toss it on the edge of the couch as I yank at my tie. I slow down as I realize Maya's lost that panicky look she's been wearing since she entered my apartment and is instead focused on me. Specifically on my hands, currently tugging on my tie. I don't bother hiding my smile as I pull a little harder, making her swallow.

This is what's going to fucking save me.

I've been dodging women wanting to get their hooks in me for so long that I didn't realize how fucking frustrating it is for the one doing the chasing. Now, I'm desperate to keep Maya from walking away before I can convince her we'd be great together.

I may not have any experience in relationships, but I sure as hell am smart enough to figure it out. If fucking Colton can be a husband, I sure as hell can be, too.

Wait...husband? Where the hell did that come from?

Tossing my tie on top of my jacket, I undo the top two buttons of my shirt, Maya's eyes on me. The idea of being someone's husband is messing with my mojo, throwing me off my game. It doesn't sound good...or maybe it does. One woman in my life from this day forward? It's crazy.

Maya in my life from this day forward, though? No way would I ever be bored.

"Maya, you're being a little...unreasonable."

She scowls at me. "Crazy. You were about to say crazy, then you changed your mind."

I shrug, grinning. "You said it, not me. But you're standing over there when there's a perfectly comfortable couch right here, waiting for your very lovely ass to sit on it."

I love the rise of her blush over her cheeks and how she ducks her head in a mix of embarrassment and pleasure at my compliment. The woman is pure sex, and she has no idea.

"We should go to my apartment," she mumbles, carefully crossing her arms and tucking her fingertips in her armpits.

"I've been dreaming of having you back in my space. Now that you're here, you want to go? Nothing broke. It's fine."

"It is not fine!" she whisper-yells. "Everything in here is so expensive. What happens when I trip again, or sneeze or something, and *another* million-dollar painting falls off the wall?"

A laugh escapes, and I quickly cover it with a cough at her glare. "Sorry. I'm sorry. It's just, you're worrying over nothing, the painting is fine." The frame cracked a bit. Not that I would ever let her know that, but it's fine. My stomach did drop a bit when it hit the floor, but that's it. I'm not one to put stuff over the people I love.

There's that word again. Love. It seems to be popping up a lot lately.

"I'd really like you comfortable in my space, Maya. How do I make that happen? What will it take to convince you to get out of the corner?"

She scowls and drops her arms, staring around my living room, cataloging the dark walls and thick curtains. I think the designer called it a lush, masculine space. I don't really know what that means, just that I walk in here, and it feels like me.

And having Maya in here makes it even better.

If only she'd come out of the damned corner.

"This place is too nice for me. It's way above my pay grade. So I can't imagine sitting in here and not worrying about how much everything costs."

"How the hell did this become my life?" I groan and roll my shoulders to ease the tension. "I like nice things. I think you've realized that. I can afford it, so why the hell not, right? Except now there's this woman that I really like, and all this shit is backfiring. Why is this such a big problem? My brothers have broken shit in here, and it's no big deal." She shoots me a look, and I backpedal. "Ok, I was a little upset, but that's it."

"A little upset? How much? How much was the stuff they broke?" Shit, shit, shit.

I clear my throat and mumble my answer, hoping she won't catch it. "I don't remember."

"Oh god," she moans, slapping her hands on the top of her head. "That means it's really expensive, and you just don't want to tell me." She's in a full panic, and there I go again, smiling. She's too fucking cute.

"It's just stuff. That's all."

"But clearly stuff you care about. You picked it all. You paid for it. You're displaying it in your home. And the idea of breaking any of it is making me nauseous," she moans.

Right. This isn't funny anymore. How the hell do I get through to her? How do I make her understand? Eyes darting around the room, I settle on a book and grab it off the shelf. I'm more of a collector than a reader, but I did read this one.

"You see this," I say, waving it in the air. "Tom Sawyer. I read this in school, and when this copy came up for auction, I grabbed it. But you're telling me that this book I paid ninety grand for is standing between us?" I have no idea where I'm going with this or how far I'm prepared to take it, but reason has left the building. "So, let's get rid of it."

I spin, heading to the kitchen, dropping the book on the counter as I search for matches. Maya's still in the corner across the room, watching me with wary eyes. But when I light the match and pick up the book, she snaps out of her self-imposed prison and runs toward me. I take a second to admire the picture she makes, hair streaming behind her, chest bouncing magnificently. If you ignore the look of total panic on her face, it's really hot.

Determined, I bring the match an inch from the corner of the incredibly rare book. "You're asking me to choose between my stuff and you. I don't think you're getting it." she slams to a stop on the other side of the island, hands flat on the wood top. "There is no choice to make. If you haven't figured it out by now, I want you. So it seems to me the only solution is to get rid of the expensive shit. It should only take me a day or so to burn everything. You don't mind sitting on folding chairs, right? Are they cheap enough for you? Or should we just sit on the floor?"

Yep, I'm losing my shit a little, but I'm dead serious.

"You're a lunatic," she says, a bit of...awe in her voice. "But you're not going to burn that book or any of your stuff." She sounds certain.

I don't know if I was planning to actually burn this book, but now?

I'm way too satisfied by the shriek she makes as I bring the match to the spine. She races around the counter, diving for me. I drop the match and the slightly smoking book in the sink because no fucking way do I want her burned, and grab her around the waist. She flails, reaching for the book. I grab her hands and pin her against the counter, a small tendril of smoke drifting between us.

"What are you doing? You're insane," she yells, her beautiful chest heaving with her frantic breaths.

I press my body into hers, and I see the moment she forgets about the book, the match, and anything else but us. "If you make me choose Maya," I whisper against her cheek, "then I will. I'll choose you."

Her breath is coming in little pants. "I...I don't want you to destroy your things."

"Then what are we supposed to do, love? Because I want you here, I want you comfortable in my space. I plan on having you here...a lot." Her eyes darken as my meaning becomes clear to her. Jesus, she's responsive. I can't fucking wait to feel her. All of her. I bring my lips a breath from hers. "Your move. What do we do?"

The woman is a master chess player, obviously. She doesn't waste words, simply leans forward and presses her mouth to mine. There's a familiarity there. We're starting to learn the shape of each other. And I didn't understand how incredible that can be. Knowing someone, knowing exactly how to make them moan, perfecting it, has never been on my radar before.

Beneath the familiarity is the intensity and fire that always amazes me coming from her. It's addictive.

Book forgotten in the sink, nothing on my mind but her, I lift her onto the countertop and press between her legs, desperate to feel her. She gasps into my mouth, and I swallow it down and press in further, demanding another reaction. She rewards me with a groan this time. I can't decide which one I like better. She's always this amazing mix of needy and surprised, and I'm memorizing each and every one of those moments because I know they won't last forever.

I plan on thoroughly corrupting her.

Starting tonight.

She pulls her mouth from mine, panting, "We're really good at that, right? All kisses can't be like that."

Chuckling, I let go of her hands and wrap her up, content to hold her as she recovers. Everything is tingling, but I'm not rabid to chase that sensation, maybe because she's in my arms, and I don't plan on letting her go. There's no clock to run out, no reason to rush.

Except for the whole blue balls situation. But so far, I've been handling that pretty well myself, thank you very much.

"No, all kisses aren't that good. Not even close. You and me? We're dynamite."

She drops her forehead and mumbles, "Yay us." Yay us, indeed. Her hands start a slow slide up and down my ribs, her fingers running over the rib and muscle like they're piano keys.

Now my head's tingling.

"So...since you missed out on all the fun in high school," I croak, "what would you say to rounding the bases with me?"

She tilts her head back to look at me, confusion swimming in her eyes. "Rounding the bases? Like baseball?" My stunned look must turn her brain online. "Oh! Right, those bases."

Her blush makes me think dirty things. All the dirty things.

"Yeah, those bases. We've got the first pretty well covered. But there's a few more we can—."

"Zach, where you at, motherfucker?"

I drop my head to Maya's shoulder, cursing every bit of technology Declan put in my place, but especially programming all my brothers to my door. "I thought I turned privacy on," I explain to Maya.

Colton's big dumb body freezes in the foyer as he realizes he's crashed our party. "Oh. Hey. Hi Maya. How are you doing? Are you smoking in here? Cigarettes will kill you, you know."

Groaning, I turn on him. "No, we're not smoking. Why are you here?"

"I need you. We gotta get Johnny out. He picked a fight

today, and if you don't hurry up and give me this plan of yours, he's gonna do it again and end up stuck in there."

Rock and a hard place here. Make out with my woman, or help my brother?

"Who's Johnny," Maya asks quietly.

"My brother," Colton answers. "He's in prison, and if we don't convince him to apply for parole, he's going to spend the rest of his life there. And that is not good. Good old Zachey here was going to come up with some brilliant plan to convince him." He turns to me, bouncing slightly on his toes, a sure sign of his agitation. "So, what's the plan?"

I'm between my woman's legs, and my brother's asking me to think. I have no fucking idea what day it is. Luckily, I'm saved by another interfering ass.

"Ordered pizza," Micah says, carefully escorting Holly past me to the couch. "Called everyone."

Fuck. Guess it's a party.

31

ZACH

"What if he works at the Dojo? Maybe he'd like that?" Kade's suggestion is met with side eyes and worried glances. I'm sure a bunch of us are thinking it, but Becca says it.

"I don't think that's a good idea. Having a man fresh out of prison, a convicted felon, working at the same place that I coach abused women in self-defense? Not sure that's a great plan."

Colton, laying flat on his back on the floor, scowls and raises his arm to shake a finger at her. "He killed one person, Bec. One. He's not a mass murderer. And he'd never hurt a woman."

And they're off.

We've all been circling around one undeniable fact tonight. Colton doesn't know his brother. It's pretty damn hard to plan out someone's future for them when you don't even know what they've been doing for the last eighteen years.

I rest back against the front of the couch, and thanks to lots of practice, I'm able to tune out the argument and instead enjoy the way Maya's legs are pressed into me. She's been quiet since everyone showed up, and I don't know what's happening in her head. We were on the verge of something... more, for a minute there, and I can't tell if she's thankful for the interruption, or frustrated by it.

Needing more connection with her, I turn sideways and lift her feet into the V of my crossed legs. *There, that's better.* Her wide eyes meet mine, and I give her a little wink, just to see if I can bring a little more red to those cheeks.

Yep, there it is.

Looking at her, it's easy to ignore the rest of the room. Which is fucking shocking since, other than Evie, who gets off shift in a couple of hours, and Mia, who's at daycare today, everyone is here.

Everyone. All my brothers, Becca, Bree, Cara and Holly.

I think this is the first time that's ever happened. We usually end up at Ransom's upstairs, or at one of my other brothers.

Never here.

Why didn't I realize that sooner? I guess it never mattered to me where we spent time, but staring at my brother as he crosses the room, I'm starting to get a pretty big clue as to why it's never here.

"Dec, why are you walking like that?" I ask quietly.

Declan freezes between the back of the couch and the wall, body straight up and down like a pencil, arms pressed close to his sides. He cranes his neck to look at me. "I don't want to break anything else," he says, eyes wide.

"Anything else?" I wrack my brain, trying to remember what he broke.

"Yeah, man. That vase, remember?"

"No, I don't," I say honestly.

His shoulders relax, and he carefully turns toward me. "It was green, with a little dragon on it. Pretty small. You had it on one of these column thingeys in the entryway. I knocked into it about a year ago." His eyes dart between mine. "Do you really not remember?"

"I remember the vase, now that you mentioned it, anyway."

He looks dumbfounded, he and Maya sharing glances. "You told me it cost you eighty grand. You seemed a little upset when it happened."

I make a hum of agreement, because yeah, the vase was hundreds of years old. So it was a little piece of history gone forever. But I don't want to make him feel bad.

"You...but..." he groans and rubs his hands over his cheeks. "I spend the whole time I'm in here afraid to move. I don't want to break any more of your shit."

"It's just stuff," I say carefully, my earlier conversation with Maya roaring back into my mind.

"Yeah, but you obviously love it, or it wouldn't be in your house."

The silence of the room penetrates, and I glance over to see everyone focused on us. I lower my gaze to Maya's bare feet, and run my finger down a blue vein running along the top. "Yeah, I like it, I guess. But you guys are my family. I wouldn't put the stuff over any of you. Are you...have you guys not been coming over because of that?" Slow nods from everyone.

Jesus.

"I didn't realize you guys were uncomfortable in my house," I say quietly, feeling like a fucking idiot. I like having nice things around me. I take pleasure in looking at them. Simple as that. But somehow they've come between me and my family.

"It's like visiting a museum," Jonas says, eyeing the art on the walls. "It feels very much like I should put my hands behind my back and stay away from the pieces. Especially those ones." He points to the pillars scattered through my large living room, and the pieces displayed on top of them.

I drop my forehead to Maya's knee, needing a moment. Her soft hands come to rest on the back of my head, gently combing through the strands.

Or trying, anyway.

I can feel the stiffness of the strands thanks to my *no-move* gel. I love the stuff. It keeps my hair exactly the way I want it. But right now, it's keeping me from enjoying Maya's touch, and that pisses me off. Just another part of the man I am that no longer feels like it fits.

I roll my head and study my family.

"I didn't know all this shit was stopping you guys from coming here."

Ransom, from his spot in the corner of the room, answers for the group. "We don't ever want to hurt you. And breaking your shit would hurt you."

"Breaking my shit would hurt me," I echo, a mix of shame and anger curling through my chest. Anger at myself, because I fucking did this. How could I be so oblivious?

I rise to my feet, eyes darting around the room, cataloging the statues and vases, wondering which one would get my point across best. Locking on an abstract statue, I move toward it, determined to show everyone exactly how much value I put on this stuff. I'm so focused on getting to the statue that I miss the shouted 'no', but there's no way to miss Maya's warm weight as she throws herself at my back and locks her arms around my hips.

I make it a couple more steps before my mind catches up. I put my hands on hers where they're clutched tight around my lower stomach and realize there's a warm weight at my ass.

"Maya," Jonas asks casually, "Why is your nose in my brother's crack?"

She mumbles an answer, and yep, I can feel the warmth of her breath through my slacks. My body reacts immediately, and I lean forward to relieve the pressure, accidentally shoving my ass further in her face. I glance back and see her legs splayed straight out. She's in a forty-five degrees lean, her grip on my waist the only thing holding her up.

Her low groan of embarrassment sends my family into howls of laughter. The hysteria ramps up as she loosens her hold and slowly slides all the way down to the floor, head bumping along the backs of my thighs, knees and calves on the way. She lays there cheek pressed to the oriental rug, and covers her head with her arms.

I try to hold it in.

I really do.

I try so hard I'm terrified I'm going to pop something. In the end, it's no use. The laughter bursts out of me and I fold over to rest my hands on my knees. My laughter seems to shake Maya out of her embarrassment. She rolls to her side, glares up at me, then pushes herself to sit neatly on the floor. When my chuckles don't stop, she reaches over and slaps the back of my leg. It barely stings, but the fact that she did it sends heat coursing through my body.

I could *so* get into that.

"What was that?" Nick asks in a wheezing voice, wiping wetness from his cheeks.

She smooths her hands down her hair, patting it in place over her breast. Does she do that shit on purpose, or does she really not realize how patting her boobs draws eyes to her? I scan the room and stare down my unpaired-up brothers, sending a clear 'stay away' glare in their direction.

"He was going to break something. Or set something on fire." Maya says, glaring at me.

"Wait...what?" Colton asks, sitting up from his spot on the floor.

"He lit a book on fire earlier!" she says, horror clear in her voice. "It was a rare book, and he just...lit it on fire."

"Why would he do that?" Ransom asks.

She throws her hands up in the air. "I don't *know*. Because he's a lunatic?"

Ransom's questioning eyes lock on me. I blow out a breath and drop to the arm of the couch. "I was trying to make a point."

"That books are flammable?" Kade asks. I shoot him a *shut the fuck up* glare, and he just laughs.

"I have all this shit because I like looking at it. But none of it matters more than you guys. I was just illustrating the point for Maya earlier."

Declan gives me a dubious look. "Really? You're saying you bought all this shit but don't care about any of it?"

I shrug, trying to loosen the tension at the base of my neck. "I like it. I enjoy it. But if it's making it so people don't feel comfortable in my home, then no, I don't care about it." I rub the back of my neck and study my brothers. "Do you all feel this way? Like you can't relax in here?" They all nod, and a wave of shame washes over me.

How the hell did I not realize?

I move to the nearest pillar and pick up the statue on it. Maya's gasp makes my lips twitch. "Relax, I'm not going to break it." I turn to the room at large. "Is it safe to say that the stuff on the walls is fine? It's the display pillars you guys have a problem with?" More nods.

"Ok, let's get this shit moved. You guys grab the pillars. Ladies, would you mind taking the art pieces and following us?"

Nobody asks questions. The women move forward and take the art carefully, as I knew they would. Even Becca. All my brothers stay way back until the expensive pieces are safely away. Then I lead everyone to my empty guest room, line the art up along one wall, and rest the pillars on the other. Everyone backs out slowly. I close the door behind me, and a collective sigh of relief echoes through the room.

"That is so much better," Declan says. "See, so much

room." He flaps his arms, waving them around in the large entryway. "Nothing to break. I can finally breathe."

I roll my eyes but secretly love how comfortable everyone looks now. They rush back to the living room, grabbing their spots. I bought these massive plush sofas for this moment, and I'm so fucking glad it's arrived. Maybe now people will come over more.

Becca drops down into Kade's lap. "You know, you have a lot of beautiful pieces in here. Now that the scary breakable stuff is gone, I can actually enjoy the other stuff."

"You too?" I ask.

She snorts and waves down her body, then the room. "Hello. bull, meet china shop."

Colton snorts at that, then squeals and skitters away as Becca leans down, looking like she's about to give him a purple nurple. It wouldn't be the first time.

We all sit, chuckling, enjoying each other's company and the new lightness in the room, when Maya speaks up.

"Your brother, Johnny. How long has he been in prison?"

Colton sobers, rolling on his side and propping his head on his hand. "Eighteen years."

She nods, brow furrowed. "Well, I don't know much about being in prison, but I do know what it's like to live a...small life. I did the same things every day. Saw the same people. Went to the same places. I knew exactly what I was supposed to do each and every day. I think prison might be like that." She gazes around the room, worrying at her lip with her teeth. We give her encouraging nods to continue.

"Well, I think that some of your ideas, while well-intentioned, might be a little...over the top. When you're coming from a place where your entire day is run by someone else's schedule, being in an environment with no structure might feel...overwhelming." She looks down, smoothing her hand along the new gray pants she picked. I have a fuck ton more clothes being delivered tomorrow. Not that she knows that.

Colton groans. "So what do we do then? Anything is going to be an adjustment for him. He's spent more than half of his life in there. He's institutionalized, and I don't know what the fuck to do for him."

"What does he like doing? Can he go to one of the garages?" Maya asks.

Colton frowns. "I thought it would be better for him to be at head office, with me, not isolated out at a garage."

Maya nods, but doesn't look convinced.

"What," Ransom asks her. "What's that look?"

She blushes but looks him right in the eye, and gives it to him straight. "There are a lot of social rules and norms in an office building. There's a flow and rhythm that someone who's never worked in that environment will have to learn. I'm not saying he can't learn it, but being at one of the garages might be a better fit, at the beginning at least."

She slides to the edge of the couch cushion and studies Colton. "When you started, no one wore a suit. The business also wasn't that big. You had years to get used to it, and to become the man you are now. At least at a garage, he can wear what he wants, and it's an environment more familiar to him."

"He's a good man, not some Neanderthal." Colton's voice is tight. I step forward with clenched hands at the bite in his voice. That tone should never be directed at Maya. Or any of the women. But Maya, once again, shocks me, showing me another side of herself.

"Do you know what it's like to walk into a room and feel like a spotlight is on you and everyone is judging you?" She raises an eyebrow and barrels on. "Do you know what it's like to have people whisper about you behind your back and suddenly not have room for you at their table? It sounds like high school crap, but every office I've ever worked in was the same. Your brother is going to have to figure out how to navigate that. It might be easier for him to do it and to find his footing in an environment more comfortable for him. That's all I was saying. I'm not judging him or his life."

"She's right," Bree says. "I've been doing a little research on life after prison—."

Cara snorts. "You watched *Shawshank*."

Bree gives her the finger. "And I read some books, asshole. I can read. Anyway, he's living in an environment where he has to watch his back twenty-four-seven. It's the heightened awareness that's…exhausting."

"Why do you sound like you're speaking from experience, Bree?" Nick asks, frowning. We all sit, eyeballing Bree. You can bet we'll be checking up on Bree a little more. She's not ok, and that can't stand.

She lifts her feet up and wraps her arms around her knees. "Because I've been living like that for a long time. If I don't expect it, every noise, every touch, is a potential threat. My nervous system goes haywire. I'm ok because I'm in an environment that I'm familiar with, at the same job I've had for years. But for your brother, everything is new. You're the only connection to the world he has right now. Unless there are other people from his past he can reach out to?"

"Shit," Maverick says, eyeing Colton. "No fucking way do we want him anywhere near other people from his past. Going back to gang life is not an option."

"I already handled it," Colton says, dropping to his back on the floor. "I bought him out."

"Is it final?" Ransom asks, trading a look with Maverick I can't read."

"I hope so," he says with a groan. "I made it clear I'm not a well they can tap again. But I doubt that's going to stop them from trying."

"Keep a close eye on it," Ransom says quietly, a thread of steel in his voice.

Colton gives him a thumbs up. "Bugged their headquarters, and I have trackers on all their cars. Declan's working on getting me into their financials. I'll be so far up their ass, I can tear it apart if I need to."

"Ew," Cara says, scrunching up her nose. "That imagery is gross and really doesn't have the impact you're looking for."

She shudders and heads for the door. "You guys will make the right decision. You love him, you want what's best for him. And personally, I think Maya knows what the fuck she's talking about. Get him out, get him working so he can find his footing, then figure out the next steps. One day at a time, people, one day at a time. I'm taking a bath, see ya." The word bath sends a bolt of electricity through Declan, who rolls off the arm of the couch and runs after her, only wiping out once on the polished floors. The man's socks have no traction.

"He's getting good and fucked tonight," Micah signs. He's not signing as much as he used to, but we still use it when we have shit we don't want to say out loud.

Holly elbows him in the stomach, and I cough out a laugh.

"Don't be rude," she mutters. She turns to Becca, Cara, Bree and Maya. "He said Declan's getting good and fucked tonight."

Micah's chest shakes with his laughter. "Right. Yes. Fucked. Sorry, ladies."

"Sounds like a plan," Kade mutters, tipping Becca off his lap, then hauling her up and over his shoulder. Becca grabs two hands full of ass and lets out a 'whoop'.

Jesus, my family's embarrassing.

The rest of my family wanders off, leaving Jonas, Maya, and I. Jonas doesn't look like he's going anywhere, and I'm about to politely ask him to leave when he speaks.

"Maya, would you like to work on my puzzle with me?"

"I love puzzles," she says, clapping her hands. I groan in frustration as they wander across the hall to his place. I trail them, because no way am I going to let Jonas scoop her.

Fucker's not gonna steal my girl.

32

MAYA

Panting, I flick the switch on the vibrator and toss it on the comforter. I throw my arms over my head and fall back on the bed, letting myself just breathe.

I do not recognize the woman I've become.

Pleasant tingles run through me, and I have to laugh. How did I go from infrequent, dare I say boring, masturbation to this?

I've been corrupted by Bree. That's for sure. That sex shop was a revelation. Who knew that a tiny little vibrator could feel that good? I sure didn't. And who knew picturing Zach tugging at that tie...so slowly...would ramp the heat up to eleven.

With a little groan, I force myself through my Monday morning routine, pulling on a silky-looking top and pant combo that feels like I'm wearing air.

I hate to admit it, but Zach's right. Wearing the admittedly ugly dresses I do has become a sort of statement to the world. It's easier to think someone doesn't like you because of the way you dress, than because of who you are.

But I didn't realize how heavy they were. Not just physically, but mentally. Pulling them on felt like I was encasing myself in cement. Like they buffered me from the world. And maybe, just maybe, that's not a good thing.

These new clothes don't magically make me a different person, but I do feel...lighter. And I think I like it.

I'm on the last bite of my bagel when my phone rings. I stare at it, honestly baffled, then pick it up, swallowing quickly.

"Abigail. Are you ok? You never phone." I didn't realize she knew how. The woman has never once phoned me, but I swear her screen smokes when she texts. She's that fast. We've been texting regularly for the last couple of days, and I'm truly feeling like we're friends for maybe the first time ever.

A small sniffle in my ear, then a watery voice. "We broke up." She's never sounded like this. Abigail is a force of nature, with an infectious laugh and a stunning smile. This is all wrong.

"Oh no," I say softly. "What happened? I thought things were good between you?" She's been with him for years. I can't imagine she would have stayed with him this long if he wasn't a good guy.

"I thought they were too," she says with a sniff, "until I caught him at home with another woman on his dick."

My stomach drops at the pain in her voice. "Oh no."

"Yeah. I had a bunch of interviews lined up, but the last one was canceled, and when I came home, I caught them." Her voice hardens. "He had the nerve to say it was an accident. Tripping on a curb is an accident. This? No way." How does a man cheat on a woman as vibrant and loving as Abigail? It doesn't compute.

"What are you going to do?"

"I don't know. I spent the night at a hotel, but I can't afford to do that every night. The job hunting is not going well at all, and I'm just so frustrated. Why did he have to fuck up?" she groans. I can picture her shaking her fist at the sky, cursing her boyfriend's name.

"Do you...have family you could stay with?" I wince. "Now that I asked it, I feel bad that I don't know the answer."

"No, I don't have anyone left. Just some cousins, but they're younger, and they're not really established yet." She sighs, her voice softening. "It's okay, you know. I never took it personally that you didn't want to get to know me before. I could see that you were a very private person, and I knew you had a hard time opening up."

"I do have a hard time," I admit. "But that doesn't excuse it. I promise I'll try to be a better friend from now on." Maybe all this Brash togetherness is rubbing off. Or maybe I'm out of my mind. I have no other explanation for what comes out of my mouth next. "You could come and stay with me. The guest room has pink glitter all over the walls." Her delighted gasp makes me smile. "You could stay for a bit, regroup. And I don't know, maybe we can find you a job here."

She's quiet, and I bite my lip to stem the tide of words that want to escape. I can't decide if I want to take it back or convince her to come. I do know that I've never shared my space, and I have no idea if I'll be ok with it.

"Are you sure?" she asks hesitantly.

Her hesitancy makes me more confident in my offer. "Surprisingly, I think I am. You...you're the only part of my old life I really miss, other than Birdie. And you're the only person." I'm such an idiot. "I would like to see you."

She sniffles. "So maybe we just call it a little vacation for now. Then there's no pressure for either of us."

"A little vacation," I murmur, really liking that idea. I've never been on a vacation. "We could do some touristy things. It's cold, but the apartment is lovely and close to all kinds of cute shops."

"Did you just use the word cute to describe a store?" she says with a gasp. "You? The woman who actually gagged when I suggested we shop for the staff Christmas presents together?"

"Yeah. That sounds like me." I shrug, forgetting she can't see me. "I'm starting to realize that I've been missing out. Zach has taken me shopping a few times, and maybe I don't completely hate it."

"Wait! Zach? Who is Zach? Why am I just hearing about him? I need details, woman!"

If I hadn't had practice with Bree and Cara, I probably would have just hung up the phone right then and there. But thanks to them, I'm a little more prepared for what friendship entails. Gossip appears to be one of the key requirements.

"He's my boss here at Brash. My direct boss, anyway. There are nine of them. And…ah, we're also dating." There's a clatter on the other end and some coughing and muttered curses.

"I think I just had a seizure," she yells, sounding far away. "I could have sworn you said you're doing your boss."

It's my turn to cough. "Dating. I'm dating my boss."

"Jesus, that's the same thing. Holy fuck. Who are you? We have so much to catch up on." More muttering, then. "I can catch a bus and be there later tonight. You better damn well be prepared to answer questions."

Oh, everything is happening fast. Really fast. Too fast.

It's ok. This stuff happens every day. Friends come to visit. This is totally normal.

"Great," I say, cringing when I hear the high pitch of my voice. Abigail just laughs. I manage to give her my address and make plans to pick her up.

Oh god. There's no bed…or anything in the guest room. I just invited her to stay, and I have nowhere to put her.

"You're distracted," Jonas says, glancing at me from the driver's seat. I've come to love our drives together. But today, after a day spent panicking over Abigail's imminent visit, I can't enjoy it. Zach, as usual, is sitting behind me. We're dating now, so maybe that should be weird. Are we supposed to want to sit together? Either way, it's comfortable and familiar. But I am being epically rude. I drop my phone to my lap.

"Yes. I'm sorry."

"No need to apologize. It was a statement, not an accusation."

"Anything we can help with?" Zach asks, his fingertips caressing my elbow through my winter coat. I turn back to smile at him, his wink making me blush. He's relaxed back in his seat as usual, looking put together and edible. Only today, he looks more touchable.

"Did you change your hair?" I ask, reaching for him without thinking. I pull back, realizing that we're in the car with his brother after a day at work, and it somehow feels not allowed. Zach snags my fingers, leaning toward me as far as his seatbelt will allow.

"Don't do that. Don't pull away from me. Don't deprive me of your touch." His searing gaze makes my stomach clench.

"Deprive you?"

"What else would you call it," he asks in a grumpy voice.

"Ah…I just…." I trail off, gaze darting to Jonas. Zach frowns.

"Jonas, do you care if my girlfriend touches me? Are you going to be disgusted? Horrified? Scarred for life?"

My brain is stuck on 'girlfriend' and I miss Jonas's reply. The word echoes around my suddenly empty brain like a marble in a bowl.

Girlfriend.

Why does that sound so terrifying? *Dating* was so much easier to process. How did this happen? Aren't you supposed to have a conversation about it? That's how they do it in those teen movies I secretly binge-watch. The boy always asks the girl to be his girlfriend. It's a whole thing. Not that I need it to be a thing, but at least I'd know. I didn't know I was a girlfriend. What do girlfriends do?

"Stop spinning out," Zach orders, shaking my hand gently.

My eyes meet his, and I can't seem to blink. I think my eyelids have fused. "*Girlfriend,*" I choke out.

His lips flatten, and he sighs. "What did you think this was, Maya? I don't date. Ever. I especially don't date employees."

"I...I don't know. I was just wrapping my head around the dating thing. Now there's more. I don't have time for all this research." Even I can hear the edge of hysteria in my voice. "I have to find a bed, and figure out how to get to the bus station, and learn how to be a girlfriend, and it's just a lot." I gulp in a big breath and hold it, counting to five, willing the dark spots in my vision go away.

"Get to the bus station," Zach repeats in a low voice. "Why do you need to get to the bus station?" The thick tension in the car is baffling. So is the watchful stares of both men.

"Abigail," I mumble, staring down at the brown purse clutched in my lap. It doesn't match my nice new clothes, and that bothers me. It never would have before. I am changing a lot. Maybe too much.

"Abigail?" Zach asks sharply. "Your friend. She's coming here?"

"Yes. Her bus gets in at eleven. I was trying to figure out how to get a bed delivered before then, but no one seems to be willing to do it. It's maddening. Doesn't anybody like money anymore? I would have happily paid double, but nooo, they called me ma'am and said I'd have to wait." I cross my arms over my chest, disgruntled all over again. Jonas looks in the rearview mirror and gives Zach a look that I can't interpret. They're having a full conversation with just their stupid eyeballs.

Ok, they're not stupid. They both have lovely, brown eyes.

The silence from the back seat is deafening. I'm afraid to turn around and look at Zach's face. Finally, Jonas breaks the tension.

"When I was in high school, I was required to take a biology class. We were supposed to dissect a fetal pig. I was... uncomfortable with the idea. I spoke to the teacher and made some excellent arguments about why it was completely unnecessary for me to do it. There's nothing that dissecting that pig would have taught me that I couldn't learn from the book. He refused to excuse me."

He glances at me from the corner of his eye, lips tight. "When I feel something is not right, or when I'm being pushed to do something that I don't believe in, there's very little else that I can think about. It goes over and over in my mind, and the problem becomes bigger and bigger until I'm completely overwhelmed. I didn't discuss it with anybody, but by the night before we were supposed to dissect the pig, I had a meltdown."

"What does a meltdown look like for you?"

He shrugs, hands tight on the wheel. "It's varied over the years, but that night I ended up rocking on the floor with my hands pressed over my ears. Zach, Nick, and Ransom were there, and they sat with me until I could calm down. Then, I told them everything. Every worry, every problem. I felt so much lighter after telling them."

"And you went to school the next day and dissected that pig like a pro?" I ask, completely able to picture it. Jonas seems like a man that can do hard things.

He chuckles and glances back at his brother. "No. The next morning, all eight of my brothers showed up at the school and talked to the science teacher and the principal. They let me write an essay in the library instead of dissecting."

"Oh," I mumble.

"One could argue that they should not have interfered and that I should not have been excused. But it didn't matter to my brothers. It was important to me, so it was important to them. So they showed up." He looks at me, brows raised, like I'm supposed to get some special meaning from what he just told me. Zach bites off a curse from the backseat. And I wish I were a real turtle and could just tuck myself into my shell and avoid everyone.

"Subtle doesn't seem to work on her, Jonas."

Jonas makes a low sound and nods. "I see. We are very alike in that way. When I need something, or when I am facing a problem, I have many people to help me."

"That's nice," I say, smiling.

"For fuck's sake," Zach mutters. "Why didn't you ask us about a bed? Or, more specifically, come to me for help sorting it out?"

I turn slowly, the seatbelt digging into my neck. "I...it's a bed. I've purchased beds before."

Zach grits his teeth and glares at me. "Yeah, you're fully capable. I am aware. But is it really that hard to ask for help?"

My mouth drops open comically as what they're saying finally hits. "I didn't know I could," I say slowly. "Ask, that is. I've never had anyone to ask for help from." Zach's eyes close slowly, and he rubs a hand on his cheek.

"We are overly involved in each other's lives," Jonas murmurs. "For us, the idea of trying to solve a problem on our own is...foreign. I lost a puzzle piece yesterday. I spent twenty minutes looking for it last night, then called for help. Three of my brothers came, and we found it in minutes."

"Where was it?"

"Stuck to the rear of my sweats. They had me bend over and look under a few tables first and laughed at me the whole time." He sounds annoyed, but he's smiling.

Men are weird.

Zach makes a choked sound. "The *point* is, we're always there for each other. Always. And the idea that you've spent all day worried about something is really fucking frustrating."

"It didn't occur to me to talk to you about it," I admit. "Even if I was in the habit of asking for help...you're a busy man. Coming to you with a problem like this seems wrong somehow."

An actual growl comes out of his mouth. "Ok. This shit ends now. I—." Jonas whistles a high to low note, cutting him off. Again, they have some silent conversation, and Zach sits back with a scowl.

"Maya," Jonas says as he pulls into the underground parking at home. "All of us, but especially Zach, like to help the people we...care about. So asking any of us for help is like giving us a little gift."

He turns off the ignition and clicks his belt, turning to face me. "I have not had a girlfriend. But I do know that if she has a problem she needed help solving, I would feel privileged to be the one helping her. Knowing that I've done something to make her life easier would be incredibly," his gaze drifts out the window, eyes far away, "satisfying." He smiles and climbs out of the van, closing the door softly, leaving Zach and me to stare at each other in charged silence.

"So," I say, breaking the silence. "What you're trying to tell me is that instead of wasting three hours calling furniture stores, feeling incredibly guilty because I was cutting into work time, I could have just mentioned to you this morning that Abigail is coming, and you would have...." I trail off because I don't know what he would have done. Would he have spent three hours on the phone?

"I would have told you we'd move over a bed from one of the empty apartments on your floor. Then I would have asked you what time she's getting in and arranged to have her picked up."

"Just like that," I mumble, tugging at the seatbelt in frustration. Zach leans forward and clicks it, freeing me.

"Just like that," he says, watching me carefully. Biting my lip, I consider my next move and every bit of ladylike behavior I've ever learned and then toss it out the window.

I'm not graceful, and I've never claimed to be, but I would definitely be elected as President of the Clumsy by anyone watching this maneuver. Bracing my hands on the two front seats, I throw my leg over the console and ponder my next move. Stepping onto the seats seems like the next logical move. From there, I do a weird duck and head-first dive into Zach's waiting arms. His low chuckles are rumbling against my cheek as I pull my legs onto the seat. He pulls me up, so I'm sitting on his lap. Aware there's an audience behind me but not caring, I cup Zach's cheeks.

"I should have known this about you. The light panels you installed, the shoes. You've shown care for me from the start. I'm sorry I didn't realize that I could come to you."

His arms tighten around me. "It's not just that. You are a very self-sufficient woman, and I appreciate that about you. But I would like to be...included in your life."

I shift my gaze to his tie and let my fingers play with the knot. "Like telling you I've been texting with Abigail and that she's coming." He nods, still watching me with those serious eyes. That little devil on my shoulder takes over, and I grip his tie. "But I should keep some things to myself, right? Like how I started my day with a lovely little...toy I found when Bree took me shopping."

No, I definitely don't recognize myself. My whole body is flushed, but with effort, I keep my eyes on Zach, and am rewarded by his widening eyes and quick swallow.

"You," he chokes out. Clearing his throat, he tries again. "You can tell me anything you want to...anything at all."

Emboldened, I slide my fingers under the collar of his shirt to caress the skin at his neck. Who knew such a simple

278 | JENNA MYLES

stretch of skin could make my heart race? "So it would be ok for me to tell you I thought about you this morning? And that the way you tug on your tie makes me feel...warm and tingly?"

He pulls me tighter, so tight there's not a hair's width of space between any part of my body and his, from hips to shoulders. His fingers thread through my hair and he tugs me down to him. This is the hottest moment of my entire life by far. I can feel every inch of him against me, but especially the hard length of him pressed against my thigh. With a small moan, I tilt my lips to his and—

"Helloooo," a voice says.

"Don't look," Zach mutters against my lips. "Ignore them, and maybe they'll go away."

"Hellooo, we can see you," another voice says. Tipping my head slightly, I glance at the side window and find Nick and Kade at the window, making fish faces and blowing on the glass so I can see the entire inside of their mouths. "Hi!" They shout, waving when they catch my eye. "Things were getting hot, but we don't have all day. Let's go move some furniture! Play kissy face later."

Giggling, I drop my head to Zach's shoulder, but not before I catch Zach throwing them the middle finger, and them giving it back while grinning like loons.

"Your family is weird," I mumble against his shoulder.

"My family is filled with cock-blocking assholes," he says darkly. I feel a quick kiss pressed to my hair, then he carefully helps me off his lap. "Come on. They won't give up. But after we get everything moved over, you and I are going to spend a little private time together."

33

ZACH

I honestly thought she was leaving, and my reaction to that scared the shit out of me.

How has she wrapped herself around me so quickly? I have no frame of reference for this, other than some completely whipped brothers who seem to be happier than they ever have been.

Maybe I've found my happily ever after, which sounds sappy as shit, and I'll deny it if anyone asks, but there it is. I'm hooked, and I don't think I want to be anywhere else. So the idea that she didn't feel the same, that she was ready to cut tail and run, hit me at my core. Thank fuck she's not going anywhere. Yet.

I glance over at her and groan. She's killing me slowly, and she has no idea. The little glances, the way she licks her lips. The brush of her hand on her throat and her hazy eyes when she looks at me? I'm fucked.

Well, not fucked. Not yet. Her friend's coming tonight, and I plan on having her all to myself for an entire fucking night when I finally get inside her. I want her screaming my name all night long. Anything less is unacceptable. So sex is out tonight.

But I need to feel her. I can't wait any longer and judging by her distraction as Nick and I put the last piece of furniture in place, neither can she. I barely notice when my brothers leave, or her murmured thanks.

"Luis is picking us up at 10:30 to get Abigail. Until then, you're mine."

She gulps adorably, looking up at me with desire clear in her eyes. "W...what will we be doing?"

I grin, and it makes her swallow and take a tiny step back. I lock my muscles in place, willing myself to stay put. There will be a time for that game later on, and you can bet I'll make damn sure when we play it. I'll make damn sure she'll love being chased. "We'll have a bit of dinner, then after, we can round a few bases."

I didn't think it was possible, but her eyes widen even more. "Not like baseball?"

"Definitely not like baseball."

HER MOAN COMES FROM DEEP IN HER CHEST AS I SLIP HER SHIRT over her head and lay her back on my couch. I throw it across the room and fall back into her, mouth at that freckle right above her breast. There's too much to admire, too much to kiss, but I've been dreaming about the skin hidden below this freckle for too fucking long.

My god, the woman doesn't disappoint. Her pale, round breasts are spilling from her basic white bra. There's nothing about it that's designed to entice, but on her, it might as well be covered in diamonds, she makes it that spectacular. They're sagging slightly to the sides, and I can't resist, cupping them both, shaping them. God, everything about her is so soft, not an ounce of silicone in sight. For a man who's used to seeing breasts stick straight up when a woman's laying down, this is a revelation.

I am never going back.

Her hands attempt to cover mine. "Small," she murmurs, blushing.

Her words startle a laugh out of me. "They're perfect. You're perfect. They're still more than a handful." I dip my head as I run my thumb under the cup of her bra, sliding it down until her light pink nipple pops free. I don't hesitate, pulling her into my mouth, laving it with my tongue, then sucking deeply. I'm rewarded by her cry, and a sharp tug on my hair.

I've been wearing that gel for decades, but I didn't apply it this morning, the memory of Maya attempting to run her fingers through it fresh in my mind. And holy hell, I'm never going back. The sharp tugs on my scalp, her breathy moans, and the feel of her under me combine into the absolute hottest moment of my life and, trust me, I've had a lot of hot moments.

At least, I thought I had.

Maya's hips are rolling under me, legs shifting restlessly. I feel my opening and I take it, sliding a leg between hers. She opens for me easily, allowing me to settle against her core. I'm cursing both our pants for keeping us apart, but I'm also damned glad for the control it allows me. I am way too close to the edge right now. Never, not in all my daydreams, did I imagine she would be so hot, so open, so receptive to my touch.

She tugs at my hair again. "I need...I...," she groans in frustration, tilting her head back on the arm of the couch. Using her grip to push me away, she reaches behind her and unhooks her bra with a frown, exposing every inch of her creamy breasts to my gaze. As soon as she settles back, I swoop in to pay her other nipple some attention. Her hips writhe again, and she makes a low sound of aching frustration. I know exactly what she needs, but I don't think I'm willing to give it to her. She's not ready. Fuck, who am I kidding? I'm not ready. Because if it's as good as I think it will be, I'll be ruined forever if she walks away after that.

I don't know if I'm ready for forever. I am, however, planning on making her very happy in the hour we have before Luis shows up. I move up to her lips, giving in and pressing a deep, breath-stealing kiss on her before pulling away with a groan. "Maya, you're so fucking hot." I can't resist teasing her a little. "Maybe we should stop now so things don't get out of hand?"

Her low growl makes my cock jump in my pants. "Out of hand? Are you insane?" I press my lips to her bare stomach to hide my smile, and I've never felt anything better. The gentle curve of it is so soft and touchable, I can't resist rubbing my stubbled cheek against it.

"I need," she mumbles, hand sliding to the V of her thighs, then up to her waistband.

I yank her fingers away from her waistband and press her hands above her head, leaving her exposed. "Don't you dare steal my fun. I've been dreaming about getting in your pants for a month."

She rears up, her torso off the couch as she gets as close to me as possible. "Then DO something already. What are you waiting for?" Jesus. This woman surprises me at every turn. I don't know why I expected her to be shy. She hasn't been in most of our other interactions. Virginal equals shy, at least according to every tv show and movie I've ever seen.

Chuckling, I drop my weight back on her, pressing her down. "Isn't the anticipation sweet, though? You can imagine how good it will feel when I touch you. Imagine me sliding my fingers down...down until they find your clit. Then they'll circle it, rubbing softly, so softly you can barely feel it at first."

"I don't want to imagine it," she says, her words coated in desire. "Just do it already. Stop teasing me." I grin again and her words turn sharp. "Stick your hands in my pants. Now."

Well, that's about as clear as it could be. I would be a total asshole to deny her. Though there will be a time and place for a little...patience. Just not today. I'm at my limit too, though I'm not going to let her know that. "Ok baby, your wish is my command."

I hear her disgruntled 'finally' but I'm too busy sliding my way under her waistband to pay any attention. I'll have her singing a sweeter tune in a minute. I take a second to caress the soft skin of her lower stomach, making her shiver, before diving into her soft curls.

"Wait," she yells right in my ear, making me wince. "Wait," she says again softly. "I wasn't prepared for this."

Please don't ask me to stop. Please. "Prepared?" I ask hoarsely.

She wets her lips and stares somewhere around my ear. "I umm...read about the kinds of grooming men like, and I even booked an appointment with a very bossy woman, but I chickened out and—."

I swoop down and cut off her ramble with a kiss. Then another. When we're both breathless, I drop my forehead to hers and slide my hand down to fully cup her mound. "I've already got my hand on you, baby. I don't give a shit if it's bare or furry, tie-dyed or braided as long as I get in there."

Her giggles muffled against my mouth, I give her exactly what I promised her I would. Gentle circles and barely there touches that get progressively harder. I let my middle finger dip inside her, thank fuck these pants are so loose, and press my palm to her mound, giving her the dual sensations she needs to tip over the edge.

Watching the woman you're falling for come apart in your arms has to be one of the most intense experiences of my life. I'm a guy, so my own release is always at the back of my mind. But I'm too busy taking in every expression on her face, and every sound she makes to worry about it. Her panting breaths gradually slow, her thighs, clamped on my hand, release. She sighs and presses a soft kiss at the corner of my mouth, not because she was aiming for it but because she's boneless and still has her eyes closed, a silly smile on her face.

That's the moment.

When I look back decades from now, I'll pinpoint this, right here, as the moment I fell completely, hopelessly in love with Maya Miller. My fingers still in her, half-naked, sweaty chests pressed together. This is the moment I gave up the fight.

"That was...like...yay," she mumbles with a dazed smile.

I let my head tip to the side to lie on the arm of the couch next to hers and trace my fingers over her face. It's strange how these features that seemed so unremarkable when I first saw her all those months ago, has become the most beautiful face in the world to me. She's unique and bold, and I don't understand how I ever thought any differently.

"I need to sit up," she says with a frown. Something in her tone puts me on edge, so I slide my hand out of her pants and raise up.

Please don't regret it. Don't regret me.

She slides out from under me and sits on the edge of the couch. I touch her back gently, not sure what the fuck is going on and she hisses, pulling away, the heat of her skin traveling from my fingertips to my brain a millisecond later. I jump off the couch and run to the dimmer, turning the lights up from the sexy vibe I had going.

She winces at the bright light and presses her arm over her breast. I should grab her a shirt, or a blanket or something, but I'm too horrified by the state of her back to move. "What the fuck Maya? What happened? I don't understand? Why did you wear the clothes if they were hurting you?"

Her face scrunches up. "The clothes are fine. I think I'm allergic to your couch." I stare at her in horror before sliding my eyes to my plush, royal blue velvet couch that took me three months to find, and way too many zeroes to buy. I take a moment to mourn, just a moment, then I dart to her.

"Show me where else," I order, dropping to my knees next to her. "Ah, wait, get off." I tug her off the fucking couch onto the floor where I can see what's happening. "Jesus, this is bad. Maybe not as bad as last time, but it's not good. Where else are you hurting?" I drop to all fours and pull the waistband of her pants away from her ass, peering inside.

She slaps at me, "Stop it. I'm okay, it's just my back. The pants protected the rest of my skin."

"Are you sure?"

The damn woman rolls her eyes at me. She's not taking this seriously enough. My fucking couch attacked her, and she's just sitting there, all calm and shit. With a growl, I take her hand and carefully tug her up, leading her to my bedroom, and push her down to sit on the edge of the bed.

"You're safe here," I tell her, heart pounding with panic. She's hurting, and I hate it. "I made sure everything's cotton. Even the area rug's cotton." I spin, running into the bathroom and grabbing the bottles off the shelf, then running back to her. I dump them on the bed next to her. She lifts one, giving me a searching look.

"I stocked up, after last time. Just in case. But I didn't think my own fucking couch would bite you. I'm so sorry. I changed the towels in the kitchen and got rid of a few blankets, but I didn't even think about the upholstery. Do you need a bath first? I can run you a bath." I spin for the bathroom, but her hand on mine freezes me in place.

She tugs me closer, and I drop to my knees, resting my hands on her thighs. "It's ok," she says softly. "This was a short exposure. It's not that bad. The lotion will be enough."

I search her face, looking for any hint that she's just trying to make me feel better, and don't find them. She's not sweating, the rest of her skin is smooth and pale. My shoulders drop and my head rolls forward as I realize she's telling the truth.

She's ok.

"Ok," I breathe, "Roll over and lay down, I'll apply it."

She quirks her eyebrow. "For real this time? You're not going to run off again?"

I feel my cheeks heat. "no, I won't run this time." She nods and with one arm still over her breasts, slides back on the bed and lies on her stomach. I grab one of the lotion bottles and squeeze a swimming pool-sized amount into my palm, then with a long look at her spectacularly rounded ass, I straddle her. "Do you promise this won't hurt you?" I ask.

"It won't hurt. Promise."

Not sure I believe her, I carefully, with the lightest touch I can manage, spread the lotion over her lower back where the skin is the reddest. I'm immediately rewarded by her sigh. Encouraged, I smooth more and more. I'm careful to make sure that every bit of skin gets lotion before I move on to the next, working in an imaginary grid pattern.

"Zach," she says softly, "why did you run off that night?"

My hands pause for a second as I register her question. Shaking my head at my stupidity that night, I smooth a new patch of skin. "I...was struggling with my attraction to you," I admit. Her back stiffens. It's nearly imperceptible, but I see it.

"You didn't want to like me?"

"No," I say quietly, "I didn't."

"Why?" There's a hint of hurt in her tone that kills me.

"At the time, there were a lot of reasons I thought we would be a bad idea. The fact that you're my employee is one of them. And I just...wasn't sure I was ready for any of this."

She's quiet, and I watch her profile carefully, counting the blinks of her eyes and her soft inhales and exhales, willing her to understand me.

And everything I didn't say.

"Sometimes, I'm not sure I'm ready for any of this either."

It takes work to make my words come out level. "I see." But I don't. The idea that she has doubts about us, especially now that I don't, makes me want to wrap her up in these blankets and haul her to my plane. I can be on a deserted island with her in a few hours. Then I can work on making her love me as much as I love her.

Kidnapping seems like a reasonable reaction at the moment. How the hell do I reel in a woman like this? One who seems to care nothing for the material stuff I can shower her in. What do I have to offer her, if not my money?

"Do…are you rethinking things…I mean me. Are you rethinking me?" I ask, staring at her profile.

She rubs her cheek on the white comforter and sighs. "Maybe I should be, but no, I'm not. We don't make sense on paper, I know that. But somehow, someway, we work anyway."

I lean down and bury my nose in her hair, breathing in complete relief. "Yeah baby, we do."

For now, we're ok.

How the hell do I make sure we stay that way?

34

MAYA

Eight hours into this sharing my space thing, and it's fine. Totally fine. I don't know what I was worried about.

Of course, she's been asleep the whole time, but that's ok. When she wakes up, we'll have breakfast, and then she can spend the day doing her thing.

Proud of myself for how well I'm handling this, I hum along to Katy Perry as I scoop out some yogurt and replay my very special time with Zach last night. I knew by the way my body tingled when we kissed that he could make me feel really, really good. But I truly had no idea. I'm no stranger to solo experimentation. But I wasn't prepared for how different it would feel with him. Something about the strength of his hands and the low rasp of his voice ramped everything up to a ten for me.

How can I ever give it up? Realistically, I know this can't go on forever. I am nothing like the women he's used to, and at some point, he's going to realize it. Maybe it would be smarter to end things now, but I don't want to. I want to ride it to the last possible stop, then jump off the train right before the track runs out. The hard part is knowing when that is.

That heart I thought was gone when Birdie died has made a reappearance. It's full of love for my new friends, my new coworkers, and yes, for Zach. It's going to hurt, a lot, at the end, I know. It's probably not only stupid but self-destructive to not try to protect it. But the idea of going back to the isolated woman I used to be holds no appeal. Apparently, I'm an all-or-nothing person. I'm either heartless or full of heart. No in-between.

"You're one of those people," Abigail says from the hallway. I screech and fumble the spoon, spraying yogurt all over the front of my housecoat. "A morning person," she continues, like I didn't just crap my pants. "People like you are annoying as hell."

I stand frozen as she shuffles to the other side of the counter and drops onto a high stool. She props her chin on her hand and closes her eyes. Her pink hair is sticking up at the back and she's wearing a faded Charlie Brown t-shirt and plaid pants.

"You snuck up on me," I mutter, grabbing a cloth to wipe the front of my housecoat. She snickers, pleased with herself, and gives me a wild grin. "Jerk."

She laughs. It's rusty, but the hint of familiarity soothes me. The woman we picked up at the bus station last night was subdued, only coming to life long enough to hug me and hi-five Zach and Luis. She fell facedown on the bed when we got home, clearly exhausted.

"Ah, the hair is…bright." I say, afraid to just come out and ask how she's doing after her boyfriend cheated.

She snorts and peels one eye open. "Yeah. I went straight to the salon after I caught him. Maybe not my brightest move, but I do like it. I always wanted to dye my hair, but Jason said I'm too old."

"You're my age," I say, angry that someone would think thirty-four is old. "We're in the prime of our lives. Too old," I grumble, carting my bowl around to sit next to her. "He sounds like a dick."

She side-eyes me. "Yeah, he is. Hey…since when do you say dick? You used to be all buttoned up and reserved."

"Honestly, I haven't really changed. I just kept most things to myself."

"Huh," she says, studying me. "You have hidden depths. Well, whatever's changed, I like it."

Laughing, I take another bite of my yogurt. "I missed you, you know. I didn't expect to. It surprised me."

"Yeah, I have that effect on people. I'm kinda like a fungus."

Dropping my head, I let the giggles roll, and her laughter joins mine. I blink quickly to chase the tears in my eyes away. This feels good. Really good.

As our laughter fades, she stands. "I better get ready. Don't want to be late on my first day," she says through a yawn.

"Wait, what? You already got a job?" Does that mean she's staying? That's an equally thrilling and terrifying thought, because, well…people.

"Yeah," she says with a snicker. "With you. Your hunky boss slash boyfriend took me aside last night and offered me the job as your assistant, temporarily anyway." Then she heads into her room, humming 9-to-5.

"How did I miss that?" I ask the empty hallway.

THIS IS GOOD. BETTER THAN GOOD. IT'S GREAT. IT'S FAMILIAR and new at the same time. You'd never know, looking at her, that Abigail had her heart broken forty-eight hours ago. She's bright and lively, directing people away from me when necessary, anticipating my needs before I ever have to ask, and generally bringing the energy on the marketing floor up to eleven.

I don't know how she does it, I honestly don't. But she just brightens up any room she's in, and she genuinely seems happy to meet everyone. Zach checked in here and there, but for the most part, left us to figure out a flow on our own.

Abigail locks her arm with mine as we stroll off the elevator onto the executive floor. She not so casually peers into offices as we pass, smiling and winking at the men inside. I catch chuckles and a few winks back. Just like that, she's comfortable. I've been here weeks, I've spent time with these men socially, and I still don't have that kind of confidence.

We arrive at my office, and she drops into my chair, spinning as she stares up at the ceiling. "This place is pretty great, huh?"

"Yeah, it is. They've been really accommodating, and they're all incredibly nice." I say, sitting on the desk.

"If you had to leave New York, I'm glad it was for this kind of setup. I'm happy for you." The little lines between her brows are pronounced.

"Your words say you're happy for me, but your face doesn't match."

She winces, but it doesn't erase the troubled look she wears. It's a version of Abigail that I don't really know or understand.

I understand loss and devastation, but I don't understand her kind of heartbreak, not really. Though I might be able to get there imagining the inevitable break up with Zach. My boyfriend.

God, that still sounds weird.

"Maya," she says, biting her lip. "I...I feel like I have to say this, and please know this is coming from me as your friend."

I grip the edge of the desk tightly and nod, bracing myself. The look on her face combined with that ominous start has my stomach in a knot.

"You seem to be thriving here. Really. And the fact that you're seeing someone is amazing. I am truly happy for you. But," her mouth twists and she exhales heavily. "My whole life was wrapped up in Jason. I lived in his apartment. He paid the bills, and now that the rat bastard cheated, I'm left with nearly nothing. The only saving grace is the bit of severance I had left, and you, a friend who could help me out of a bad spot. I just can't help worrying about you."

"Why are you worried?" I ask, though a tendril of understanding is starting to unravel.

"What happens if he breaks up with you? Or you break up with him? You're living in an apartment he owns. He's your boss. He could make things really difficult for you, or hell, even fire you."

"He wouldn't do that," I say quietly. He already assured me of that.

She reaches over and covers my hand. "I hope not. I hope that things stay really good and that he's your forever guy. But I just think you're in a scary situation. I don't ever want what happened to me to happen to you. I mean, let's face it, men are whores."

Bitterness laces her voice. Again, I want to tell her she's wrong, that Zach's not like that. At least not with me, but it feels a little hollow. More than one person has referred to him as a man whore. Hell, he said it too. And Bree told me about the clubs. None of this is new information.

So why does it feel new?

"You know what, I'm just being silly," she says, grabbing my knee and shaking it. "Your guy is nothing like Jason, I'm sure. So forget everything I said." I force a smile, but I can't quite let it drop.

"I have my own money," I tell her. "If something happened, I would be ok."

She nods, wilting into the chair. "That helps a lot. I just…if something happened, and I hadn't said something, I don't know if I could live with myself. But you're right. You'll be ok, no matter what. You've been alone before, you can totally do it again."

She's being kind. She has no idea how those words hurt. *Alone*. Always alone. I don't want to go back to that. I have a life now. Friends. People who look happy to see me, which is such an amazing thing. I don't want to give that up.

"Right. You're right. I appreciate it, Abigail, I do."

She exhales, her relief palpable, and grips the arms of the chair. "These ceiling panels are really cool. Where did you find them? I bet your headaches are so much better."

"They are cool. But I didn't find them. Zach put them up himself after my first day of work. He…I've never had anyone see me like that." I have to show her who he is. She has to know. Or maybe I'm just trying to remind myself. "He saw that I was struggling and he just…fixed it. I didn't ask him to. He stayed up all night to do it. He didn't want the credit. He didn't want to talk about it. He just did it."

"That's really nice of him," she says softly.

"He's really nice," I say, looking down at my shoes, and flex ing my toes. I still haven't gotten used to having shoes that fit so well. The calluses caused by blister after blister from the old shoes are nearly gone.

Abigail claps her hands. "It's settled then. He's amazing, and I'm completely jealous of y — woah. Who is that?"

I follow her gaze and find Cara walking toward us. She's in full Cara mode, red lacy top under a black bustier. Her leather pencil skirt cups her hips tightly, arrowing down to her knees. And on her feet, leopard skin patterned stilettos with the red sole.

"Cara," I murmur as she approaches. Abigail's still staring, and Cara arches a brow at her. "This is my friend Abigail. She was my assistant back in New York, and she's working here now, for a while at least."

"Abigail," she says, in her low, throaty rasp.

Abigail shakes herself and holds out her hand. "Hey, hi. Wow! You're just...stunning. I thought I was into guys, but you're seriously making me rethink that. I mean," she waves her hand in the air in a vague hourglass shape, "wowza."

Cara stares at her, face flat for a minute, then slowly, a grin takes over her face. The laughter follows soon after. "Jesus, you're something else. Nice to meet you. Killer hair, by the way."

Abigail flushes and pats her pink hair, tumbled around her shoulders like raspberry cotton candy. "Thank you, I just broke up with my guy, and I needed a change, desperately."

Cara hums and taps her hand on her thigh. Her nails are a dark, nearly midnight blue. I tip sideways to look past her, giving Janey a little wave as she stops at the doorway. I introduce her to Abigail, and she works her magic in minutes, getting Abigail's entire life story and offering a sympathetic ear as she spills the details of her betrayal.

"I'm so sorry that happened to you," Janey says, pressing her hands on her chest. She looks heartbroken on Abigail's behalf.

"I am too," Cara murmurs. "But my sister gave me some advice once that I think is appropriate in this situation."

"Lay it on me," Abigail says with a wave of her hand.

"It was something to the effect of 'when you fall off the horse, get out there and ride a cowboy.' I don't know. I didn't take it at the time, but I think it's pretty solid advice."

Abigail cackles and claps her hands. "Well, I think it's spectacular advice. I think I need to head out and pick up some men. Any idea where I could go?"

Cara just smiles like the cat that ate the canary. "Oh, I have some ideas."

35

MAYA

"Is it always this loud?" I yell in Janey's direction.

She smiles, wincing as she gets bumped into. Again. We tried to stick to the corner, but Abigail is bouncing around like an overeager puppy, and I'm afraid we'll lose her. "I think so. I don't really go out much, but... Keith took me to a couple of clubs, and yeah, they're pretty loud." The hesitation in her voice before she says his name is weird, but I'm too distracted to question it.

"It's so loud," I yell again. I want to cover my ears, but I'm also completely fascinated by the mass of humanity around me.

"Cara is so cool," Abigail says, bouncing to me and grabbing me in a hug. "I mean, she has her own club. How cool is that? Do you think she and her boyfriend are serious?"

I laugh and shake my head. "You're not gay. Why do you keep pushing this?" Should I tell her I had a similar reaction when I met Cara the first time? Nah.

"Because I would totally go Bi for her. The woman is sex on stilettos. I either want to do her, or be her. I don't know, I'm all mixed up. And I'm four drinks in, so either seems like a valid choice."

She spots Cara threading through the crowd and yells to her, "Hi Cara. Hey! How are you? You're so cool. This place is awesome. I love you. Oops," she dissolves into giggles and collapses against me, burying her face in my breasts.

I stand there dumbly, holding my friend, wondering if it's too late to change my mind. When Cara suggested we come to the club, I should have politely declined. Stupid new me. This is not my scene at all. Though watching my friend make a fool of herself is mildly amusing.

Cara rolls her eyes and stops next to Janey and me. She studies our faces, and her gaze softens. "Why don't we move you guys to the VIP area? You'll have a little more room to breathe up there."

I nod frantically and, clutching Janey's hand in one of mine, loop my other arm around Abigail. We move as a wobbly, giggly amoeba toward the back of the club.

Cara's approached every few steps, but she somehow keeps us moving as she smiles and laughs with men and women along the way. Finally, we're up some steps past one of the tallest men I've ever seen in person and sitting on a velvet couch.

I sigh in relief as Abigail lets go of me and drops to the cushion. I rotate my shoulder as I stare around the space. The music is a little quieter here, which is weird since it's still in the same space. The lighting is lower, and yeah, there's more room to breathe. Sitting on the edge of the sofa, I can look down a few feet into the mass of people, but not be totally overwhelmed by them.

"This is much better," Janey says, the same relief I'm feeling in her voice.

Cara waves a waitress over. "Take care of them. Anything they need, put it on my tab." The waitress nods and takes our drink orders, then hustles off. "My bartenders are getting slammed, so I can't stay. But I'll check in with you later."

"Bye, Cara," Abigail yells, waving her whole arm. Cara laughs and waves over her shoulder as she walks away.

"How did I not know you were this embarrassing?" I ask Abigail, barely recognizing my friend.

She snorts and searches for her straw with her tongue while staring out at the crowd. "I don't know. Because you used to be a bit of a cold fish, so we didn't really hang out. Besides, this isn't me. This is brokenhearted, ready to hump someone, me. Regular me will come back at some point, I'm sure."

Janey chokes on her drink. "Ready to hump?" she repeats, sounding shocked. I get it. Janey and I are a lot more alike than I even understood. I thought that because she had a boyfriend, she was more...worldly, maybe?

"Yes. My boyfriend stuck his dick in another woman. A bony, bleach-blonde woman. And I need to get that image out of my head. So I'm going to go out there and pick a man to fornicate with." She nods, pleased with her plan, and sways herself to the railing to look for her target.

"I swear she's not usually like this," I mumble to Janey.

Janey covers her cheeks with her hands and laughs, but it sounds brittle. "She's a little wild, but it's understandable. She put her trust in someone, and she was betrayed. It's hard to come back from that."

"You sound like you're speaking from experience."

She shrugs, attempting to look casual, but I see beneath it to the pain she's hiding. "Yes, well, sometimes we have to learn things the hard way."

"I'm sorry," I say, leaning in. "For whatever happened."

She nods stiffly and visibly shakes off the moment. She looks like she's about to say more when Abigail screams in absolute joy.

"Hey! I know you guys! C'mere!" She's waving her arms frantically, smiling like a loon at...Zach, Jonas, Nick and Declan, standing across the club near the bar.

Oh, my god. Who invited them?

As always, my eyes are locked on Zach. The men are all handsome, but I never get tired of looking at him. And it's not just 'cause he's beautiful.

Declan leans over the bar and takes Cara's mouth in an X-rated kiss. They part, and even from up here I can see the heat between them. Smiling, she rubs at the corner of his mouth, then nods her head toward us. Abigail's shouts get their attention at the same time, and they all glance over. I hide with a squeak, which is dumb, I know. I'm dating one of those men. I work with all of them. But I don't know what the rules are here. Do I kiss him? Cara didn't seem to mind when Declan kissed her. Or would that be too forward?

Staring down into the crowd, it's obvious it's not. More than one couple is kissing and doing other...stuff on the dance floor.

I use Abigail's body as a shield as I watch the men work their way through the crowd. They're a head above most of the women, and they all move with a natural grace that anyone would envy. They seem to command the space, and the women are drawn to them like bees to nectar. What's it like going through life having everyone want you? I honestly have no frame of reference, so I can't imagine it.

Zach's in one of his suits again. Honestly, I never paid attention to men's clothing before meeting Zach. And now, all I can think about is how he looks all rumpled, tie askew, shirt unbuttoned, hair wild. I want him to unravel for me every night.

My own private strip tease.

My cheeks heat imagining being alone with him, and I'm grateful for the low light. No one in here knows I'm having dirty thoughts.

He's moving through the crowd a lot like Cara did. Smiling, flirting, and acting like every woman he talks to is special. I've seen this before, the night of the Gala, but tonight, it hits differently. All those women coming onto him are nothing like me. The teased hair, the skimpy outfits. They look like they belong here. They look like they belong with him.

I pinch my thigh, determined to shut down those thoughts. As much as I wish they weren't, Abigail's words this evening seem to be stuck in my head.

This is lunacy.

I went from having no social life or connections to a boyfriend. But not just any regular Joe. No, I had to pick a suit-wearing, art-collecting billionaire. The fact that he's my boss barely registers in all of that.

Maybe I'm a fool trying to ignore our differences. But as I watch the way Zach and his brothers watch out for Jonas in the crowd, I think I'd rather soak up every last second of being with this caring man.

Because he is caring. As I watch, the brothers seem to have a well-rehearsed system of getting through the club. Zach's in the front, flirting, paving the way. Jonas is right behind him in his gray t-shirt and cream cardigan. Flanking Jonas on either side is Declan and Nick.

Jonas isn't by any means relaxed, but it's clear he trusts his brothers, and all of them work together to get Jonas through the crowd without being touched by strangers. That's one of the things I noticed at work. Casual brushes in the coffee room or in the hallways are just a fact of life in a busy office. But Jonas takes pains to make sure he has space. Though that doesn't seem to apply to me, Cara, or anyone else he's close to.

Maybe it's my imagination, but the air around me seems to shift. Slowly, carefully, I move my gaze back to Zach and find him locked on me. The heat in his eyes sucks the breath out of my chest. I choke a bit, thankful he can't hear me from all the way over there and give him a wobbly smile and a wave.

He doesn't wave back, he's too cool for that. But the way his lips curl at the corner is better than screaming and yelling. Because none of the other women in that crowd get that smile. It's just for me.

The guys move faster, and I sit back to catch my breath. The intensity of his focus heats my already hot cheeks, and I slide my eyes over to Janey, hoping for a distraction. Only she looks a million miles away as she glares at her phone screen, aggressively tapping out a text.

"Are you ok?" I ask her. "You seem...upset."

She startles, clutching the phone to her chest. She smiles, but it's forced. "No...well, yes." Her laugh is shaky. "I don't know what I'm talking about. It's just..."

I smile at her encouragingly. I don't have it in me to pry. My habit of keeping to myself makes it impossible for me to dig when someone so clearly doesn't want me to. But I want her to know I'm here, willing to listen.

She bites her lip and drops the phone onto her lap. "Keith and I broke up. I'm just trying to...sort some things out." She's blinking furiously, and I wish I knew the right thing to say in this situation.

"I'm sorry, Janey."

She shakes her head. "It's fine. That's the way life goes, you know. People break up all the time."

She takes another sip of her drink and stares at the floor. First Abigail, now Janey. There are relationships falling apart all around me. Who the hell am I? Thinking Zach and I will be any different? I mean, realistically, what's the likelihood that I find a forever man my first time out?

Not very, I'm thinking.

There's no more time to contemplate my relationship status as Zach appears in front of me. He's sliding onto the couch next to me, casually unbuttoning his jacket. He leans in and presses an intimate kiss to my lips. I breathe him in, cupping his cheek, memorizing the way he feels. I don't care who's watching. I don't care that his brothers are standing feet from us.

I don't want this to end. Ever.

"You're here," I say in his ear when we separate, smoothing the fabric of his jacket over his shoulder.

"Cara called us. She didn't think having you ladies here alone was a good idea," he murmurs, rubbing his nose against my neck. I'm enjoying the shivers traveling up and down my back, so his words don't register right away.

I pull back, frowning at him. "We're grown women. We don't need babysitters," I tell him, a little offended at the implication. He raises his eyebrow and very pointedly stares at Abigail. She's dangling over the railing on her stomach, yelling in sheer joy as Nick holds onto her legs, laughing. Declan's right there with them, laughing too, not attempting to put any stop to their nonsense.

"Oh. Maybe *she* needs a babysitter," I mumble. Zach laughs and curls an arm around my shoulder.

"It's a good excuse to spend time with you," he murmurs.

"You saw me all day." Why am I breathless? This is middle school boyfriend/girlfriend stuff. Get a grip, woman.

He shakes his head, fingertips playing with the hair on my shoulder. "No, we worked all day, and Abby kept you busy."

"Abby? She asked you to call her Abby?"

"Yeah. She said no one called her Abigail but you and the old man in her apartment building."

I hum a response, but inside, I'm shrinking a little. Why wouldn't she tell me she doesn't like being called Abigail? It seems like such a simple thing, but not knowing my friend prefers a nickname feels like a pretty big friendship fail.

Zach runs a finger over the wrinkle between my brows, smoothing them. "Hey, what's going on in your head?"

I let my eyes wander to the other end of the couch, where

Janey and Jonas are chatting. He's got a goofy smile on his face, and my heart gives a little pang. They would be a truly adorable couple, and they make a lot more sense than Zach and I do. Zach and I are like a champion show dog and a rescue getting together. What would those babies look like?

"Maya," he asks again. My eyes snap back to his.

"Dogs, I was thinking about dogs."

His lips quirk. "I think maybe I should be offended. I'm sitting here, putting my best moves on you, and you're thinking about animals?"

"These are your best moves?" I ask in surprise. His eyes widen, and he barks out a laugh.

"Ouch," he says, shaking his head. "Way to kill my confidence, woman."

"I think you'll be fine," I say dryly, loving the banter. The man knows he's got the best moves. They're the only moves I've experienced, but I don't need to compare them to anything to know they're the best.

"Something's wrong," Jonas says, his voice carrying from the other side of the couch. Zach sits up straighter, his arm tightening around my shoulder. Jonas is frowning at Janey, his hands clenched into fists on his knees. "You are not acting like yourself. I don't like it."

The pain and disappointment I saw earlier on her face is still there. He's right, something is wrong. But it doesn't look like Janey has any intention of sharing her problems.

"I'm dealing with some things, Jonas," she says, giving him a weak smile. "I'll be fine. Actually, I think it's time for me to go h...to leave." She stands, and Jonas immediately jumps up.

They're such a contrast. Janey's not a small woman, maybe a couple of inches shorter than I am. But everything about her is softly rounded. Jonas towers over her, his lean, corded strength looking even more powerful compared to her.

His face is pained as he hurries to smooth things over with her. "Wait. I apologize. I did not mean to upset you. I can go."

She smiles softly and puts a hand on his arm. His whole body stills as he stares at her. "I'm tired. It's time for me to go. Stay and enjoy your evening. I'll see you at work tomorrow."

He nods reluctantly. "I'll escort you to your car."

She's already shaking her head. "No, that's not necessary. I don't have my car today. I'll just order a ride." She pulls out her phone, and Jonas visibly puffs up with his deep inhale. The man looks like he wants to pick her up and carry her anywhere she wants to go.

"I'll drive you," he says decisively, nodding his head, the matter settled as far as he's concerned. But Janey frowns and rakes her hand through her golden brown hair.

"Jonas, I appreciate your concern. But I have a ride coming. I'm fine."

He plants his hands on his hips, his lip curling into the smallest of sneers. "He's coming to get you, right? Tell him he needs to get out of the car and open your door. Good men treat their girlfriends with respect." The dual certainty in his voice, that he knows what's right, and that her boyfriend isn't meeting the standard, is clear.

Janey flinches, and her face flattens. "Yes, I suppose you're right. Good men do." She nods her goodbyes and makes her way through the crowd to the coat check. Jonas's eyes are locked on her the whole way. Zach and I are locked on Jonas. The muscles in his shoulders are bunched, tension radiating off of him.

"Brother," Zach says softly. Jonas tips his head but doesn't move until Janey is out of sight. Then he spins to us, a fierce look on his face.

"I don't like this. He isn't treating her right. I should follow her and make sure she's safe." He takes a step away, fists clenched again.

"Stop!" I yell. He freezes and turns to me. "Don't do that.

She is having a rough time, and I think it would be better for her if you just let her go for right now."

"But she needs to be safe," he insists.

"She'll be ok. She's smart and will keep an eye out for danger. But if you go after her right now, I'm afraid that..."

He takes a few steps toward me and crouches down in front of me. "What?" He asks quietly, completely focused on me, like the answer I give him may change everything. And maybe it will.

"She broke up with him," I say, cataloging the minute changes in his features. The widening eyes, the flaring nostrils. His muscles bunch like he's about to bolt after her. "If you go after her right now, when she's hurting, you might damage your friendship."

"I don't want to be her friend," he says flatly. "I want to be her husband."

I choke a little at that, and glance at Zach, who's sitting stiff and silent beside me. There's no surprise on his face.

"Wow. Okay," I lick my lips, trying to gather just the right words to explain to him. "If you care about her that much, then you'll have to be careful. But can I just point out...if you want to be her husband, then being the best friend she's ever had is the best place to start. Because if she can't trust you...if she thinks you don't respect her, then I can't ever imagine she'd be willing to marry you. Hypothetically I mean since there's a long way to go between here and marriage."

"But I waited, and I think this is my moment," he insists.

I stare at him, baffled, vaguely aware of Abigail tugging Nick and Declan to the dance floor. I've never seen her dance...it's incredibly entertaining, but right now, my focus is on Jonas. He picks up on my confusion and explains.

"Zach said that I can not interfere, but I can watch and wait for my moment. Now is my moment."

"I see." I shoot a look at Zach, registering how tightly he's holding his body. "I think you're right and wrong. She's broken up, but she's also heartbroken. Being her friend is the best thing you can do right now."

"I do not want to be friend-zoned." My mouth drops open, and Zach winces.

"Brother, where'd you pick that up?"

"I saw it in a movie. It's a bad thing."

"I don't think it is," I say firmly. "I think that if a woman puts you in the friend zone, it means she trusts you. That's a good thing. A really good thing."

He studies me, frowning. Then nods with finality. "Ok. I will work to get in Janey's friend zone." He stands, "It's too loud here. I want to go." Then he turns and moves easily through the crowd, his arms held away from his body, creating a little bubble for himself as he moves through the mass of bodies.

"Talking to your brother is refreshing."

Zach snorts. "That's one way of putting it. Also maddening. And frustrating. And hilarious."

"He has no filter," I murmur.

"No, no filter. Which honestly, I love about him. But brutal honesty can be hard to handle sometimes."

I sigh and lean into him. "Any kind of honesty is hard, I suppose."

Zach's body tenses behind me, but I don't look back. I can't. I want to imagine that everything is going to be okay for a while longer. So I do the only logical thing. I take his hand and pull it around my waist and lean in to whisper-yell to him.

"Did I tell you I have a list of things I want to do? It's not really a bucket list. It's more a list of regular things I haven't done."

Interest sparks in his eyes. "Do you want me to guess what's on it?"

"No," I say with a laugh, reading the dirty thoughts all over his face. "Some of the things you're thinking about are on there, but I'm realizing that I missed adding a lot of things. There are so many things I haven't done that I want to."

The interest on his face his turns to warmth. "Like what? Lay it on me," he says, grinning. I lose my train of thought for a second as I wallow in the warmth of that smile. *Let me have this just a little while longer.*

I press a soft kiss to his lips, loving the way he inhales when our lips touch. He reacts to me just as much as I do to him. He draws me in deeper until the pounding music and the laughter fade to nothing in the background.

I pull away, panting. "Dancing," I mutter. "I've always wanted to go dancing." I look up at him through my lashes, feeling nervous. "Will you dance with me?"

His slow, sensual smile makes my breath catch in my chest. "Anytime, baby," he murmurs, pulling me to my feet. He pulls me in front of him and lines my back up against his front. He's hard everywhere, and a low moan escapes me. He chuckles evilly and leans down to nip at my shoulder. "I'll help you knock off *everything* on your list. And I'll bet I can introduce you to a few things that aren't on there."

We're on the floor, pressing and rubbing together. My blood is pumping in time with the throbbing base. Every once in a while, I catch a glimpse of Abigail's moves, and it breaks me from my daze. Nick and Declan seem perfectly content to make fools of themselves as they all seem to be competing to be the worst dancer. The people around them have wisely moved away from the flailing limbs.

She sends me a wild grin, and I send her one right back. Look at us. We're actually living.

"Eyes on me, baby," Zach orders, tilting my chin up so he can meet my eyes. "I want all of your attention for as long as I can get it tonight."

"Okay," I say, dazed.

I am so riding this train to the end.

The likelihood of me being able to jump off before getting hurt is slim to none. It's far more likely I'll be riding on the top of the train, bull riding style, arms in the air, yelling at the top of my lungs as it crashes into the bottom of the canyon.

I can't bring myself to care.

36

ZACH

My kidnapping plan is starting to take shape.

Maybe that should freak me the fuck out, that I'm so willing to commit a crime to keep this woman, but it doesn't. Actually feels pretty logical. She's been distant this week, and I can't figure out where I fucked up. But getting her alone on a deserted island...ok, a luxury deserted island with a stocked fridge and a plush bed, sounds like the right move.

"She's pretty incredible, isn't she?"

I manage to keep from flinching and turn to meet Abby's knowing eyes. She's always measuring, calculating, and I can't help wondering if I'm coming up short. I'm new at all this relationship shit, but I'm pretty sure that getting in the best friend's good graces is pretty damn important. Abby's the closest thing to a best friend Maya's got.

"Yeah, she is. That's why I chased her so hard."

Abby crosses her arms and studies me. "You chased her. And you got her. What are you going to do with her now, boss man?"

The bite in her tone when she says 'boss man' raises the

hairs on the back of my neck. I glance back at Maya, leaning over the spreads, surrounded by her whole team, then back at Abby. "Outside."

She nods and follows without complaint, which is a small blessing, I guess. I've felt this conversation coming, but fuck if I know what I'm going to say. I hold the door to an empty office open and wave her in. She drops into the chair behind the desk and folds her hands on top. I suddenly feel like I'm at a job interview. Not that I've ever been to one, but I imagine the power dynamic would feel exactly like this.

"You've had something to say to me for a while," I say, tucking my hands in my pockets and leaning back against the door. I raise my eyebrow and give her an impassive look, the rest of my body relaxed, determined not to let her know how uncomfortable I am.

She bites the inside of her cheek as she studies me. "I can't really figure it out," she finally says, tapping her fingers on the desk. "People talk, and the people on this floor talk about you, a lot. Like, tons. So I know a little about you. And based on everything I've heard, the fact that you're openly dating Maya is blowing their collective minds."

I grind my molars together and shove my anger down. "You're her friend, so I'm going to try really hard not to be really fucking offended."

Her eyes flare, and she leans back in the chair and crosses her arms. "Offended? Why? Because I mentioned your past? Because I looked you up, and from what I can tell, you seemed quite happy to be fucking around."

She blows out a breath and drops her arms. "Look, I'm not a fan of your past, but I'm not judging you for it. But I just don't understand why you're chasing Maya now. She is nothing like those women you're used to."

"No, she's not," I bite off, that ball of rage growing larger. But beneath it is that pool of worry I always carry. Abby's words are splashing down in it, the water level raising dangerously close to spilling over. "That's obvious to anyone who looks."

She tilts her head and rises from the chair to sit on the edge of the desk. I have to give her credit for her giant lady balls. Most men wouldn't think of confronting me, let alone an employee, but she's doing it without a flinch. Does that make her crazy, or just a really good friend?

"Why? Why are you with her? Is it just a temporary thing? Because if it is—."

"Enough," I snap. Her mouth closes in shock, and I regret my tone...a bit. "I thought you were her friend?" I say harshly.

She raises an eyebrow and tilts her head. "I am her friend."

"No, I don't think you are. If you were, you'd understand exactly why I can't get enough of her. Yes, she's unlike any of the women in my past. I didn't spend more than a few hours with any of them. But Maya?" I scowl and tug at my tie. "I spent an hour last night listening to her ramble about superhero capes. I still don't have a fucking clue what she was talking about, but not once did I wish she would shut up. Not once did I get bored. Why is that so hard for people to understand? She has this amazing brain, and she's funny. She sees the world with this...freshness that I just don't. And she's got an ass that's just...spectacular." I take a deep breath and level my tone. "People don't change until they have a reason to. I have a reason to *now*."

Abby's mouth drops open somewhere around the middle of my ramble. She looks like she's at a loss for words, which is really fucking amazing since she's talked pretty much non-stop since I hired her. "Oh my god," she says slowly, a smile curving her lips. "You love her."

I just stare at her because, yeah, I love Maya. But I'll be

damned if I tell Abby before I tell Maya. I don't know all the relationship rules, but even I know that's fucked up.

My stare doesn't seem to bother Abby at all. She grins and does a little happy dance. The woman is a crap dancer. She cuts it short suddenly and turns to me.

"I might owe you an apology," she says, wincing.

"For today? Sure. Lay it on me."

She scrunches up her face. "I'm not sorry about confronting you. But...I have been a little...upset this week. And I've been doing a bit of venting about my ex...and men. And I may have said some things about you."

The way she draws out 'may' makes dread pools in my chest. I can't get a full breath. "What kind of things, Abby? Be specific."

She winces. "Well, I've mentioned the fact that you're her boss a few times...like a lot. And the fact that she's living in an apartment you provided...which is totally luxe, by the way." Seeing my mounting fury, she hurries on, her words tumbling over one another. "It's just...if you ever broke up with her, she'd be up shit creek. You have to see that."

"I would never do that to her," I say coldly.

She stands straighter, still only coming to my chin. "You say that now, but people change. There are no guarantees. I should know. I spent ten years with a man I apparently didn't know at all. I put all my eggs in his basket, and he just chucked the damn thing off a cliff." She drops her eyes. "I won't get in between you, I promise. That was never my plan. I just...worry about her."

I nod at her curtly, my fury cutting off my voice, and yank open the door, striding to the elevator. I need some space, and maybe to punch something. I manage to grunt at my brothers as we pass on the Executive floor, but I don't stop moving until I've slammed the door to my office. "Fuck! Fuckity fucking hell. Shit!"

I brace my fists on the windowsill, the last couple of weeks flashing through my mind. I thought things were so good. At least, they were. But lately, there's been some hesitancy in Maya when we've been together. I've felt like I have to be on my best behavior somehow, like she's just waiting for me to fuck up, and now I know why.

"Fuck!"

"Let's take a walk," Ransom says from the doorway. I spin, glaring at him, not in the mood to talk to anyone. I open my mouth to tell him that, when he points a thick finger at me, "Now."

"Fine," I snarl at him, following him out. A few of my brothers pop their heads out of their offices. Nick, Jonas and Kade fall into line behind me and we all hit the stairwell, pounding down the twelve stories. By the time we hit the ground floor, some of my mad has worn off. Not all of it, but some.

We're uncharacteristically silent as we cross the back parking area, past a few delivery trucks at the loading dock, and into the warehouse.

A few of the warehouse guys nod but otherwise don't pay much attention. Seeing us walk through to the room in the back is not unusual, though it's happened less this year. Ransom scans his palm on the scanner, and shoves open the door. He tugs off his jacket as he moves to the middle of the room. Kade slams the door shut behind us.

"So," Ransom says, carefully removing his cufflinks. He lines them up neatly on the stool next to the boxing ring and stares at me. "Fists or words?"

My eyes travel over the ring, then my brothers. "I don't want to fight any of you," I say flatly. "We're not kids anymore."

Jonas pushes up his glasses. "You and I fought last weekend because I ate your leftover Pad Thai."

"It was really fucking good," I yell, glaring at him. "Besides, that was fun."

Jonas's lips twitch. "Agreed."

"What's fucking with your head today?" Kade asks, leaning on the ring. When we bought this place, it was bigger than we needed. We were still all scattered in different apartments across the city and we decided to create a private hangout space back here. It started with a few couches and a TV. The boxing ring came later. Now, since we live on top of each other and hang out all the time, this room only gets used when we need to punch it out.

Privately.

I snarl at him, deciding punching it out is a great idea actually, and yank off my tie. "I'll start with you," I say, flinging my shirt on the floor on top of my tie.

He grins and rocks back on his heels. "Well, all-fucking-right. Fight it is." He strips off his jacket and shirt. We both kick off our shoes and climb into the ring. Jonas, Nick and Ransom all move to one side, hands clutching the ropes.

Kade's big, a few inches taller, and definitely more muscle-bound, but I'm faster. We dance around the ring, eyeing each other. I'm going to wipe his stupid grin off his face right— . "Like, how bad is kidnapping, really?" I ask. "What if I just take her on a vacation, and whoops, we don't come back? That's not the same thing, right?"

Kade drops his head and frowns. "Yeah, it is. I fucking checked. You get her to leave, voluntarily, you're ok. But if she tries to come back home and you stop her, that's some bad shit."

Nick chokes out a laugh. "Did you research this before or after you married Becca?"

Kade sighs and runs his fingers through his hair. "Last week." He scowls as we laugh, but, seriously? It's funny shit, especially when it's someone else.

"The car thing again?" Kade's been trying to get Becca to

drive something new and safer. But the woman is stubborn as hell, and even though she's married to a man who can clearly afford to buy her one, she doesn't seem to want anything from him.

"No, actually. She hasn't been driving it lately." His mouth quirks as he flashes a look at Jonas. "For some reason, it won't start. I get it running, then the next morning, dead in the water."

Jonas widens his eyes and very deliberately stares at the ceiling, avoiding our gazes. He whistles casually and cracks us up.

"You're still pulling that shit?" Nick asks, laughing.

Jonas scowls at him, then over at Kade. "That car is not safe. She should not be driving it. You need to handle that."

"I'm fucking trying, man. She won't let me buy her one."

Jonas tilts his head, eyes drifting to the corner of the room. A small smile curves across his mouth. We all stare at him, which takes him a while to notice. He just shrugs. "Are you fighting?"

Kade and I eye each other and nod. We dance around each other a little more, hands up, ready to work out our frustrations. "Wait, what exactly is going on with you and Maya? You guys seem really good together." Nick asks.

"I don't fucking know," I snarl, dropping my hands to glare at him. "Things were great and now it seems like she's pulling away from me. Now I find out fucking Abby has been filling her head with doubts."

"What doubts?" Ransom asks quietly, hands tucked into his pockets.

"All of them! That I'm a fucking womanizer, that I'll get bored with her. That our power dynamic is fucked up." I groan and bend over, resting my hands on my knees. "It is fucked up, but not the way Abby thinks. Maya has all this power over me. One word from her and she's got all of me. Nothing exists but her. She…"

I clear my throat and force out the words. "She bought me dog slippers. To match hers. They're fucking hideous. And I wear them. And," I can barely get the rest of it out. "They're so fucking warm. I think about the fucking things all day, and I can't wait to put them on when I get home." I drop to sit on the padded mat. "I don't recognize myself anymore."

Kade drops to the mats, too, resting his back against the ropes. My brothers exchange glances and climb in, sprawling out. They study me carefully. Finally, Kade breaks the silence.

"You are different. But I like it." I shoot him a look, and he grins. "You've always been a bit of a stuffed shirt. Always dressed so nicely, hair always perfect. Even when we're lounging at home. It's fucking weird, man. I mean, I've never seen you wear anything with a hole in it."

"Is that the bar? I'm fancy because my clothes don't have holes in them?" My brothers exchange glances, then nod.

I groan and lay on the mat. "You're all sloppy assholes."

"My favorite sweatpants have a hole in the crotch," Jonas says dreamily. "If I forget my underwear, my balls fall through the hole, and it hurts like hell. But the pants are so soft I don't want to throw them away."

Our laughter echoes through the room. Jonas just smiles and rests back on his elbows. "I like Maya." He says. "She's good for you. And I think you're good for her. She seems more comfortable in her skin now than when she first came, and I think a lot of that has to do with you."

"You mean the clothes? She does seem to like them."

Jonas rolls his eyes. "Not the clothes. You love her, and she is brighter around you. She shines."

"He's right," Ransom adds. "She was very...aloof when she first came. The woman clearly came here for something different, so it's not all because of you, but she is brighter when you're around. But you're brighter when she's around, too. You seem a little less concerned about appearances too, which is healthy."

"You guys make it sound like I spend every minute staring in a fucking mirror."

"Nah," Nick says, "it's not that bad. But can I ask you something?" I nod, but he's already talking. Why did he bother asking? "What would happen if you wore the slippers to family dinner? Or didn't comb your hair? What would be so wrong with it?"

I shift uncomfortably. "Nothing...I guess."

"Why do you look like you just smelled a fart?" Kade asks. I glare at him, and he gives me the finger with a grin.

"Good question," Ransom says. "Why are you so horrified by that idea."

"I...fuck, it just feels like I would be too..."

"Exposed," Jonas says flatly. "You would feel exposed. You have spent so many years trying to be perfect that you can't imagine not living that way. It's become a habit."

We all stare at him. "You've been talking to Colt?" Nick asks.

Jonas shakes his head. "No. But I read all of his textbooks."

"For fun?" Kade asks, eyes bulging. Colton has a lot of psychology textbooks. A lot.

"No. I was attempting to figure out why I am fixating on Janey."

"What did you learn?" I ask him.

"That I empathize with her. That I respect her. And that I appear to be in love with her."

Kade sucks in a breath, chokes, and drops to his stomach, coughing. None of us bother checking on him, all too busy staring at Jonas, stunned.

"You just...said it," Nick says in awe. "Just like that."

"Should I not?" Jonas asks with a frown.

"It's fine," Ransom assures him. "But you haven't told Janey that, have you?"

"No. I have been advised that I must get into the friend

zone first. Maybe, if she spends more time with me, she might grow to have some affection for me."

Kade opens his mouth, probably to spew some shit about the friend zone, so I kick him. I glare at him, and he glares back, but shuts his mouth. I turn to Jonas, and open my mouth to tell him how lucky Janey would be to have him, but the door flies open.

"There you are. Jesus, leave a fucking note next time." Colton throws the door closed, narrowly missing Maverick as he enters, then dives into the ring, scrambling towards me. I crab walk back, but not fast enough. He hooks my ankle and drags me into him, wrapping his arms around my waist and dropping his head on my stomach. He lays there on top of me and sighs. "It worked."

Ransom's gaze sharpens. "It did?" He whistles through his teeth. "Holy fuck."

"What worked?" Nick and Jonas ask in unison.

"Johnny," Colt mutters against my stomach. I can hear the relief in his voice. "We went today. He agreed not to fuck up. He's getting out."

"Wait...like now?"

"He made a petition. Now we just have to wait. We've had the judge put in a good word. It looks promising," Maverick says.

I reach down and pat Colton on the head. His short spiky hair feels weird. I don't think I've ever touched any of my brothers' heads before. It's a weirdly intimate thing. "That's good news. Really."

"Yeah," he says with a sigh. "Your plan worked. He couldn't imagine life outside of there. I think he sees he might still have a future." His hot breath wafts over my stomach, and I really want to get up now. Colt must have the same idea, because he starts to roll away, then flashes back and blows a massive wet raspberry on my stomach.

"Fucker! That is just wrong," I yell as I flail, shoving him away. He rolls away with a giggle and flops onto the mat, arms spread, a big smile on his face.

Chuckling, Ransom reaches over and slaps his foot. "We need to celebrate, man."

Kade hoots and dives out of the ring. "I'll send a group text. And I'm pretty sure we have a few bottles left in here."

Where is he? Then man is usually always around, but today he's vanished. Maybe I should be grateful for that. I don't really want him to come. No, it's better I do this alone...well, not alone. With Abby.

Abby. Not Abigail. I've been using her nickname for the last few weeks, and it finally rolls off my tongue. And every time I use it, she smiles. It feels like we're part of a secret club. Course, there's no shortening Maya. But maybe she can call me M or something. I think I'd like that.

"Ready for this?"

I shoot her a look, and she shakes her head. "I know. But this partnership is good for the company. You said I could take some initiative, and I know how much you love causes like this."

"Yeah, I do. But I don't think I'm ready for it." My hands are sweaty. I wipe them down the side of my pants.

Abby's face gentles, and she puts her hand on my arm. "Maybe you're not ready. But I'm not sure you ever will be. Today really is about supporting them. You don't have to do anything but smile and hand over a check."

"Smile, and hand over a check. I can probably do that." I can put on a happy face and pretend we're somewhere else.

I snort out a laugh, because no, I can't. There's no way that will work. But I recognize that look on Abby's face. There's no getting out of this. So I paste a stiff smile on my face and push through the back door to the parking area, expecting to find Zack's driver, Luis. He's been put on call for us, and honestly, I love it. I hate ride shares. There are too many chatty drivers. What happened to just ignoring each other?

I miss those days.

I run into Abby's back with an "oomph." Lifting my head, I see exactly why she stopped. Coming across the parking lot from the loading dock is every one of our bosses, even Micah. A shirtless Zack and Kade are leaning on each other, giggling. All of them are laughing, and with the exception of Jonas, walking with a loose, awkward gait.

"Oh my god," Abby says gleefully, "they're shitfaced." She pulls out her phone and starts taking a video. I snatch it and shove it into my pocket. She turns and pins me with a thunderous scowl.

"Don't you scowl at me. What exactly are you planning to do with that video?"

She drops the attitude and smiles innocently, but I can see the gleam of evil in her eye. A shudder runs down my back, and I pull out the phone, making sure she sees me delete the video. I hand it over and glare at her until she shoves it into her pocket with a scowl.

"Hellooo," Nick calls, waving at us. We wave back as the rest of the guys start waving, too. I go to lower my hand, and they look so crushed that I raise it and keep waving. Now we're stuck in this weird waving loop, and I have no idea how to get out of it.

Thankfully, a bird with a death wish flies between them, making a few of the men shriek, some laugh, and all of them except Jonas drop into a crouch.

"Are you the only sober one?" I call.

He nods, then turns his gaze back to his brothers. "They're quite embarrassing, but they aren't that drunk. They'll sober up in an hour—" Just then, Maverick tips backward onto the icy pavement, pulling Zach over with him. They lay there giggling, and Jonas sighs and props his hands on his hips. "Okay, maybe two hours." He takes a few steps toward us, leaving his giggling brothers behind, and eyes the SUV idling and a grinning Luis. "Where are you heading?"

Abby gives him a sunny smile. "Brash has made a significant donation to a rescue organization here in town. We need to head over and present them with a check. And I'm planning on petting some puppies."

Jonas looks intrigued and asks her the name. "I'll join you. Wait, a minute." He jogs back to his brothers and together they seem to come to some sort of decision. "I'll grab the van, be right back," Jonas yells as he runs across the parking lot.

"Wait, what's happening?" I ask, looking at the men picking their way over the ice toward us.

"We're going to see the dogs," Ransom announces cheerily. He's still clothed, but he's carrying his jacket and his sleeves are rolled up.

How are they all so attractive? Did he have a list of criteria when he was building this family? Like, must have granite jaws and brown eyes? Must fit right in on a runway? A loud burp and giggle from Colton make me laugh. Yeah, they're attractive, but they're still just men.

"I love dogs," Micah says with a sigh. A bunch of them echo the sentiment while weaving back and forth.

"They're coming with us?" I ask out of the side of my mouth. Abby's snorting with laughter as she nods her head. "Crap. Let's go." I hurry to the door Luis is holding open. I can feel Zach's eyes on me as I dive in. Abby, still giggling, jumps in after me.

"Hit it Luis," she says through her giggles. He laughs and jumps into the driver's seat.

He peels away, getting us to the rescue in record time. I'm honestly impressed with him, and stop to tell him so. "Thank you for getting us here so quickly."

He winks, and I see hints of the suave man he used to be...ok, still is. "Anything for the boss's lady."

I give him a smile and retreat to the front of the building as I absorb the impact of his words. *The boss's lady.* Is that what I am?

Am I somebody's?

I know I'm supposed to argue that I'm not. That I'm an independent woman and I'm my own person. But I don't give a flying fuck about any of that.

I want to belong.

I want to be someone's lady. And I really want someone to call mine too.

"Oh my god," Abby whispers.

I follow her gaze to the curb behind the SUV. Oh, my god is right. "It *is* like a clown car," I mutter, watching in awe as Jonas hits the button to open the sliding door. There are seven very large men in the back of the minivan, and we watch, they carefully climb out, the van bouncing as each one exits. The van gets a foot taller once everyone's on the curb.

Zach is the last to climb out from where he was sitting in the passenger seat. Our eyes immediately meet and like every time he looks at me, my stomach flips...in a good way. Maybe I do have someone to call mine. At least for now.

He gives me a cautious smile, and I frown before I can stop it. I don't understand these smiles lately. He's seemed so...careful around me, and I hate it. When did the brash playboy get to be so cautious?

He stops in front of me, and I automatically reach out to finger the buttons of his shirt. It's become a habit lately, but it settles me, having this little connection with him. "Why was your shirt off before?" I ask him, conscious of all the eyes on us. Abby, bless her, steers the brothers toward the front door of the rescue. She's walking a little bent over with the weight of Maverick and Nick's arms over her shoulders.

Zach winces and covers my hand, cradling it against his warm chest. "I was a little...frustrated. Kade was helping me work it off."

"Work it off...without your shirt?" I ask with a raised brow. "And then you all ended up drinking to...blow off steam?"

Zach shakes his head absently, "Mostly to celebrate. Colton's brother's going to be getting out soon. Thanks to you, mainly. Your idea of him working at the garage was the right one. He agreed to try."

"That's really good news. Colton must be relieved."

He nods, absently as he traces his fingers over my face. "You're so pretty. How'd you get so pretty, huh?"

I clamp my mouth shut to stop the instinctive denial. I'm not pretty. Not according to current beauty standards, but I'm not going to point that out to him. "I haven't changed."

He snorts, tips his head back, and wobbles. "Woah," he mumbles, reaching for me to steady himself. He wraps his arms around my shoulders, sighing when he's got my head tucked against his neck. "That's better."

"Yeah, it is." I never spent much time thinking about how men smelled. Don't get me wrong, of course, I registered pleasant or unpleasant smells, but only in the context of how close I had to be to someone. It only mattered if I was seated next to them at a meeting or on a subway.

But with Zach, I seem to be developing an obsession with all his smells. The aftershave lingering on his cheeks. The faint hint of sweat at the end of a workout, and now the yeast smell of alcohol. All simple smells, but on him, suddenly they're my favorite.

"You changed Maya," he mumbles. "A lot. I didn't know

what to make of you at first. You were annoying, and you kept losing things, *and* you own the ugliest clothes on the planet." He lifts his head and frowns. "The Universe. Your dresses are the ugliest in the universe. If the aliens came to earth and found you wearing that damned bug dress, they'd turn around and go home."

I roll my eyes at him, because what else am I supposed to do? He catches me and blows a raspberry. "They're ugly, you know it."

His eyes widen, and he takes a step back. "Don't you? You know they're ugly, right?" His grip on my shoulder is firm, and clearly he's waiting for me to answer him. I let my lip tremble a little and hide my eyes.

With a sad sound, he pulls me in for another hug. "Shh. It's ok. Shit. You didn't know. You are so lucky to have me. I can make sure you always match. Don't worry."

Snorting with laughter, I drop my head on his shoulder. "Yeah, I'm not worried. You are such a snob, you know that?"

He frowns down at me, eyes slightly crossed. "It's not snobbery, it's good taste."

"Whatever," I mumble, sinking into him. I'm thoroughly enjoying this stupid conversation, and I don't plan on moving at all if I can help it. There are enough people inside to han—.

"Maya, stop fondling your boyfriend, and come on. We're waiting on you."

I groan and twist to glare at Abby. She waves me in frantically, but I'm serious. I don't plan on going. But before I know it, Zach walks us right through the front doors.

The first thing that registers is the muffled barks coming from the double doors past the small reception area. I drag my eyes away from them, and glance around at the giants filling the space.

Kade's shirt is still off. The rest of them are leaning on the walls, or studying the posters. Zach wanders over to Jonas and leans against him. Jonas takes his weight easily, but as only a brother would, knocks him into the wall with a thump a second later.

I always wanted a sibling, and watching the brothers over the last month has been eye-opening. The roughhousing and the picking on each other should maybe make me think twice, but it doesn't. Not really. I would have traded the silent oppressiveness of my house for the chaos of a family like this in a heartbeat.

Abby leads me to a baffled-looking woman somewhere between thirty and forty. She's wearing plain black leggings and a T-shirt featuring the rescue's logo. Her dark hair is pulled into a messy bun, and as I get closer, I see fur covering every bit of her clothes.

I like her already

"Maya, this is Cadence. She runs the rescue."

Cadence takes another look at the men on the otherwise of the small room, then focuses on me. "Ah, hello. I'm sorry, I wasn't expecting this many people. Are you sure-"

She's interrupted by a thump. We both look over and see Micah falling backward. On the way down, he bangs into the back of Maverick's legs, making him buckle. Maverick falls straight down on Micah, who lets out an oomph.

Cadence frowns, "Are they drunk?"

"Yes," I admit, wincing. I can't imagine this is the kind of image that the Brash Group wants to project to the world, but the jerks insisted on coming. With our luck they're going to end up on the front page of tomorrow's newspaper.

Her brow clears, and she nods casually. "Oh," she turns back to me and extends her hand, "It's great to meet you. I can't tell you how much this donation means to us. Things have been so tight lately. I..." her voice gets thick. She clears her throat and widens her glassy eyes. I do the same thing. I'm working. I can let the tears go later. "Anyway, I really appreciate it. This donation will help me keep things running for a while."

I take her hand, holding it more than shaking. She's completely unfazed by the drunk men laying on her floor, and she chokes up because our donation will help her rescue more dogs.

This woman has her priorities straight.

"You are so welcome," I murmur. Zach wanders over and stands beside me for a minute, then wanders away. I stare at his retreating back as he exits. *Is he leaving?* This whole thing has gotten away from me, and if I've learned anything about these men, it's that trying to predict how they'll react makes me twitch. "I really respect what you're doing here. I...I understand how important finding the right human for each dog is." I force a smile and drop her hand. She gives me a gentle nod and a smile.

"You've had dogs?"

"One," I say stiffly.

She smiles again in understanding and gives my arm a little squeeze. "I thought maybe I could-" she stops and tilts her head, a little smile playing on her lips as the brothers, not so quietly, shuffle to the double doors.

We watch, me with my hands covering my cheeks in embarrassment. Abby with glee, and Cadence with a bemused smile as they casually — Nick's even whistling — push open the door. One by one, they slip through, somehow not once noticing us staring.

"Are...is... Hell," Cadence says, propping her hands on her hips. "Are they who I think they are?"

Abby and I exchange a look, but it's Abby who answers. "Yeah."

Again, Cadence nods, looking shockingly calm. "Ok. So a pack of billionaires just broke into my kennels?"

Jesus. Do these guys have a PR department? I should ask. If they don't, they really need one. "Well, 'break' might be a little harsh. They just got...curious."

Zach enters and beelines to us, still not that steady on his feet, his hands tucked behind his back. "Where'd everyone go?"

We point to the back room, and he blanches. "Back there? With the barking and the fur?"

Oh, we are so going back there. Zach Lee, in his expensive suit, covered in dog fur, is not something I want to miss. I widen my eyes at Cadence, hoping our shared love of dogs is enough of a connection to convince her to play along. Thankfully, she shakes her head with a smile and steps forward. "Follow me."

Zach gives me a goofy grin, then steps right behind her, following her suspiciously closely. I can't see past his giant back, but he's doing some sort of weird dip with every step, and his arm is moving. Suspicious, and really worried about us all getting arrested, I sidestep to get a clear look at what he's doing.

I slam my eyes shut in horror, and okay, it's really funny too. But we are definitely getting arrested. Maybe it won't be so bad. Lots of people end up in jail for a night, don't they? Maybe I should have added it to my list. I open my eyes just as Zach makes another swipe.

The damned man has a lint roller, and is swiping at the dog hair on Cadence's back. I watch horrified as he peels a layer of sticky tape off, then swipes again. "Zach," I whisper yell. He turns back, but so does Cadence. I glare at him, telling him with every fibre of my being to keep his stupid lint roller away from her, but apparently, my message isn't getting across because as I watch his arm comes up, and he runs that roller down Cadence's arm.

Abby's shaking with silent laughter. I am so embarrassed I can't make my mouth move. What am I going to say, anyway? Sorry, my boyfriend is a freak?

Actually, that might work.

As I open my mouth to explain, or apologize, Cadence casually turns to face Zach and spreads her arms. A smile breaks over his face as he proceeds to lint roll every inch of her clothing, peeking at her for permission before running in quickly over her chest. She stands patiently, a slight smile on her face, until he's done. The man's smile is blinding when he's finished. He even presses a kiss to the handle of the roller.

"Nice job," Candace says, grinning. "Follow me." She turns and pushes through the door. Zach's just standing there, grinning, oblivious to everything. I stop beside him and grab the elbow of his jacket. He turns to me, gets a good look at my face, lets out a '*meep*' and bolts through the doors, clutching the lint roller to his chest.

Abby's laughter isn't silent anymore. She attempts to speak through her giggles. "He went out...he got it...from the car." Her eyes are watering. "He travels with a lint roller." I gave her a second to get a hold of herself. "I was so wrong about him. You two are perfect for each other."

"This is supposed to be work, Abby. Get yourself together." I'm trying for stern, but I can't pull it off, my giggles slipping out.

This man. Even drunk, he needs things to be tidy. How would that work if we lived together? Would he give me a room I can be messy in? Would he sneak into my drawers and color-code my panties?

I mentally slap myself, not ready to go down that mental road. From what I can tell, my time is better spent figuring out how to get all the men back home in one piece.

Abby wipes her eyes and sighs. "I'm trying. I swear. But this whole thing has gone completely off the rails. I don't think there's anything to do but go along for the ride."

I freeze for a second as I process her words.

She's right. If this train's about to go off the rails, I promised myself I'd hang on and enjoy the ride.

I just didn't image the ride would include corralling all my bosses at a dog rescue.

And look at the bright side. They're such a big distraction, I haven't had time to feel sad about Birdie.

Abby and I take deep breaths and push through the doors, ending up in a big room lined with enclosures. The barking increases in pitch as we enter, one little dog near the front making a ton of noise. Once glance at his small body and dark coat, and I realize I spoke too soon.

38

ZACH

She can't have it. I will give that woman almost anything. I'll give her the last breath in my body, but she can't have my lint roller.

A man has to draw the line somewhere.

I clutch it tighter to my chest and scan the space, cataloging my brothers. They're all scattered, crouched down next to the dog jail cells. Or maybe, in this case, they're more like dorm rooms. I wish I'd paid more attention to where we were going. I hope these dogs aren't going to visit the big dog park in the sky. That would be way too sad.

I'm not really sure why we're here. We donate to places like this all the time, but we don't usually show up in person. Not enough exposure in it. The flashy Galas that seem like they spend as much as you earn are more likely to get you on the front page.

I walk carefully down the aisle, peeking through the doors. There are all kinds of dogs. Big, small, fat and muscled, quiet and fierce. I stop and eye a small dog with the biggest ears I've ever seen. I shudder at her long, blonde hair. She probably sheds like a motherfucker. Wait...she? I lean down, way down, trying to look under her for a thunderstick, and end up tipping over onto the concrete floor.

It doesn't smell good.

At all.

Why did I have to drink so much? I should be keeping my wits about me and figuring out how to make Maya fall in love with me. Not doing a shot with my brothers. Fine. Shots.

"Eww," I mumble as I shove myself up. I come face to face with the small dog. Her head tilts to the side as she stares at me. It's actually pretty cute, so I tilt my head too. Her ears twitch, and she tilts the other way.

She's funny.

We play that game for a while. It only stops when she barks and puts her little feet up the gate, and yep, it's a girl. No weenie in sight.

"Hey, little girl. What's your name?" I rear back and scan the paperwork on the jail door, and need to squint to make out the words. Why the hell did I drink so much? "Pe... Peaches? They named you fucking Peaches?" Her little tongue hangs out, and she smiles. I didn't know dogs could do that. I smile back, because I'm not a fucking monster. "That's an awful name. You need a more dignified name. Like Lily or Grace. Those would suit you way better."

Giggles distract me, and I tip sideways to see Colton and Declan on the floor, dogs wiggling in their laps. Declan has a big, gray, highly muscled dog on his lap, but the giggling is coming from Colton, who's letting a tiny dog with a very big tongue lick his ear.

"Ugh. Gross." Why would he let it do that? I mean, they lick their own butts, don't they? Seriously gross. I turn back to my...the...dog. "You look like you have better control of your tongue, don't you?" I eye the latch on the gate, hesitating as I eyeball her long coat. She doesn't have to climb on me, but maybe I can just pet her. Her hair looks really soft and my fingers are tingling, the same way they do every time I look at Maya's hair. Is that weird?

Nah, that's totally ok.

Maya.

I love her. She's the best thing ever, and I'm sure her hair is way softer than this dog's. And she's cuter too.

Jonesing for my fix, I scan the room for her. My Maya. The wonderful, sexy, bossy, lovely —.

What the fuck?

I lurch to my feet, grabbing the gate for balance, though I don't need it. I'm suddenly stone-cold sober. I take a few steps, stopping next to Abby. She's standing still, hand over her mouth, her eyes full of sympathy. And my woman is curled up on the floor in the corner, crying her fucking eyes out.

"What the hell happened?" I growl at Abby. To be fair, it might not be her fault, but the woman is still on my shit list from this morning, so I'm not too sorry for my tone.

"She's upset, asshole," she growls back. The woman has no respect. Doesn't she know she's supposed to fear me? I am her boss.

But I don't waste any time arguing with her and instead go straight for Maya. She's curled up a foot away from a cage that holds a little black dog. The dog's peering out at her, giving soft little whines.

The most gut-wrenching sobs are shaking Maya's shoulders. I drop to the concrete next to her, something wet seeping into my pants, but I can't be bothered to care. All I can focus on is the pain she's feeling and figuring out how the hell to stop it.

I run through my options in my head. Do I put my arm over her shoulder? Do I rub her back? Do I just sit with her? All the options are a confusing jumble.

"Fuck it," I mumble and scoop her onto my lap. She gasps,

and stiffens briefly, then sags in my arms. She wipes at her cheeks roughly, trying to erase signs of her pain. I cup her hands in one of mine and bring them down to her chest, holding tight. She doesn't have to hide her feelings from me, ever. "Baby, tell me what's wrong. How can I fix it?"

She lets out a cross between a sob and a snort and drops her head on my chest, staring off at the far end of the rescue where my brothers are all gathered. "You can't fix this," she says, her voice thick with tears.

Not fix it? Not a fucking option. I can't handle her this upset and not have some way of making it better. "The hell I can't. I'm stupid rich, remember? Money can fix almost everything. So just tell me what's wrong. Your tears are killing me." She rolls her head until her forehead is resting on my chest. She sighs heavily and closes her eyes.

"I miss my dog," she mumbles against my crisp white shirt.

"Ah. Okay. Is it back home?" As soon as the words are out, I realize I'm a fucking idiot. She wouldn't be sobbing like this if she was missing an alive dog. Damn these alcohol-soaked brain cells. "I mean, I'm sorry. She's not back home, right? She's…" I almost let go of her hands to make a slashing motion across my neck, but stop myself in the nick of time. There would be no coming back from that. She would get up and walk right out of here, and I wouldn't blame her.

Briefly removing my hand from her back, I pinch my thigh until tears fill my eyes. The pain does what it's supposed to and helps me chase away a bit more of the drunk.

I can't say I understand this level of grief for a dog, but I've never owned a pet, and I have no fucking clue if this is normal or…I have no idea. But I do know how to handle emotional meltdowns. I'm a pro at that. With Jonas, the first step would be to make sure he was comfortable with contact, but I can cross that worry off my list. Maya's spine has the consistency of overcooked spaghetti right now as she rests against me.

So fucking grateful she's letting me comfort her, I wrap her up and press a kiss to the top of her head, then rest my cheek there.

"Tell me. Tell me all about..."

"Birdie," she murmurs, a fresh tear falling. I don't wipe it away, letting it stain the white of my shirt. Another soon follows it. How can one word, a simple name, carry so much love and pain all at once?

"Tell me about Birdie."

Another deep, long sigh. "I got her the day after I moved into my apartment. I..." her voice drifts off. I have so many questions. I want to know everything about her, but how the hell do you know how much to push? I never wanted to know a woman like this before, so I have no idea what my right next move is. Is she hooked enough that I can push and won't lose her?

"You were living alone? It must have been nice to have company."

She lifts her head and sniffs. "It was. I don't think I really understood how lonely I was until I got her."

"I get that. We get used to one way of living, so we don't know what we're missing. It's only when we find something new, something better, that we realize what we have." Her eyes soften, and she presses a kiss to my jaw. I have to clear my throat. "You'd never had a dog before?"

"No, my mom wouldn't allow it. Then I was in the dorms. But...it's dumb..." she trails off, a slight blush staining her cheeks.

"Baby, nothing you have to say is dumb. Tell me." Her eyes search mine, and I make sure she sees the truth of my words. If I can listen to her talk about superhero capes for an hour, I sure as fuck can listen to her when her heart's broken.

She gives me a weak smile. "I didn't plan it. I had just moved in and had walked down to the grocery store to get a few things, and there was this little boy and his dad selling puppies out of a cardboard box. I mean, I've seen that in movies, but I didn't know people did it in real life. I passed by them on the way into the store, but I couldn't stop thinking about it." A little line develops between her eyebrows, and I can't resist stroking it with my forefinger. Her eyes cross as she stares at my finger. She laughs lightly at herself, and I smile. She sounds better, even if just a tiny bit. But I'll take it. "Even though I finished college and my mom was gone, in my mind she was still all controlling. Because she didn't like dogs, I always just figured I wouldn't get one. Is that weird? That I let her have so much control over my life?"

"No, I think that's pretty normal. When you're in a family, other people's needs and wants matter. The difference is my brothers care about me too. They care if I'm happy, and they work to make sure I'm in a good place, too." I brush the hair back from her face and tuck it behind her ear. "What made you go back out and pick one?"

She scrunches up her face. "I think it was more of a rebellion at first. Moving into the dorms, going to college and then getting my own place, all of those things were little rebellions, but for some reason, getting a dog felt like the biggest screw-you ever. It's probably not a mature reason to get a dog, but there it is." She smiles. "Birdie was the smallest in the box, but she had this white patch on her chin that made her look like an old man. I was petting them all, but she was such a little stinker, pulling on her sibling's tails, or biting my thumb. She had an attitude. I really respected her for that."

I smile, because how can you not? Of course, she picked the dog with attitude. She sees herself as a quiet, awkward woman, which admittedly she is. But she also seems to search out people with opinions and attitudes. Her assistant is a perfect example.

"She went with me everywhere. She even came to work with me. My boss didn't love it, but I made a good argument about morale, so he let it go. Everyone there loved her." There's a slight bite to the word 'her'. She's already told me how separate she felt in the world. "She'd prance into a room and make everyone smile. Even at the end…"

I tuck her tighter, wishing I could take away the pain in her voice. She snuggles in, and my heart pounds because she's letting me comfort her. Other than Jonas, I've never done this for anyone. But being there for Maya, being someone she can lean on, makes me feel ten feet tall.

"What happened to her?"

She wets her lips, her gaze far away. "She got cancer. My Vet told me that the cancer was aggressive and she only had a few months left, but I couldn't…I had to try. So I found this amazing holistic vet, and they tried all kinds of treatments. They gave me three extra years with her."

"When did she die?"

"A week before I contacted you."

I sit up straighter and, with one finger, tip her chin up so I can meet her eyes. "She's why you wouldn't accept the job?"

"Yeah. I didn't want to move her."

I nod slowly because, finally, for the first time, I feel like I see her. All of her.

She's beautiful, inside and out.

"You turned down a salary more than three times what you were making for your dog?"

"Yes," she says, frowning.

A clump of dog fur floats through the air between us. We both watch it slowly, delicately land on the knee of my pants. Maya looks from it, to me, a little wobble on her lips that morphs into a stunning smile.

"That's killing you right now, isn't it?" She asks. I nod

because, yeah, it kinda is. I eye my lint roller longingly. It's just out of my reach, dropped when I saw Maya's upset. If there was any doubt in anyone's mind how much I love her, the fact that I dropped the lint roller for her is proof of my feelings.

She laughs. "I can't believe you travel with a lint roller. And that you used it on that woman."

"Yeah, well, the alcohol probably had a little to do with that. But she really needed it." The woman walks past us, carrying a stack of bowls, and I do a double take. "What the fuck?" My eye starts twitching, and my hands flex rhythmically.

Maya's giggles morph into full belly laughs. "Oh my god, your face." She's snorting into my shirt, shaking, and it distracts me a little from my horror.

A little.

"How is it even possible? It's been what? Ten minutes? How is she as covered as before?"

Maya reaches up and presses a kiss to the twitch at the corner of my eye. Everything in me relaxes as I'm surrounded by her. Her hair rests against my cheek, and I just breathe her in. "She works in a kennel honey. I'd say it's a miracle she stayed hair free for ten minutes."

Suddenly I don't give a fuck about the hair on my knee or on that woman's clothes. All I'm thinking about is Maya and that word, *honey*. My hands flex again, but this time not because I want my lint roller, but because I want more of her. I give into temptation and slide my hands along her side, meeting at her ribs just below her breast.

"You just called me honey," I say softly, watching her face carefully. I've been called that before, but never like this. Never with affection and warmth and just a hint of exasperation. I fucking love it.

Her eyes widen slightly, then dart side to side, like she's about to run. I tighten my grip, because no fucking way is she getting away from me. But she doesn't run. Instead, she takes a deep breath and looks me dead in the eyes, almost challenging me to look away. "Yeah, I did. I'm going to do it again. Because I'm riding this train right over the cliff. You have a problem with it?"

It's work, but I manage to keep a straight face. "Riding the train? Are we headed over a cliff?"

She nods seriously. "It's inevitable. At some point, you'll move on, and I'll be heartbroken. But until then, I want to enjoy every second of this."

Frowning, I scan the room for Abby and pin her with a glare. She shoots me the finger and runs away. Brat. She put this shit into Maya's head. There is no way I'm letting her get away from me. And breaking her heart? The idea turns my stomach. Because if I break her heart, if she walks away, there will be nothing left of me.

I scan the dull yellow walls and bare concrete around us. This is not the place for this conversation. We should be home, tucked into bed. There should be roses or something. And in the background? Some sexy music.

Instead, we're sitting on the floor, dog hair flying, as we listen to a symphony of my drunk brothers making kissy noises, barking dogs, and laughter.

Not at all what I had planned, but honestly, I don't care. It's perfect because she's here.

"There's a lot to unpack there," I say, grinning. "But let's try." She gives me a cautious nod. "First, I think your plan, to enjoy every second of us, is perfect. I have the same damn plan. But this train? If you're planning to ride it off a cliff, then I'm going too."

She frowns at me. "It's my train. I'm the one riding it. You can't ride it too."

The mulish expression on her face makes me laugh. "Why not? It sounds like a hell of a ride."

"Because you're the freaking train. I'm riding the train, cowboy-style right to the end. You can't ride yourself."

My chest shakes with the effort of holding in my laughter. "So, just to clarify, you're going to be riding me until we crash and burn?"

There they go again. Those eyes widen, and a wash of red covers her cheeks. I get a brief glimpse of it before she slaps her hands over her cheeks and groans. "That came out wrong. I meant I was riding you...the train. I mean, I'm riding the train."

One laugh chokes out. "Cowboy-style, though, right?"

She screams in frustration and drops her chin to her chest. "It made sense in my head."

"Oh baby, it makes perfect sense. I'm on board. You go ahead and ride me anytime you want. Actually, maybe we could stop somewhere, get you a cowboy hat and some boots, so you can have the full experience."

Her blush remains, but there's a glint of interest in her eyes. Good. We're damn well going to enact that little scenario. Over and over.

"What kind of outfit would you wear?" she asks, looking intrigued.

I let the laughter roll, dropping my head on her shoulder. "Baby, I'll wear any damn outfit you want. I promise."

Her hand cups the back of my head. "So you...you want me, then?" The hesitancy in her voice sends rage through me. I've fucked this up already, obviously, if she can't see how amazing she is. And how head over heels I am for her.

I rear back, frowning at her. "Why the fuck would you think I don't?"

She scowls right back and throws her arms out. She drops between my legs, ass to the concrete. Turtled, she tries to climb out, but I swing one of her legs over my head and down to my hip, so she's straddling me, then pull her up straight on top of my rock-hard cock. Let's see her try to deny I want her now.

She freezes, then very carefully tilts her chin down to me. This was such a stupid idea. Now that I've got her on me, I can't remember what the hell we were talking about. She feels too good, and I think I'm about to blow imagining getting her naked and back in this position.

"Umm…what are we doing?" she asks. My eyes are locked on her chest, that magnificent chest, moving in rhythm with her rapid breaths.

"I have no idea," I breathe, mentally imagining my clothes covered in fur, trying to calm the fuck down. Only it's not working. I'm pretty sure I'm sitting in a puddle of dog piss. There's fur on me already, and I don't even care.

I am such a goner.

She moves. Just the tiniest flex of her hips, and I groan. I band my arms around her back and pull her down on me, making sure she can't move.

"Don't torture me. I'm a man on the fucking verge."

"You do want me," she says, a hint of glee in her voice.

I snort and roll my eyes. "Of course I want you. I wanted you when you wore ugly dresses. I wanted you in those fucking shoes. I wanted you when you looked like a fucking lobster. This is not new information."

Her scowl comes back and she pinches my cheek. "Then why do you keep backing off? Every time we're…you know, about to park the car in the garage," she lets go of my cheek to make the universal fucking gesture, thrusting one finger into the circle made by her other fingers, "you back off."

How can I laugh this hard and be this turned on at the same time? "Park the car. Jesus, Maya." I tip my head back and suck in a breath, trying to get both my laughter and my dick under control. Finally, I think I have it. "I didn't want to fuck this up. I had this idea that because you're inexperienced, we should take things slowly."

"Why?" There's a hint of hurt in her tone, and beneath that hurt, embarrassment.

All traces of my smile die, and I risk loosening my grip on her hips so I can thread my hands through her hair. "Because you matter. This matters. More than anything ever has." I shift my gaze to her forehead and force out the rest. "I've never had sex with someone I love, Maya. And I'm terrified I'll fuck it up." It's such an overused word, love. But it matters, and keeping it in has been torture. I want her to know. I want everyone to know. But I'm pretty sure I would feel less exposed walking naked in the middle of downtown.

Her soft gasp and whispered, "Zach," run over my skin. Her hands come to rest on the sides of my neck. "Look at me."

I do, because I was serious. Anything this woman wants, I'll give her. Even if what she wants is to see the embarrassment swimming in my eyes. But thank god I do. My discomfort washes away at the wonder in her face.

"You...you love me?"

"Yeah, I do. I have for a while." She looks like a kid on Christmas morning, my words landing like gifts around her, each one lighting her up brighter and brighter. "You're the light in my life, Maya. I want all your days. All your nights. I want the privilege of holding your hand when you're ninety, and I want to lie beside you every night."

"Oh," she says softly, a tear falling down her cheek. I catch it, letting it hang on my fingertip before wiping it away. "Did...do you know I love you?" she asks hesitantly.

You know that feeling you get? When you set down a really heavy weight and almost feel like you could float away? That's how I feel right now. "I didn't know that. I hoped, but I wasn't sure."

"Words are important, aren't they?"

"Yeah baby, they are."

"I haven't heard those words very much in my life." She

licks her lips, the layer of moisture in her eyes making them gleam under the fluorescent lights.

"I'll make sure you hear them all the time. Multiple times a day. So often that you're sick of me saying them."

She drops her forehead to mine. "I won't ever get sick of them."

"And me? Will you ever get sick of me?"

She laughs softly. "No, I won't ever get sick of you." She leans back, eyes locking with mine. "I love you, Zach. Big time. Bigger than anything I ever imagined."

Her next words are cut off by hysterical laughter coming from my brothers. She looks back at them, specifically at Colt rolling around on the floor, clutching his balls, while Declan holds the tiny dog with the big tongue. I think that furry little fucker is laughing. There's definitely a story there.

Maya shakes her head at the commotion, turns back to me, and quirks her brow. "What do you say we head home? Maybe we can park the car in the garage." It takes me a second, only a second, then I'm right there with her.

"Fuck yes. Let's go. Right now. Come on." I help her climb to her feet, but she's too busy giggling to help me. Finally, I just pick her up and set her on her feet. I take her hand and tug her toward the doors, stopping briefly to grab the lint roller.

"Where you going? Zach? Zachie? Can I come?"

I shoot Nick a glare over my shoulder, which cracks him up. Now all my brothers are watching us leave, waving with stupid grins on their faces. "Idiots," I grumble.

I come to an abrupt stop at the doors as the woman from earlier stands in our path. I give her a nod. I take the lint roller and carefully press it into her hand. "This is for you."

She looks down at it back at me. Her lips quirk, and she bows slightly, which should look awkward as hell, but somehow, coming from her, looks completely natural. "Thank you. Much appreciated, kind sir."

I smile, because she's weird, and I'm coming to like weird, then slide past her and out the door.

"Zach," Maya murmurs, a grin on her face. "You gave her your lint roller. That's big of you. How will you cope without it?"

I shoot her a grin over my shoulder. "I have three more in the car."

39

MAYA

My palms are sweating. A lot. I rub them down my pants as I stare at Zach across the elevator. He looks a bit like a stranger, features pulled tight, eyes burning as he nearly glares at me. The tension between us is so tight. I think I'm supposed to enjoy this tension. This anticipation. But apparently, all tension leads to stupid stuff coming out of my mouth.

"There are so many euphemisms for this..." I say, waving my hand between us. "Parking the car in the garage. Putting the hot dog in the bun. But some of them are kind of offensive. Like *Taking the Bus to Tuna town,* or *Bumping Uglies.* Why would you call it that? It doesn't really make it sound like something two people would want to do. And *tuna?* That's offensive. Do men really think a woman will want to have sex with him if he compares her lady town to fish?"

The intensity on Zach's face fades as I speak, a grin blooming. His warm chuckles fill the elevator. The tightness in my chest loosens.

This is going to be ok.

He takes my hand and leads me off the elevator to his front door. His eyes are locked on my face as he opens the door and pulls me in. The door is barely closed when he presses me against the wall in the foyer, mouth descending to mine.

"Wait!" I yell.

He freezes, eyes searching mine, looking for an explanation.

"We're not stopping this time, right?"

His grin could only be described as *rakish*. It does something funny to my legs, and I lean a little more heavily on the wall.

"No baby, we're not stopping. Not unless you want to."

"I don't want to...so can you please lock the door this time? I really like your family, but they show up at the most inconvenient times. I really don't want to be all..." I wave my hands up and down my body, "exposed and stuff when one of them walks in. I mean, I'm okay with awkward, but having one of my bosses...other than you...see my taco would make it hard to look them in the eye."

Laughing —I really love his laugh, and the fact that I can get him going so easily— he backs up and engages the fancy lock. *Privacy Mode Enabled* flashes on the screen. "You are a wise woman. There, they can't get in. It's just you and me." He pushes his hands into his pant pockets, eyeing me, a gleam of challenge in his gaze. "So, what are you going to do with me?"

My mouth drops open as I stare at him. "Do you...do you really not remember? I haven't technically done this, but I have a lot of ideas, but the whole...riding thing seemed like a pretty solid plan."

Zach's grin drops and he presses into me, lining our mouths up. His hands plant on the wall on either side of my head, his lips barely touch mine. "Baby, if I'm in charge, I'm afraid I'm going to go too fast or do something you don't like."

I can't catch a full breath. That's got to be why I'm light-headed. "I..." I lick my lips and try again to speak through the tightness. "I really like everything you've done so far."

He presses a barely-there line of kisses from the corner of my mouth to my ear, stopping briefly to nip at my earlobe. "I can take over. I can do everything I've dreamed of doing. Or," another nip at my earlobe. I lock my knees, willing my legs to hold me. "You can do whatever you want with me. You can be totally in charge."

The idea is tantalizing, but also a little uncomfortable. "I... what if I don't know what to do? I don't like the idea of you being some robot I order around."

A low chuckle, and this time the nip is followed by a suck that pulls a deep, guttural moan from my chest. I clamp my lips shut. He tries to hide it, but I catch the smirk on his face. Suddenly, there's a different kind of fire roaring in my belly. This man is so confident most of the time, and he understands how easily he affects me. It's his turn to moan.

"Step back," I order, voice husky. I can't help that part. I want him, badly.

He bites the inside of his cheek and does as I order. Giving a little pep talk to my knees, I push off the wall and kick off my flats. Then slowly, with a sway in my hips I might have practiced in front of the mirror, I lead him to the bedroom. I'm hyperaware of him prowling behind me. Close enough to feel the heat coming off him, but he doesn't touch. That tension is back again, but this time, I'm not worried about a stream of stupid words. This tension is one I'm creating, and he's feeling it as much as I am.

I turn at the foot of the bed and back up until my calves are touching the mattress. Time to drop the big girl panties, and take what I want. I slide my hands beneath the waistband of my pants, and lock eyes with Zach, seeing all the love, and heat, and anticipation that I'm feeling. For a second, just a second, it all feels too big. Too impossible. How did I get here? How did we find each other? It's too perfect for it to be an accident.

"Don't tease me baby," he says, voice dark and husky. I said the same thing to him weeks ago, and now, being on the receiving end, I understand how hot that is. But I am going to tease him. A lot.

"This isn't a tease. It's a promise. Tonight, all of it is coming off. But first, I want you to take your shirt off, slowly. I kinda wish you had the tie on, but we'll make do." A grin lights his face, and he strides into the closet, emerging seconds later with a dark blue tie in his hands. I watch, in complete lust, as he ties it neatly.

"You...wow, you did that fast. Like...you're efficient. And good with knots." Crap, crap, the tables are turning here and I didn't mean for that to happen, but seriously watching the man put on a tie is as good as watching him pull it off. He's the whole package.

His hands freeze on his tie, all humor drained from him. "I had a plan, you know. I was going to take this slow. I was going to let you be in charge. But you had to go and ruin it, looking at me like you want to lick me. Now, you've done it."

The bite in his words makes me press my hand against the ache low in my stomach. "Done what?" I ask. But I know. And I want.

Those hands move again, pulling roughly at the tie he just knotted, yanking it free from his collar. "Pushed me over the edge," he growls, advancing toward me.

"Oh...no," I mumble, staring at the v of his throat as he stalks toward me. His hands go to the buttons. "No," I yell, throwing up my hand. He freezes and opens his mouth, but I thread my fingers through the two sides of the shirt, and with every bit of might I can muster, yank.

I may have overestimated how much force it takes to tear open a man's shirt. Or underestimated my strength. Either way, the result is the same. Buttons pinging against the far walls of his bedroom. Zach is staring at me wide-eyed, a mixture of shock and awe on his face. "I always wanted to do that", I say, cheeks hot.

Zach swallows and wet his lips. "That was the hottest thing that's ever happened to me." Dumfounded, I'm about to ask him details, then realize it doesn't matter. My hot boyfriend, the man that loves me, looks like his mind is blown, and we haven't even got to the good stuff yet.

I got this.

He pounces, and with a giggle, I fall back onto the bed. We're roving hands and hot breath, and laughter as we get stuck in the rest of our clothes. But finally, I get to see all of him.

And oh my god.

I know for sure most men don't look like this. I let my eyes trail over his body, from the broad shoulders, to the strong chest, and over the ridges of his abs. All of it is beautiful. Wait, no, men aren't beautiful, right?

All of him is super manly and handsome.

That thought makes me giggle, but all my humor vanishes as I get to his waist and what lies below it.

Okay, now I'm a bit nervous.

"So I know you're not crazy big. I mean, that store Bree took me to has…really big thingeys, but I am wondering if there might be a way of easing into this, so to speak." Or maybe we have to literally ease *him* into *it*.

Zach doesn't look like he's paying any attention. In fact, I know he's not. He's got a glazed look on his face as he stares at my boobs, and I can't quite decide how I feel about it. Do I cross my arms over my chest? Do I bounce up and down and let them wiggle? I go for the wiggles because, honestly, if he's going to kick me out of his bed, I'd rather it happen now and not later.

I do a bit of a shimmy on my back against the cool white sheets. That glazed look morphs into a look of absolute hunger. Okay, he's not going to kick me out. In fact, he looks like he wants to tie me to the bed and keep me here forever, which, honestly, I'd be up for. His admiration helps dissolve the last little bit of the shyness I was holding onto.

His hand trails reverently from the hollow of my throat down to my sternum and rests there. "You are so fucking beautiful. I can't decide what I want to touch first."

I'm not having the same problem. Taking the bull by the horns, or in this case, the man by the penis, I wrap my hands around him. He jumps as his breath comes out in a shudder.

I wasn't prepared for how hot he is or how smooth his skin would be. Peeking at him carefully to make sure he's on board, judging by the dopey look on his face he is, I let my fingers roam over him. I dance them along his shaft and to the tip, gently rubbing, squeezing, and caressing. Then, more to satisfy my curiosity than anything else, I bend down and give him a lick.

I'm not sure what I expected it to taste like. Wait, yes, I do know.

Gross.

Gross is how I expected him to taste. But nothing between us is gross. He's salty and I realize I could happily do this for the next hour.

I settle down onto my tummy and explore him, learning what makes him groan. Learning that the tip of my tongue pressing just underneath the head makes him moan. Knowing these things about him, that intimacy is heady because I know that tomorrow I can do it again. And the day after, I can do it again. My technique is going to be so darn perfect with all this practice that he'll be my willing sex slave for the rest of his life.

Finally, he fists his hands in my hair and pulls me up to

his mouth. "You're killing me. You've got to stop, or this is gonna be over too soon."

Soon? I already feel better than I ever have in my entire life. If it ended now, I would be okay.

Wait, no, that's a lie.

I want to get to the finish line. I pull back from him and rest my palms on my knees, legs spread. His eyes narrow as they focus on the juncture of my thighs. Thanks to the clenching of my belly, a trickle of wetness leaves me. I'm not embarrassed about it. At all. I want to know what that mouth feels like. I want that tongue running over my folds.

Thankfully, Zack is on the same wavelength. Suddenly he's there between my thighs, taking me backward. He rests his hands on the tops of my thighs and places a kiss on my mound just above where I want him most. "Wait," I yell.

His look is a cross between *I'm going to murder you* and *are you fucking kidding me*? I laugh and hurry to explain. "You're going to pay a visit to lady town, right?"

Zach snickers and leans his cheek against my inner thigh. "That's the plan. You have any objections?"

"Um...no. I'm excited for you to visit. I just want to make sure..."

"Make sure of what?" he growls, clearly done with my interruptions.

"That your bottom half's not planning to visit, too. Because I want to ride the train, remember?"

He wheezes out a breath. "The memory of that conversation is seared into my brain, baby. I guarantee you I haven't forgotten."

"Good," I say cheerily, then wave my hand at him. "Carry on." Then I throw myself onto the bed again, snuggling into the sheets.

I thought it would feel good. I thought I'd like it. But holy hell, that's got to be the best feeling in the world. Thank goodness he knows what he's doing. A suck at my clit makes me clamp my thighs around his head with a grunt. A little giggle escapes and I slap my hand over my mouth to stop the words from bubbling up. Who knew I was chatty during sex? But I am not going to ruin the mood again. No chance.

Zach scolds me with a little nip, just beside my clit. It makes me jump with a squeak, but I can't decide if it hurt, or if it felt amazing. Maybe it's both. Maybe it hurts too good.

"Don't do that. I want to hear all of it. Your laughter. Your tears. I want all of you. Even if you're giggling while my tongue is on your clit."

My cheeks heat and another giggle escapes. He rolls his eyes at me, and I take a second to admire his shiny cheeks. He's sure sweaty....wait. That's not sweat. That's me. I'm all over his cheeks. Oh, my god. Yep, here they come.

"I'm so glad you know what you're doing. I should send thank you letters to all those women. I mean, you're really good at this. Thank goodness. I don't even want to imagine what it would have been like to let some teenager get into my pants in high school. I can't imagine that would be much fun, all crumpled up in the back of some car while he...Oh god. Wait. How..."

I have no words. Zach, apparently not interested in anything I'm saying, dives back in, putting his lips and tongue to spectacular use. But what makes me scream, what sends me over the edge, is the thick fingers that push into me, twisting and rubbing.

As I detonate, losing track of everything but my connection to him, I reach out, needing to feel him. He doesn't hesitate, not for a second, instead surging up and pulling me into his arms. He holds me through the shaking, petting my hair and murmuring in my ear. I have no idea what he's saying, but it doesn't matter. Because I feel loved. Completely.

As I come back to my body, I gaze up at him. He's watching me so seriously. I reach up and smooth my thumb over his eyebrow.

"Thank you," he says, "Thank you for trusting me. Thank you for being with me."

I smile at him. He's sappy, and I love it. But I'm a little distracted right now. I rise up, shoving him over to his back, and throw my thigh over his hips. "You can thank me by letting me ride you."

"Dammit woman, I was trying to have a moment here," his frown isn't terribly convincing. Neither is the humor lacing his tone. But I try for contrite and apologetic, anyway.

"I'm sorry," I murmur, wrapping my hand along his base and rising up. "I'll make it up to you later."

I tease my core with the tip of his cock, circling my clit and sending little electric bolts down my back. I'm not worried anymore. Not about his size, not about the way he feels. Not about the way I feel.

Everything about the two of us is just right.

Locking eyes with him, one hand pressed to his chest, I guide him inside me. My hips rocking instinctively, helping lubricate the way. When he's fully seated inside me, I lean forward for a kiss. "We fit," I whisper against his lips. It's a strange feeling. Overwhelming, but also right.

He nods seriously, pushing my hair back. "Like we were made for each other."

"I like that idea. A lot. Every choice we made, every path we chose, led us here. To this moment together."

"I won't ever do anything to make you doubt us. I swear it."

"I know," I whisper, rocking, sending rockets of sensation through my body. "I see you. I see the man you are." I grip his other hand, using it to stabilize myself. "Now stop talking so I can focus on rocking your world."

His full-body chuckle makes me gasp. I feel it everywhere. *Everywhere.* Another thing we'll have to repeat.

Over. And over.

I never had riding lessons, so I'm figuring things out on

the fly, but judging by his gasps and moans, he's enjoying the ride. And Oh. My. God. So am I. "This is so much better than my vibrator," I gasp, leaning down to steal a kiss. "This is good, right? Like, I'm really good at this."

"You're fucking amazing," he says through gritted teeth.

"Yay me." I might have said more, but honestly, everything is muffled. All that feels real, feels present is the pressure growing in my core, and the tingles in my feet and fingertips. "Oh, my god. It's coming." I read the books. I know a simultaneous orgasm isn't a real thing most of the time, but that doesn't matter. As long as we both feel good in the end, I consider tonight a success. And right now, I'm starting to feel so good.

I lose my rhythm as the waves build, finally crashing over me. I can't do more than grind down, milking every drop of sensation. I'm aware of Zach's strong hands on my hips, holding me to him. And of the musky smell in the room, a mixture of both of us. But I can't focus on any of it.

Finally, my shaking stops. I'm ready to collapse into a ball and sleep for a million years. Or clean the house. Weird.

"Baby," Zach says hoarsely. I force my eyes open and lock on his tense features. I give him what I'm sure is a dopey smile.

"I can't feel my legs," I say with a snorting giggle. Everything is brighter and funnier right now.

I shriek and grab Zach's shoulders as he rears up. He yanks me down to him, pushing deeper inside me. Everything wakes up with a gasp. Maybe I'm not that tired.

"My turn," he says darkly.

He's definitely ridden horses. The man can move his hips. And all those muscles he worked so hard to build are gleaming, bunching, moving. I feel like I'm in the middle of the tornado, Zach being the tornado.

But he's also my anchor. All I can do, all I want to do, is hang on tight and enjoy the ride.

So that's exactly what I do. All of my senses are pinging, cataloging everything about this moment. Watching the bead of sweat trickle down his temple. The salt taste of it against my tongue. His rough groans and grunts in my ear. The massive power of his muscles under my hands. And beneath all of it is us. That smell is uniquely ours.

I watch him fall apart. I watched him dissolve and I hold him tight as he comes back to earth. Maybe that's why I don't notice the hand that presses between us. Or the gentle press of his finger against my clit.

Now it's my turn to dissolve.

Again.

And I know he'll hold me tight and keep me safe until I come back.

SEX IS GREAT. FANTASTIC. AMAZING.

But laying here with him? The casual way he runs his fingertips up my back? The nearly absent minded press of his lips against my temple? This is pretty damn incredible, too.

I'm soaking it all in. Capturing each moment with a mental photograph. Not because I think this will be the last time, but because I want to remember the first time. When it all felt so new, so incredibly life-altering.

I hope it doesn't change, but I also hope it does. I hope I always lose my breath when he touches me, as much as I hope that I'll feel like something's missing when we're not together. Like a piece of me is gone.

I want that familiarity desperately.

We still don't match. The handsome, put together playboy, and the frumpy, slightly odd woman. On paper, we're complete opposites. Maybe in real life, too. But it doesn't matter. I know his heart, and he knows mine.

The rest of it doesn't matter.

Zach's looking lost in thought. I turn his chin toward me

with one finger, loving how easily he moves. How quickly he looks for our connection.

"What are you thinking about?"

His lips quirk, and he gives me the absolute last answer I ever expected.

"Dogs."

40

MAYA

"A re you sure about this?" I ask for about the millionth time.

Zach smiles, which is a miracle. I wouldn't be this patient with me. Not at all. "Yes, I'm sure." He steps out of his walk-in closet —the man has way too many clothes— and leans in the doorway, arms crossed.

"But, they're messy. And needy. And noisy."

His low chuckle makes my toes tingle. There is not a part of my body untouched by this man. He even sucked on my toes. My toes! It didn't seem strange to let other parts of him into me, but somehow, him sucking on my toes was both the hottest and most embarrassing moment of my life.

"Baby, I could say the same for you. My apartment is a wreck since you came along."

"Now you're just being dramatic. It's not that bad."

He raises an eyebrow and stalks toward me slowly. "The cushions on my very expensive organic cotton couch are always messed up. Your shoes are everywhere—."

"That's your fault. You bought all of them."

"There are cut marks on my butcher block countertops."

"Hey, no fair. Nobody ever cooked in there before me.

Your knives were brand new." I'm disgusted all over again. "Why would you have a kitchen that nice and not use it? There's something really wrong with that."

He grins and backs me up against the bedroom wall. I love it when he does this. Looms over me with that heated look in his eye. Like I'm the best thing he's ever seen.

"You're proving my point. You have brought chaos and mess into my life." He leans down, burying his face in my hair. "And I'm so fucking thankful for it. For you." Wetness fills my eyes at his words. He pulls back and makes a low sound when he sees my tears. "Hey. No, don't cry baby."

"I can't help it," I choke out, sniffing. I'm positive my nose is as red as Rudolph's as I try to stem the tide of tears, but it's no use. "Sometimes it's too overwhelming."

His face turns guarded, and I grab two fistfuls of his sweater and hang onto him. He doesn't resist my hold, letting me pull him closer. He never does. Anywhere I want him, whatever I need him for. He's there. Always.

"I've never had this. You know that. But I think sometimes you don't realize how overwhelming it can be, to be loved. I mean, you're always here. You're always smiling at me and touching me. You look at me like a movie star, and sometimes, just for a minute, it doesn't make sense."

He frowns and cups my cheeks. "I thought we were over this? I love you—."

I press my fingers over his lips. "No. I know. I really do. You're fantastic at telling the people you love how much they matter to you. I didn't know men could be like you. But sometimes, it just feels like I'm living someone else's life. Like I'll wake up and I'll be back in my apartment in New York, alone."

His gaze softens, and he exhales heavily. "I get it. I feel the same way too, sometimes. Like you're too good for me. Too perfect." I raise my brows at that, because perfect is not a word people use to describe me. Ever. He laughs and shakes his head. "We just need time. Before you know it, we'll be an old married couple."

He freezes, eyes widening to match mine. Neither of us are breathing as we stare. Finally, I break the silence.

"Um. So, yeah, you just said the M word." He nods, and swallows, but doesn't say a word. "Should we pretend that never happened? Like, whoops, it just fell out of your mouth by accident? I can totally do that."

No, I can't. He said the M word. Who could ignore that?

"Do you *want* it to be an accident?"

I press my suddenly dry lips together as I search his gaze. Is there a right answer to this? If there is, I don't know it. So as usual, I wing it.

"No, I don't think I do." My words land like darts, popping his balloon of tension. "It hasn't really been that long, so maybe it's a bit soon, but knowing you feel that way is...good."

"Good," he repeats. "Ok. So I said it. But there's no panic. It's not an official proposal."

"Right. Good."

"Besides," he says with a grin, "the official proposal would be a lot bigger. With a symphony, or fireworks. Maybe a flash mob."

"My skin is itchy," I mumble, imagining all those eyes on me, all that pomp and circumstance. It sounds horrible.

Zach cackles at the look on my face and presses a quick kiss to my lips. "Hurry up, woman, we've got a dog to adopt."

I follow, dazed, as we board the elevator and he hits the button for the lobby. Zach's vibrating with energy, bouncing lightly as he watches the numbers drop.

"So...ah. Flash mobs aren't really my thing."

"No? Maybe a proposal on a Jumbotron? They could broadcast the whole thing, and send it into millions of homes. Everyone could see." He's teasing me. I see it in the glint in his eye. But just the idea…I reach up and scratch the back of my neck.

"Maybe a flash mob would be fun," I squeak, staring at the numbers. Zach laughs hysterically, and I shoot him a glare. "You suck, by the way."

He pulls me into a hug. "When I do it, I promise you it'll be perfect. Don't worry."

I drop my head to his chest and snort. "Sure. No problem." Tipping my head back, I meet his eyes. "It doesn't need to be perfect, Zach. It just needs to be perfect for us. The rest of it doesn't matter. And there's no rush. We're basically living together already. There's no panic."

"Basically," he mutters. "You haven't spent the night in your apartment in weeks. Remind me again why you aren't moving all the way in?"

"Abby. I don't want to completely ditch her."

"Ditch her? You'd be moving a couple of floors up. It's not ditching."

"We'll see," I say, scrunching up my nose. Abby might seem tough, but she's not. I don't want to just abandon her. But I'm sure there will come a day when leaving makes sense. "Besides, all my stuff was just delivered. I'd like to unpack and settle in."

"It would be easier to settle into my place," he mutters, crossing his arms over his chest. He's sulking, but somehow, on him. It's still sexy.

The doors opening saves me from answering. I don't know what I want to say. Moving in with him sounds wonderful, but now that I really have a true friend, I don't want to leave her in the lurch. But one day, hopefully one day soon, she'll be okay and I'll run my butt upstairs for good.

I'm not dumb. I'm not letting him get away from me. Ever.

I grab his hand and pull him out of the elevator with a wink. "Besides, sleepovers are more fun."

He pulls me tight to him until our bodies are lined up.

"Sleepovers aren't enough. I want all of your days and nights."

"Two months," I whisper, breathless. "Two more months, then I'm yours."

"Two weeks," he whispers back, kissing the skin below my ear. What are we talking about? Why aren't I giving him exactly what he wants?

"One month."

It's only after he smiles and says 'deal' with a smirk that I realize I've been played. I can't be too mad about it though. In my heart, in my gut, all I want to be with him, too. I'll make sure Abby's ok in the meantime.

"Young love," a woman's smooth voice says. Zach and I startle and turn toward her. It's the woman with the Weiner dogs. I give her a sunny smile and drop to my knees beside the elevator to greet the babies.

"Mrs. McCauley, how are you? How's business?" Zach asks, gently sliding me out of the way of the elevator doors.

"Business is good as always Mr. Lee. How are you? It seems like a lot has changed for you and your brothers lately." She looks pointedly between Zach and me.

He grins and runs his hand through his hair. "Well, a few of us have coupled up. And Micah's expecting a baby with his Holly."

One of the loveliest, kindest smiles I've ever seen wreaths her face. "That is truly wonderful news. Please pass on my congratulations to your brother." She looks down at me with raised brows. "And you young lady, I had high hopes for you and one of my grandsons but judging by that kiss I just witnessed, you're off the market."

Zach scowls at her, making her laugh. "She's off the market. Totally. Tell your grandsons to find their own women."

She sighs long, and pained. "They've done a horrible job of it. All over thirty, and not one of them has found someone to love. I fear that they may never find love and get married."

"There's time. I never expected to find someone. And then suddenly, there he was. Maybe it will be the same for your grandsons."

"I hope so young lady," she says, giving me a wink. "Well, I will leave you to your day. Please excuse me. And Miss…"

"Maya. My name is Maya."

"Maya," she repeats. "I'm Constance. And I expect you to come and join me for tea one of these days. Mr. Lee will give you my contact information." She taps her cane, and gets on the elevator like a queen, her dogs trotting happily behind her.

"She's so nice."

Zach snorts. "She's terrifying." I frown at him, because really? He grins. "That nice old woman is one of the most terrifying people I've ever met. She and her husband started a steel business fifty years ago. Now, she's the largest steel supplier on the entire eastern seaboard. She makes teamsters quake in their boots. The woman's as rich as we are."

"Wait. What?"

Grinning, Zach explains. "She still runs the company, but her grandsons are next in line. But they're all over the world, acting crazy. She's pretty pissed about it."

"Wow," I murmur, staring at the closed doors. "I really want to have tea with her."

"She owns the entire sixteenth floor. You'll find her there."

"The whole sixteenth floor," I repeat dumbly. I am so having tea with that woman. I can't imagine the life she's lived, and I want to know more about her. To have built that kind of company long before women were CEOs is an amazing accomplishment.

Zach moves to the door, holding a hand out to me. "Come on, love. I need you with me."

I move to him, taking his hand. Stopping for a moment, I

savor our connection. It's not just holding hands, it's so much bigger. "How does that work?" I ask, tightening my grip. He tilts his head questioningly. "This," I say, shaking our joined hands. "How does holding your hand make me feel like everything is perfect? Like I can handle anything the world has to throw at me?"

"I don't fucking know how that happened. But I need you to make me a promise." His hand tightens around mine, and I give him a nod. "Promise me that if I ever do anything that makes you lose that feeling, you tell me. And you give me a chance to fix what I broke."

This is more than moving in. This is more than a marriage ceremony. We both know it. This is a commitment. A promise, just between us. I'm sure we'll have a ceremony one day, but right here, right now, is when two separate people commit to a future together.

It's for us, and it's everything we need.

"I promise," I say, gazing into those gorgeous brown eyes. That slow smile sends a happy shiver down my spine. I can't wait to spend decades more just like this.

Luis clears his throat from his spot next to the open SUV door and gives us a happy smile. The man seems to always be smiling lately. "It's a lovely day, isn't it? A perfect day, actually, and if you want to keep your appointment, we'll need to get going."

"If you don't want to do this, if you think it's a bad idea, then we don't have to go."

Is it a bad idea? Maybe. But he won't have to do this alone. I'll be right there with him.

I tug him to the door of the car, smiling at Luis as we pass. "I have faith in you," I tell Zach. And I do. Absolute faith. He might make a mistake. He might get frustrated, but if he makes this commitment, he won't ever give up.

41

ZACH

"**A**re you listening?"

I nod at Colton, but if I'm honest, I'm not. Not even a little. How the fuck am I supposed to concentrate when I have Maya's lucious ass pressed against my cock? She laughs at something Holly's saying, and her body shakes, creating even more friction. I'm not going to last. There's no way.

The woman is fucking insatiable. I never imagined that having the same partner day after day would be like this. This exciting. This all-consuming. She's all I think about. I have to stop myself from dragging her into my office, or a closet, or an empty office twenty times a day.

And Maya? She's fucking radiant. Every day, she seems to shine brighter. I didn't know that was even possible. She was my North Star. Now? She's the fucking Sun.

"You're not listening," he complains, rubbing his face against Gracie's soft fur.

I was right. That long blonde fur sticks to everything. But she's soft and sweet, and has better manners than my brothers.

"I am listening. And stop hogging my dog," I grumble, reaching out to snag her from his lap. I ignore his pout. I swear I haven't had more than five minutes alone with her since I adopted her. When Maya's around, which thankfully is often, they're usually cuddling on the new couch together. I'm the fucking third wheel.

It doesn't bother me a bit. Seeing her light up for this odd little dog just makes me fall deeper in love with her. And I'm learning to live with the dog hair. I invested in a new lint roller company, so I've guaranteed my supply.

"I wanted him here for Christmas. This is just wrong." Colt grumbles, wandering away from me now that the dog's been taken away. I'm sure one of my other brothers will show up in a minute, wanting to hog the dog. Until then, I tuck her against my chest. Maya's other hand comes up and cups Grace's bum.

"They can't get enough of her," she says with a smile. Her eyes shift to Colt's retreating back. "He's pretty tense."

"Yeah, the closer we get to Johnny's release, the worse he's getting."

"He's afraid that it won't happen." It doesn't sound like a question. I shoot her a look, and she shrugs, the sleeve of her silky top sliding off her shoulder. The memory of that last night, the night before meeting Maya, pops into my head. The woman at the club that night knew the score, and understood the rules of the game, so when the strap of the dress slid down her arm, all she did was hit me with a sultry smile.

My woman, the one who makes my ears burn when she looks at me, yanks on her sleeve, tugging it into place yet again. It immediately falls, and she huffs in annoyance. My fingers intercept hers, sliding under the material to tease her soft skin before slowly, carefully sliding it up her arm and into place.

The little catch in her breath is quiet. So quiet, I shouldn't be able to hear it. But I do. I always do. That sound is a happy prelude to an amazing night ahead of us.

As soon as we ditch my family.

"Why don't we get out of here?" I press a kiss to her shoulder and watch in satisfaction as her eyes flutter.

"Aren't we supposed to be helping decorate the tree?"

I raise my brows and study the twenty-foot tree in front of the windows. I still don't know how the fuck Ransom got it up here. I'm guessing a helicopter. It's so big, we can't actually reach the top half to decorate it, so some of my brothers have decided that throwing the ornaments from the second floor is the best way to solve the problem.

"I don't think they need our help. Honestly, we'd just be in the way, wouldn't we?"

She bites her lip and watches as Maverick leans dangerously over the rail to toss a popcorn garland he made. We had to buy a popcorn maker. And a needle and thread. And popcorn. And watch a tutorial, but he was really damned motivated. Something about having the women in our lives, and especially Mia has motivated us to celebrate Christmas like we never have before.

"I have to hand it to you. You guys can sure make things complicated. I don't think this is what Holly intended when she suggested a tree."

She may be right there, but she might as well learn now. This is how we do shit. We go big. We go loud. We go over the top. In all things.

And I can't be mad about it, seeing the wonder on Maya's face at every ornament, every cup of cider, every strand of popcorn. Somehow I don't think my woman has had enough merry Christmases, and I want to make up for it, in a big way. I can't wait for Christmas morning.

Course, we haven't actually celebrated a traditional Christmas before, so we're learning on the fly now.

The slam of a door brings my head up. Jonas storms into

the room. I've never seen him look like this...so tense, so frustrated, but also resolved.

"Brother, what's going on?"

His lips are a thin white line. The rest of the room quiets as he answers. "She's not safe."

"Who's not safe?" I ask calmly, trying like hell to keep my voice level.

"Janey. I went to her apartment tonight. But she's not there. The landlord said she was evicted weeks ago." His hands clench into fists. "I can't find her. Where is she? She won't be back at the office until January. That's too long to wait. We have to make sure she's okay now."

Holy fuck.

Maya and I exchange a look. She slides carefully off my lap, and puts Gracie on the floor. Gracie goes straight for Jonas, pawing at his shins to be picked up. Some of his tension drains as he looks down at her. He scoops up the dog, letting her lick his chin. Maya's hand tucks into mine, and she leans close, worry etched on her features.

Ransom stands, and moves to Jonas, laying a heavy hand on his shoulder. "Come sit down, brother. Let's talk it out."

Jonas shrugs off Ransom's hand. "I don't want to sit down. Janey does not have a home. Why aren't we out looking for her?"

"I'll grab my computer. I'll start digging. I'll figure out what's going on, I promise," Declan says. He doesn't waste any time jogging from the penthouse. Jonas seems to deflate a little now that he understands we're taking him seriously.

"Tell me what happened tonight," I ask. I don't know what the hell I can do, but if I can fix this, I will. No way can I stand by and do nothing.

"We...argued tonight. She left, but I realized she had forgotten her jacket." His features pinch tight. "It's cold outside. She needs her coat Zach."

"I could call the shelters," Evie offers quietly. Jonas visibly flinches at the idea of Janey in a shelter.

"Why would she be there? I am her friend. She knows she can come to us…doesn't she? I…I don't understand."

Maya rises and moves to Jonas, taking his hand and drawing him to the couch to sit. "We don't always know what people are going through. She might have been embarrassed, or maybe she's sitting warm and cozy in a new apartment."

"Cozy and warm? Maybe," he mutters, staring at the floor. His hands are twisting and rubbing. His shoulders are up around his ears. I watch him carefully, ready to support him in anything he needs.

He pushes to his feet. "I can't stay here. I'm going out to look for her. I'll drive all night if I have to."

Evie nods from her spot at the table, phone pressed to her ear. "I'll call you if I learn anything."

Jonas nods grimly. "Declan needs to call me if he figures anything out."

He takes a step to the door, and all of us stand. Like we share a brain, we all follow him. He stops, turning slowly to face us.

"What are you doing?"

We all trade glances, but it's Ransom that answers. "We're going out to look too. We all know how you feel about her, Jonas. But it's more than that. She's one of ours, and until we know she's safe, we won't rest."

Some of Jonas's tension dissolves and his shoulders square. "Okay. If we're doing this, we're going to do it right. We'll work in grids."

Maya pulls me aside as Jonas starts organizing the search party. "I just talked to her today. She was vague about her Christmas plans, but I didn't think anything of it. She's been off lately, but I thought it had to do with the breakup."

"I didn't see it. But you can be damn sure, we won't leave a single stone unturned. We'll find her. Guaranteed."

"I hope we do, for Jonas's sake."

I see it in her eyes. Her worry that what we find might be bad. I have the same fear, but right now, I have to hope that everything will be okay.

Because if anything happens to her, I know, in the deepest part of my soul, I'll lose my brother.

ABOUT THE AUTHOR

Jenna lives in Canada with her family, both human and furry. She's a proud adoptive and foster parent, and has a soft spot for people from hard places.

f facebook.com / authorjennamyles

instagram.com / authorjennamyles

tiktok.com / jennalovesromance